STATE OF THE UNION

FIRST FAMILY SERIES, BOOK 3

MARIE FORCE

State of the Union
First Family Series, Book 3
By: Marie Force

Published by HTJB, Inc.
Copyright 2022. HTJB, Inc.
Cover design by Kristina Brinton
Cover photography by Regina Wamba
Models: Robert John and Ellie Dulac
Print Layout: E-book Formatting Fairies
ISBN:

The First Family Series

Book 1: State of Affairs
Book 2: State of Grace
Book 3: State of the Union
Book 4: State of Shock

More new books are always in the works. For the most up-to-date list of what's available from the First Family Series as well as series extras, go to *marieforce.com/firstfamily*

CHAPTER ONE

Author's Note: I wanted to remind you of my note in *Someone Like You*, Roni's Wild Widows book, that the timeline and events in that book would not match up exactly with the First Family Series. That was intentional. Please experience them as separate from each other. Also, a reminder that my version of the Metro PD is entirely fictional. None of the events portrayed in this or other books are real or happened in the real-life department, or if they did, my presentation here is purely coincidental. Happy reading! —Marie

The White House bomb shelter reminded Sam of the one they'd been in the previous summer—and not in a good way. It had all the comforts of "home," except you could never forget for a second that you were enclosed inside a box that could withstand a nuclear blast, buried deep under the most fortified house in the world.

Merry freaking Christmas.

In consultation with the Secret Service, Nick had decided not to disrupt the guests sleeping in every bedroom in the residence with the news that a bomb had been discovered outside the main gates. It was quickly disarmed, but the Secret Service wanted the first family in lockdown until they thoroughly searched the rest of the grounds. They'd brought only their kids and Skippy the dog. After being awakened from a sound sleep, Aubrey and Alden were in tears wondering how Santa would find them in this strange place.

"He'll find you," Nick assured them. "In fact, I heard he stops at the president's house first."

"Is that true, Lijah?" Alden asked their older brother.

"If Nick says it's true, it must be. He's the president after all."

Sam smiled, thinking of what the media would say about that. Some reporters were predisposed to doubt every word that came out of Nick's mouth—and hers, for that matter. "The best thing you guys can do is go back to sleep," she said. "Little boys and girls have to be asleep before Santa can come."

"I'll lie down with you guys." Elijah led his younger siblings into one of three rooms off the main area that included a mini Situation Room and a bank of official-looking phones. From the doorway, Elijah said, "Wake us up if we're allowed to go back upstairs."

"Will do," Nick said.

"So did Santa already come?" Scotty, their fourteen-year-old son, asked.

"I'll never tell," Sam said.

"Oh, come on. I'm not a baby anymore. I know it's you guys."

Sam gasped. "Shut your filthy mouth. That's not true!"

"Mom... Be serious."

"I'm not talking to you about Santa. He's real, and he's magic, and that's all I'm going to say about it."

"Dad, will you talk to her?"

"You know as well as I do that talking to her when she's like this is pointless."

"True."

"I can hear you guys," Sam said.

"Who do you think is trying to bomb us?" Scotty asked, his dark brows furrowing in a serious expression.

"Could be anyone," Nick said with a nonchalant shrug designed to assuage Scotty's concerns. "Could be someone who didn't like my speech about reasonable gun control after the shooting in Des Moines, or it could be someone who doesn't like that I was never elected as VP and thus shouldn't be president."

"Or it could be the family member of someone I've locked up," Sam said to let Nick off the hook. "It could be Detective Ramsey, who finally succeeded in getting himself fired after he broke into my office and trashed it. Or it could be former Lieutenant Stahl's brother or uncle who's pissed that he's doing a life sentence for trying to kill me twice, as if that was my fault." Sam mirrored Nick's shrug. "Like Dad said, it could be anyone."

"You guys have a lot of enemies," Scotty said bluntly.

"I suppose we do, even though we'd rather we didn't have any," Nick said.

"It's the nature of both your jobs," Scotty said. "Haters are gonna hate, but I think most of them would like to *be* you."

"Everyone thinks it's so cool to be president until they're president and find out it's actually super stressful," Nick said.

"It's also pretty cool," Scotty said. "I mean, you're the only person in the world that the Navy Band plays 'Hail to the Chief' for, and you get your own armored car, helicopter and airplane, as well as this sick house that comes with a bakery, twenty-four-hour pizza, Coke on demand *and* a pool, bowling alley and theater. It's not all sucky."

Nick chuckled at Scotty's recitation of the benefits. "No, it certainly isn't, and I'm not complaining. I don't want you to think I am."

"Nah, I get it. When some country halfway around the world does something crazy, that's your problem. I can see how that gets old."

"Not to mention when someone does something right here in the US, that's my problem, or when a hurricane or tornado wipes out whole towns or a blizzard takes down the power grid of a major city. All that is my problem."

"That's a lot of problems for one person to manage."

"But, hey, there's twenty-four-hour pizza and Coke on demand."

Scotty laughed. "Touché." To Sam, he said, "Does he win every argument now that he's president, or does it just seem that way?"

"He's been on a winning streak lately. We'll have to work on that while we're on vacation."

"You guys must be *so* happy to be on vacation," Scotty said. "Even happier than I am to have no algebra for twelve whole days."

"Never been happier," Sam said. "The last month has been a bit chaotic."

"You mean the part about Nelson dying, Dad suddenly becoming president, us having to move to the White House, getting a dog, several murders, a school shooting and a standoff in Iran?"

"Other than that, Mrs. Lincoln, how was the play?" Nick asked in a teasing tone.

"What the heck does that mean?" Scotty asked, seeming confused.

"That's an awful reference to the assassination of President Lincoln while they were at Ford's Theatre," Nick said.

"Oh jeez. That's in very poor taste, and I declare assassination to be a swear word while Dad is the president."

"All in favor say 'aye,'" Sam said.

"*Aye*," they all said.

"And it passes unanimously," Sam declared.

"We don't like that word," Scotty said in all seriousness. "In fact, it's become my least favorite word in the English language."

"We hate that word," Sam said.

"I don't want you guys worrying about stuff like that," Nick said.

"What?" Sam said. "Us worry?"

"I'm surrounded by the finest security in the entire world. Nothing is going to happen to me."

"Dad, you're the president and everything, so I hate to say don't be naïve, but really... Don't be naïve. Of course it can happen to you. People hate you simply because of the office you hold and that you belong to a party they don't align with, or you do things like say we need reasonable gun control when everyone knows we need reasonable gun control."

Sam felt sick just thinking about the many things that could happen to Nick or the many people who hated him for the reasons Scotty noted as well as plenty of others.

"I think we need to limit his time online," Nick said, affecting a lighthearted tone when the subject was anything but.

"At what point will he officially be smarter than us?" Sam asked.

"Uh, duh, I went past you a year ago."

Even though she was still in the red evening gown that had made her feel so sexy earlier, she tackled her son and took him right down onto the rug, the way she would a perp on the job. Holding his arms behind him, she said, "You're not so smart that you saw that coming."

Scotty was laughing so hard, he couldn't breathe.

Sam much preferred that to his serious concerns about Nick being murdered.

"Say uncle."

"Why?"

"I don't know. That's what you're supposed to say when you find yourself in a pickle like you're currently in."

"I'd think a feminist like you would request the word 'aunt.'"

Nick snorted with laughter. "He's got you there, babe."

"Maybe so, but who's the one flat on his face, pinned to the carpet by his mommy?"

"Only because I don't want to hurt you."

"Oh please. Show me what you've got, tough guy."

"Dad says we should never be rough with a woman or a girl. It's not gentlemanly."

"What are Dad's rules for when a woman is beating the crap out of you?"

"Even then," Scotty said.

Sam let him go. "Well, you guys are no fun at all."

"We disagree," Nick said with a meaningful look for her.

"Ew, don't make it gross." Scotty stood and dusted off his pajama pants. "Just so you know, I could've gotten you off me if I'd wanted to."

"No way."

"Is there a gym at Camp David, Dad?"

"I think so."

"Then I challenge you to a wrestling match when we get there, Mom. I think Dad would agree that an official challenge is different from being rough with a woman in the way that he means."

"I agree," Nick said, "and I'll serve as the referee."

"Only if you don't give her extra points because she's your main squeeze."

"Hmm, I can see how that'd be a concern for you. Your mom is a heck of a main squeeze."

"I'm out." Scotty held up his hands in surrender. "And I demand impartial officiating for the wrestling match. I'll ask Elijah."

"That's probably a good idea," Nick said.

"It's concerning that you wouldn't pick your kid over your wife like any other father would. You need to think about your priorities, Mr. President."

"I love you equally," Nick said.

"That is a damned lie. Everyone in the world knows you love her more than anything."

"Scotty, come on. I love you just as much."

"No, you don't, but that's okay. You love me more than enough. Merry Christmas and good night. Wake me up when they let us out of here."

"Why would he say that?" Nick seemed genuinely distressed. "He knows I love him more than anything."

"The whole world knows we love each other more than anything, but that doesn't mean we wouldn't take a bullet for any of those kids, or think of them first in a fire, or do anything we could to keep them safe." She curled up on his lap and put her arms around him. "Focus on the other thing he said. You love him more than enough."

"It's kind of upsetting that he thinks I wouldn't pick him and the others first, right along with you."

"He knows you would. He's just pushing buttons. That boy knows who loves him."

"Yeah, I guess. I love him so much. I can't imagine life without him anymore. It's like he's always been here, part of us."

"I know, and I hate that he's already fourteen, that we missed most of the first twelve years with him."

"I do, too, but that doesn't mean we don't love him with everything we've got to give."

"He'd never want you to be upset by something he intended to be good-natured teasing, Nick."

"You're right."

"It was nothing more than another jab at how disgusting we are," Sam said.

"We are pretty gross."

"*Super* gross, and I wouldn't have it any other way."

He brought her in for a kiss that quickly turned into tongues and the rampant desire that was ever present between them—so much so that anyone who knew them could see it. Unfortunately, the whole world knew them now, and their smoking-hot love affair was the source of late-night jokes.

"In case I forget to tell you later, you taking him down wearing an evening gown was super sexy."

"Was it?"

"Oh yeah." He cupped her ass and gave it a squeeze through the red silk, feeling around like he was looking for something. "No panties?"

"No panty *lines*. They're there."

His brows lifted. "*Oh*, the in-between kind? I like that kind."

"Hands off, Mr. President. Don't start something the Secret Service could interrupt at any second."

"Ugh, why do people have to leave bombs for us when my wife is looking extra sexy *and* wearing a thong? Don't they know it's Christmas?"

"Maybe they did it *because* it's Christmas."

"I hope they figure out who it was sooner rather than later so we don't have to be worried about that all week."

"Yeah, me, too."

An hour later, Sam was dozing with her head on Nick's shoulder when a knock on the door roused her.

"Come in," Nick said.

John Brantley Jr., Nick's lead Secret Service agent, stepped into the room. "We're all clear, Mr. President, Mrs. Cappuano."

"Thanks, Brant."

Sam got up from Nick's lap and stretched out the kinks before going to wake Scotty and Elijah. Eli carried Alden, and Nick took Aubrey as they trooped up the stairs to the residence. They'd lived there for only a month, so Sam didn't expect it to feel like home yet, but she had a strange feeling of homecoming after having been detained in the bunker. Anything looked good to her after that.

They got the kids settled in bed and said good night to Scotty and Eli.

"Wake me up when Alden and Aubrey are up," Scotty said. "I don't want to miss a second of our first Christmas with them."

"Will do," Sam said, kissing his cheek. "Merry Christmas."

"Same to you."

After Scotty closed his bedroom door, Sam and Nick turned to Brant.

"What do you know?" Sam asked.

"Nothing yet. The device has been disarmed and taken to the lab for further analysis. We should know more in the morning."

"So it was an active explosive device?" Sam asked.

"Yes, ma'am."

"Thank you, Brant," Nick said. "We'll see you in the morning, or I guess I should say later this morning."

"Yes, sir. Merry Christmas to you both."

"You, too. Go home while you can."

"Yes, sir."

Nick guided Sam into their suite and closed the door.

She went right to the bedside table where she'd left her cell phone charging earlier and put through a call to the Metro PD headquarters. "Explosives," she said when the dispatcher answered.

"Please hold."

"Higgins."

"Hey, it's Holland. What're you hearing about the bomb outside my house?"

"You mean the one outside the White House that got me called in on Christmas Eve?"

"Yes," she said, exasperated by his need to state the obvious.

"I heard it was sophisticated and could've done some major damage if it had detonated."

That wasn't what she'd wanted to hear. "Who's got it?"

"The FBI, but my team and I were on the scene earlier when it was being defused. I don't know much else, but I'll let you know if I hear anything from them."

"Please do."

"Hope you have a merry Christmas despite all this."

"We will. You, too. Thanks for the info."

"You got it."

Sam slapped the phone closed and thought about what Higgins had told her. A sophisticated bomb that could've done some major damage had been left outside the gates to their home, the most protected place on earth.

"How did someone get close enough to the White House to leave a sophisticated bomb at our gate?" Sam asked.

"Am I expected to have an answer to that question?" Nick replied, ducking his head out of the walk-in closet where he'd stripped down to his underwear.

"I'd like an answer to that question from someone," Sam said. "It's bad enough we have to worry about someone harming us every time we step foot outside the gates. We ought to feel relatively safe inside the gates with all the security we have."

Nick sat next to her on the bed and put his arm around her. "Even the best security isn't foolproof."

"That's not a good answer."

"How about we try to put these worries aside for now so we can get some sleep? Eli warned me the kids will be up crazy early."

"Sure," she said, knowing he was right. They needed to sleep while they could, or they'd be wrecks tomorrow with a houseful of guests. But she wouldn't stop worrying until she knew who'd left the unwelcome package at their gate.

CHAPTER TWO

Christmas at the White House was utter mayhem with so many kids underfoot. Alden and Aubrey had led the charge to the third-floor conservatory, where Santa had left labeled piles of gifts for each child. One of the White House staff photographers captured the fun so parents could enjoy their children and not have to worry about taking pictures. Other than the daily security briefing, which he'd attended at five a.m., and barring any unforeseen crises, Nick had the rest of the day off to spend with his family.

His six-year-old half brothers, Brayden and Brock, couldn't believe that Santa had not only found them at the White House, but he'd gotten them all the toys they'd asked for. Nick's dad, Leo, and stepmother, Stacy, laughed at the boys' excited commentary.

Sam's nephew Jack, dressed in full Spider-Man regalia, came over to hug her. "Thank you for the funnest Christmas *ever!*"

She returned his tight hug. "Thanks for coming to my house for Christmas."

If the excitement was off the charts, so, too, was the mess.

"Thanks so much for having me, Sam," her mother, Brenda, said. "Last night and this morning were incredible."

"Glad you could join us."

"My first Christmas with all my girls and my grandchildren," Brenda said, looking a bit misty.

"It's nice to have you here," Sam said sincerely. It was their first Christmas together in more than twenty years after a rift had kept them apart.

"This is amazing." Sam's "uncle" Joe Farnsworth sipped coffee with his wife, Marti, as they watched the chaos unfold. That he was also her chief of police was secondary at a time like this.

"We provide headache medicine for those who need it," Sam said.

"No need," Marti said, grinning. "We've never been part of anything like this before. It's delightful." The Farnsworths had been unable to have children of their own and had treated the Holland girls like beloved nieces all their lives.

"I'm glad you think so. It's great to have everyone we love in one place. How was the Lincoln Bedroom?" Joe and Marti had been the runaway winners of the dance contest Sam had held to determine who got to sleep in the legendary room.

"It was *fabulous*," Joe said.

"He'll dine out on his night in the Lincoln Bedroom for the rest of his life." Marti squeezed Sam's arm. "We so admire the way you and Nick have risen to the occasion to embrace the massive changes to your lives. We're so proud of you both."

"Aw, thanks. We're trying to cope as best we can. Sharing it with our loved ones helps us keep it real." Sam leaned in, whispering to Joe, "What're you hearing about the bomb?"

"Not much, which is annoying. The FBI has taken over the investigation, and we haven't heard a word."

"Keep me in the loop if you hear anything later," Sam said.

"Will do."

"This is the best birth control in the history of birth control," Sam's beloved partner, Freddie Cruz, said when he joined them with his wife, Elin.

"Hush, Freddie," Elin said. "This is what Christmas is all about—the magic."

"That's right." Sam watched Aubrey show off the doll Sam had bought online, hoping it was the one she wanted. Judging by the child's shout of happiness, she'd gotten it right.

"I can't believe you pulled off such an epic Christmas morning, Sam," Elin said. "Although I shouldn't be surprised. You're Wonder Woman."

"Wonder Woman had a ton of help from Celia, Shelby and the White House staff," Sam said. "They're the ones who made it happen."

Speaking of the staff, they appeared on the scene with garbage bags and a hot breakfast they served buffet-style while parents talked their children into putting down their new toys for a minute to have something to eat.

Sam supervised Alden at the buffet, while Eli took care of Aubrey.

They brought plates to the coffee table and sat to eat bacon and pancakes shaped like Santa, along with a side of fruit.

"Is there anything missing, ma'am?" the chief usher, Gideon Lawson, asked.

"Everything is perfect, Gideon. Please pass along our thanks to the staff and send everyone home as soon as you possibly can. We'll take care of ourselves for the rest of the day."

Sam had told him they didn't want the staff fawning over them on a day they should be spending with their own families. Thus the plan for breakfast rather than an elaborate dinner later in the day. With the first family spending Christmas at the White House, most of their Secret Service detail could have some time with their families that day. That was why they'd put off their departure for Camp David until the next morning.

"As you wish, ma'am, but we'll have a few people here if anything should come up."

"Thank you for everything, Gideon. It was wonderful to have everyone together."

"It was our pleasure, ma'am. Merry Christmas."

"Same to you and your family."

After breakfast, Sam, Nick, the kids and Skippy posed for the White House photographer for an official family photo that would be released on their POTUS and FLOTUS accounts. The staff had already written messages that would extend Christmas wishes to the country and the world from the president and first lady. It still boggled Sam's mind to realize that a casual photo of their family would make international news.

By noon, most of their guests had departed for other engagements, leaving only Sam's sisters and their families, who'd been invited to spend the day. Sam's stepmother, Celia, who lived with them at the White House, had left with her sisters to visit an elderly aunt and would return later.

"This has been an incredible Christmas," Sam's eldest sister, Tracy, said. "And I wouldn't have thought that would be possible without Dad."

"I know," Sam said. "I agree. It worked out well, all things considered."

"The White House gave us something new and different in a year when we really needed it," Angela said. "So thanks for that, Nick."

"I do what I can for the people," Nick said from his post on the floor where he and Alden were playing with Alden's new train set.

"That line is trademarked and copyrighted," Sam said as the others laughed.

"Skip would want his best girls to be happy," Nick said.

"Yes, he would," Sam said, sighing. "Even if we were much happier when he was here, bossing us all around."

Angela pointed to Sam. "What she said."

"Sometimes I still can't believe he actually died," Tracy said. "After everything he'd survived, how is he just gone?"

"I know," Sam said. "The defendants are due in court in January. I'll need to know if you guys want to be there."

"I do," Tracy said. "I want to be there for everything."

Angela hesitated. "Normally, I'd want to be there, but right now... I'm not sure I can handle it." She was pregnant with her third child, due in June.

Spencer, Angela's husband, crawled past them as he chased their son, Jack, who was still wearing his Spider-Man costume. Their baby daughter, Ella, was asleep in her mother's arms after an exciting morning. Angela laughed at the face Spencer made at her as he went by. "He's so good with Jack. They make up a new game every day."

When she'd first met Spencer, Sam had thought he was full of himself. Sometimes he could still be that way, but she couldn't deny his devotion to Angela and their children.

Nick came to sit next to her on the sofa.

Sam leaned into him, suddenly exhausted after the busy weeks that had led up to the holiday. She'd give just about anything for a nap.

"We need to get going to Mike's parents' house." Tracy stood to give her kids Brooke, Abby and Ethan the signal that it was time to go. They left a short time later with hugs and thanks to Sam and Nick for a fun Christmas. "We'll see you at Camp David next weekend. And I can't believe we're going to Camp David for New Year's."

"Believe it," Sam said as she hugged her sisters and walked them downstairs, carrying bags of gifts and overnight bags.

"This was so much fun," Angela said.

"More to come at Camp David," Nick said.

Spencer shook his hand. "Thanks for including us."

"It's more fun with you guys along for the ride," Nick said.

After they'd left, they went back to the third floor, where the kids were playing with their new toys and watching a movie.

"I've got them if you guys want to take a break," Eli said.

"Are you sure?" Nick asked.

"Yep. You must be exhausted after all the festivities."

"I wouldn't mind a break," Nick said, giving Sam the side-eye at the unexpected opportunity for some alone time.

"Me, too," Sam said.

"We're going to hit the pool after this," Scotty said. "We'll catch up to you in a bit."

"Sounds good," Sam said, taking Nick by the hand to make their escape before one of the Littles could object.

"Did that just happen?" Nick asked as they headed downstairs.

"Don't say a word that might jinx it. And isn't it nice to have an older kid around to keep an eye on the younger ones? Our family planning was spot-on."

Nick laughed at that.

Nothing about their family had been planned, but it had worked out beautifully.

They'd no sooner closed the door to their suite when Sam's cell phone rang. "It's Jeannie. I have to take it."

"Make it snappy, and that's an order from the president."

Sam smiled at him as she took the call from her detective. "Merry Christmas."

"Same to you. Hope you guys had a great day."

"We did. How about you?"

"Lots of fun with the family. They're all jealous that we got to do Christmas Eve at the White House. What a great time. Thank you again for having us."

"It was fun. Thanks for coming."

"I wanted to let you know I'm going to Richmond tomorrow to do some more digging into the Carisma Deasly case. As I mentioned last night, I met with a former boyfriend of Daniella Brown's, and he believes she had something to do with Carisma's disappearance. He said she was obsessed with that kid, and he used that word—obsessed. He said she lives in Richmond now and told me where to find her."

Sam sat on the bed. "What's your plan?"

"I haven't got one yet. I'll play it by ear and see what happens."

"Is Matt going with you?"

"He is."

"What did you tell him?"

"That we're tying up a loose end from the Tappen case," Jeannie said.

"I'm still worried about this blowing up in our faces after we were told to stand down on this investigation." Carisma's disappearance was one of many still-open cases overseen years earlier by now-disgraced Lieutenant Leonard Stahl, who'd recently been convicted of attempting to murder Sam—twice.

"I understand the situation, and I promise to clear anything with you before it happens."

"If you think you've found Daniella, we'll call in Jesse Best and the U.S. Marshals. We can't be the heroes in this one."

"I hear you. I'll let you know if we need the marshals."

"Sounds good."

"In the meantime, have a great time with your family and try not to worry."

"What? Me worry?"

Jeannie laughed. "I've got you covered."

"Thanks, Jeannie, and be careful."

"Will do."

Sam closed the phone and sat there for a full minute, thinking about whether she and Jeannie would land in a shit-ton of trouble for pursuing this case after being told not to.

"What's going on?" Nick asked when he came out of the bathroom.

"Jeannie and Matt are going to Richmond tomorrow to look into a lead on a missing-person case from eleven years ago."

"Oh wow. Why did I hear you telling her you're worried about it blowing up in your faces?"

"Because we were told to not pursue the case."

"Um, why?"

"Remember how I solved one of Stahl's old murder cases in an afternoon?"

"I do. That was amazing."

"I agree, but the press is making a thing out of how easily I solved a cold case, and it's making us look bad rather than good. They don't want another 'easily solved' cold case coming when the FBI is due to release the report of their investigation of the department next month."

"Ah, I see."

"But we have a girl missing for eleven years, and Jeannie thinks she's maybe found the person who took her."

"You're going forward with the investigation despite the order?"

"Something like that," Sam said with a sheepish look. "If she thinks she's got something solid, we'll call in the U.S. Marshals and let them take it over the finish line. That way, they get the credit, and we won't have the press asking how many other cases are sitting on the back burner waiting to be solved once the MPD decides to give a shit."

"What will Malone and Farnsworth say if they find out she's in Richmond chasing down leads after they told you guys not to?"

"They won't be happy, but as Jeannie said, how are we supposed to go on with our lives knowing we might've found this girl? She's no longer a girl, but a full-grown woman now, if she's even still alive."

"Playing devil's advocate… You could call in the marshals now and tell them what you have and let them take it from here."

"We could do that."

"But you're not going to?"

"Jeannie is invested. I want to give her the chance to see it through, almost to the finish line."

"You know what you're doing, so I won't question it. I'll just say I hope it works out okay and that you guys find the missing girl without getting yourselves in trouble."

"I'll try not to cause any bad publicity for you."

"I don't care about that, and you know it. I care about *you*."

"I'll be fine. Jeannie and I both believe that finding that girl is what matters. And on that note, I'm back off duty and wondering how we should spend this unexpected moment alone on Christmas Day."

"I thought we could start with this." He handed her a long, slender package wrapped in gold paper with a gold bow on top.

"What is it?"

"Open it and find out."

"I thought we agreed to *one* present this year?"

"I loved your gift, and I can't wait for a weekend away together very soon."

"And I loved the suede boots. They're gorgeous."

"I needed something more than the boots to properly thank you for everything over this last month and to butter you up for the next three years."

Intrigued, Sam removed the paper to reveal a blue velvet Tiffany box. "What've you done?"

"I had a little fun. Open it."

Sam lifted the lid on the box to reveal a stunning diamond bracelet. "Holy smokes. That's gorgeous."

Nick took it from the box and put it on her wrist. "Every time you look at it, I want you to remember how much I appreciate you—

always—but especially lately. And I want you to remember how much I love you."

"It's beautiful. Thank you. How'd you manage to pull this off?"

"I had a little help from Tracy and Angela. They helped me narrow down the choices, but I made the final call."

"You did good." Sam held up her arm to let the bling catch the light from the fire burning in their fireplace. After hearing how much she loved the wood fireplace, the staff came in each night to light it for her before bedtime. Since it was a holiday, they'd done it early. At first, she'd been worried about them coming in unannounced, but the staff never entered the occupied suite unless they'd been asked for something. They had an almost supernatural ability to know when to stay away.

"Last night and today were fantastic," Nick said, kissing her. "Thanks for all you did to make it happen."

"That was mostly Gideon and the staff."

"But it was your idea."

"That was the easy part. The staff gets the credit for bringing my idea to life."

"I hope we can do it every year that we're here."

"That would be nice," Sam said. "Everyone seemed to enjoy it."

"They were dazzled."

"This place is rather dazzling."

"Nothing was more dazzling last night than my first lady."

"She did look rather smashing, didn't she?" Sam asked with a laugh.

"She was the belle of the ball, the apple of my eye, the love of my life."

"Sigh. You know I'm a sure thing, right?"

Nick laughed. "I never take that for granted."

"You probably could at this point."

"I never will." He stood and held out his hand to help her up so he could remove the sweater and leggings she'd worn for the morning festivities. Her bra and panties landed on the floor with the rest of her clothes, and Sam pressed her naked body against his. "Let's go by the fireplace."

"Wherever you want, love."

Sam grabbed a pillow and throw blanket that they snuggled under next to the fire. "You have no idea how badly I needed some time alone with you after these last few insane days."

"I think I have a small idea."

Sam wrapped her hand around his erection. "There's nothing small about it."

His laughter turned to a groan as she stroked him, letting the diamond bracelet rub against his sensitive flesh. "Sam..."

"Hmm?"

"Don't finish me off too soon."

"Don't tell me what to do, Mr. President. You're not the boss of me."

"Ain't no one the boss of you," he said, quoting Joe Farnsworth's famous comment to Sam.

Sam laughed. "That's right, and don't you forget it." Determined to help him relax, she bent over him and took his cock into her mouth, using her lips, tongue and hand to bring him the ultimate pleasure. She'd avoided that act with other guys. But like everything else with him, she loved the way he reacted when she did it—and she enjoyed knowing he wasn't thinking about anything else but her and them.

With him carrying the weight of the free world on his shoulders, it was important to her that he get as much reprieve as possible, and she loved being the only one to give him a full escape from the unrelenting pressure. She viewed managing the president's stress as her most important role as first lady.

The phone on the bedside table rang, the one he was supposed to answer no matter what.

He groaned. "Please don't stop."

She doubled down with her hand, lips and tongue and finished him off in spectacular fashion, if she said so herself.

The phone continued to ring with an unrelenting urgency.

His deep sigh said it all as he got up from their camp in front of the fireplace to take the call.

"Yes?" The single word was full of annoyance over the interruption. He listened for a full minute before he said, "I'll be right there."

Sam sat up and wrapped the blanket around her shoulders. "What's going on?"

"The North Koreans thought Christmas Day would be an excellent time to test an ICBM, which is in violation of the U.N.'s Security Council resolutions, and apparently, that's my problem." He came over to her, squatted to kiss her and brushed the hair back from her face. "I'm sorry, babe. They want me in the Situation Room."

"It's okay."

"No, it isn't. Can we pick this up later right where we left off?"

Smiling, she said, "I'll be here all week."

"I can't wait for some downtime with you and the kids."

"Go deal with the North Koreans and their icy BM."

Nick cracked up. "It's an intercontinental ballistic missile, capable of carrying nuclear weapons, thus the alarm."

"Ah, gotcha."

"Just so you know, I'd much rather be dealing with you than the North Koreans."

"That's not much of a compliment."

Smiling, he kissed her again, then went to the bathroom to clean up and get dressed so he could go deal with the North Koreans. And people thought being the president was so exciting. From her point of view, it was nothing more than a gigantic pain in the ass, even if the service at the White House was second to none.

In her opinion—and probably Nick's, too, though he'd never say so—the cons outweighed the pros by a mile.

CHAPTER THREE

After spending Christmas Day with her husband and family, Detective Jeannie McBride had gone back to work on Christmas night, reviewing her notes on the case for the hundredth time. On each pass, she added to her list of questions and came to the same unavoidable conclusion. Before she went to Richmond, she needed to see Carisma's mother.

LaToya Deasly had put herself through paralegal school, had bought a townhouse for her and her three children and, by all accounts, was a dedicated mother. Over the eleven years her daughter had been missing, LaToya had repeatedly claimed her former friend, Daniella Brown, had kidnapped her child.

No one had listened.

Jeannie had realized that a week ago. Not only had no one listened, it seemed no one had cared about another missing Black teenager. What would LaToya say now if an MPD detective showed up at her house, claiming to care after all this time? Jeannie wouldn't blame the woman for slamming the door in her face.

But she had to try. LaToya could help her understand the dynamics of her relationship with Daniella as well as Daniella's with Carisma.

Jeannie had interviewed Daniella's ex-boyfriend, who'd confirmed that Daniella had been fixated on Carisma, referring to her as her daughter, not as her friend's daughter. It had been odd, the boyfriend had said, the way she'd had herself convinced the child belonged to her. They'd argued over Daniella's obsession with someone else's kid and ultimately had broken up over it. He believed she'd had something to do with Carisma's disappearance and had said so at the time.

No one had followed up with him. Then-Detective Stahl hadn't even noted the man's comments in the sparse reports he'd bothered to file on the case.

As she went over her notes again, Jeannie felt sick over the way this case had been handled—or hadn't been handled. If she was still alive, Carisma was out there somewhere, waiting for someone to care enough to look for her.

Jeannie cared enough, and she'd rather ask for forgiveness than permission to pursue the leads she had so far.

The next morning, she was up early to shower, hoping the nausea she woke with every day would subside before she left for work.

"How are you feeling, hon?" Michael asked.

"Same as every other day."

"Did you eat something?"

"A piece of toast that's stayed down so far."

He came over to kiss and hug her. "I sure hope this kid is worth what he or she is putting you through."

Jeannie was thankful that the scent of his cologne, always one of her favorites, didn't make her nauseated the way so many other scents did lately. "I hear they're worth it."

"What's on tap for you today?"

"I've got a few things to do in town, and then I'm going to Richmond to poke around a bit."

"Is Matt going with you?" he asked of her partner.

"To Richmond, yes."

"You'll be careful?"

"Always."

"Take good care of my baby mama."

"I will. Love you."

"Love you, too. Thanks for a great Christmas."

"It was a good one. Next year will be even better with Junior with us."

"I can't wait."

After he left, Jeannie gave herself thirty minutes to see if she was going to be sick or not. Some days she was, others she wasn't. She never knew what to expect from one day to the next. She sent a text to her partner.

Stopping to take care of something before I pick you up at HQ.

Matt responded right away. *You want me to come?*

I got this. See you at the house.

Jeannie hated to make things about race and gender, but as a Black woman herself, she thought she might get further with LaToya without her white male partner with her. Thirty minutes later, she pulled up to LaToya's block off Good Hope Road in the Fairlawn neighborhood and parked. She approached the black door bearing a Christmas wreath with trepidation, hoping she'd have the chance to speak with LaToya.

She rang the bell and waited off to the side, always leery of people shooting through closed doors, especially since that'd happened to Sam and Freddie.

The door swung open.

Jeannie recognized LaToya from press coverage of the kidnapping. She had put on considerable weight since then and had a world-weary look to her that told the story of her long ordeal.

Jeannie held up her gold shield. "Detective McBride, Metro PD, to see LaToya Deasly."

"I'm LaToya." She eyed Jeannie suspiciously. "Did you find my daughter?"

"Not yet, ma'am, but I'm working on her case and was hoping for the chance to speak to you."

"Are you the one who got abducted and raped?"

The question hit Jeannie like a fist to her already churning gut. "Yes, ma'am."

"I followed the coverage of that. They said you were gutsy."

"I survived." *Just barely*, Jeannie thought.

"Come in."

Jeannie followed LaToya into a warm, inviting living room that led into an eat-in kitchen.

"Can I get you anything? Coffee? Water?"

"Water would be great. Thanks." The offer of refreshments was much more than she'd expected from LaToya, who had every reason to despise the MPD and everyone associated with it.

"Have a seat."

Jeannie joined her at the kitchen table.

"I have to say, it's a shock to find an MPD detective on my front porch. I've gotten nowhere with your department for years."

"I know, and I apologize for the failures of others. I wish I had a better explanation for you than people being overworked, but there's nothing I could say that would ever make this right."

"No, there isn't. But if you find my daughter, I might find a way to forgive the sins of the past."

"I want very much to find your daughter, and I've been reviewing everything I can about her disappearance. I spoke with the former boyfriend of the prime suspect."

"Daniella," she said in a dead-sounding tone. "My ex-best friend, who I've always believed kidnapped my child. There's no way it's a coincidence that she disappeared around the same time."

"I don't believe it is either."

"I did everything for her. Took out a loan to pay for two trips to rehab, gave her a place to live when she got out, helped her find a job with my company. I come home one day, and she's gone, and so's my daughter. At first, I thought they'd left to get food or something, but when one hour became two and then three, and neither were answering their phones, I knew it was something else."

"You called the police at nine twenty," Jeannie said, consulting her notes.

LaToya nodded. "They sent Patrol officers over to take a statement, said they'd check into it and then... nothing. I waited two days before I called again, asking if there was any information about my daughter. No one knew what I was talking about. I had to give the entire report again. They sent a detective named Stahl over. He asked a bunch of questions, took some notes, said he'd put out an alert for Daniella's car and track her phone and Carisma's. Again, I waited days without another word. I left messages for Detective Stahl that went unanswered. I called the mayor's office, the chief of police, the FBI. No one returned my calls."

Jeannie tried very hard not to lose her composure. The sick feeling that overtook her had nothing to do with pregnancy. The treatment LaToya had received from all levels of law enforcement was an outrage. "I wish there was something I could say that would be adequate, but there's nothing anyone could say that would explain how this could've happened."

"People don't care. That's how it happened."

"I care. This case has become personal to me, and I'm determined to see it through until you have some answers."

"Why now?" LaToya asked, understandably suspicious.

"We started a review of former Lieutenant Stahl's cases after his conviction."

"I read about that, too. He tried to kill the first lady—twice."

"She wasn't the first lady then, but yes, he did."

"And the deputy chief was involved in her father's shooting. I'm not surprised the MPD is a mess if those are the people running it."

"Not everyone in the MPD is like them. Most of us are dedicated professionals who give our cases one hundred percent for as long as they're ours, and Carisma's is mine now."

LaToya blinked back tears as she looked away. "I've waited a long time for someone to care about my daughter. She'd be twenty-four now, but when I think of her, she's still thirteen and full of attitude, sass and sweetness. I love all my children, but she was my first, so that made her extra special."

"I'm expecting my first, so I get that."

"I'm happy for you that you were able to put your life back together."

"It wasn't easy, and some days it's still a work in progress, but I'm trying."

"It's been hard for me to move forward without knowing what happened to my baby or if she's still alive. Even if she isn't... It would help me move forward if I knew."

"I'll do all I can to get you some answers. Let's start by going over everything you remember about the last few days before Carisma and Daniella disappeared, and we'll go from there."

SAM WOKE the day after Christmas feeling confused and out of sorts about why her alarm hadn't gone off, until she remembered she was on vacation, and her mood immediately improved.

Nick was curled up to her, his arm around her waist.

Since she hadn't seen him again after he was called to the Situation Room the night before, she wondered what time he'd gotten to bed.

When she tried to ease out of his embrace without waking him, he tightened his arm around her.

"Don't go."

"Gotta pee."

"Come back."

"I will."

Sam used the bathroom and brushed her hair and teeth before returning to bed.

He raised his arm, inviting her to rejoin him.

"What time did you get to bed?"

"Four."

"Yikes. What's going on?"

"Not worth getting into. It's handled. For now, anyway."

"And we're not at war?"

"Not at the moment."

"Excellent work."

His grunt of laughter made her smile. "In case I forget to tell you, this job sucks."

"But the room service is something else."

"There is that, and today, we get to fly on *Marine One* and check out our super-cool presidential retreat for the first time."

"I guess it's not all bad. As Scotty pointed out, you're the only person in the world the Navy Band plays 'Hail to the Chief' for, not to mention ruffles and flourishes."

"True. That tops being called to the Situation Room while my wife is sucking my—"

Sam kissed him. "Do not say it."

"Why not? Are you shy?"

She snorted. "Hardly." She let her eyes wander around the room. "You just never know who's listening around here."

"No one is listening in here."

"So they say."

"These rooms are off-limits." His hand wandered under her T-shirt to cup her breast.

She didn't believe that any part of the White House was completely off-limits to spying eyes, but she'd take his word for it. "Anything more about the bomb?"

"Not yet. What time is it?"

"Eight fifteen."

His hand froze. "Seriously?"

"Yes, why?"

"I'm due in the Oval in fifteen minutes for a lesson on how to salute properly."

"You need to be taught that?"

"After we went to Des Moines, Commander Rodriguez mentioned I needed some training," he said of the naval officer who was one of his military attachés. "I guess past presidents have been mocked mercilessly for improper salutes."

"Why do you need to learn this today?"

"Because I'll be saluting the marine who greets us as we board *Marine One,* and apparently, my salute needs a bit of work."

"Oh. Okay. Do we really have to go to Camp David in the helicopter?"

"That's what the Secret Service prefers. It's quicker and more efficient than a motorcade."

"But the first lady hates to fly."

"As you learned the day we went to Des Moines, *Marine One* is a luxurious adventure, and I think you'll grow to love it."

"I'm certain I won't."

"I'll be there to hold your hand."

"That does make everything better."

He kissed her and got out of bed. "Sorry to have to go again. I'll make it up to you when we get to Camp David. I promise."

"Your job is one gigantic cock blocker."

"You said gigantic cock."

Sam laughed as he headed for the shower, but she wondered if they'd ever have uninterrupted sex again.

"THE OUTER EDGE of your hand needs to be angled this way," Lieutenant Commander Juan Rodriguez said, demonstrating.

Nick followed suit.

"That's good, but your elbow needs to come forward a bit, and the top of your arm should be more horizontal. May I, sir?"

"Of course."

Juan adjusted Nick's arm according to his instructions. "And don't forget, you always salute with your right hand, unless that arm is in a cast or sling."

"Got it."

"How's he looking?" Dr. Harry Flynn asked as he came into the Oval Office.

"I think he's got it," Juan said, saluting Nick, who returned the salute.

"Normally, the Navy doesn't salute indoors except for special occasions, but this is just for practice. The Army and Air Force salute indoors, outdoors, on base, off base."

"That's good to know," Nick said.

"As the commander in chief, they're always saluting you, not the other way around," Juan added.

"In my mind, I'm saluting you guys for the job you do to keep us safe."

"Thank you, sir. I'll see you on *Marine One*."

Juan and the other military attachés who rotated through the assignment accompanied Nick everywhere he went as the keepers of the "football" that contained the nuclear codes.

"The fun never ends around here, does it?" Harry asked when they were alone.

"You have no idea."

"Heard about the North Koreans messing with Christmas. Everything okay there?"

"For now. That's always a precarious situation, as you know. Ready for some R&R at Camp David?"

"We can't wait," he said of himself and his new fiancée, Lilia, who was also Sam's first lady chief of staff.

"How's engaged life treating you?"

"Never been better. I'm so, so glad I waited for her."

"She's great, and I'm glad you waited, too. She's perfect for you."

"In every possible way. I'll admit I used to think you and Sam were so... What's the word I'm looking for?"

"Ridiculous?"

Harry laughed. "I wouldn't say that, exactly, but close. And now... Now, I get it. When it's right, you don't care who knows you're madly in love."

"Speaking of that, we've heard *Saturday Night Live* is going to debut the actors playing us this weekend, and the focus will be on our too-hot-to-handle romance."

"Stop," Harry said, sputtering with laughter.

"I believe the term used to describe the skit was 'dry hump.'"

Harry lost it laughing. "That's going to be the highlight of my holiday season."

"I thought getting engaged would be."

"Nope. That will be."

"What's so funny?" Terry O'Connor asked when he joined them.

"*Saturday Night Live* and the dry hump," Harry said, losing it all over again.

"Have you told Sam?" Terry asked Nick as he clearly tried not to join Harry in the hysteria.

"She knows it's coming, but the words 'dry hump' haven't been brought to her attention. If they had, I certainly would've heard about it."

"As your chief of staff, I recommend you mention it to her sooner rather than later," Terry said.

"It's on my list for when we get to Camp David, along with some uninterrupted time with her and the kids."

"We'll do what we can to make sure that happens," Terry said, "but we've got a lot to do this week, beginning with the first draft of your State of the Union address. George is coming up the day after tomorrow to spend the day with us."

"I want to write that myself," Nick said.

Terry's raised brows conveyed his opinion of that plan. "The whole thing?"

"Yes."

"I still think you should sit with George and discuss your ideas."

"I'll give him a few hours, but not a whole day. I promised Sam a real break, and that's what we're going to do. And I hope you're working on getting us to Bora Bora for our anniversary in March."

"Being the director of the White House Medical Unit sure has its perks," Harry said, grinning, "such as traveling with the president everywhere he goes, including Bora Bora."

"We're working on the logistics for that," Terry said. "The Secret Service has sent an advance team—"

"Wait, what? An advance team to Bora Bora?"

"Yes, sir, Mr. President. As you know, that's a routine part of their planning for international trips."

"But this one is unofficial."

"Doesn't matter," Terry said. "They still go through the steps and will ship The Beast out there on a C-17 or C-5 ahead of your arrival."

The Secret Service allowed Nick to ride only in the car it provided.

"That seems like a lot of work and expense for an anniversary trip," Nick said, already anticipating what the press would make of it.

"The same effort went into it when you were VP," Terry reminded him.

"I didn't like it any better then, but I was under much less scrutiny than I am now."

"Do you wish to change your plans, sir?" Terry asked.

Thinking of the many sacrifices Sam had made since he'd unexpectedly been launched into the Oval Office on Thanksgiving, he shook his head. "Sam is looking forward to it, and so am I." They were going while Eli was on spring break, so he'd be home to help with Alden and Aubrey. Everything was planned, down to the Secret Service doing advance work, apparently.

He would take his lumps with the press to give his wife a memorable anniversary. In the two years they'd been married, their lives had changed dramatically due to his unprecedented rise through the political ranks to the top job. That same dizzying rise had led to claims of illegitimacy from political rivals, since he'd never been elected as vice president.

Rather, he'd been tapped to complete the term of ailing Vice President Gooding. Thankfully, there was precedent for his situation, dating back to when Gerald Ford replaced indicted Vice President Spiro Agnew and then ascended to the presidency when President Nixon resigned.

Nick's communications team repeatedly referred to Ford when questions of illegitimacy surfaced almost daily in the press room.

"Back to the State of the Union," Nick said. "We need to use this opportunity to reintroduce me to the American people and to state my intentions to work on behalf of everyone, not just the people who agree with me. I have some thoughts about how I'd like to do it that you might not like."

"We look forward to your input, Mr. President," Terry said. "I'll let Will know to expect that you'll be writing most of it yourself."

"Please do." Nick had been thinking a lot about what he wanted to say to the country in his first State of the Union and had declined to have it postponed when the Speaker of the House had inquired as to whether he'd like more time before the nationally televised address. He was ready to stand before a joint session of Congress and the American people and stake his claim to the job he'd told them he didn't want shortly before it became his.

He had some work to do to prepare for that event, now just over a month away on the first of February, and he was ready to get down to it.

But not until he had some much-needed vacation time with his family—and he had to find a minute to tell Sam about *SNL* and the dry hump. He couldn't wait for that conversation.

CHAPTER FOUR

A s Sam stood in the doorway of the South Portico, preparing to cross the South Lawn to *Marine One* on that cold but sunny late December morning, she tried not to think about flying in a helicopter. She'd done it once before and had lived to tell, but despite what Nick said, it would never become routine to her.

Their social secretary and close friend, Shelby Faircloth Hill, would accompany them on this first trip since she'd coordinated their arrival with the team at Camp David.

"You're going to love it," Shelby said to Sam. "I was there last week to make sure everything is ready for you guys, and it's just wonderful. I also took care of picking up all the groceries you asked for."

"Thank you for handling that." Sam said. "It'll be nice to get out of the gilded cage for a few days. I'm determined to do some cooking for this family for once."

"I'm sure they'll enjoy that. You all seem to be adjusting beautifully."

"We're doing all right, but it's... a lot. Nick hasn't been out of here since we went to Des Moines. That's the hard part for him. But we're certainly not complaining as we walk out to our own personal helicopter."

"Don't worry," Shelby said, laughing. "I get it. I'm looking forward to a night off from motherhood, you know the job I couldn't wait to have?"

Sam laughed. "I feel you."

"Avery and Noah are driving up tomorrow for the week, and by the time they arrive, I expect to be fully twitching from withdrawals from my darling Noah."

"Enjoy the break, Shelby. You've more than earned it."

"Thanks for inviting us to join you guys. Avery is delirious with excitement to see Camp David, but don't let on that I told you that. You know how hard he works to be cool about everything."

"I do, and your secret is safe with me. P.S., of course we invited you guys. You're family."

"Mr. President," Brant said. "We're ready for you."

Nick reached for Sam's hand. "Shelby, walk with us."

Without his invitation, Shelby would've hung back. Sam was glad he'd asked her. She'd become like a sister to Sam and Nick, and they loved her.

Wearing the new long red wool coat her designer, Marcus, had sent over, Sam followed Nick's lead and waved to the press assigned to record their every movement, knowing their walk across the lawn would make the news. Reporters called out to Nick, asking for comments on the bomb, North Korea, former Secretary of State Ruskin's latest swipe against him and whether he had anything to say about an editorial in the *New York Times* about an unelected president having his finger on the nuclear button.

He ignored them while smiling and waving like he hadn't a care in the world, laughing at Skippy galloping along with Scotty, excited for an adventure.

Sam, Celia and the kids went ahead of Nick up the stairs, but Sam fell back to watch him salute the young marine who greeted him at the bottom of the stairs. Sam gave Nick's salute an A-plus.

"Mrs. Cappuano, I'm Colonel Stone Walker, your new chief pilot, and it's my pleasure to welcome you on board *Marine One*." He was tall, with dark hair and eyes, and wore an impressive uniform covered in pins and ribbons.

Sam shook his outstretched hand. "Pleasure to meet you, Colonel. This is my stepmother, Celia Holland."

"Lovely to meet you, ma'am," the colonel said as he shook hands with Celia.

"You as well," she said. "This is all *so* exciting."

"We're glad to have you on board."

Watching Celia's delight at the perks that came with life in the White House was fun for Sam. She was thrilled her stepmother had agreed to be part of their grand adventure.

Nick entered the aircraft, and the colonel introduced himself to Nick, who shook his hand. "What's your handle, Colonel?"

The man seemed slightly embarrassed. "It's, um, Taco, sir, due to my unreasonable love of them."

Nick smiled. "I love me a good taco myself. I think we'll be great friends."

"I'd enjoy that, sir. We have perfect conditions for our flight to Camp David."

"That's what the first lady wants to hear. She's not a big fan of flying."

"I promise you'll be perfectly safe, ma'am."

"That's good to know. Thank you."

"Please make yourselves comfortable, and we'll have you there in no time. When we arrive, you'll be greeted by Captain Martin, CO of Camp David, and the staff, all of whom will come out to the pad to welcome you, since it's your first visit."

"Got it," Nick said. "We're looking forward to meeting them."

The kids were excited about the gifts the crew had left for them, including *Marine One* toys and T-shirts to commemorate their first ride.

Nick checked to make sure everyone was buckled in, then sat next to Sam and put on his seat belt. A low rumble of conversation came from a compartment in the back, where White House staff and pool reporters rode. Lilia and Harry were back there, along with Terry and several other West Wing staffers and Secret Service agents.

It was nice to have friends along for the ride.

"Scotty, hang on to Skippy," Nick said. "She's apt to be startled by the engines."

"I've got her."

Scotty and the twins were fascinated by every aspect of *Marine One*, from the plush leather seats to the beverage and snack service to the way the chopper lifted off the South Lawn with effortless grace.

"This is *so* cool," Scotty said. They had to speak a little louder than usual to be heard over the engines. "We're the only ones in the whole world who get this kind of service."

"Don't let it go to your head, champ," Nick said. "It's temporary."

"That doesn't mean we can't enjoy it while it lasts."

"Did you bring that report you wrote about Camp David for social studies like I asked you to?" Nick asked.

"I did, but I have no clue why I have to bring schoolwork on vacation."

"Because I want you to tell us about the camp before we get there."

"You already know about it."

Sam gestured for Scotty to proceed. "The rest of us don't know squat about it."

"You've got the floor, son," Nick said.

"If you insist, Mr. President," Scotty said with a grin, knowing how Nick hated to be called that by close friends and family.

"I do insist, and I'm the boss of the whole country."

"Talk about not letting it go to your head." Scotty rolled his eyes and cleared his throat dramatically as he held up the typed pages of his report. "I'll give you the highlights. Located in Catoctin Mountain Park, Camp David is eighteen hundred feet above Thurmont, Maryland, and it's actually a Navy base called Naval Support Facility Thurmont."

"Wait, there's a mountain in Maryland called Catoctin?" Sam asked. "How have I lived here all my life and never heard of it?"

"You also didn't know that the Naval Observatory is the keeper of the Master Clock."

"I still want to know whose idea it was to send him to school," Sam said as Shelby cackled with laughter.

"As I always say, it certainly wasn't my idea," Scotty replied. "Anyway, the first president to have a retreat located outside of Washington was Hoover, who founded Rapidan Camp in 1929 in an area that became the Shenandoah National Park after the Hoovers deeded it to the National Park Service. FDR didn't like that place, and besides, he spent most of his off time at his home in Hyde Park, New York, or on his presidential yacht, the USS *Potomac*. During World War II, it was decided that it was too dangerous to use the yacht because of the possibility of being attacked by bombers or U-boats, so they went looking for another location and ended up at the place that's now Camp David. Roosevelt called it Shangri-La. President Eisenhower thought that name was too fancy, so he renamed it Camp David, after his grandson, who later married one of the Nixon daughters.

"Roosevelt hosted Winston Churchill at the camp, and Presidents Carter and Clinton hosted the Middle East peace summits in 1978 and 2000, and many other world leaders have come to Camp David. There's all sorts of cool stuff there, like a gym, a bowling alley, a heated pool, a game room and a movie theater, but if you're thinking it's going to be fancy like the White House, it's not. The word 'rustic' is most often used to describe the accommodations. The president's cabin is called Aspen, and that's where we'll stay, and your office is located at Laurel, Dad, but I'm sure they'll show you where that is as they drive you around on Golf Cart One."

Sam recalled making a deal with Scotty to go to the gym together on vacation. She hoped he'd forgotten about that.

"Wait," Nick said. "That's really a thing? Golf Cart One?"

"Yep," Scotty said.

"Do I get to drive?" Nick asked.

"Yep," Scotty said again.

"Yes," Nick said with a fist pump. "I miss driving."

"I want to drive, too," Scotty said. "It's never too soon for you to start teaching me how. And since we can't use an actual car, this will have to do."

"We'll see what we can do," Nick said, smiling.

Sam looked out the window for familiar landmarks and recognized the Baltimore-Washington Parkway, which was strangely devoid of traffic, thanks to the holiday week.

"When can we go to the game room?" Alden asked.

"As soon as we get there," Nick promised him. "We just have to get settled first and figure out the lay of the land."

"What does that mean?" Alden asked. "Lay of the land?"

"The location of everything. I'm sure they'll give us a tour."

Forty-five minutes after liftoff, Sam felt the chopper start to descend into an area that appeared at first to be all trees. In the mountains, there was snow on the ground, which she hadn't expected. "There's snow," Sam said, gesturing for the twins to look out their window.

"I sent boots and snow clothes up for the kids," Shelby said.

Sam glanced at her friend. "God bless you for all you do for us."

"That's my job—and it's my pleasure."

"Did you guys have a nice Christmas?"

"We did. Avery's family was here, and it was lots of fun with Noah this year. I can't believe that by next Christmas, we'll have two little ones underfoot." She patted her pregnant belly. "I'm ready for this person to make his or her appearance."

"How can you stand not knowing what you're having? I'd want to know the second I could." Not that there was much chance of that ever happening for Sam, who'd had a rough go of it in the fertility department. That had made her extra grateful for the four children who'd come into their lives through adoption for Scotty and guardianship for the twins, who'd brought Eli to their family.

"There're so few surprises in this life," Shelby said.

"I guess."

"You're too impatient to wait for things like that."

"I'd go mad!"

"Look," Nick said. "There it is."

From the air, Sam saw a sprawling campus of wooden cabins, trails and other buildings that made for a much bigger "camp" than she'd expected. Although she should've known it would be, as protecting the president and his family required a ton of people and resources.

The helicopter made a smooth landing on a gigantic helipad, and when the pilots cut the engines, the sudden silence was almost jarring.

Sam gestured for the others to file off ahead of her until only she and Nick were left on board. "Colonel Walker, I have a question for you."

"Yes, ma'am. And please, feel free to call me Taco. Everyone does."

"Taco, what if I need to get out of here for some reason, like a big crisis at work or something?"

"If you're here, we're here," he replied. "We can only use *Marine One* if the president is also on board, so if he's willing to leave with you, we can fly you back on *Marine One*. If not, we can bring in another chopper to transport you, or the Secret Service can take you via motorcade."

Sam felt squirrely at the thought of how much time any of those options would take. "Thank you for the info."

"Of course, ma'am. We're here for you, so let us know if there's anything we can do."

Nick shook his hand. "Thank you for the smooth flight, Taco."

"My pleasure, sir. Enjoy your time at camp."

"Will do."

With Nick's hand on her lower back, Sam headed for the air stairs to take in the storied camp she'd heard about all her life but had never given two thoughts to how it ran or what went on there.

A naval officer with gold stripes on her uniform sleeve approached them. Petite, with brown skin and a warm smile that lit up her dark eyes, the woman said, "Mr. President, Mrs. Cappuano, I'm Captain Tisha Martin, the commanding officer of Naval Support Facility Thurmont, and it's my great pleasure to welcome you to Camp David." She shook hands with them and the kids. "My team and I are here to make sure you fully enjoy your stay."

"Thank you for having us," Nick said. "We're looking forward to it."

After introducing them to her full team of military and civilian employees, Captain Martin led them to a line of golf carts. "Elijah, would you like to follow us with the kids and Skippy?"

"Sure," Eli said. "We can do that."

The reporters who'd traveled with them on board *Marine One* and a lone TV camera recorded their every move. Even away from the White House, the world was still watching, Sam thought, determined to shake off that unsettling feeling to enjoy this getaway with her family.

Staffers and Secret Service agents boarded the other golf carts.

"Would you like to drive, Mr. President?" Captain Martin asked.

"I'd love to."

"I'll take the back seat so you can direct him," Sam said to Captain Martin.

"That's the hangar where *Marine One* will be during your stay here at Camp David. If you're here, there'll always be a complement of pilots available to transport you at a moment's notice if necessary." As they made their way into the camp, Captain Martin pointed out the chapel, health clinic, gym, fire department and the barracks where the Navy and Marine personnel permanently stationed there lived as well as the officer housing. The wooden guest cabins, painted a mossy green color, had names like Birch, Dogwood, Rosebud, Walnut, Hawthorn, Hickory, Sycamore and Linden, which was fitting, as the camp sat within an oasis of trees. "You'll never hear a plane overhead, as Camp David is a secure air space. Over there is the playground, which the kids will love, and the Leatherwood basketball court."

"Check out the presidential seal on the court," Nick said, pointing it out to Sam.

She couldn't help but note how happy he seemed to be there, which lifted her spirts, too. He loved to play basketball, and having a court right there would be great for him. If only she could shake off the anxiety that came from being so far removed from her own home base in DC. It was the same feeling she'd had on trips to Bora Bora the last few years, but it was even more so here. When they were on those trips, she was far enough away to let go of her work responsibilities. Here, she was close enough to get to DC if needed, but it would take some doing, and that was the part she found stressful.

Shake it off, she told herself as she took in the scenery and coziness of the camp. *You deserve a vacation like everyone else.*

Captain Martin directed Nick to a cabin with a rough-hewn sign on the front designating it as Cedar. "Welcome to the presidential cabin, home away from home to every president since FDR." She pointed to a small pond in front of the cabin. "President Roosevelt had that built because he wanted a water source nearby, as he was desperately afraid of fire."

They followed her up the stairs to a porch and inside to a surprisingly dated cabin that had just the right amount of coziness and comfort with a stone fireplace being lit by a young Navy sailor, a sunny living room with comfortable-looking furniture and bookshelves she would check out later. Captain Martin showed them the kitchen and pantry, neither of which was anything flashy, as well as four bedrooms. Scotty and Eli decided to share a room, as would the twins.

"This is lovely," Sam said.

"I'm glad you like it," Captain Martin said. "Camp David isn't to everyone's taste, but those who are able to relax and fully soak up the atmosphere tend to really love the escape it provides from the grind of the White House."

"I can already tell we're going to love it," Nick said.

The sailor lighting the fire stood to greet them. "Welcome, Mr. President, Mrs. Cappuano."

Sam and Nick shook hands with him.

"What's your name, sailor?" Nick asked.

"Petty Officer Third Class Mick Torres, sir."

"Where're you from, Petty Officer Torres?"

"Tulsa, Oklahoma, sir."

"Thank you for your service." Nick gestured to the White House photographer who'd accompanied them and posed for a photo with the young man. "I'll make sure you get a copy of that."

"Thank you so much, sir."

After the sailor left, Captain Martin said, "You've made his entire career with that photo, sir. It means a lot to the team that runs Camp David to have you and your family here, Mr. President."

"Please tell your crew they're welcome to speak to us like the normal people we are, and pass along an invitation to anyone who'd like to play basketball with me tomorrow morning around ten."

"I'll do that, sir. I'm sure you'll get a crowd."

"Great, then we can have a tournament."

"I'll leave you to get settled." She pointed to a phone on a side table. "Pick that up to let us know if you need anything at all. The White House has sent a full kitchen staff to take care of you, and they'll have lunch ready within the hour."

"Thank you again for the warm welcome," Nick said, shaking her hand.

They called the kids in for the photo they took with Captain Martin before she and the photographer left them to get settled.

"What do you think?" Nick asked when the kids had gone to inspect their rooms.

"This is just what we need."

He put his arms around her and held her tightly. "I couldn't agree more."

CHAPTER FIVE

Driving south on I-95 toward Richmond, Jeannie debated how much to tell her relatively new partner. Detective Matt O'Brien seemed like a good guy, but they hadn't yet found the easy groove she'd had with her former partner, Detective Will Tyrone. He'd chosen to leave the force after their colleague Detective Arnold's murder. But because she was taking Matt with her as she did something they'd been ordered not to do, she felt guilty about not telling him the truth about their mission.

However, she reasoned, by not telling him, he could say later that he hadn't known.

Ugh, what to do? This reminded her of when she and Will had discovered that Skip Holland had ignored some rather significant evidence in another cold case and had kept that information from Sam out of respect for her father's reputation. That had come back around to bite them in the ass—hard.

This mission could cost her much more, as the order to stand down on the Deasly case had come from the chief.

"Are you going to tell me why we're going to Richmond?" Matt asked after twenty minutes of silence.

"I'm trying to decide whether I should. It would be better for you if you didn't know."

"I'm not sure what to do with that."

Jeannie sighed. "Here's the thing... I want to tell you, but I have no idea if I can trust you with information that I shouldn't be giving you. Does that make sense?"

"Not even kinda, and yes, you can trust me. We're partners, Jeannie. That means I've got your back. I know it's been a rough year for you guys, losing Arnold and then having Tyrone decide to leave. But you can count on me. I swear it."

"We could get in trouble for this—big trouble. We're defying an order that came straight from the top by following leads to Richmond."

Matt thought about that for a full minute. "Does the LT know where we're going and why?"

"She does."

After another long pause, he said, "Then I guess she's out on whatever limb we're on with us. Right?"

"I've been advised to proceed with extreme caution. This is a fact-finding mission. Once I know for sure I've found the person I'm looking for, then she and I are going to consult on next steps."

"Isn't she at Camp David?"

"She's aware of what's going on and is expecting my call later today. If, or when, this blows up in our faces, it would be better for you if you could say you were asked to come along but weren't told where we were going or why."

"And you think people will believe I did what I was told, got in the car and asked no questions?"

"Isn't that what you did?"

"I was expecting you to fill me in on the details."

Jeannie wanted to believe him when he said she could trust him. What choice did she have? He was her partner for better or worse, and in months of working together, he'd given her no reason to question his loyalty. "It's up to you, Matt. I can tell you, or you can choose not to know. The latter would be better for you if this goes bad, which it's apt to."

"I'll take my chances. Lay it on me."

Jeannie told him everything she knew about the disappearance of Carisma Deasly—and Daniella Brown—and how former Detective Stahl had failed to do even the most rudimentary investigation despite filing reports to the contrary. "I met with Carisma's mother, LaToya, this morning."

"I would've gone with you."

"I know, but I decided it would be better if I went by myself. I thought she might be more forthcoming one-on-one."

"Was she?"

"She had a lot to say, and none of it good for us or the other law enforcement agencies that failed her so profoundly. No one did *anything*, Matt. Like *at all*. A thirteen-year-old girl goes missing, her mother has a pretty good idea who took her, and *no one* cared."

"That's unbelievable."

"I'm so angry about it. It's why I couldn't stop this, even when I was told to."

"Why did they tell you to stop? I don't get it."

"You know how Sam solved the Calvin Worthington case in an afternoon after fifteen years?"

"Of course. That was incredible."

"It was, but it makes the department look ridiculous that the case was so easily solved the minute someone decided to care. Add to it that the victims in both these cases are Black kids, and it looks even worse."

"So they'd rather we *not* solve the cases than make the department look bad?"

"As you know, it's been a rough few months with Stahl convicted, Conklin and Hernandez charged in relation to Skip Holland's case, and the FBI investigating us. People are bracing for the FBI report, which is due in January and not expected to do us any favors. The chief wants us to stand down on the cold cases for now, but how am I supposed to do that when I think I might know where Daniella is?"

"You can't," Matt said bluntly.

"And if we turn it over to the FBI or the marshals, we could still look bad because it took only a couple of days of effort to close an eleven-year-old case, even if they're the ones who get the credit. People are going to be, like, where was the MPD all this time, you know?"

"It's a valid question."

"It certainly is. Even though I don't agree that standing down on this case is the right thing to do, I can see where the chief is coming from. He has to manage the political and media fallout, which was significant after Worthington."

"You'd think people would just be thankful the case was solved."

"You would think, but what they see is a department so inefficient that a case that could've—and should've—been solved fifteen years ago was left undone for all that time until someone bothered to care. It's a bad look for us, no matter how you spin it. And solving Carisma's case, if we solve it, won't help with the PR mess the chief is already dealing with."

"But that's no reason to ignore what we've already learned."

"That's my thinking as well." She glanced over at him. "We're defying orders that came directly from the chief. I need you to say you understand that."

"I do."

"I appreciate you coming with me, which was Sam's only request —that I not go alone."

"Where you go, I go. That's what partners do."

For the first time since Will Tyrone had told her he couldn't bear to continue on the job after his close friend Arnold was murdered, Jeannie felt like she had a true partner again. "I should probably tell you I'm pregnant so you'll know why I'm green every morning."

"I wondered because I've noticed you having rough mornings. Congrats. That's great news."

"Thanks. We're excited and scared and all the things."

"You'll be great parents."

"Thank you. I hope so. Talking with LaToya this morning was so upsetting. I tried to put myself in her shoes, not knowing where my child was for eleven years. She's twenty-four now, if she's still alive, and LaToya has had to miss her all that time and live with the not knowing. I'd go mad."

"I don't know how people handle some of the stuff life throws at them. The things we see on this job... It's a lot sometimes."

"It's a lot *all* the time."

"True," he said with a laugh.

"People join our squad thinking it's going to be so cool, and sometimes it is," Jeannie said. "Working with Sam is amazing, especially now that she's first lady and bringing all that glam to us. But most of the time, it's heartbreak and drudge."

"Yeah, but it's also satisfying to get justice for our victims and their families."

"It is, even if it doesn't change the fact that the victims are still dead and their families changed forever. That's one of the reasons why I was intrigued by the Deasly case. Maybe she's still alive, and we can reunite her with her family. That's not something we get to do very often as Homicide detectives."

"What's our plan for Richmond?"

"Before Christmas, I spoke to the ex-boyfriend of Daniella Brown, LaToya's former friend. LaToya did a lot for Daniella, giving her a place to stay and paying for two trips to rehab with money she didn't exactly have lying around while supporting three kids on her own. LaToya and Daniella's ex confirm that Daniella was obsessed with Carisma and referred to her as her daughter."

"And the mom didn't say anything about that?"

"At the time, she let it slide, thinking Daniella loved Carisma, and so what if she called her a daughter? That didn't change the truth about who her mother was."

"I can see that."

"Carisma looked up to Daniella, loved to talk fashion and movies and celebrities with her. As a working single mom, LaToya appreciated the attention Daniella gave to Carisma."

"What about LaToya's other kids? Did she have a rapport with them, too?"

"She did, but she was closest to Carisma. They were 'special' friends, is how LaToya put it."

"Was she ever concerned about Daniella taking off with her?"

"Not for a second. It never occurred to her that something like that could happen, mostly because LaToya was basically supporting Daniella, too. Like, where was she going to go, you know?"

"Does LaToya think it's at all possible that someone else took both of them?"

"She acknowledges that's possible, but not probable. For one thing, they weren't together when they went missing. Carisma was walking home from school and was seen talking to someone in a car. A witness didn't see her get in the car, but it's assumed that she did."

"Do we have a description of the car?"

"The witness wasn't sure what kind of car it was, but it was an older sedan, maybe a Corolla or Civic in either navy or black."

"That narrows it down to thousands of possibilities."

"Yep. Daniella was at LaToya's the afternoon of Carisma's disappearance, but then she went out to get coffee that same night and never came back. LaToya said that in all the confusion over Carisma's disappearance, it took her a full day to realize Daniella was gone, too. That's when she started to suspect the two events were related."

"If it's related, I'd want to know who was in the car and how they were attached to Daniella."

"With the ex-boyfriend's help, I did some digging into people she was close to at the time, and one of them was an uncle who was only a couple of years older than her. He drove a navy-blue Corolla at the time."

"What do we know about him?"

"Reggie Parks, age forty-two now, in and out of trouble all his life, beginning as a juvenile and escalating into drugs, robbery, B&E."

"So, it wouldn't be much of a leap to add kidnapping to the list."

"Right."

"Where is he now?"

"Locked up for the latest B&E. If things don't pan out in Richmond, my next stop is at Jessup to see him. The ex-boyfriend told me Daniella had people in Richmond and where to find them. He isn't sure they still live there, but I figured it's worth a shot to scope the place out."

"Definitely."

"Thanks," Jeannie said. "You know... for caring about Carisma."

"It's about time someone cared about her."

"That's how I feel, too, and I'm strangely unconcerned about getting in trouble if there's any possibility of finding her and reuniting her with her mother and siblings."

"Right there with you, partner."

NICK LOVED everything about Camp David, from the no-frills accommodations to the hiking trails to the basketball court and the barbecue pit that was built during the Eisenhower administration and never upgraded. A feeling of historical significance hung over the place as he stood on the same porch FDR had once occupied with Winston Churchill. He took a deep breath of the fresh, cold air and felt himself begin to truly relax for the first time since his life—and that of his family—was turned upside down by President Nelson's sudden death.

The ability to move around freely outside was such a gift after being under lock and key at the White House. Most days, his outdoor time consisted of the one-minute walk to and from work on the West Colonnade. That was often the only fresh air he got all day as he passed the Rose Garden on the way to the Oval Office. In comparison to that, Camp David was paradise.

He'd known, of course, that being president would be confining. Being vice president had been confining, but this was even more so. The intense confines of the presidency had to be experienced to be truly understood. There were days when he wondered what would happen if he simply stood up, walked out the doors of the Oval Office and headed for the gates to freedom.

The Secret Service wouldn't let him get far before they'd be on him, redirecting him back to the gilded cage where he belonged, like a cockatoo who'd staged a naughty escape. He was entertained by the fantasies of the many ways he might escape, walk away and never look back. Except he'd never leave his beloved wife and children. Escaping with a party of six plus a crazy dog would be far more complicated than a solo mission.

Sam came up behind him and slipped her arms around him, resting her head on his back. "What're you thinking about out here in the cold all by yourself?"

The hug and the question reminded him of the first week they'd been back together after her ex-husband had tried to blow them up. "I like it here. I can breathe here."

"It is pretty."

Someone who didn't know her as well as he did wouldn't have heard it, but to him, her anxiety came through loud and clear. He turned to face her. "What's wrong?"

"What? Nothing. We're on vacation. What could be wrong?"

"Samantha, you might be able to get away with that with anyone else, but not with me. I can feel distress coming from you."

She scowled at him. "Knock that off. I don't like it when you know me too well."

"Tough shit," he said, smiling. "I know you better than anyone, so tell me what's wrong."

"I just have this odd feeling right here." She rubbed her chest. "Came on when I realized how hard it would be to get back to the District if I need to."

"Why would you need to? You're on vacation."

"Right, but you know... Always on duty, like you are. But unlike you, I can't just hop aboard *Marine One* and get back to town in forty-five minutes. It would take a motorcade and coordination and *time*."

He rested his hands on her shoulders. "Let me set your mind at ease. If you need to get back for any reason, I'll go with you so we can use the chopper, okay?"

"You don't want to do that. Not to mention, the press would have a cow over you taking me back to town on your chopper."

"I'll do whatever it takes to make it so you can relax and enjoy yourself this week after a very, *very* rough couple of months. That includes lending you my helicopter with a personal escort back to town, if it comes to that." He kissed the tip of her nose and then her lips. "Are we good now?"

"We're better than we were. Thank you for understanding."

"I get it, babe. Even when you're not on duty, your squad is your responsibility, and you take that seriously."

"I do, and even though I left them in Gonzo's perfectly capable hands, I sort of freaked out when I realized how far removed from civilization we are up here."

"Don't worry about a thing. Just breathe in the fresh air and the woodsmoke."

"I do love the smell of woodsmoke."

"I know you do. You want to go for a walk with me and do some breathing?"

"Since we've lost the kids to the game room, probably for the week, that sounds good."

He extended a hand and escorted her down the steps. "Which way you want to go?"

"Surprise me."

He was certain his Secret Service detail was close by, but for the moment, the agents were out of sight. "Brant and the others probably love it here as much as I do. It's so sealed off and protected that their jobs become that much easier here."

"Probably. I had no idea what to expect of this place, but it's much bigger than I thought it would be and obviously a very involved operation. What do the people stationed here do when we're not here?"

"I suppose they prepare for the next time we come."

"That seems kind of boring."

"From what I understand, it's considered a great honor to be stationed at the president's retreat, even if there are stretches of time between visits."

"I'm just saying—an occasional visit wouldn't be enough to keep me from being bored senseless the rest of the time."

"Duly noted, love."

They strolled aimlessly through wooded trails that went on for miles.

"It's nice to be outside," he said.

"I don't know how you can stand being so cooped up in the White House."

"I can't stand it, but what's the alternative?"

"We have to get you out of there more often."

"I'm sure we'll find a groove with that, eventually."

"Sooner rather than later. I can't have you going loco on me."

"Who else would I go loco on?"

"Haha, very funny."

"Speaking of funny, we heard that *SNL* is releasing their first

Cappuano administration sketch this weekend with an interesting theme."

Sam stopped walking and turned to him, giving him a wary look. "What theme?"

"Don't shoot the messenger. Promise?"

"What theme, Nick?"

"Um, I believe the words used were 'dry hump.'"

"What? *Dry hump*? What the hell is that about?"

"Terry thinks it's, um, a nod to our rather obvious affection for each other."

"Stop it."

"I'm sure it'll be hilarious."

"It'll be mortifying!"

"That, too, but what do we care? We're madly in love, and we don't care who knows it."

"Scotty will kill us for this."

"It'll be fine. We'll find out later."

"Wait. Today's Saturday, so it's *tonight*? Isn't the whole world on vacation this week?"

"Apparently, they couldn't wait for the New Year to air this skit."

"I love how you wait until the last possible minute to tell me about it."

"Technically, the last possible minute would've been at eleven twenty-nine tonight."

CHAPTER SIX

Before Sam could form a cutting reply to his outrageous statement, her phone rang with a call from Jeannie McBride, which was a relief. At least her phone worked on the mountaintop. "Please hold," she said to Nick as she took the call. "What's up?"

"We've located Daniella Brown," Jeannie said, sounding elated. "It's definitely her."

"What're you thinking?"

"We need to bring in reinforcements on this. How do you feel about me calling Jesse Best?"

"I feel good about it, but before we do that, I need to consult with the captain and chief."

"Is there a chance the chief will put the kibosh on the whole thing?"

"I honestly don't know, but I don't think so. He'll be pissed, though."

"Please tell him I take his orders very seriously, but I was already so far down the road with this case when the order came down that I couldn't, in good conscience, stop when I had a chance of locating Carisma."

"I'll pass that along."

"I'm willing to take the hit on this, Sam. I don't care if I ever go beyond detective. I have so many other things in my life that matter more than this job. I couldn't have lived with myself if I didn't see this through."

"You're not in this alone, and I'll tell him. I'll call you back."

"Okay."

"What now?" Nick asked after Sam slapped the phone closed.

"Jeannie thinks she's found the woman who took Carisma Deasly, and now I've got to call the chief and let him know what's happening and hopefully get the go-ahead to call in the U.S. Marshals to take it from here. Maybe if they get the credit, he won't fire us both."

"Yikes," Nick said.

"You said it." She flipped open her phone and put through the call to the captain, who didn't pick up. So she called her uncle Joe.

"Happy Boxing Day," he said. "I'm still high off my night in the Lincoln Bedroom."

"I'm glad you enjoyed that."

"It was the highlight of our lives. Thank you for the honor."

"I'm hoping you'll remember that and how much you love me when I tell you why I'm calling."

"Oh, come on, Sam! I was having a good day. I saw my niece on the news with her family, walking across the White House lawn to *Marine One*, and that put me in a damned good mood."

"I'm glad you're in a good mood, because I need to talk to you about that order you gave concerning Stahl's cold cases."

"What about it?" he asked, all hints of frivolity gone from his stern tone.

"It's like this... And I did try to call the captain first. When we received that order, Detective McBride was already far along on an eleven-year-old missing-person case involving a teenage girl. For Jeannie, it became a matter of deciding whether she could live with herself if she didn't see it through to completion."

Sam grimaced at Nick, who grinned at the face she made.

"With that in mind," Sam continued, "Detective McBride is in Richmond with my blessing and believes she's located Daniella Brown, the friend of Carisma Deasly's mother who went missing around the same time as Carisma and was widely believed by Carisma's mother and others who knew them both to be involved in the girl's disappearance."

"What are you asking me?"

"I'd like to bring in Jesse Best and let the U.S. Marshals take it from here. With your permission, of course."

"*Now* you're asking for permission, Lieutenant?"

"Yes, sir, and apologizing at the same time. I hope you can understand the way Detective McBride and I felt, knowing she might be close to getting answers for a family that has waited too long for them."

"I do understand that, but I had a very good reason for telling you to hold off."

"And I respect that, as does Detective McBride. We aren't looking to bring any more negative PR down on the department. That's why we're asking to call in the marshals. We're more than fine with them getting the credit for anything that happens next."

"I'll authorize the call to the marshals if Detective McBride—and I assume Detective O'Brien—aren't part of the raid."

"Understood."

"I hope you do understand, Lieutenant, that there're only so many hits this department can take under my watch before the mayor, the city council and the residents begin calling for new leadership. I assume that's the last thing you'd want to see happen."

"The very last thing, sir."

"I expect you and your team to follow my orders, regardless of who we are to each other."

"Yes, sir."

"Are you just saying that to appease me?"

"No, sir. I take your orders seriously, as does Detective McBride. I hope you can empathize with the position she was in, having already done a considerable amount of work toward finding this missing person when the order came down."

"I do empathize, and I'm not a monster, Lieutenant. I intended the pause on examining Stahl's cold cases to be temporary, until we get past whatever fresh hell is coming our way in the FBI report."

"Maybe it won't be that bad."

"I'm under no illusions. And while I have you, I should let you know the union is pushing back hard against Sergeant Ramsey's firing and intends to appeal it in court unless he receives due process."

Sam couldn't believe what she was hearing. "They honestly think they have a case when he was caught vandalizing my office?"

"He says he didn't do it."

"They have his prints!"

"He says that could've happened during the regular course of business as the two of you work together."

"Anyone who knows either of us is aware that we do *not* work together."

"I wanted you to be aware that he may be back on the job while we dot the i's and cross the t's."

"Thanks for the great news."

"Try not to worry about it. We have other ways of getting rid of troublemakers, and I intend to do whatever it takes to permanently rid us of him as soon as I can."

"But you're planning to keep me and McBride around?" Sam asked, hoping for a moment of levity before they ended the call.

"For the moment, but as usual, you're both skating on the thinnest of ice."

"We like to live dangerously."

"Keep me in the loop with Best and the marshals. I'll let Jake know that I spoke to you and gave the go-ahead."

"Thank you for everything. I don't care what anyone else says about you, you're the best."

"I do what I can for the people."

Sam's mouth fell open in shock. "That is *one hundred percent* trademarked."

"Did you or did you not allow one of your officers to defy a direct order from yours truly?"

"You should feel free to use that line to your heart's content, sir."

"Somehow, I thought you might say that. How's Camp David? Is it as cool as it seems?"

"It is. Since you're on vacation this week, too, you and Marti ought to take a ride up one day and check it out for yourselves."

"Seriously?"

Nick nodded in agreement.

"Of course. Our camp is your camp. Let me know when you'd like to come."

"Sam... Wait, is this and the Lincoln Bedroom blackmail to butter me up for future insubordination?"

"Blackmail is such an ugly word, Chief."

His snort of laughter made her smile. She was relieved to know they were—as always—in accord.

"Please come up. We'd love to have you."

"We'll do that. I'll text you. And let me know about Best."

"Will do."

"Tell McBride I'm not going to fire her and that I said good work."

"I'll do that, too. Talk to you later." She glanced at Nick. "I need two more minutes."

"I'm enjoying the fresh air. Take your time."

"Is fresh air your new drug of choice?"

"It is."

Sam put through the call to Jeannie. "I talked to the chief, and he gave the green light to call in Jesse and the marshals to take it from here. He wants you and Matt nowhere near the raid. You're to pass on the info and then step aside."

"Got it and will do."

"I'm sorry to have to do this to you, Jeannie. You and I will know this is your arrest."

"That doesn't matter. All I care about is getting Carisma back to her mother, if she's still alive and in there. I'll make the call to Best and tell him the request comes from the top."

"Keep me posted?"

"Will do. Is he pissed?"

"He understood you were already into it and couldn't let it go when you were on to something. He said to tell you that you did good work, he's not going to fire either of us, but as usual, we're skating on the thinnest of ice."

"Where we do our best work."

Sam laughed. "Indeed. I'll wait to hear from you."

"Thanks for the support."

"You got it." Sam slapped her phone closed. "And with that, I'm back on vacation."

"P.S., you suck at being on vacation."

"I know! I'm sorry. It just doesn't come naturally to me."

"No kidding, really?"

"Your sarcasm is noted and appreciated."

Nick put his arm around her as they walked along a trail that seemed to go on forever. "Look up, see the sky, smell the scent of evergreen, let it all go. Work is in good hands with Gonzo, Jeannie and the others. And you're in good hands with me."

"I love being here with you and the kids. You know that, right?"

"Of course I do."

"You guys are my favorite place in the whole world, no matter where we are. It's just that I feel 'off' if I'm not also smack in the middle of a case that requires every ounce of my focus and attention to bring it to a successful resolution. It's like I'm lost without that rush."

"You might need a twelve-step program to address this issue."

She elbowed him. "Stop. I'm being serious."

"So am I. You're a thrill junkie, Samantha. You have no off switch when it comes to your work."

"I really don't. I need it like you need fresh air and a view of the sky. I honestly don't know what I'd do without it. I'd be like a balloon when you let the air out of it, flailing all about."

"I hope you know how proud I am, how proud we all are, of the work you do and how hard you fight for justice for your victims and their families. And now there's the grief group, too. You're making a big difference, Samantha."

"Thank you for the kind words, but it's a team effort, and I have the best team ever. I just wish we could do even more than we already do. There's so much to be done and only so many hours in the day."

"You're doing more than enough."

"This stuff with Calvin Worthington and Carisma Deasly makes me wonder what else there is, you know? What's been overlooked, causing families to suffer needlessly for years?"

"You can't save everyone, babe."

"And I know that. I really do, but we can sure as hell try, can't we?"

"Nothing has fallen through the cracks on your watch over the last two years."

"No, but there was stuff from Stahl's watch that should've gotten more attention. That eats at me now that I know he ignored cases. How could anyone live with themselves after doing that?"

"Don't forget he's the same person who tried to kill you—twice."

"Yeah, that's true. Speaking of people who hate me, the union is fighting Ramsey's firing."

"On what grounds?"

"That his fingerprints could've been left in my office during the regular course of business."

"Even if the entire department can attest to the fact that he never had regular business with you, except for mouthing off at you in the hallways?"

"Yep."

"Hopefully, that doesn't go anywhere."

"I guess we'll see."

The thought of that son of a bitch coming back to work was one she didn't care to entertain.

LATER THAT NIGHT, after the twins were asleep, Sam and Nick sat with Scotty, Eli, Harry, Lilia, Terry, Lindsey and Shelby to watch *Saturday Night Live*. Lindsey had driven up for the night but had to head back to work the next day because her deputy, Byron Tomlinson, was leaving in the morning to be the best man at his brother's New Year's weekend wedding.

The show's cold open began with a handsome dark-haired actor who bore a striking resemblance to Nick sitting at the Resolute desk, reviewing a huge stack of paperwork with intense focus.

"Mr. President?"

"Yes, Terry?"

"Oh my God, I'm on *SNL*," Terry said, "and they gave me a pot belly. What the hell?"

"We've received reliable intelligence that the North Koreans are planning to declare war on Alaska."

"What've the Alaskans done to offend the North Koreans?"

"We aren't entirely sure, sir, but the Joint Chiefs are in the Situation Room, waiting to brief you."

The actor playing Nick looked to his right, obviously tuning out Terry as the camera panned to show a blonde bombshell actress playing Sam standing in the doorway to the Oval.

"Am I disturbing you, Mr. President?" she asked in a breathy, sexy voice. She had a gun strapped to her waist and a gold badge pinned to her chest.

Real Sam gasped as the others giggled. "Oh. My. *God.*"

"Please disturb me."

"Um, Mr. President, the North Koreans..."

Nick waved his hand to dismiss Terry. "Give us a minute."

"Yes, sir."

Terry left the room, closing the door.

Nick crooked his finger to bring Sam over to him.

She sat on his lap behind the Resolute desk, and they kissed passionately.

Real Sam groaned loudly. "Someone please *shoot me right now.*"

The others roared with laughter.

"It's amazing how true to life this is," Scotty said, earning a bop on the head from his father.

As the kissing went on, the two actors began to gyrate to the tune "My Humps" by the Black Eyed Peas.

"Stop it!" Sam said, screaming. "I can't look!"

The next scene showed Terry sitting in the Situation Room with a group of stoic military officers.

"Is he coming?" one of them asked as the screen behind him shows bombs heading for Alaska.

"Yes," Terry said, "I believe he is most definitely coming."

They shifted back to the Oval Office, where the Nick and Sam characters were disheveled, blissed out and panting. In between gasps of air, they said, "Live from New York, it's Saturday Night!"

"We can never show our faces in public again," Sam said.

Nick couldn't stop laughing.

Sam whacked him. "It's not funny!"

"Sorry, Sam." Shelby wiped tears from her eyes. "But that was the funniest thing I've ever seen on that show."

"You can't say that and be my friend, too."

"Welp, it was nice knowing ya."

Lilia and Harry were so weak from laughing, they could barely sit up.

"Lilia, tell them that wasn't funny."

"I wish I could, Sam," Lilia said. "But that was funny."

"I hate everyone and everything," Sam said.

"Maybe if you could find some decorum when you're around your husband, these things wouldn't happen," Scotty said.

That set everyone off again on a fresh wave of hysteria.

Nick put his arm around Sam.

She pushed him away. "This is all your fault! If you weren't president, we wouldn't be dry-humping on TV!"

"Ew," Scotty said. "I'm so outta here."

"Right there with you, brother," Eli said.

"What's a dry hump, anyway?" Scotty asked him.

Eli led him from the room with his hands on Scotty's shoulders. "We'll talk about that later."

Moaning, Sam dropped her head into her hands.

"I've never laughed so hard in my life," Lindsey said. "I'm weak."

"They gave me a pot belly!" Terry said. "I don't have a pot belly!"

"It's okay, honey." Lindsey patted her fiancé's flat abdomen. "I'll still love you if you get a pot belly."

Sam's phone rang with a call from Freddie. "What?"

He and Elin were laughing so hard, they couldn't speak.

Sam slapped the phone closed. "I hate everyone."

"Even me?" Nick asked.

"*Especially* you!"

Their phones were blowing up with texts from family and friends full of laughing emojis.

"I can't," Sam said. "I'm going to bed."

"I'll go with you," Nick said.

"You're not invited."

"Now, babe, none of this was my doing."

"All of it was! You're the one who's the goddamned president around here."

They left their friends laughing as they went into their room and closed the door.

"I hate your guts to hell and back," Sam said.

Laughing, he put his arms around her from behind and rested his chin on her shoulder. "No, you don't."

"Right now, I do, and I expect that to last a week or two as everyone I know mocks me."

"They wish they were us." He turned her to face him, lifting her chin to accept a soft, sweet kiss that made her knees weak even when she was mad with him. "We're the luckiest people in the whole world because we have each other." He kissed from her lips to her neck. "Wanna hump?"

Sam couldn't help the snort of laughter that burst from her.

"There we go. We have to laugh at these things, babe. Remember what I always tell you—they can't touch us unless we let them."

"It's mortifying."

"But funny. And PS, I'd never let the North Koreans bomb Alaska while I humped you."

"That's good to know."

"Are you ready to forgive me?" he asked, continuing to kiss her neck as he moved his hands over her back and down to squeeze her ass.

"I need more convincing."

His hands wandered under her top and up to cup her breasts. "I'm very good at convincing you."

"You never have to try very hard."

"And thank goodness for that." With practiced ease, he had her clothes off in a matter of seconds. As he backed her up to the bed, he pulled his shirt off and tossed it aside. "I've been dying for this for days. If that phone rings right now, I'm gonna let North Korea bomb Alaska."

Sam looped her arms around his neck and pressed her pelvis against his erection. "No, you won't."

"I really would."

The one thing Sam could fully appreciate about vacation was the uninterrupted time with him that was so rare in their regular lives. Sure, that damned phone could ring at any moment, but in the meantime, she put everything else aside to fully indulge in the pleasure she could find only with him.

He knew just where and how to touch her and was the only person in the world who could make her forget that mortifying skit so quickly. What did she care about that when she had the man himself making sweet love to her?

If there was anything better than this, she'd yet to find it. Even with all the changes and upheaval they'd experienced lately, this was the one thing that never changed. They were always in perfect harmony.

"Sam," he said, his lips burning a trail over her neck. "I love you so much. You'll never know..."

She held him even tighter. "I know."

"No, you don't. They haven't invented the words yet."

"That, right there, is why I'll forgive you for the stupid *SNL* skit."

"Don't make me laugh when I'm being serious." He kissed her for a long time, scrambling her brains while the rest of her tingled from the pending orgasm. "I don't care if the whole world thinks we're a couple of horny toads."

"*You're* the horny toad. I'm just the long-suffering wife."

He pushed into her so hard, she gasped. "Are you suffering right now?"

"Terribly. The sacrifices I make..."

When he pressed his fingers to her core, he detonated an orgasm that had her seeing stars, moons and planets in several solar systems. She floated in a sea of bliss for a long time before she opened her eyes to find him watching her.

"Welcome back."

"Mmm."

"Are you still suffering?"

"Greatly."

Laughing, he kissed her and then gathered her into his warm embrace. "I get no credit for the sacrifices I make to satisfy my insatiable wife."

"Mmm, right." She was so blissed out, she could barely form words. That was another of his superpowers.

Somehow, she ended up under the covers and tucked into bed with him curled up to her. She was so comfortable, contented and delighted to be on vacation with her love that she slept like a dead woman.

CHAPTER SEVEN

J eannie and Matt sat outside the house in Richmond for the hours it took for the U.S. Marshals to request and receive a warrant and then mobilize to conduct the raid in cooperation with Richmond police. In that time, Daniella Brown came out to get her mail and then went back inside.

"You can confirm the subject is still in the house?" Chief Marshal Jesse Best asked. At six and a half feet tall with blond hair and intense brown eyes, he projected an aura of competency that put Jeannie at ease. She'd noticed in past encounters with the imposing marshal that he never wasted time with small talk.

"I can confirm that she entered through the front door three and a half hours ago and hasn't come out again. I can't confirm that she didn't sneak out the back in that time, but we've seen no other movement."

Jeannie called up dated photos of Daniella and Carisma and showed them to Jesse. In a normal investigation, there'd be age-progressed photos, but they'd never been done in this case. "This is who we're looking for. The suspected kidnapper and the victim. They're eleven years older now. Carisma would be twenty-four, if she's even there."

"Got it. Are you coming?"

"We've been ordered to stand down and turn it over to you."

"Huh," he said, which was his way of expressing surprise that any law enforcement agency would give another credit for their bust.

Anyone else would want to know why. Jesse Best wasn't anyone else.

He turned and walked away, armed with the info he needed to get the job done.

"Sucks to have to take a back seat," Matt said.

"It does, but all that matters is finding Carisma and arresting Daniella. I don't care who gets the credit."

Jeannie's body was rigid with tension as she waited for the raid to go down with the stealth that made the marshals so good at what they did. Aiding state and local authorities in apprehending fugitives was part of the marshals' mission, but they were primarily focused on protecting the federal judiciary and apprehending federal fugitives.

Around eleven, she'd texted Sam to tell her the marshals would be going in sometime during the night.

I can't wait to hear what happens, Sam had replied.

I'll text you in the morning with an update.

Call if you need me.

Will do.

Jeannie watched through binoculars as Best led his team toward the house, gesturing for other officers to cover the back. She'd wondered if they were going to bust in or knock on the door.

Best answered her question when he knocked.

The woman Jeannie had identified as Daniella answered, saw law enforcement on her doorstep and freaked out. When she tried to slam the door in their faces, Best had her cuffed in a matter of seconds. He stepped aside so his team could go in as Daniella continued to flail and scream.

"Nothing says 'I'm guilty of something' than acting like that when cops show up at your house," Matt said.

"No kidding," Jeannie said. "I'm sort of relieved she acted that way. That tells me we nailed it."

"*You* nailed it. I'm just along for the ride."

Jeannie gasped when one of the marshals came out holding an infant. Another was right behind with a toddler in each arm. The children were turned over to local authorities.

"Oh my God," Matt said. "What is this? Who are those kids?"

"I have no idea," Jeannie said, shocked. She'd heard nothing about Daniella having children of her own.

Daniella's screams pierced the quiet neighborhood.

Yet another marshal emerged from the house, carrying a young woman.

Jeannie was out of the car and walking toward them before she made the conscious decision to go. She had to know. Flashing her badge to the marshal, she asked the woman, "Are you Carisma Deasly?"

The odor coming from the woman, who was emaciated, couldn't be described in mere words.

"Yes," the young woman said as tears streamed down her face. "It's me."

"She was chained to a bed in a back room," the officer carrying her said. He had tears in his eyes.

Jeannie blinked back her own tears. "Your mom has never stopped looking for you, Carisma. Would you like to speak to her?"

The young woman nodded. "Please."

Jeannie made the call and handed the phone to her, noting how weak she seemed.

"Mama, it's me. Carisma."

Her mother's screams could be heard through the phone.

JEANNIE ARRANGED for MPD Patrol to transport LaToya to Richmond as quickly as possible. While she waited at the hospital, she placed a call to Michael.

"I was hoping you'd call," he said. "How's it going there?"

"You won't believe it. Not only did we find Carisma, but there were nine other children in the house."

"That Daniella took from people?"

"We don't know yet, but we believe that's possible."

"Jesus, Jeannie. This is huge."

"I know. It's unbelievable and overwhelming. They were all filthy and starved and abused. It's just..."

"Baby..."

"I'm okay."

"It's all right if you're not."

"It's just a lot worse than I expected. I was hoping to find Carisma, but this..."

"You've stumbled upon a nightmare and saved ten lives in the process. I'm so proud of you, sweetheart."

"Thanks."

"When will you be home?"

"I'm waiting for Carisma's mother to get here, and then we should be able to leave."

"And Matt is still with you?"

"Yep. He's been great today. I feel like we finally became real partners while we waited for this to go down."

"I'm happy to hear that. I know how tough it's been for you since Will left."

"Yeah, it has been. I'm getting a call from Patrol. I've got to run."

"Be safe, love, and wake me up when you get home."

"I will. Love you."

"Love you, too."

Jeannie took the call from the Patrol officer transporting LaToya.

"We're five minutes out."

"Please bring her to the main entrance."

"Will do."

"Thanks so much."

Jeannie put her coat back on and stepped outside into frigid air to wait. She saw the flashing emergency lights before the car came into view. The officer killed the lights as he turned into the hospital driveway. She opened the back door and offered LaToya a hand getting out of the car.

The other woman fell into her arms, sobbing. "I just can't believe you found her. Thank you, Detective. Thank you so much."

"I have to warn you," Jeannie said. "She's in rough shape."

"But she's alive. That's all I care about. Take me to my baby."

Jeannie led her by the hand to the bank of elevators. As she passed Matt, sitting in the lobby, he gave her a thumbs-up.

"Be right back," she said to him.

"Take your time."

In the elevator, she pressed the button for the fourth floor.

"How bad is it?" LaToya asked.

"As bad as it gets."

LaToya let out a whimper and began to weep again. "Why would she take her and then treat her like that?"

"I wish I knew."

"And there were other children?"

"Nine others."

"My God. Where did they come from?"

"We're still trying to figure that out."

"You saved their lives," LaToya whispered.

"I wish it had happened a long time ago."

"Let us give thanks that it happened now," LaToya said. "It wasn't your fault it didn't happen sooner. I'll always be grateful for what you did for me and my family, Detective."

Jeannie had never felt hollower or more emotionally drained after successfully solving a case. She led LaToya to Carisma's room, where a Richmond officer stood watch outside. "This is her mother," Jeannie told the officer she'd met earlier.

He opened the door for them.

Jeannie followed LaToya into the room. Carisma, who'd been bathed and lightly sedated as her many wounds were cleaned, was asleep in the big hospital bed.

LaToya's hand covered her mouth as she looked at her daughter for the first time in eleven years. Tears streamed down her face when she approached the bedside.

Carisma stirred, her eyes opening to blink her mother into focus. "Mama."

"It's me, baby." LaToya leaned over to kiss her and caress her face. "It's me."

"Missed you," Carisma whispered.

"Oh, baby, I missed you so, so much, and I've never been happier to see anyone."

They hugged each other for the longest time.

Satisfied to see them reunited, Jeannie tiptoed from the room, wiping away tears as she stepped into the hallway.

"It's unbelievable," the Richmond officer said. "The way she kept those kids."

"Horrifying."

"I heard you were the one who led the marshals to that house. Great bust, Detective."

"Thank you." Jeannie understood that this was the kind of bust that made cops into celebrities, that launched their careers into all-new stratospheres, but as she collected her partner and headed home to DC, all she felt was heartsick over the whole sorry mess.

WHILE THE KIDS SLEPT IN, Sam and Nick watched in horror as the story unfolded live on CNN. They'd woken to a text from Jeannie that said to turn on the TV. In all, ten children ranging from three months of age to Carisma at twenty-four had been found living in utter squalor in the Richmond house. So far, they'd publicly identified only Carisma as one of the victims and noted that Daniella Brown was facing numerous felony charges.

Jesse Best stepped up to a bank of microphones outside the house where the ongoing operation proceeded behind him. As he briefed the media on the raid that had led to the rescue of the children who'd been held prisoner and detailed the conditions inside the house, Sam's stomach turned, especially when he noted that the three dogs who were found in the house were obviously well cared for, unlike the children, who'd been starved and viciously abused.

Sam noted that the usually stoic and unemotional marshal looked exhausted and ravaged by what he'd witnessed in that hell house.

"I'll take a few questions," Best said.

"What led you to the house?"

"We were acting on a tip from DC's Metropolitan Police Department."

"*Oh shit,*" Sam said on a long exhale. "Shit, fuck, damn, hell."

Her cell phone rang with a call from Captain Malone.

"Hey," Sam said.

"This is a shit storm of such epic proportions," he said without preamble, "I can't begin to articulate them all. I know you're on vacation, but I need you back here to help manage the fallout."

Sam glanced at Nick, who nodded. "I'll be there later this morning."

"Thank you."

The call ended with a click that echoed through her brain like a shotgun blast. He and the chief were dealing with yet another potential PR disaster at a time when they could least afford it.

Her phone rang again, this time with a call from Jeannie. "Hey."

"Hey," Jeannie said, sounding subdued.

"Are you still at the house?"

"No, I'm home. I left after Carisma's mother arrived. I know their reunion is worth the fallout coming our way, but I can't help but worry."

"Malone just called and ordered me back to work immediately."

"Oh shit, Sam. Are you coming?"

"Yeah, I'll be there this morning."

"I'd say I'm sorry about all this, but being there when LaToya and Carisma were reunited was one of the best moments of my career, even if I'm sick over the rest of it."

"You did good, Jeannie. You saved nine kids and Carisma from a nightmare."

"But I caused another one for the department."

"We'll get through it. Try not to worry and instead celebrate the enormous accomplishment. You trusted your gut and followed your heart. Missing kids will be reunited with heartbroken parents. I don't care what anyone else says, there's no downside here."

"If you say so."

"I say so, and I'm the boss. I'll gladly take any hit that comes our way for this outcome."

"Thank you for always having our backs," Jeannie said, sounding emotional and exhausted.

"That's my job. I'll see you in a bit."

"See you then."

Sam closed the phone.

"How is she?" Nick asked.

"Devastated and worried about the fallout."

"I have to believe that when the dust settles, the MPD will be seen as heroic for cracking this case."

"That may be true, but first they're going to drag us through the mud asking why it took so fucking long for us to care about a missing Black girl. It's been a lot lately... I just keep wondering what's going to send the mayor and the city council over the top, and they start demanding the chief's resignation."

"You need to advocate for him every chance you get. Use your first lady bully pulpit to talk about what a great chief he is and how much he's done for the department."

"I'll do whatever I can for him, but I'm worried. If this is the straw that breaks the camel's back, it leads right back to me and Jeannie. This is exactly the kind of thing he was hoping to avoid."

"But Jeannie rescued nine little kids and Carisma from hell on earth. I have to believe that's going to take precedence over the rest."

"It won't, Nick. She's been missing eleven years, and this is the first time the department made a sincere effort to find her. This is going to blow back on us big-time."

The phone rang on the bedside table.

He let out a deep sigh as he got up to answer it. "Yes?" After a long period of silence, he said, "I'll be right there." After he put down the phone, he said, "I have to go over to Laurel for a briefing. North Korea is at it again. They've fired yet another missile test."

Sam looked up at him, offering a wan smile. "We suck at vacation."

"We sure do."

"Maybe we can salvage the second half."

"I sure hope so."

CHAPTER EIGHT

They left Camp David aboard *Marine One* at eleven. The plan was for the helicopter to land on the South Lawn long enough for Sam to disembark before lifting off again to return Nick to Camp David.

Earlier, she'd explained to the kids that she had to go into work for a day or two, but would return to pick up the vacation already in progress. With Tracy, Angela and their families due to arrive at the camp that day, the kids were looking forward to some cousin time and had plenty to keep them occupied.

If Sam was bitter to be missing the time with her family, she kept that to herself. The story of her life going forward would be the push-pull between work—including her "job" as first lady—and the desire to spend more time with her children and family. It was the conundrum of working mothers everywhere, and she was no different. Well, except she was managing the push-pull on a much larger stage than most mothers—and with much more help.

Nick held her hand during the flight and gave it a squeeze as the White House complex came into view.

"This is my stop."

He kissed her forehead. "Be careful with my wife. She's my whole world."

"Don't worry. I'm going back to fight a PR battle more than anything."

"If there's a way to injure yourself doing that, you'll find it."

Sam snorted out a laugh. "True, but I'll do my best to avoid the paper cuts."

"Call me later?"

"You bet."

He kissed the back of her hand and then released it as Taco brought *Marine One* to a soft, easy landing. "Love you."

"Love you, too. Try to relax and have some fun with the kids in between North Korean missile launches."

"I'll try. But it won't be any fun at all until you get back."

"I'll be there as soon as I can."

The door to the air stairs opened, and Sam leaned in to kiss him before she stood. "Thanks for the lift, Mr. President."

"Anything for you, babe. Be safe out there."

"Always." She gave him a jaunty wave and headed down the air stairs as her lead Secret Service agents, Vernon and Jimmy, deplaned from the back.

As soon as they were clear of the landing area, *Marine One* lifted off again.

Sam turned and gave a wave, hoping Nick could see her, before heading inside to grab what she needed for work. Since they hadn't been expected back, there were no reporters outside screaming questions at her. But there would be at HQ. She nodded to the usher who greeted her at the door. "Morning, Harold."

"Morning, ma'am. Welcome back."

To her agents, she said, "I'll be down in two minutes."

"We're ready when you are, ma'am," Vernon said.

Sam rushed up the red-carpeted stairs to the residence to retrieve her weapon, cuffs, badge wallet, notebook and keys from the locked drawer in her bedside table and was on her way back down in under a minute. Though she felt terrible about leaving the family vacation, something akin to euphoria came over her when she was heading to do the job she loved so much—even when the shit was hitting the fan.

She had no idea what to expect when she got to HQ, which was a rare feeling. Usually, she knew exactly who and what she was when it came to the job. She knew who her friends were and kept them close while monitoring her enemies, of which there was one less with Ramsey fired—for now, anyway. If they let him come back to work after he'd ransacked her office and threatened her more than once—with witnesses—she might lose faith in the system designed to weed out those who didn't belong among their ranks.

Human nature being what it was, there were going to be bad

apples in any organization, but the disappointment when those things happened was profound nonetheless. How could Stahl live with knowing that murders and kidnappings in their city had gone uninvestigated for *years*? And yes, that was a rhetorical question considering the many other ways Stahl had turned out to be morally deficient. But how could you be paid to do a job and then just not do it? In their line of work, not doing the job allowed kidnappers and murderers to run free to terrorize innocent people.

As she considered Stahl's many fuckups, she also had to accept that her dad and others in command had either turned a blind eye or had been unaware of his lack of effort. Or they'd been so overworked during times of tight budgets that they hadn't noticed. Whatever the reason, the blowback could put a dent in Skip's legacy, and that possibility made her sick.

As she approached HQ, she was shocked to see media trucks lining the road a half mile from the building. "Holy shit," she whispered. This was even bigger than the turnout right after Nick had become president, and they'd come looking for scoops on the first lady police officer.

If she was looking for proof that this would be a day unlike any other, the media crowd was her first clue. She could only imagine how furious the chief must be. As she always did in times of intense press coverage, she drove around to the morgue entrance in the back, but even that was staked out. "Shit."

She was thankful for the presence of Vernon and Jimmy, who would get her inside without being accosted. Vernon signaled for her to wait for them. *No problem,* she thought. Not that she couldn't defend herself, but this was a whole other level of intense.

When the agents were in position outside her car, Sam opened the door to a barrage of questions that were every bit as brutal as she'd expected.

"What took so long to find Carisma?"

"Were you called back from vacation at Camp David?"

"Did your father know that no one bothered to look for Carisma?"

"What else has the MPD ignored?"

"Does the MPD have a racism problem?"

That, right there, was why the chief had ordered them to stop investigating Stahl's cold cases. *Motherfucker.*

"Did the president give you a ride back to DC on his helicopter?"

Sam ignored the questions and let Vernon and Jimmy move her

through the throng into the morgue door, where Lindsey waited to greet her.

"I knew from the roar coming from outside that it had to be you."

"You must've gotten up early."

"Four a.m.," Lindsey said with a yawn and sleepy grin. "I heard you were coming in, and I'm very sorry to see you here when you're supposed to be on vacation."

"I'm sorry to be here," Sam said. "I meant to ask you at the camp why you were coming in on a Sunday?"

"With Byron away for his brother's wedding, I needed to be back in town, so I came in to do some paperwork that I can't ever seem to get ahead of. And P.S. the Brown bust is *amazing*."

"Even if it's eleven years too late."

"Yeah."

"What's being said online?"

"You don't want to know."

"And the word on the street here?"

"Also not great."

"Fucking hell." Sam used her chin to gesture to the morgue. "You got a minute, Doc?"

"For you? Always."

They went through the sliding glass doors into the antiseptic-smelling morgue, Sam's least favorite room in the building. "There's a very good chance I could get fired for this."

"No way. For one thing, the chief would never fire you, because he loves you. For another, having the first lady working for us is the best PR we'll ever get. And third, you guys did the right thing pursuing those leads. No one knew it would blow up into something like this."

"The chief was afraid of this very thing."

"You know what? Who cares if it's a media shit storm? Jeannie saved the lives of *ten people*, nine of them little kids and babies. That's what matters here. That's the *only thing* that matters, and if you say that, over and over, eventually people will hear you."

"Yes, I suppose you're right. I'm worried about this blowing back on my dad and his legacy."

"I know," Lindsey said with a sigh. "I thought of that, too. Where was the brass when Stahl was ignoring these cases?"

"There's no way my dad would've stood idly by while he did that, so all I can think is that Stahl talked a big game, filed bogus reports and made them believe he was doing everything he could."

"Find those bogus reports. That'll help to make a case that Stahl's incompetence was deliberate and strategic."

"That's a good idea. We'll look into that."

"Fight back, Sam. Keep reminding people, including the chief, that you aren't responsible for the sins of the past, and by trying to make them right, you're saving lives. She was *starving* Carisma and the others. They were living in filth the likes of which none of us can begin to imagine. You guys did *good*, no matter what anyone says."

"Jeannie gets all the credit, but I needed this pep talk. Thank you."

"It always helps to address an issue with action."

"Wait, I think that's one of my trademarked lines."

"No, that one's all mine."

"Thanks, Linds. I owe you one."

"You don't owe me anything. Do what you do. That's all you need in this or any situation."

Sam gave her friend a quick hug. "Thanks again."

"Anytime. Go kick some ass and take some names."

"On it."

Sam left the morgue feeling energized by Lindsey's support. Her friend was right—they had done good, and screw anyone who said otherwise, even her own bosses. While that thought worked in her own mind, she wasn't sure how that attitude would be met when she put it into action.

Her squad was hard at work when she stepped into the pit. "Hey."

At the sound of her voice, they all turned to her in surprise.

"What're you doing here?" Freddie asked.

"I hear we've got a mess to clean up," Sam said.

"You're goddamned right you do," Captain Malone said as he came into the pit. "In the office. Now. McBride, you, too."

As Malone stormed toward Sam's office, Jeannie grimaced at her.

"I got this," Sam said as they went into her office, where Gonzo was seated at the desk.

"May I help you all?" he asked as Jeannie closed the door.

Ignoring him, Malone turned to Sam. "You can help me by telling how it is that my direct order *to stand down* in the Deasly case was basically ignored."

"I spoke to the chief about what Jeannie had uncovered prior to the order," Sam said. "He authorized us to turn the case over to the marshals, which we did. Jesse Best tied the case to us in his press conference. We followed the order we were given by the chief, and he said he would bring you into the loop."

"He did, but this... *shit storm*... is exactly what we were trying to avoid when we gave you the order," Malone said.

"We understand that, but Jeannie saved the lives of ten people, Captain. That's the headline here."

"No, Lieutenant," he said with unusual fury, "that is *not* the headline here. The headline is actually going to be 'Ten people rescued when MPD decides to give a fuck about missing Black girl.' *That's gonna be the goddamned headline.*"

Sam had never seen him so pissed. "I'd like to remind you that we're not the ones who didn't give a fuck about the missing Black girl. We're the ones who decided *to* give a fuck."

"Try telling that to the mayor and the city council and everyone calling for my head and the chief's head on a silver platter. How, they want to know, could we have let a case like this go unsolved for *eleven years* and then closed it in a matter of days, like we did the Worthington case? This has happened on *our watch*, and *we're responsible.*"

"What's more important?" Sam asked, her stomach cramping with anxiety as she went toe to toe with her beloved captain. "To save lives or protect our careers?"

Jeannie gasped.

"I guess we're going to find out which is more important to the people who matter," Malone said.

"I have to believe it'll matter more to them that we solved these cases than it does how long it took. Nine little kids were rescued, along with Carisma. Surely that counts for something."

"You'd better hope so," Malone said as he stormed out, slamming the door behind him.

"*Whoa,*" Jeannie said. "I've never seen him like that."

"Me either," Sam said.

"What's our plan?" Gonzo asked Sam.

"I want the reports Stahl filed on these cases when they first happened."

"I'm way ahead of you, LT," Gonzo said. "I pulled them first thing, and they're some of the best fiction you'll ever read." He handed printouts to her and Jeannie detailing the many steps Stahl claimed he had taken to investigate the Worthington and Deasly cases. "This is what your dad and others were seeing. This is why they didn't press him about what was being done, because to read his reports, everything was being done."

"LaToya Deasly told me she only saw him once and then never

heard from him again," Jeannie said, scanning the report. "But he details multiple lengthy meetings with her. Where was this? I never saw anything about this in the files I had."

"There was nothing in the Worthington files either," Sam said.

"The reports were archived," Gonzo said.

Sam felt a zing of electricity that went straight down her backbone. "Only captain or above can archive files."

"Which means someone intentionally archived these reports—someone at the captain level or above," Gonzo said.

"Is it possible to see who did it?" Sam asked, recalling when this had come up before, but fairly certain it wasn't possible to tell.

"Not at our level."

"How were you able to find out they were archived?" Sam asked.

"I asked Archie to dig deeper and see if he could find anything buried on Worthington and Deasly," Gonzo said, referring to Lieutenant Archelotta, who ran the IT division. "These are what he found."

"There's got to be more," Sam said. "This was intentional. Stahl created these reports, and then someone buried them. I want to know who did that."

"It was probably Conklin," Jeannie said of their disgraced former deputy chief. "He would've been a captain then."

"Conklin hated Stahl as much as anyone," Sam said. "I can't believe he would've done anything to help him cover his tracks."

"What if Stahl had something on him?" Gonzo asked.

"I suppose that's possible," Sam conceded. "Is it possible to archive something without going through a captain?"

"No."

"We might never know the whole story," Sam said, "but this is enough for us to show Malone and the chief that Stahl was documenting efforts that never actually happened. It might get the dogs off our backs."

"Or would that open a bigger can of worms?" Gonzo asked.

"That question is above my pay grade," Sam said. "Good work on this, Gonzo. It helps to have something to work with."

"What's next?" he asked.

"I'm going to venture into the lion's den with this info and turn it over to them."

"Go with God, Lieutenant," Jeannie said.

The three of them laughed.

"Listen, Jeannie," Sam said. "This was a remarkable bust, and you need to be proud as hell for what you did for Carisma, her family and the nine other kids and their families. Don't let any of the bullshit take away from that. Do you hear me?"

"Yes, ma'am. Thank you for your support."

"You got it. I'm damned proud of what you did here, and you should be, too."

"Me, too," Gonzo said. "Very good work, Jeannie."

"Thanks, guys. Although... I'm never going to forget the condition Carisma and the others were in," Jeannie said, her eyes filling with tears. "It was horrifying. How human beings can treat others that way... The murders are tough, but this was unlike anything I've ever seen."

"I want you and Matt to spend some time with Dr. Trulo," Sam said, referring to the department's psychiatrist.

"I don't think we need that."

Sam would like to think she'd learned from past mistakes. She would always regret not doing more to support Gonzo after Arnold's murder. "Nonnegotiable," she said to Jeannie. "Make the appointment. Together or separate. You decide."

"Yes, ma'am."

"I'm going to see Malone. If I don't come back in thirty minutes, send reinforcements."

"Will do," Gonzo said, chuckling.

Sam left the pit and headed for the captain's office, surprised to see the door closed, which was rare. She knocked.

"Enter."

She opened the door. "Do I need my vest to come in?"

"I'm not in the mood for jokes, Holland."

"I'm aware. The question was serious."

"Come in and shut the door."

She did as she was told.

He was seated behind his desk, one leg raised by bracing his foot on an open desk drawer. "What do you want?"

She laid the reports on his desk.

"What's that?"

"Reports that Stahl filed in the early days of the Worthington and Deasly investigations. They were separate from the files we pulled."

Malone held her gaze for a beat before reaching for the reports.

Sam stayed as still as she possibly could while he reviewed them.

"Where did you find these?"

"Gonzo asked Archie to do some digging. They were archived separately from the case files."

"What *are* these?" he asked, sifting through the papers.

"We aren't sure, sir, but that's what the bosses at the time were seeing. Jeannie confirmed Stahl only met once with LaToya Deasly, and then she never heard from him again. His reports include detailed notes on multiple meetings and follow-ups that never happened."

He stood so abruptly that he startled her. "Come with me."

Sam stepped aside to let him lead the way straight to the chief's office. She nodded to Helen, the chief's admin, as they went by. That she looked more spooked than usual did nothing to settle Sam's nerves.

Malone walked right into Farnsworth's office.

Sam closed the door behind them.

"Tell him what you told me," Malone said.

"Gonzo asked Archie to look for anything he could find on Worthington and Deasly, and he found these reports in the archives. They were separate from the case files that we pulled when we reopened both investigations."

"If they were archived," Farnsworth said slowly, "that had to be done by a captain."

"Yes, sir."

He glanced at Malone. "What is this, Jake?"

"I don't know, sir, but we're going to look into it, starting with everyone who was a captain eleven years ago."

"One of them is dead," Sam said.

"There's no way your father had anything to do with hiding Stahl's bogus paper trail," Farnsworth said, his gaze heated.

"Maybe it'd be easiest to go to the source," Sam said. "Ask Stahl why he created bogus reports and who helped him hide them. He's facing life in prison with nothing else to lose, and knowing him, he'd love to take someone else down with him."

"What do you think?" Farnsworth asked Malone.

"It couldn't hurt anything to try. But who's going to be the one to go there?"

"It can't be me," Farnsworth said. "I'm the one who fired him and had him charged."

"He and I have too much history," Malone said, "and it can't be Sam, for obvious reasons."

"Gonzo?" Sam asked. "He didn't work for him for long and doesn't have history."

"Yeah, that'd work," Malone said, "if we agree that he's doing all right with the trial going on and everything."

"I'll ask him and see what he thinks," Sam said.

"Give him an out if it's too much right now," Farnsworth said.

"I will."

"The media is crawling up our asses looking for a statement about the Deasly case," Farnsworth said.

"I'd like Detective McBride to make that statement," Sam said. "This was her bust, and she should get the credit."

"That's fine with me," Farnsworth said, "but I'll go out with her to take the inevitable questions about why it took us so long to find Carisma." He handed her a sheet of paper. "Public Affairs drafted this statement to get things started, and I approve of the language. Ask Detective McBride to start with this."

"I'll get her," Sam said, "and talk to Gonzo about Stahl." As she headed for the door, she avoided eye contact with the captain while wondering how big of a deal this was going to turn out to be for her and her team. Whatever the fallout, she wouldn't have done a damn thing differently, not when it meant her actions and Jeannie's had freed nine little kids and a young woman from hell on earth.

CHAPTER NINE

"You need to stop fuming, Jake," Joe said when they were alone. "Back in the day, you and I would've done the same thing Holland and McBride did."

Jake sat, exhaling a deep breath. "The two of them are insubordinate as all hell, and you know it."

"Yes, they are, and they're also exceptionally good at their jobs. It's a fine line we walk with that combination."

"Still... We told them to stand down."

"I told you Sam called me. We talked about it and agreed to turn what McBride had over to the marshals. Jesse Best blew our cover, but you can't blame him. He was giving credit where it was due."

"Yeah, I get all that. What I'll never understand for the rest of my life is how Stahl *faked* entire investigations and even filed the paperwork to go along with his bullshit. And then, of course, I wonder what else there is."

"And that's the crux of the matter, which is why you need to direct your anger where it belongs—and not at Holland or McBride."

"I'm pissed about the insubordination, and I'm gonna be for a few days."

"While you fume about that, I want you to *quietly* talk to the captains from that time, including Conklin, and find out who helped Stahl hide the paper trail. I want you to personally handle that, with no one else involved."

"Is this a criminal investigation?" Malone asked.

"Potentially. I mean, why were his fake reports separate from the case files? It makes no sense."

"How long is this guy going to continue to haunt us, anyway?"

"I'm afraid we've only seen the tip of the Stahl iceberg."

As SAM MADE her way back to the pit, she encountered Freddie coming toward her. "We've got a body in Rock Creek Park. We weren't sure if you wanted to take that, or if you're outta here after the press briefing."

Sam checked her watch and saw it was almost one thirty. Her goal was to be back at Camp David for dinner. "I've got some time." In the pit, she called for Jeannie.

"Yes, ma'am?"

"You'll be handling the press briefing on Deasly."

Jeannie's expression went blank. "Me?"

"Yes, you. It was your bust, and you should get the credit."

"But the captain and chief—"

"Would like you to do it. The chief will go out with you and field any questions about the past handling of the case."

"Oh. Okay."

"Just go out and tell them what you did and how you found Carisma. That's what they want to hear."

"When do they want me to do it?"

"Now would be good." Sam had never seen Jeannie look so flummoxed. She handed Jeannie the statement that public affairs had come up with. "I'll go out with you, too, if that would help."

"Yes, please."

"They want you to start with that statement and take it from there."

"Okay."

Jeannie gathered notes and reports she wouldn't need. She knew the case by heart. Sam was certain of that. Cases like these worked their way into your bone marrow, where they would stay forever. As she went into her office to grab her coat, Sam could recall the intricate details of cases she'd worked years ago for that very reason.

When Jeannie was as ready as she'd ever be, Sam said to Freddie, "Be ready to go to Rock Creek Park right after this."

"Yes, ma'am. Good luck, Jeannie."

The rest of the squad called out words of support as Sam and Jeannie walked toward the main lobby to meet the chief.

"Very nice job, Detective," Farnsworth said, shaking Jeannie's hand.

"Thank you, sir. I'm, ah, sorry about the fallout."

"I'll take care of that. Let's do this."

The chief led them through the main doors and into the media scrum that gathered there every day. Reporters started shouting questions at them the second they crossed the threshold.

One stood out among the others: "Lieutenant, did the president give you a ride home from Camp David on his helicopter?" Shit, she'd have to give Nick a heads-up about that question being asked multiple times.

Farnsworth held up his hands to quiet them. "Detective McBride has a statement, and then we'll take any questions you have."

Jeannie stepped up to the stone podium that served as their briefing spot in all seasons.

Sam glanced up at the dark clouds that hung overhead, wondering about the weather forecast.

"Following the conviction of former Lieutenant Stahl, we've given some of his cold cases a fresh look," Jeannie said.

Sam could hear the nerves in her friend's voice.

"One of them was the disappearance of then-thirteen-year-old Carisma Deasly. I approached the investigation as if it was a new case, speaking to Carisma's mother, LaToya, and other people who were close to the family at that time. I quickly became focused on Daniella Brown, a friend of LaToya's, who lived with the family and who also went missing around the same time. LaToya always believed that Daniella took her child, and that's the lead I followed in my investigation."

"Was she angry that the MPD didn't do more at the time her child went missing?" one reporter asked.

Jeannie looked to the chief.

"We're taking a close look at the early part of the investigation hoping to answer those questions," Farnsworth said.

"I spoke to a former boyfriend of Ms. Brown's," Jeannie said, "who told me he believed she was living in Richmond. He was critical to us finding her, Carisma and the other children who were rescued. After my partner and I visually identified Ms. Brown, we consulted with the marshals, who oversaw the raid that led to the arrest of Ms. Brown, the rescue of Carisma Deasly and nine other children."

"Did you suspect there would be other victims in addition to Carisma?" a reporter asked.

"No, we had no idea. That was a shock to us as much as everyone else."

"How's it possible that you were able to solve this case so quickly after so long?" Darren Tabor from the *Washington Star* asked.

Normally, Sam liked him. As much as she hated the question, if she were him, that'd be her first question, too.

Farnsworth stepped up to the podium alongside Jeannie. "We're looking into a number of disgraced former Lieutenant Stahl's cold cases and finding some irregularities, including reports on investigative work that we now know was never done."

"Will Stahl face additional charges?" a reporter asked.

"That hasn't been determined yet," Farnsworth replied. "We're in the earliest part of our investigation."

"Will other cold cases be examined?"

"Yes, they will."

"How was it possible that Stahl's commanders at the time, including yourself, the late Deputy Chief Holland and others, were unaware of him cutting so many corners?" Darren asked.

"During the time in question, the District was experiencing an intense budget crunch that had detectives working alone, largely on the honor system. Frankly, it never occurred to me, Deputy Chief Holland or any of the other commanders that a detective in our department would pretend to investigate a case while in fact doing nothing. We're horrified by these discoveries and will do everything in our power to get justice for the victims of these crimes. Make no mistake about it—Leonard Stahl is a criminal, and he has been for much longer than we first suspected."

"What does it say about you, Chief, that you had a criminal working for you for all this time?"

"I'm well aware that the buck stops with me, and I'm as appalled as anyone at his behavior—the things we already know and the new things coming to light. This department is full of hardworking, dedicated law enforcement officers who put their lives on the line for the people of this District every day. Are there some bad apples? Absolutely. But there're far more honorable officers than not. We can't change the past, but we'll do everything within our power to right these terrible wrongs. That's all we have to say for now."

He gestured for Sam and Jeannie to precede him inside. "That went as well as it could under the circumstances," he said once the doors were closed.

"I'm sorry for any angst my investigation has caused," Jeannie said.

Farnsworth's warm gaze passed over them. "I was wrong to tell you to stand down on this investigation."

Sam stared at him, stunned by the confession.

"I was worried about the PR, which was the wrong thing for me to focus on. Saving the lives of Carisma and the others and locking up a dangerous criminal is far more important. While I don't condone my officers circumventing a direct order, I understand why you did it, and I commend you for doing the right thing by these victims."

"Thank you, sir," Jeannie said. "I hope you know that I hold you in the highest regard and would never want to do anything that would cause trouble for you or the department."

"You're not the one causing the trouble, Detective. Our old friend Stahl is responsible for this shit storm. Not you. We'll get through it."

"Does this mean you want us to look at the rest of the cases?" Sam asked.

"Yes, but I want to be kept fully in the loop so we can anticipate the fallout."

"Yes, sir. We've got a body in Rock Creek Park I've got to deal with first," Sam said.

"I thought you were off this week?"

"So did I. I'm heading back to Camp David later."

"You might not get there today. Have you seen the weather forecast?"

"No, why?"

"The winter storm watch was just upgraded to a blizzard warning."

"MR. PRESIDENT, I'm sorry to interrupt, but we've received word from the National Weather Service that the capital region is under a blizzard warning, beginning later tonight," Brant said. "We'd like to get you back to the White House so you aren't stuck here in an emergency."

Nick wanted to weep. Even though Sam was in DC, he wasn't in any great rush to leave the tranquility or fresh air at Camp David. He'd spent the afternoon sledding with the kids, and just being outside was such an incredible gift. "When are you looking to go?"

"Within the hour."

It was all he could do not to throw a two-year-old tantrum. "I'll rally the kids."

"Thank you, Mr. President."

Nick got up and went into the bedroom Eli and Scotty were

sharing. They each had one of the twins in bed with them as they watched *Elf* for the tenth time this holiday season. "Guys, I hate to say it, but they want to take us back to the White House because of a blizzard warning."

When the four of them moaned at the news, Skippy raised her head off the floor to see what was going on.

"Let's get packed up."

"Can we come back soon?" Scotty asked.

"God, I hope so," Nick said.

He received a text from Sam letting him know the press were on the trail of him giving her a ride home from Camp David in *Marine One* and asking questions. He passed that on to his communications team to deal with.

Nick, the kids, Scotty and the others in their party boarded *Marine One* just over an hour later, along with Harry, Lilia, Terry and other staffers and Secret Service agents for the ride back to DC.

"Might be a few bumps, Mr. President," Taco said when he greeted them. "We've got some low clouds to contend with."

"It's a good thing the first lady isn't with us," Nick said.

"No kidding," Scotty said. "She hates to fly."

Skippy jumped into his lap for the ride home.

"Don't worry about a thing," Taco said. "We'll get you home safe."

Five minutes into the flight, as they rocked and rolled through the clouds, Nick was very glad Sam wasn't with them. He withdrew the secure BlackBerry he used to communicate with her to send a text. *Evacuated from paradise due to blizzard warning. On* Marine One *with the kids. See you at home.*

Terry came into the main cabin and took a seat next to Nick. "The FBI has a lead on the bomb. They've tracked it to one of your most outspoken critics who firmly believes no one should be living in the people's house unless they were elected by the people. He has a long track record of violent protest."

"So that's going to be the theme of our administration, then—the unelected president."

"It's going to be a storyline, not a theme. As you've said, it's also an opportunity to think outside the box and carve your own path, especially if you're determined not to run for reelection."

"I'm determined not to run, but if I were to get reelected, I would serve."

"What does that mean?"

"I'm not going to campaign for it. If the party nominates me, and they want to support my candidacy, great. But I'm not going to spend a year and a half chasing it. I'm going to spend that time doing the job I wasn't elected to do."

"You're a rare bird, Mr. President," Terry said with a grunt of laughter.

"I know. Your father tells me that all the time. I drive him crazy." Nick turned in his seat to face his chief of staff and close friend. "Here's the thing—when the time comes, people are either going to want me, or they're not. I can spend hundreds of millions of dollars and time I'd rather spend at home campaigning, but in the end, it's going to come down to how I handle the next three years. I'll let my record speak for me."

"You're aware that's not how this works, right?"

"Of course I am, but, Terry, I'm already the president. If they dump me, so what? People will call me Mr. President for the rest of my life. I'll be out of office in my early forties and can make millions writing books and speaking. What do I care if they don't reelect me?"

"I like the way you think."

"I'd rather do the job and be with my family than chase a second term that's going to be decided solely by how the next three years unfold. If they want to keep me around, they'll reelect me. If they don't, they'll show me the door."

"And you really don't care either way?"

"I care about doing the best possible job I can while I'm here. We both know that's not going to matter to a lot of people, but if there're enough who approve, maybe we get a second term. If we don't, Sam and I ride off into the sunset with the kids and go live the rest of our lives. Either way, we get an amazing opportunity to do some things. Such as... In the State of the Union, I want to talk about what my life was really like growing up."

"That's risky, Nick. They might use that info against you."

"Did you hear what I just said about not caring about risks or reelection or anything other than trying to do the best job I can for all Americans?"

"What I want to know is whether I'm going to have ulcers by the time we leave office."

Nick's low chuckle made Terry laugh. "Nah, don't sweat it. If we're approaching it from a we-don't-care-if-we're-reelected point of view, what can go wrong?"

"Pass the Tums."

. . .

SAM RAISED the collar on her coat as she walked toward the yellow crime scene tape in Rock Creek Park. Freddie had the car he'd borrowed from his mother and would join her when he arrived. It was too damned cold to stand around and wait for him.

Patrol Officer Keeney lifted the tape for her. "Nice to see you again, Lieutenant."

"You, too." Sam was trying to remember when she'd last encountered the young patrolman. During the sniper shootings, she thought.

"Right this way, ma'am."

Sam followed him down a wooded path, watching for patches of ice as she went.

"I saw you and your family going to Camp David on *Marine One*. That must've been so cool."

"Yes, it was." She didn't want to talk about *Marine One* or Camp David when there was a murder victim in need of justice. "Where's the person who found her?"

"With the paramedics. She was pretty shaken. Her dog ran off and led her to the victim."

Great. Our crime scene has been compromised by a dog. She pulled on latex gloves. "Have you called the ME and CSU?"

"Yes, ma'am. They're on the way."

"Thank you."

Another Patrol officer stood watch over the victim, a white woman who was facedown and naked from the waist down, which meant she'd probably been sexually assaulted. Because it was her job, Sam took the required photos and then handed a pair of latex gloves to the patrolman before asking him to help her turn the woman over.

Her clothes were torn, her breasts were covered in abrasions, and her neck was badly bruised, indicating manual strangulation. The poor woman had endured a brutal attack.

A glove covered one hand, but the other was bare.

Sam pulled a paper bag from her coat pocket and carefully inserted the woman's ungloved hand into the bag to preserve any evidence. She checked the pockets of the woman's jacket, found a small wallet with a DC driver's license that she held up to the beam of the patrolman's flashlight, which was needed as storm clouds and tree cover made it almost as dark as night in the thicket.

Audrey Olsen, age twenty-four. The address listed was in Adams Morgan. Sam took a picture of the license and then bagged the wallet and the woman's phone to be added to evidence.

"What've we got?" Lindsey asked as she joined Sam.

"Twenty-four-year-old Audrey Olsen, found by a woman walking a dog that broke loose and led her to Audrey. I took photos and bagged the one hand that was bare."

Lindsey took note of the woman's leggings and underwear wrapped around her feet. "Poor baby. Who did this to you?"

"We're going to find out," Sam said, filled with the outrage that powered every investigation. This young woman had been out for a run in a public park, minding her own business when her life was senselessly stolen from her. The person who'd done that to her would have Sam's full attention until he was brought to justice, vacation or not. Audrey was hers now.

Freddie came jogging up to them. "Sorry. I witnessed an accident on the way here and had to wait for Patrol to get there." He was driving his mother's red Prius until he found the perfect car to replace the ancient Mustang that'd recently died.

Sam updated him on what she'd learned so far. "Let's go talk to the woman who found her."

On the main path, they headed for the ambulance's flashing red lights. A middle-aged woman sat on one of the stretchers, her shoulders wrapped in a blanket, the dog seated in front of her.

"She's a wreck, Lieutenant," the older of two paramedics said. "Very upset."

"Understandably. We just need a minute with her."

They stepped aside to give Sam access to the ambulance. She glanced at Freddie. "I'll do this so we don't overwhelm her."

"Sounds good."

She climbed into the back of the bus and took a seat on the stretcher across from the woman, who gasped when she recognized Sam.

"I'd introduce myself..."

"No need. I wish I was meeting you under different circumstances."

"As do I." Sam pulled a notebook from her back pocket and a pen from her coat pocket. "Can you tell me your name?"

"It's Lillian Pearson. My dog, Josie, and I were walking through the park like we do most days, when Josie started pulling me toward the brush. She pulled so hard, I lost my hold on her, which never happens. I was frantic as I ran after her, yelling for her to come back, and nearly tripped over... the woman." She choked on a sob. "I couldn't believe what I was seeing."

"Did you see anyone else on the path around the time you discovered her?"

"There were two women jogging. I see them almost every day, and we always say hello, but I didn't see anyone else. My husband... He doesn't like when I walk in the park when it's getting dark, but I've been doing it for thirty years. I love it here so much, but now..." She shrugged and dabbed at her eyes with a tissue. "I don't know if I'll ever come back."

"We're going to want you to come back to help us identify the women you saw jogging so we can find out if they saw or heard anything."

"Whatever I can do to help."

"Freddie?" Sam called to her partner. "Will you arrange to meet Ms. Pearson here tomorrow around this time to identify other potential witnesses?"

"Yes, ma'am."

"This is my partner, Detective Cruz."

"Yes, I know who he is."

"Can we please have your address and phone number?"

Lillian recited the information.

"I'm going to ask the Patrol officers to see you home, unless you feel like you need medical attention." Sam gestured to Freddie to set that up.

"I don't. I was just... I was shocked."

"Understandably so. Officer Keeney will see you and Josie home." Sam handed the woman a business card. "If you think of anything else that might help, please call me. My cell phone number is on the back."

"I will. Thank you for all you do. We're very excited about your husband's administration."

"That's nice to hear. Thank you." Sam helped her down from the ambulance.

"Right this way, ma'am," Keeney said, taking the dog's leash from her and extending his arm to her.

Sam appreciated his care with the traumatized woman and made a note to say so to the Patrol commander.

CHAPTER TEN

Lieutenant Haggerty, the Crime Scene Unit commander, approached her.

Sam led him to the body, which Lindsey hadn't moved yet.

"Ah, damn," Haggerty said when he saw the young woman. His gaze darted around the area, already looking for evidence. "We'll take it from here."

"I'm going to notify the family." Sam's stomach turned the way it always did at times like this. Having to give people news that would change their lives forever never got easier, no matter how many times she had to do it. She walked back to the cars with Freddie. "I can take it from here if you want to go home. My family is out of town."

Freddie held up his phone. "Actually, they're on their way back to the White House."

"What? Why?"

"Blizzard warning. They didn't want Nick trapped on a mountaintop in an emergency."

"Ugh, he'll be so bummed." Then another thought occurred to her. "So, wait, my entire family is currently on a helicopter?"

"Well, your sisters aren't on the helicopter."

"You know what I mean!"

"They'll be fine, Sam, and I'll go with you to Audrey Olsen's place. Elin is working late tonight, and besides, no one should do that job alone."

"I'm still stuck on my family being on a helicopter without me." She withdrew the secure BlackBerry that she used to communicate with Nick and found the text from him. "I guess the vacation is over before it started."

They got into Sam's car to drive to Adams Morgan.

"That's such a bummer."

"True confession?"

"Always."

"I was freaking out up there."

"About?"

"About getting back here if need be. And I know when we go to Bora Bora, I can't get back, but that's different. I'm not less than an hour from the District when I'm in Bora Bora. I just had the weirdest feeling of being trapped there, whereas Nick loved it. He was so happy to be out of the White House. I feel bad he has to come home early."

"You're very weird, but you know that already."

"I do know that. I can't explain the panicky feeling I had up there, but then, of course, Nick tuned right in to it and said he'd give me a ride home if it came to that."

"Which it did. You told me you wanted me to tell you when the press is hammering you guys, right?"

"I guess..."

"They're going off about him flying you home on *Marine One*. Waste of taxpayer dollars and such."

Sam sighed. "I was coming home to work *for* the taxpayers, but no one considers that."

"They want to know why you weren't driven home."

"Because the chopper was quicker!"

"You know that, and I know that..."

"They're just looking for things to pick at us about."

"Yes, they are. That's what they do with whoever lives in the White House. Nonstop picking."

"This is why I never wanted him to have the job in the first place. The scrutiny of everything we do is just maddening."

"I can't imagine what that must be like. Here's what I'd do if I were you... Live your lives. That helicopter is his to use as he sees fit. They can't make him use it when it suits them and then come for him when it suits him. All you can do is ignore the noise and do your thing."

"That's easier said than done when you work for the people who are criticizing you."

"You don't work for the media."

"No, but they're firing up the people we *do* work for."

"Those people know how hard you work for them. *You* know why you needed to get back to town fast, and you did what you had to do. That's what the chopper is for—to transport you guys where you need to go. Remember that."

"True. It's not like he can just jump in the car and give me a ride home if he wants to."

"People don't understand the severe restrictions you guys live under."

"I didn't understand it fully until I was living it."

"Which is why I say do your thing and ignore the noise. You're following the security rules set forth by the Secret Service."

"True," Sam said, sighing. "I just wish people would try to understand that the president—and first lady—can't just do whatever the fuck they want when they want and have to follow all these protocols to do anything." She pulled into a parking space three blocks from Audrey's apartment in Adams Morgan. "Who do you think we're going to find at her place? Parents, significant other, roommates?"

"I don't know, but I hate doing this to anyone."

"Same."

They zipped up tight against the cold and walked to the building. Outside the main door, they pressed the button for apartment six.

A male voice responded. "Yes?"

"Metro PD. May we speak to you for a moment?"

After a long pause, the man said, "Uh, yeah. Come on up."

He buzzed them in.

"Boyfriend," Sam said. "Or husband." *Ugh.*

They went up the stairs to the second floor, where a young, dark-haired man waited for them in a doorway. His eyes widened when he recognized Sam.

They showed their badges. "Lieutenant Holland, Detective Cruz. May we step inside for a moment?"

"What's this about?" he asked as he moved aside to let them enter.

"What's your relationship to Audrey Olsen?"

"She's my girlfriend."

"And your name?"

"Wes Hambly."

"Do you live here, Wes?"

"Yes, with Audrey. She's out for a run."

"Can we sit for a second?"

"Um, sure." He showed them to a cozy living room with colorful pillows on the sofa bearing sayings such as "Life is Good," "Be Positive" and "Onward and Upward."

Those freaking pillows broke Sam's heart.

"What's this about?" Wes asked.

"I'm sorry to have to tell you that Audrey was murdered in Rock Creek Park."

He tilted his head as if trying to process what she'd said. "Audrey isn't dead. You must be mistaken. She just went for a run, like an hour ago. She's training for a marathon, so she's gone awhile sometimes."

Sam held up the evidence bag containing Audrey's wallet. "Is this hers?"

"I... Yes, but... She's not dead. She can't be dead."

"I'm very sorry to have to tell you that she is, but we need someone to provide a positive identification. Would you be able to come with us to do that?"

"Audrey's really dead?" he asked, his voice wavering.

"Yes." Sam hated this more than just about anything, but she'd learned to be direct when delivering dreadful news.

He dropped his head into his hands. "She was just here."

They gave him a minute to get himself together. "Are there other people who should be notified?"

"Oh God, her mother... She's the only child of a single mother."

Fucking hell.

"If you'd like, I can call her," Sam said, hoping he'd decline her offer.

"It... It probably should be me."

"Where is she?"

"Pittsburgh. Audrey... She's from Pittsburgh. We met in college at American. We've been together five years. What am I supposed do without her?"

Sam couldn't begin to imagine what he would do without her. She wouldn't wish the journey he had before him on anyone.

"Should I... Should I call her mother now?"

"I think so." Sam ached for the mother in Pittsburgh whose life would never be the same after that phone call. "Is there someone you can ask to be with her before you call her?"

"I have a number for her neighbor. She and Audrey are close to her. I'll text her."

Wes got up, went to the kitchen and returned with his phone. He stared at it for a long time before he found the number he needed and started a text to the neighbor.

Sam decided to help him. "Tell her, 'I'm Audrey's boyfriend, Wes, in DC. Something terrible has happened, and I have to call her mother. Can you be with her?'"

Nodding, he typed the message and sent it.

They sat in silence, waiting for a response that came five minutes later. *Oh God. Of course. I'm going now.*

They waited another endless ten minutes before Wes placed the call to Audrey's mother, putting the call on speaker.

"Wes, what's wrong?"

"Denise..."

"*What, Wes?*"

"It's Audrey."

"What about her?" In those three little words, Sam could tell that the woman somehow already suspected.

"The police are here, and they said..." He broke down into heart-wrenching sobs, as if the news had finally registered with him.

Sam took the phone from him. "Ma'am, this is Lieutenant Holland with the DC Metro Police. I'm very sorry to have to tell you that Audrey was murdered."

The scream that came through the phone pierced Sam's soul.

"*No, no, no. I just talked to her earlier. She's not dead.*"

"I'm sorry."

"No."

"Wes is going to come with us to positively identify her. Is there anything I can do for you in the meantime?"

"Please tell me this isn't true."

"I wish I could."

"God, no, not Audrey. Not my baby."

Sam could hear the other woman's voice in the background, offering comfort where none could be had. "We will be in touch again later," Sam said. "I'm so very sorry for your loss."

"What do I do now? What do I *do*?"

"Just wait to hear from us again. We'll be in touch soon."

"Could I please speak to Wes?" she asked, her voice laced with sobs.

"Of course." Sam handed the phone back to Wes and then glanced at Freddie, who looked stricken. The day this sort of thing wasn't overwhelming for them was the day they needed to find another line of work.

"I know," Wes said tearfully. "I will. I'll call you after I see her. Yes, of course. Love you, too." He ended the call and wiped tears from his face with the sleeve of his T-shirt. "How can this be real?"

"I wish I had an answer to that question," Sam said. "If you're able to come with us, we can get this over with." To Freddie, she said, "Contact Lindsey and let her know we're bringing him in."

Freddie nodded and walked out of the apartment, probably glad to have something else to do besides witness Wes's nightmare.

"Is there someone we can call to be with you for this?" Sam asked Wes.

"My brother lives locally. I could call him."

"Ask him to meet us at MPD Headquarters."

He nodded and placed the call.

Sam tried to tune out what he was saying and the fresh wave of grief that came with telling his brother the dreadful news. She stepped out of the apartment to give him a minute and leaned her head back against the wall, drained by the emotional tsunami that came with murder.

She took a second to check both her phones and found a new message from Nick. *Landed at the WH. See you when you get home.*

That gave her one less thing to worry about. *Will be home soon,* she responded.

Wes emerged from the apartment, wearing a winter coat, with his keys and phone in hand.

Sam pushed off the wall, led him downstairs to her car and got him settled in the back seat.

Freddie walked toward her, on the phone. "We'll be there shortly. Will do." He stashed the phone in his pocket. "She'll be ready for us."

"Let's get this done."

On the way to HQ, they drove through lighter-than-usual traffic, a sign that a storm was coming and people were most likely in panic mode. If there was so much as an inch of snow in the region, the grocery store shelves were cleared and school canceled. A blizzard would be treated like Armageddon.

Normally, she and Freddie would laugh about the panic surrounding a snowstorm, but they were silent as they drove Wes to HQ.

Sam pulled up outside the morgue entrance and glanced at Freddie.

"Be right back," he said.

He would make sure Lindsey was ready for them so they didn't have to drag this out for Wes.

"Who could've done this?" Wes asked, breaking the long silence.

Sam looked at him in the rearview mirror. "We don't know yet, but we're going to find out."

"How will you do that?"

That was a question she was rarely asked by grieving family members, who often didn't have the capacity to wonder how an investigation would unfold. "We'll begin with physical evidence collected during the autopsy as well as crime scene evidence, witness statements and video surveillance of the area. There are security cameras all over town. We'll take it one step at a time, one puzzle piece at a time, until we have the full picture of what happened."

"What if you can't find him?"

"We'll find him."

"Did he rape her?"

"We believe so. Her pants and underwear were around her ankles."

His sharp inhale was his only response to that news.

Freddie came to the door and waved them in.

"Are you ready to go in?"

"No, I'm not," he said, but he got out of the car and walked inside with Sam.

At the door to the morgue, Sam turned to him. "When we go in, Dr. McNamara, the chief medical examiner, will ask you to identify Audrey. You'll see only her face. Do you have any questions?"

"No."

Sam stepped forward to activate the automatic doors to the morgue. As usual, the antiseptic smell of the place triggered her aversion to this hideous task. "Wes, this is Dr. McNamara. Lindsey, this is Audrey's boyfriend, Wes."

Lindsey shook his hand. "I'm very sorry for your loss."

"Thank you," Wes said stiffly, as if her condolences offended him.

He would get used to receiving them over the next few days, but he wasn't there yet, Sam thought.

"Right this way." Lindsey led them into the freezing exam room, where a body on a table was covered by a sheet. "Are you ready?"

He gave the barest of nods.

Lindsey drew the sheet back just enough to reveal Audrey's face.

Wes let out an inhuman sound as his knees buckled.

Sam and Freddie held him up.

He broke free of their hold and went to her, leaned over to rest his head on her chest and wailed.

Sam glanced at Freddie, noting the tears in his eyes.

They gave Wes all the time he needed with Audrey before leading him out of the morgue to the conference room in the pit.

"Can I get you some water?" Freddie asked.

"Sure. Thanks." The words were dull and flat, like his expression.

Sam followed Freddie out of the room. "I want him to give permission for us to look at her phone."

"I'll get the form and the water."

"Thanks."

When she entered the conference room, Sam took a seat across from Wes, who was staring at the wall with tears rolling down his face. "I'm so, so sorry for your loss."

"Thank you."

"I know it seems absolutely impossible to imagine right now, but you're going to get through this."

"I don't think I will."

"You will," Sam said, "because you have no choice."

Tears continued to slide down his cheeks as he let that thought settle.

"Is your brother on his way?"

"Yeah, he was just leaving class when I called. He's coming." Wes dropped his head into his hands, his shoulders heaving with sobs. "How could this have happened to Audrey? She's the best person I've ever known. She'd take a bug outside to set it free rather than kill it. She volunteers to teach English as a second language to immigrant children. Who kills someone like her?"

"Someone who has no regard for human life." Sam believed a stranger had killed Audrey, but she still had to go through the motions. "Has she had problems with anyone lately? Friend, coworker, family member?"

"No, nothing like that. She's all about peace and tranquility and helping others. She was in graduate school to be a social worker because she's been so moved by her ESL students. All she talks about are the things she wants to do to help make their lives better. I just... I can't believe someone killed her."

It would take, Sam thought, months, if not years, before Wes wrapped his head around what'd happened to Audrey.

"I'm sorry to do this to you when you're already in shock, but the first hours of an investigation are critical, so I need to ask you some questions."

"Yeah, sure. Whatever I can do."

"Were you home the whole time Audrey was out jogging?"

His head shot up, and his shock multiplied. "You think *I* killed her?"

"I'm only asking where you were."

"I was still at work when she texted me that she was leaving. We have a huge project due early next week, and we worked most of the weekend."

"What time was that?"

He checked his phone, seeming to realize he was looking at the last text he'd ever receive from Audrey. "Four."

"And where do you work?"

"On M Street, for a political action committee. We lobby Congress on behalf of the natural gas industry."

"What time did you leave the office?"

"Not until about five thirty."

"Are there coworkers who can corroborate that you were there until then?"

"Yes," he said through gritted teeth.

Sam pushed her notebook across the table. "If you'll write down their names and numbers, we can contact them."

"I didn't kill Audrey. I loved her more than anyone."

"I believe you, Wes, but by confirming your alibi, we can eliminate you as a suspect, which is our goal."

That seemed to appease him somewhat. He took the pen she offered and used his phone to get the numbers she'd requested.

"Thank you. Do you know the passcode on her phone?"

"It's zero-two-two-zero. My birthday."

Sam wrote down the numbers as Freddie stepped into the room with a paper he handed to her and a bottle of water he put in front of Wes, who didn't seem to notice it.

A Patrol officer came to the door with a tearful young man. "He's here for Wes Hambly."

Sam nodded and gestured for Wes's brother to come into the room. Like Wes, his brother had dark hair and eyes.

Wes shot out of his chair and met his brother with a sobbing hug.

"This can't be happening," his brother said.

"I saw her. It's real. I can't..."

Sam gave them five minutes before she cleared her throat. "I'm so sorry to have to do this right now, but as I said to Wes, the early hours of a homicide investigation are critical."

CHAPTER ELEVEN

The two men released each other and wiped their faces.

"Your name?" Sam asked the brother.

He sat next to his brother. "Brecken Hambly."

"And you're in college?"

"Yes, I followed my brother to American."

"What year?"

"Sophomore."

"And you've been in class this afternoon?"

"Yes, since two."

"Aren't you on winter break?"

"We can take intensive classes during the break, and I'm taking two. One of them started today." He glanced at his brother. "Why?"

"Ruling you out," Wes said with a world-weariness he most likely hadn't had before Sam and Freddie had shown up with soul-crushing news.

"Oh, okay. Yeah, I was there from two until about twenty minutes ago."

"Is there someone who can verify that?"

"I have a friend who's in the class I had this afternoon."

Sam pushed the notebook across the table. "Write down his or her name and number for us."

Brecken did as she asked and then returned the notebook to her.

"Wes said he can't think of anyone who Audrey might've had a problem with in recent days or weeks. How about you?"

Brecken rubbed his palms on his jeans. "Wes would certainly

know better than I would, but no, I haven't heard or seen anything unusual recently."

"When was the last time you saw Audrey?"

"Last Sunday," Brecken said. "We watched football at their place, like we do most Sundays. Audrey always makes us snacks." His voice caught as he seemed to realize that would never happen again. "When I came to college, she helped me set up my dorm room and went to the store to buy me stuff she thought I needed." He wiped away a tear. "She was very sweet and made me feel at home here."

Sam ached for the violent loss of such a wonderful young woman. "Talk to me about her family," she said to Wes. "You said she's the only child of a single mom, right?"

"Yes," Wes said.

"Any family members—cousins, aunts, uncles, grandparents—she was close to?"

He shook his head. "She always said it was just her and her mom. They were incredibly close. Talked every day, sometimes more than once. Audrey referred to her mom as her best girlfriend."

This just got worse by the minute. "How about friends?"

"She has tons of them," Wes said. "She makes friends easier than anyone I've ever met. She makes everyone feel important to her."

"She's a great listener," Brecken said. "Whenever I had girl trouble, she was the one I went to for advice. She always knew what to do."

Sam made notes about everything they told her. "Wes, would you sign this form to give us permission to review her texts and other messages on her phone?"

"Yes, of course." He signed the form and pushed it back to her.

Sam wrote the code Wes had given her on the form and gave it to Freddie, who left to deliver it to Malone to get a warrant to back them up just in case they needed it before it went to Archie's team in IT for examination. "Did she work?"

Wes nodded. "At a school for rich kids in Northeast called Whitmore. That job is why she volunteers with the immigrant kids. She said she wants to give something back to the kids who don't have every advantage money can buy."

"So, she didn't like the job?"

"She hates it. Entitled kids, entitled parents, nonstop drama. She's been looking for a new job, but it's hard to move during the school year. I've been trying to get her to quit and go to school full time, but she doesn't want me supporting her." All the air left his lungs in one big exhale. "She should've let me take care of her."

"Do you have somewhere you can stay tonight? We'd like to send crime scene investigators into your apartment tonight."

"Why?"

"Often, we don't know why until we know why. Does that make sense?"

"I guess."

"Do we have your permission to do that?"

"Yes, of course."

"He can stay with me," Brecken said. "I'm in an apartment now."

"Write down your address and phone number. I need Wes's number, too."

Brecken provided the info and gave her the notebook.

"Can you give me keys to your home?" Sam asked Wes.

"Ah, yeah, sure. This one is for the vestibule, and this one is for our place."

Sam wondered how long would it take for him to realize he now lived alone.

"Thank you for your cooperation at such a difficult time. Audrey would be proud of you for trying to help catch the person who did this to her."

"I hope so," he said, wiping away more tears.

Sam stepped out of the conference room and signaled for Detective Cameron Green. "Will you please have Patrol give Wes Hambly and his brother a ride home?"

"Yes, ma'am. Also, I wanted to remind you that Gigi is due back to work tonight."

"Yes, that's great news. I'll stick around until she arrives so we can hand off to her and Dani."

"I'll line up Patrol."

"Thank you." Sam returned to the conference room. "We're going to get you a ride home, and I'll check in with you in the morning."

"Audrey's mother... She texted that she's going to come here."

Sam handed him her card while doubting anyone could get to DC with a blizzard heading their way. "Have her call me when she arrives."

He nodded.

"I wish there was more I could do for you than tell you we'll try our very best to get justice for Audrey—and for you."

"Thank you."

When the time was right, she'd talk to him about the grief group she'd founded with Dr. Trulo for victims of violent crime.

"Are you okay?" Freddie asked after Sam saw Wes and his brother off with the Patrol officer.

"Another day, another wonderful person murdered in our city," Sam said, "and multiple lives changed forever as a result."

"You're supposed to be on vacation," Captain Malone said from behind her.

Sam turned to him. "I know, but we caught a new case—"

"That your team is more than capable of handling."

"Nick and the kids came back to town because of the storm, so I can give it a little time this week."

"As long as you take some downtime, too."

"I will." Sam looked up at the man who'd been so much more than a boss to her. "So, you're not pissed with me anymore?"

"When did I say that?"

"All righty, then."

"You and McBride defied a direct order. That won't be soon forgotten."

"She found ten missing kids." Sam shrugged. "I'd do it again if I had it to do over."

"Good to know." He ran his fingers through his gray hair, frustration rolling off him in waves. "I'm trying to keep our chief from being fired, Sam. Do you get that?"

"I do, but I also have to support my team, and Jeannie was too far down the road with this case to let it go. At the end of the day, we have to be able to look ourselves in the mirror and like what we're seeing."

"I get that. I really do, but the firestorm is *so* not what we need right now."

"I'm sorry about that. I truly am. The last thing *in the world* I want is for the chief to get fired or be under any more scrutiny than he already is. But we had to see this through. I can only hope that the lives saved will outweigh the other side of the story."

"The side in which we were incompetent for eleven years and let this woman continue to kidnap and torture children? You think anything is going to outweigh that?"

"We weren't incompetent. One member of our department was."

"One is all it takes, Sam. You know that as well as I do. The U.S. Attorney is calling for a review of all of Stahl's cases, including his successful prosecutions."

Sam gasped. "*Everything?*"

"Every fucking thing. If he cut corners on cases he didn't bother to investigate, what did he do with the ones he *did* investigate?"

Her stomach began to hurt again. "I... uh... wow. I don't even know what to say."

"This could get very, very ugly, but I don't have to tell you that."

"No, you don't. Jeez... What a mess."

"Another mess, you mean."

"Yeah." She looked up at him. "We can't change what was done in the past, but we can sure as hell do whatever we can to make things right."

He nodded but seemed as low as she'd ever seen him. "This happened on my watch, on Joe's, your dad's. We're all going to take a hit, so you need to be ready for people coming for your dad."

She would never be ready for that. "No one despised Stahl more than he did."

"Maybe so, but it was still his job at one time or another to supervise him, just as it was my job and Joe's. We're all on the hook for this."

"Let's do an interview with Darren about how horrified we are and how horrified my dad would be to know what Stahl was really doing while he was filing false reports about his efforts." Since Sam never voluntarily did anything with the media, the idea got his attention. "We can say there's never been a day that we didn't come here and do our very best for the people of this District. That kind of thing. If we get out ahead of it, we might stanch the bleeding a bit. And we can praise Jeannie for the rescue of Carisma and the other children."

"It's not a terrible idea. I'll pitch it to Joe." He seemed considerably brighter than he had a second ago.

"It always helps to have a plan."

"Yes, it does, and it's a good one. I'm sure he'll go for it."

"Let me know, and I'll set it up with Darren."

"Are you going home?"

"As soon as I give Dani and Gigi their marching orders. Gigi is back tonight."

"Glad to have her back."

DETECTIVE CAMERON GREEN met Detective Gigi Dominguez in the parking lot, opened her car door and gave her a hand getting out of the car.

She winced from the pain in her midsection that had persisted following the recent removal of her spleen.

"You're coming back too soon, hon." Her face was pale, her dark eyes big. He was crazy about her and had urged her to take more time off.

"I'm fine. It's just an occasional twinge now. Is that the LT's car? I thought she was on vacation."

"She came in to help deal with the fallout over the Deasly case."

"What an incredible bust for Jeannie. I'm so proud of her."

"We all are, but it's causing chaos for the department."

"I saw that. People are saying some ugly stuff about the chief and others, including Skip Holland."

"I know. It's horrible. If they'd had any idea what Stahl was doing, they would've intervened immediately. They've discovered he was filing bogus reports about investigations when he wasn't doing *anything*."

"Oh my God. That's crazy! I was thinking about that earlier and wondering how he could live with himself. I never could've."

"Me neither. I feel bad going home at the end of a shift when a case is still open."

"Yes, exactly." She smiled up at him, and even though it was freezing and starting to snow, Cameron didn't want to be anywhere else. "What are you up to tonight?"

"Jeffrey and I will be a couple of sad sacks alone on the sofa because our best girl is working."

"Aw, you guys are so cute. You should watch some hockey while you have the chance."

"But you've got me hooked on HGTV. Hockey doesn't look as good to me anymore. Nothing looks as good to me as you do." He kissed her, which was all they'd done so far since she was still recovering from the serious injuries inflicted by her ex-boyfriend. God, he wanted her so badly, but he would wait for as long as it took for her to feel well again and be ready for all the things he wanted with her.

"I've got to go."

"I know." He put his arms around her. "Please be careful. No setbacks."

"I'm on desk duty for another month, so don't worry."

"I will worry." Reluctantly, he pulled back to kiss her again. "I'll see you in the morning."

She gave him that sexy little smile that made his heart race. "Can't wait."

"Break it up, lovers," Gigi's partner, Dani Carlucci, said as she approached them. "We've got work to do, girlfriend."

"Let's get to it," Gigi said as she walked away with Dani, giving him a wave over her shoulder.

Cameron swept the snow off his car and got in, turning the heater to high. A long, boring evening loomed until he could see her in the morning at shift change. Working opposite schedules was going to suck, but they had weekends to look forward to and would make it work.

Somehow.

"You two are hot and heavy, huh?" Dani asked as she held the door to the morgue for Gigi.

"Not as hot and heavy as I'd like to be. He treats me like I'm made of blown glass and might shatter at any moment."

"That's the way he ought to treat you after what you've been through."

"I'm much better than I was."

"But you're not quite there yet, and he sees that."

"I guess."

"So you're in love, huh?"

"Like I've never been in my entire life. I had no idea, Dan. None at all."

"That's amazing. That's how it should be."

"Is it weird that I'm a tiny bit thankful to Ezra for losing his mind and forcing me to end that relationship once and for all so I could have this exciting new thing with Cam?"

"Yes, it's very weird to be thankful for the beating you withstood."

"I'm not thankful for *that*. But I am thankful to be free of him and to have the chance to be with Cameron."

"He's such a good guy. I've always thought so, but seeing the way he's cared for you these last few weeks has made me love him even more than I already did."

"I'm glad you do. That means a lot."

"They caught a new homicide today," Dani said as they walked to the pit. "A twenty-four-year-old woman raped and murdered in Rock Creek Park."

"Oh God," Gigi said, her good mood deflating just that quickly. Working murder did that to you. It reminded you that even when things were going better than they ever had in your own life, other people's lives were falling apart. And it never became routine, no matter how many years she came into work to news of yet another senseless killing. Her own recent brush with mortality had Gigi's emotions hovering close to the surface as she walked into the pit for the first time in weeks.

Her colleagues embarrassed her with applause.

"Thanks, everyone."

"Glad to have you back, Gigi," Sam said. "You're looking well."

"I'm feeling much better."

"Take it nice and easy until you're back to a hundred percent."

"Yes, ma'am." It never got old reporting to the wonder known as Lieutenant Sam Holland. Gigi loved that the rest of the world would have the chance to find out what an amazing person she was now that she was first lady.

"Let's get you ladies up to speed."

Sam and Freddie went over what had been done so far in the Olsen investigation.

"Archie should have the dump on her phone soon, so start there. Go through everything and find out if she was beefing with anyone." She handed over the phone numbers Wes and his brother had provided to account for their whereabouts during the time of the murder. "Confirm their alibis. And then get with Archie's team to see where we are in the review of cameras in the park. After that, if you have time left, look into recent reports of any activity in the park."

"I was just coming to talk to you about that," SVU Detective Erica Lucas said as she entered the pit, holding papers she handed to Sam. "Report of an unsolved rape we caught in the park two weeks ago."

Sam eyed the pages before handing them over to Dani. "We'll want to compare DNA if there is any from Audrey."

"Will do," Dani said. "We'll take it from here."

"I'll be in for a few hours in the morning if I can get here in the storm," Sam said, "but I'm taking my laptop in case I can't."

"Got it," Gigi said. "We'll be ready to update you by seven."

"Everyone else, go home and be careful getting back in the morning. We're hearing this storm is going to be one for the ages."

"Could I have a minute, LT?" Erica asked.

"Of course. Come in."

Gigi glanced at Dani. "What do you suppose that's about?"

"Not sure, but we'll find out soon enough."

CHAPTER TWELVE

"What's up?" Sam asked Erica, a detective she liked and respected.

"Hearing rumblings that Ramsey is coming back to work while his firing is being appealed."

Sam groaned. "Just when we thought we'd seen the last of that son of a bitch."

"But he has rights, don't you know."

"Whatever. We have rights, too, and one of them is the right to come to work and not have to deal with assholes."

Erica snorted out a laugh as she sat in Sam's visitor chair. "Exactly. With all this shit about Stahl and his past cases coming to light, we don't need people like Ramsey making the rest of us look bad."

"Agreed. Hopefully, the appeal won't go anywhere."

"From your lips to God's ears. So, tell me the truth. How was Camp David?"

"Pretty and rustic. What I saw of it, anyway. Nick loved it."

"Did you?"

"I wanted to."

"But?"

"I felt a little odd about being on a mountaintop, removed from everything here."

"Odd. Is that another way of saying you were coming out of your skin?"

"Maybe," Sam said, laughing. "I *so* want downtime with my family, but the isolation there was crazy. Which, of course, was exactly what

Nick needed. I'll suck it up occasionally so he can get out of La Casa Blanca."

"Good plan. Is it all still surreal?"

"It's becoming a little less so as we get used to it—as much as anyone gets used to it. Thankfully, they're mostly leaving me to do my thing here and not expecting me to be a traditional first lady—not that there's anything wrong with being a traditional first lady."

"I get you. It's not your thing."

"No, it most definitely isn't. I have a great team there helping to keep me engaged without me having to be engaged, if that makes sense."

"It does, and it lets you have the best of both worlds. I'm gonna go and let you get home to your family."

"Thanks for the info you brought us."

"Let me know if anything comes of it. We're still looking for the guy. He did a number on our victim. She was in the hospital for more than a week."

"But she got away."

"Because she had self-defense training. He took her by surprise, so she couldn't fight back until after he'd assaulted her. She believes he intended to kill her, but she hasn't been able to tell us much else. She's severely traumatized."

"Is that in the report?"

"Yep."

"Thanks again."

"You got it."

After Erica left, Sam put her coat on and grabbed her bag, phone and keys. "I'm out," she said to Dani, Gigi and Freddie. "And you," she said, pointing to Freddie, "need to go home, too."

"I'm going. Can you give me a lift to the Metro? I figure it'll be easier to get back that way tomorrow."

"No problem. Let's go."

They walked out into snow falling much more intensely than it had been earlier.

"The whole region is going to be paralyzed by this," Freddie said.

"I know. It'd be comical if it wasn't such a pain in the ass. At least it won't be as bad as it would be during a regular workweek." She'd no sooner said the words than she was airborne, having slipped on a patch of ice under the snow. "Fuck," she said when she landed hard on her hip and elbow. "Goddamn motherfucking snow."

Freddie had come around the car to help her up.

Vernon and Jimmy rushed over to help, too.

Sam shook them off. "I'm fine." But her hip and elbow hurt, bad. "Why do I have to find the one random patch of ice?"

"Are we heading home, ma'am?" Vernon asked.

"With a stop at Judiciary Square to drop off Detective Cruz."

"Very good."

She unlocked the car and eased herself into the driver's seat, wincing from the blast of pain. "Shit, fuck, damn, hell, goddamn it."

"Sam."

"This is no time for a lecture about the Lord's name! I just busted my ass!" She reached for the key and nearly blacked out from the pain in her elbow. "And my arm!"

"Do you need the ER?"

"No, I don't need the motherfucking ER."

"'Scuse me for asking."

"You are not excused!"

"How glad am I that you're on vacation and not my problem this week?"

"I'll be in for a few hours tomorrow to keep things moving on Olsen." He would understand, better than anyone, that it had taken less than five minutes for Audrey—and Wes—to become *hers*. Yes, she trusted her team to do right by their latest victim, but Sam needed to help. And then she'd go home and hang out with her husband and kids.

"Oh joy," Freddie said in response to the news that she'd be in tomorrow.

Sam drove to the Judiciary Square station and pulled up to the curb. "Get out."

"You have a good night, too."

"Buh-bye now."

Whistling the tune of "My Humps," he closed the door and jogged toward the station with no worries about falling and busting his ass. Bastard. What should've been a ten-minute ride home stretched to thirty minutes because people *could not drive in snow* to save their lives. She witnessed four accidents and was glad they weren't her problem. Patrol officers would have their hands full tonight.

By the time the distant glow of the White House came into view, her entire body hurt, and how was that possible when she'd cracked her hip and elbow? Was this the first time she was glad to see the place they now called home? "I think it is," she said with a gruff chuckle.

Knowing Nick and the kids were in there, along with a warm meal and a cozy fireplace, greatly improved her mood.

Until she moved to get out of the car.

Holy shitballs of pain, Batman.

She hobbled to the door, where Harold greeted her with a concerned expression.

"Are you all right, Mrs. Cappuano?"

That was a very good question. Was it possible she'd broken something? No, because she had no time for that. "I think so," she said, eyeing the staircase to the residence, "but there's an elevator, right?"

"Yes, ma'am. Right this way." He not only led her to the elevator, but he accompanied her as if she couldn't find the second floor on her own. God forbid she should push a button for herself. She no sooner had that thought than she was chastising herself for it. The White House staff took great pride in their work, and Sam appreciated everything they did for her and their family. "Are you sure you're all right, ma'am?"

"Took a fall in the parking lot at work and landed hard, but I'm okay."

"Ah, the ice got you, did it?"

"It did."

"Sorry to hear that." The elevator doors slid open. "There you are, ma'am."

"Thanks for the lift, Harold."

"My pleasure, ma'am. I hope you feel better."

"Thanks. Me, too."

Sam limped down the hallway, wondering where everyone was. Usually, she could hear them before she saw them. She was about to text Nick when he stepped out of their suite and smiled when he saw her coming. His smile quickly faded when he realized she was limping.

"What happened?"

"Goddamned ice in the goddamned parking lot at work."

"Oh no. What hurts?"

"It'd be easier to tell you what doesn't hurt."

"How about a hot bath?"

"That sounds like heaven, but where are the kids? I totally missed today with them."

"They're fine. They're upstairs playing Chutes and Ladders with Eli and Celia. All is well."

"Then please lead me to that hot bath." Her hip hurt so badly, she wondered if she'd fractured it. Please God... She did *not* have time for that. While Nick got the bath ready, Sam sat gingerly on the bed, wincing when her battered hip touched the mattress. "Yow." This reminded her of the time she'd been hit by a car while chasing a perp. She'd survived that, and she'd survive this, too.

But damn, it hurt.

Nick came out of the bathroom and knelt before her to remove her boots.

"I need a photo of the leader of the free world kneeling before me."

He grinned as he looked up at her, the most devastatingly handsome man she'd ever laid eyes on. "This is just for you, babe."

"It'd better be."

"No worries there, as you surely know."

"This is going to put a damper on vacation activities."

"That's okay."

"It isn't. Our whole vacation has gone sideways."

"No, it hasn't. We're all together, and that's what matters. Who cares where we are?"

"Um, you do. You were loving Camp David."

"We can go back again sometime soon."

"You're taking this better than I expected."

"I was disappointed to leave, because I was enjoying the change of scenery, but all my favorite scenery is here with me, so I'm good."

She ran her fingers through his thick dark hair. "You're easy to please."

"As you well know, it doesn't take much to make me happy."

Sam smiled and leaned in to kiss him. One of her greatest joys in the life she shared with him was seeing him deeply loved by a family of his own, which was something he'd never had before.

"Let me go check the tub, and then I'll help you get naked, which is my favorite activity of all."

No matter what disaster she brought home with her, he always made her feel better. That was one of his many superpowers where she was concerned.

When he returned, he helped her up and then gently removed her clothes, wincing at the huge red marks on her hip and elbow that would soon blossom into massive bruises. "My baby took a hell of a hit."

"It attacked me out of nowhere. One minute, I was walking to the car, and the next, I was flat on my ass. Or I guess it was my hip.

Figures I couldn't have landed on all that cushion I've got back there."

He gently patted her bottom. "We wouldn't want anything to mar this national treasure."

She laughed. "Have you had it officially designated as such?"

"Not yet, but I'm going to talk to Terry about an executive order."

"I'm sure he'll be thrilled about that." The silliness with him helped to take the sting out of another difficult day at work. She took the arm he offered and let him lead her slowly into the bathroom. "I'm like a ninety-year-old."

"Nah, you're like a thirtysomething who fell on ice. Let me see."

When he got a better look at the red mark on her hip in brighter light, he gasped. "Holy shit, babe. That looks bad. Are you sure we shouldn't get you checked out?"

Sam twisted to see the huge red spot on her hip that would no doubt turn colorful by the morning. "I'm sure I can't be bothered with a trip to the ER."

"Let me get Harry up here. We do have a medical unit at our disposal, you know."

"Not tonight. I'll deal with it in the morning if it's not better.

"If it's still bad tomorrow, we're doing something about it."

"You're not the boss of me."

"In this case, I am," he said, dropping pain pills into her hand and giving her a glass of water.

"Thank you."

With his help, she managed to get in the tub and ease into the heated water. But she had tears in her eyes by the time she got settled.

"I hate when you get hurt," he said, running a finger over the stitches in her arm from the bullet that recently grazed her.

"I do, too, especially when it's my own fault."

He sat on the mat next to the tub. "The blame for this one belongs firmly on the ice."

"Bastard."

As he chuckled, his BlackBerry chimed with a text. "Scotty is looking for me." He typed a reply. "I'm telling him you're home, and we'll be ready for dinner in about half an hour."

She closed her eyes and gave in to the pleasure of the bath. "That sounds good, and this feels wonderful. Thank you."

"Always a pleasure to tend to my lovely wife."

"This week is going to be a little more complicated than we hoped."

"Because of the fall?"

"That and a case we caught today." She opened her eyes and turned to him. "A twenty-four-year-old woman raped and murdered in Rock Creek Park."

"Oh no."

"I had to tell her live-in boyfriend of five years."

"That had to be rough."

"It never gets easier, not that I hope it will. It shouldn't be easy. I'm going to work a few half days to keep things moving there."

"I understand."

"Will the kids?"

"They know your work is important."

"I feel this incredible push-pull inside me all the time. If I'm here, I feel like I should be there. When I'm there, I worry constantly about what I'm missing here."

"I believe that condition is called working motherhood."

"Before we had kids, I would've said I understood how hard it is for working moms, but I didn't know squat—and I still don't. I have tons of help that allows me to do three jobs sorta well. What do people do who haven't got any help? Single moms are superheroes."

"They sure are. You know... You're able to invite guests to the State of the Union. That might be a great opportunity to shine a light on the challenges single moms and working moms face."

"I'd like that."

"Do you have people you'd like to invite?"

"I can't think of anyone off the top of my head, but my sisters and Shelby will. I'll ask them."

"Think about who else you'd like to ask."

"How many can I have?"

"Like maybe five?"

"Oh, cool. All right. Maybe the mom, Cath, I met in Des Moines who lost both her children in the shooting."

"That's a good one. I'll ask Terry and Lilia to invite her."

"I'll think about who else."

"No, you won't. Terry talked to Lilia, and she's on it."

Sam splashed water in his face. "Stop acting like you know me so well."

Laughing, he used the towel he'd gotten for her to wipe his face. "I do know you so well, and I understand your unique... limitations."

"Meaning my one-track mind that's focused ninety percent of the time on my job?"

"You said that, not me."

Sam released a deep sigh. "I wanted kids so badly, and I'm so, so happy to have our family, but will I always feel that I don't give them enough time?"

"Probably, but here's how I see it. You have a special gift, and by using that gift, you help make this a safer town for everyone who lives here and visits. It'd be a crime for you to not use that gift the way you do."

"That's very kind of you to say, but I want to be a good mom, too."

"You are, and the kids love you. Everyone is happy, healthy, settled in this new place we call home for the time being and content to be together this week. The twins are thrilled to have Eli home, and so is Scotty. All they need is to know we're here and we love them."

"You make it sound so simple."

"It is. We're there when they need us, and they're surrounded by people who'd kill for them when we can't be here. They know our jobs are intense, and Scotty told me the other day that he thinks we're the coolest parents ever."

"He said that?"

"He did. I meant to tell you."

"What brought that on?"

"I was talking about you trying to close your cases before the holidays while getting ready to host our entire crew for Christmas Eve and me dealing with the issue in the Gulf of Suez and how everything was nuts. I told him we're sorry to be so busy all the time. That's when he said it's fine. He said, 'I have the coolest parents of all my friends. They're jealous.'"

"Wow."

"Yeah, so we're not a conventional family—"

Sam laughed. "That's putting it mildly."

"But our family works for all of us the way it is. I don't want you to feel guilty for doing the work you were born to do. We're giving the kids a life they'll never forget."

"For better or worse."

"For much better. Don't stress. We're making it work."

"How are you so chill about all of this?"

He shrugged. "I've given in to the reality of our situation. We're both doing important work that matters to a lot of people. Our kids are well cared for and well loved, and that's what matters. I actually get to see them more than I did before I was president, which is a perk of living above the store."

"That's true. Thank you for the pep talk. I needed it after having to leave our vacation."

"You were thrilled to leave our vacation."

"I was not!"

He tweaked her nose. "Yes, you were. You were like a caged bear up there."

"That is not true!"

"Samantha... Remember who you're talking to."

"Don't be sanctimonious. It's not a good look on you."

His smile, though... That was the best look ever. "My sweet, sexy grizzly bear."

"I hate when you know me so well."

"No, you don't."

"Yes, I actually do. And P.S., I saw how much you loved it there, and I'll go back anytime you want."

"Good to know."

"Now get me out of here before I prune."

He stood to give her a hand. "We can't have that."

The pain was intense. "Ah, fuck me to tears."

"Happy to. Anytime."

Grunting out a laugh, she said, "Not tonight, cowboy."

He wrapped a towel around her and kissed her cheek. "I'll take a raincheck."

CHAPTER THIRTEEN

With Sam hopped up on ibuprofen and sporting ice packs on her hip and elbow, they spent a relaxing night with the kids, watching *Christmas Vacation* for the umpteenth time and laughing as if it was the first time they'd ever seen it. From the third-floor conservatory, they could see the snow blanketing the District.

She received several texts from Dani with updates about the investigation that she would deal with in the morning.

After the movie ended, Nick and Eli carried sleepy twins to bed while Sam and Scotty followed them via the elevator.

When Scotty extended his arm to her, Sam's heart melted. "Hang on to me. We don't want to make it worse than it already is."

She hooked her arm through his. "Thanks, pal."

Skippy pushed past them and nearly took Sam and Scotty with her.

"Good thing you were holding on to me," Scotty said. "She's a maniac. I can't do a thing with her."

"We need to get her some training."

"Probably, but I'd hate to break her spirit."

"We don't want to break her spirit, but we do want her to behave."

"I like that she's the wildest puppy in town."

"You would like that."

"She keeps things interesting around here."

"Can I ask you something?"

"Sure."

"Do you care if I work a little this week when I'm supposed to be on vacation?"

"Why would I care?" he asked.

"Because I'm supposed to be hanging out with you."

"I'm fourteen, Mom. It's okay if you're not with me all the time. I have a life of my own now."

Sam wanted to scream with laughter, but he was dead serious, so she bit her lip.

"Plus, since it's snowing, we'll have plenty to do outside. There are snowmen to be made, snowball fights to be had, and Eli said he's going to build us a snow fort. You hate being cold, so it's better for all of us if you go to work. If you can walk tomorrow, that is."

"That last part was unnecessary."

"Was it, though?"

Sam laughed. "You're just like your father."

"You really think so?" he asked, looking up at her with big eyes.

"Oh, hell yes."

"That's really cool. I can't think of anyone I'd rather be like than him. Or you, too, of course."

"Please, God, don't let you grow up to be like me."

"That wouldn't be so bad. We had a career day thing at school last week. Some guy from the FBI came in, and his presentation was *sick*. I'm not ruling out a career in law enforcement."

"I'd rather you go into politics. It's safer."

"Eh, not really."

"Yes, it is, and I need to believe that, so don't argue with me."

"Whatever you say, boss lady." They got off the elevator, and he walked her down the hallway, stopping outside the door to her and Nick's bedroom. "How about I tuck you in for a change tonight?"

"That's the best offer I've had all day."

"Somehow I doubt that, but we're not talking about *that*."

He was endlessly amusing, delightful, insightful, sweet and loving. She couldn't imagine that any mother loved her son more than she loved this boy. After she painfully used the bathroom and brushed her teeth, Scotty helped her into bed and pulled the covers over her.

"You're a mess."

"Thank you. I know. Let me tell you what—I don't care how old you are, falling sucks."

"I'll take your word for it. I haven't done much falling."

"Not yet, but you will when you get old and stupid like I am."

He leaned over to kiss her cheek. "Sleep tight and don't let the bedbugs bite."

"Best tuck-in I ever got."

"Lights out in ten minutes," he said sternly, making her laugh again.

"Hey, Scotty?"

"Yeah?"

"I just want you to know... The day you showed up was one of the very best days of my entire life, and every day since then has been even better."

"Thanks, Mom. Right back atcha."

Nick came into the room and stopped short at the sight of Sam already in bed.

"I tucked her in," Scotty said, "but no funny business tonight, Mr. President. She's injured."

"Yes, sir," Nick said, his lips quivering from the effort it took not to laugh.

"And with that, I'm out."

"Love you, buddy," Nick said.

"Love you, too."

"That boy..." Sam smiled. "He's amazing. He insisted on tucking me in for a change, and he told me he doesn't mind if I work a bit this week because, and I quote, 'I'm fourteen and have a life of my own now.'"

"Stop it. He did not say that."

"Yes, he did!"

"I love it."

"And he said that while he hasn't ruled out a career in politics, there was a *sick* presentation from the FBI at career day, and he's thinking he could see himself as a federal agent. I told him politics is safer, but he said not always. I shut that right down, because I need to believe it's way safer."

"He's growing up fast and will be making those decisions sooner rather than later."

"I'm not ready for him to grow up."

"Ready or not..." Nick ducked into the bathroom and returned five minutes later, wearing only a pair of flannel pajama pants. He got into bed and curled up to her, moving carefully so he wouldn't cause her any pain.

"Did you set an alarm?" Sam asked.

"Yeah, for seven. I have a security briefing at eight."

"No rest for the weary, huh?"

"More like no vacation from the horrors that go on in this world."

"Right? We both see and hear the worst of the worst."

"Someone's gotta do it."

"I guess," she said.

"You know, someday it won't be us doing it."

"What do you mean?"

"Stop," he said, laughing. "You won't be working the streets at ninety."

"Who says?"

"I say. We're going to turn it over to other people one day, and we'll get to do anything we want."

"What'll we do?"

"I have no idea."

"Do you really want to be stuck with me full time without the job to keep me sane?"

"Um, well... Not really."

"Great. Glad we had this conversation. You can do your retired thing, and I'll keep you in the style to which you've become accustomed."

"With butlers and ushers and chefs and florists?"

"On a cop's salary?"

"Well, maybe not quite *that* level, but I can live happily with much less as long as I have you."

"You know that our lives are never going to be normal, right?" she asked.

"Shut your mouth."

"Nick... Tell me you know that after this, there'll be presidential libraries and speaking tours and memoirs and endless obligations."

"We'll make it work."

"Where have I heard that before? Was it when you promised you were going to do one year in the Senate and then we'd get back to normal?"

"Am I ever going to hear the end of that?"

"Not *ever*."

"Good to know."

"You hoodwinked me, and now I'm living in the freaking White House and trying to pretend that's normal. People at my *job* are whistling the tune to 'My Humps,' and if you laugh, I'm getting out the rusty steak knife."

His lips quivered, but lucky for him, he held back the laugh. "It's perfectly normal."

"You need to be very, *very* thankful that I love you so much, mister."

Nick pushed himself up on an elbow. "I'm thankful every minute of every day that you love me so much." He punctuated that with a soft, sweet kiss. "You're the best thing to ever happen to me."

"Likewise, even if you're a lying hoodwinker."

Smiling, he kissed her again. "And you love me."

"God help me, but yes, I do."

SAM DREAMED about Audrey and other victims who'd crossed her path. She dreamed of Stahl, Ramsey and Conklin. Good people, evil people, coexisting in the same community, and her in the middle of it, charged with bringing order to the chaos. Nick's alarm ended the dream abruptly, startling her and reminding her of the painful injuries she'd sustained the day before.

Her sharp gasp had Nick sitting up. "Is it worse?"

It was much worse. How was that possible? "I, um, I'm not sure."

"Wait for me." He got out of bed and came around to help her sit up.

She wanted to scream from the pain.

"Babe, you need a doctor."

"No. I don't want to deal with it. I've got a body in the morgue that needs my attention."

"If you have a broken hip, you're not going to be much good to her."

"It's not broken. It's just a bruise." When she tried to straighten her injured arm, she immediately regretted that, too. Sam wanted to scream from frustration as much as the pain. She had too much to do to deal with this crap.

"Samantha, you need a doctor. Let me arrange to have you taken to GW. We can call ahead to your buddy Dr. Anderson."

"I don't want to."

"Yes, I know."

"Help me up."

He took hold of her uninjured arm and helped her stand.

The second she put weight on her right leg, she nearly passed out from the pain radiating from her hip. But when she sat back down, it wasn't any better. "Mother-effer."

"Let me talk to Brant. We'll get you to the hospital."

"No ambulances or production."

"Got it."

While he took care of that, she placed a call to Carlucci.

"Morning," Dani said. "I was just about to call to see if you're going to make it in today."

As a rule, cops didn't get snow days. "I was planning to, but I fell on the ice yesterday and can't seem to sit or stand, so my husband is making me get it checked."

"Oh damn. That sucks."

"Yes, it does. Where are we with Olsen?"

"Lindsey ran the DNA, and it matched the case Lucas brought us yesterday, but of course, the owner of the DNA isn't in the system."

"Because we never get that lucky."

"Right? However, we have his DNA from another case that dates back almost two months. It's like Lucas's case, where the woman fought back hard and managed to get away, but not before he raped her."

"So, we have a serial rapist on our hands who's just escalated to murder." Sam wanted to talk to his previous victims to get as much information as she could, which was what she'd be doing today if not for these goddamned injuries.

"With no way to know if that's his first murder."

"Right. Where was the older case from two months ago?"

"Dupont Circle."

"Which is not far from the park. Talk to Malone about putting out a warning."

"Will do. We also went through everything on Audrey's phone, and nothing stood out except an exchange on Slack with a coworker who disagreed with her approach to a parent and told her so in no uncertain terms."

"What's Slack?"

"An internal messaging app that companies use for their employees to communicate."

"Ah, okay. Was the coworker male or female?"

"Male."

"I want to talk to him."

"I figured you would, so I tracked down his info. The school is closed because of the holiday break. He's probably home today."

"How much snow did we get?"

"Fourteen inches."

"Seriously? Everything must be closed."

"It is, and the mayor is asking nonessential personnel to stay off the roads."

Nick came back into the room. "All set. The Secret Service will take us to GW."

"Hang on, Dani." To Nick, she said, "You have your security briefing."

"I put it off until eleven."

"You don't have to come."

"Yes, I do, or you'll have Vernon take you to HQ rather than GW."

She scowled at him and then heard Carlucci cracking up. "You'd better not be laughing at what he said."

"I heard nothing."

"Why does everyone in my life lie to my face or my ear?"

"It's how we manage you," Nick said. "Now let's get going."

"I've got to go," Sam said to Dani as she scowled at her husband. "Pass everything off to Gonzo and the others. Tell them I'll be in as soon as I can."

"Will do. Hope it's nothing serious."

"It had better not be." Sam slapped her phone closed and let Nick help her into leggings, a sweater and boots. She was in a cold sweat from the pain by the time she was dressed.

Nick reached for her cell phone. "Give your friend Dr. Anderson a call and ask him to get us in with a minimum of fuss."

Sam put through the call, even though it was the very last thing she wanted to do.

"How's my favorite first lady today?" Anderson asked when he answered the call.

"It seems that I might've busted my ass."

"What's that?"

"I fell on the ice at work yesterday and can't put any weight on my right leg today."

"Oh shit. Can you get here?"

"That's the plan. The Secret Service is bringing me because the ball and chain insists on coming."

Nick sent her a filthy look as Anderson laughed.

He told her which entrance to use and to call when they were getting close.

"Thanks."

"Anything for my favorite patient."

"Now that's just a damned lie."

He was laughing when she ended the call.

"Everyone is a comedian," she said to Nick. "I have to pee and brush my teeth."

He helped her up and then put his arm around her to act like a crutch on her right side. "Ball and chain, huh?"

"If the chain fits..." Moving carefully, they made their way to the bathroom, where she discovered sitting on a toilet was no more pleasant than sitting on the bed. In fact, it was much less pleasant than the bed had been. By the time she finished, she had tears in her eyes. She reached back to flush. "I might need you to get me up."

"Here I come."

He helped her off the toilet like that was no big deal, but it was mortifying.

Tears spilled down her cheeks. "I'm so fucking pissed with myself about this. It's bad enough when I get hurt on the job, but this was just so stupid."

Nick kissed away her tears. "Accidents happen to the best of us, babe."

"When do they happen to you?" she asked as he helped her to the sink to brush her teeth.

"I had that thing with the ribs playing hockey last winter, remember?"

"*One* time. It happens to me monthly. I've got too much shit to do to deal with this. We've got a serial rapist on the loose who just killed someone." The whole thing was infuriating. "How am I supposed to get downstairs?"

"The ushers are bringing up a wheelchair."

"You can't let me be photographed in that chair."

"I told them to clear the area."

"My hero," she said tearfully as she kissed him.

"Don't worry about anything. Let's just rule out a fracture, and then you can go about your business making everyone's day."

"That's my specialty, especially when they're murdering scumbags."

CHAPTER FOURTEEN

Gary, one of the ushers, was waiting in their sitting room when Nick walked her out.

"What about the kids?"

"I told Eli we're leaving for a bit and that he's on duty for when the twins wake up. Scotty will sleep for hours yet."

"Sorry to hear you're feeling poorly, ma'am."

"Thank you, Gary," Sam said as Nick placed a pillow on the seat and then helped her into it.

Sam gasped when her backside contacted the pillow. She wanted to cry from the pain as much as the inconvenience of being injured.

Nick insisted on being the one to push her to the elevator and then to the South Portico, where the Secret Service had positioned SUVs to block the view of the door. They smoothly delivered her to the back seat and shut the door before anyone noticed them.

"I never thought I'd be thankful to a blizzard," Sam said when they were on their way in a five-car motorcade, which was small in comparison to the usual production. "Otherwise, we never would've gotten away with you pushing me out the door in a wheelchair."

"Very true. The media scrum is taking a snow day." He looked out the window as they made their way slowly to the White House gates.

It seemed that would be the theme of her day—*slowly*. She wanted to scream with aggravation, but when the car hit a bump, she wanted to scream from the pain. There wasn't another car to be found on 17th Street, which was piled high with snow on either side. After flipping open her phone, she called Malone.

"Morning," he said gruffly.

"Hey, so I fell in the parking lot last night, and now I'm on the way to GW for X-rays of my hip."

"Oh shit. It must be bad if you're going in willingly."

"I'm going in under significant duress."

His grunt of laughter made her smile for the first time that day. "Tell Nick we're all sorry for him."

"I'll do that. Listen, Carlucci and Dominguez have connected our perp from the Olsen murder to two unsolved sexual assaults. We're looking at a serial offender and need to put out the word."

"Yes, she mentioned that. I'll review the reports and get with public affairs on that. I assume you'll be out today?"

"I'm coming in right after this."

"I guess we'll see about that."

"No, I'm definitely coming."

"You're on vacation, Holland."

"I want to work on Olsen. I never got a chance to talk to Gonzo about seeing Stahl. You want to do that?"

"I'll take care of it."

"I'll see you shortly."

"I can't wait."

Sam slapped the phone closed. "Comedians everywhere I look."

"You inspire us with your dry wit, babe."

"Whatever you say. There'd better not be any needles, or I'm going to hold that against you for weeks."

"I'll take one for the team if we can get you feeling better."

"Don't be nice to me when I'm pissed off."

"Yes, dear."

A low snort from the front seat was followed by a throat clearing.

"Are we entertaining you, Brant?"

"Always, ma'am."

"He's going to write one hell of a memoir about his time with us," Sam said to Nick, as she often did.

"Your secrets are safe with me, ma'am."

Nick smiled at her, which made her feel better. That's what he did. He made everything better, even a potentially busted ass.

She flipped open her phone and called Freddie.

"Morning. How about this snow?"

"I'm very angry with the snow and the ice at the moment, as I'm on my way to GW to get my ass checked."

"Oh damn. From the fall?"

"Yep."

"Crap. It must be bad if you're getting it checked."

"I can't stand how everyone thinks they know me so well."

"You're rather consistent in your disdain for all things medical."

"I want a full report ready for me on where we are with Olsen. Thanks to this blizzard that's shut down the entire city and the busted ass, we can't do much today, but I want a plan in place to hit it hard tomorrow."

"Yes, ma'am."

"I'll call you later."

"Good luck at GW. Let me know if you need anything."

"I need my ass not to be broken so I can get back to work."

"I'm not able to assist with that request."

"Later." She slapped the phone closed and fumed the rest of the way to the hospital. The drive took twenty minutes longer than it should have because DC was crippled by one inch of snow, let alone fourteen.

"Do you guys remember the back way in, Brant?" Sam asked.

"Yes, ma'am."

Seeing they were getting close, Sam called Anderson. "Almost to the door you sent me to the last time."

"On my way."

She closed her phone. "Don't quote me on this, but being married to the president does have its advantages."

"Is that right?" Nick asked. "Such as?"

"First-rate transportation and security, as well as being snuck into the ER through back channels that keep me out of the limelight."

"Anything else?" Nick asked, brow raised.

"Nothing I can say in front of the kids."

"And the kids thank you for that," Brant said.

"That one's getting very sassy," Sam said. "We need to do something about him."

"I'll get right on that," Nick said.

Joking with him and Brant was better than thinking about what fresh hell awaited her in the hospital. True to his word, Anderson was there with a wheelchair. With Nick and the Secret Service accompanying them, he took them to a service elevator that the agents had to check before they'd let them board.

"We're going straight to X-ray," Anderson said.

"You're going to want to do her elbow, too," Nick said, earning him a glare from his wife.

"My elbow is fine."

"It is absolutely not fine," Nick said, glaring back at her.

"Now, kids, don't bicker," Anderson said. "We'll take a good look at everything."

"You will not," Sam snapped at him.

"I'm nothing if not *thorough*," Anderson said with the charming smile that did nothing for her.

The X-ray technicians were speechless when they realized who their patient was and who had accompanied her.

"Close your mouths," Anderson said, giving them instructions about the areas he wanted X-rayed. "Right side?"

"Yes," Sam said through gritted teeth.

"We're going to need to get you into a gown, Mrs. Cappuano," one of the young women said.

"I'll help her," Nick replied.

The three women nearly swooned when he said that.

Dear God in heaven give her patience, because Sam was about to blow.

They were led to a changing room and given one of those gowns that left the ass on full display, which would probably come in handy in this case. Nick helped her up and out of her clothes.

"You're very good at this nursing thing."

He kissed her pout. "I only provide these services for certain patients."

"It really hurts," she said, winded from the effort to stand while he helped her change.

"I know, sweetheart. I'm sorry."

Nick stayed right by her side when they wheeled her into the freezing room for the X-rays.

"I'm sorry, Mr. President, but you have to wait outside," one of the women said, her tone deferential.

"That's fine." He kissed Sam's cheek and whispered in her ear, "Behave so we can get out of here."

That earned him another glower from her.

By the time they had gotten films of her elbow and hip, Sam had tears streaming down her face from the agony of being turned and twisted into position.

"I'm sorry that was so painful, Mrs. Cappuano," one of the techs said. "I hope you're feeling much better very soon."

"Thank you." Sam felt clammy and sick to her stomach when she rejoined Nick and Dr. Anderson in the hallway. "Can't wait to do that again soon."

Anderson led them to a private exam room that wasn't in the Emergency Department.

Sam would be forever thankful to him for helping to protect her privacy.

"Let's take a look," he said, easing her gown up so he could see her mangled hip.

"This is the moment all your dreams come true," she said, mortified that she had to show the doctor her ass.

"You know it, hot stuff. Holy moly, you don't do anything halfway, do you?" Then he looked at her equally colorful elbow. "Ouch. I'm not going to put you through an exam that requires moving it until I see the films. I'll see if they're in yet. Be right back."

Nick stood by her side, holding her hand while they waited.

"Thanks for coming with me."

"Of course I came with you."

"You say that like it's no big deal for you to come."

"It isn't."

Sam rolled her eyes at him. Anything to take her mind off the throbbing pain in right side and her anxiety over what those X-rays would show.

Anderson returned ten minutes later. "There's good news and bad news. What do you want first?"

"Good."

"Your elbow is fine. Just a nasty bruise that'll hurt for a few days. Your hip, on the other hand, is fractured and will require surgery."

"Wait. *What?*"

"You heard me. Sorry to be the bearer of bad news."

"How long will I be down?"

"Four to six weeks."

"No way. I don't have that kind of time."

"Sam, your hip is *broken*. You have to get it fixed if you ever want to walk again."

"This is ridiculous! I can't be down for four to six weeks! I have shit to do."

"It'll go by so fast, babe," Nick said. "You'll bounce right back and be on your feet again in no time. I'm sure of it."

"How can a thirty-six-year-old person *break their hip*?" Sam sounded hysterical even to herself. She could only imagine what they thought of her reaction. "Isn't that something that happens to old people?"

"It can happen to anyone who lands just so when they fall. I'll contact Ortho and get a surgeon lined up for you. I'll be right back."

When they were alone, Sam turned to Nick. "I got hit by a fucking car and didn't break my hip. How is this possible?"

"It was just a fluke thing, babe, but I'm sure you'll sail right through this. You can work from home and oversee your cases and still drive everyone crazy. It'll be fine." He brushed hair back from her face and kissed her cheek. "Don't worry about anything."

"Right. What do I have to be worried about?"

Things moved quickly after that. Sam was shocked to learn she'd be having surgery *that day*, not in a few days when she'd have had time to wrap her head around it. "I should've stayed at Camp David," she muttered to Nick.

"I'll remind you of that the next time you're wanting out of there."

She called Malone.

"What'd they say?"

"Did you know that a thirty-six-year-old person can break a hip and need surgery to fix it?"

"Stop it."

"I'd love to, but alas…"

"Sam, no way. I'm so sorry. That sucks."

"Totally sucks. Put Gonzo in charge of the Olsen investigation and the squad. I'll be back to busting balls from home in a day or two. For now, I'm out."

"Keep us posted on how you're doing."

"Will do."

She closed the phone and wasn't surprised to receive a call from her partner two minutes later.

"Shut the hell up," Freddie said. "Are you kidding me?"

"You have no idea how much I wish I was."

"What can I do?"

"Whatever you can for Audrey Olsen and her family. That's what I need—a full-court press on her case."

"We're on it. Don't worry about anything. Will you have Nick text me after the surgery?"

"Yeah, I will."

"I'll be in to see you later with a full update."

"Excellent. I won't be down for long."

"I'm sure you'll be back to kicking our asses in no time."

"You swore, young Freddie."

"I figured the occasion called for it."

"It certainly does. I've got a shit, fuck, damn, hell for anyone who'll listen. Is Gonzo nearby?"

"Yeah, hang on."

"Jeez, Sam," Gonzo said. "What a bummer, huh?"

"Literally."

"Don't make me laugh, because it's not funny."

"Listen, you gotta stay on the Olsen case and this shit with Stahl and all the other crap."

"I got you covered," he said. "Don't worry."

"Did Malone talk to you about going to see Stahl?"

"Yeah, he did."

"How do you feel about that?"

"I'm not sure it'll do any good, but I'll take one for the team."

"And you're sure you feel up to that?"

"I'm okay. I know you're all still worried about me, but I'm doing much better than I was."

"What are you hearing from the trial?"

"The defense is bringing in a parade of bullshit character witnesses to sing the praises of what a good guy he is, but Faith tells me the jury isn't being swayed by the theater of it. They know who this guy is and what he's done."

"I can't believe they wouldn't allow admission of his past crimes," Sam said.

"They have more than enough to convict him for killing Arnold. I'm not at all concerned about it not going our way. Once that's done and the first anniversary is observed, I'll be able to really breathe again. But in the meantime, I'm feeling good and back in the game."

"You have no idea how glad we all are about that. If the visit with Stahl is triggering in any way, I want you to leave. Nothing is worth risking your hard-won progress."

"I hear you, and I can handle him. Don't worry."

"Keep me posted."

"I will. We'll be in to visit."

"I'll probably be home tonight."

Standing at the rolling computer station, Anderson shook his head.

"Or tomorrow."

Again, Anderson shook his head.

Sam wanted to scream. "I guess I'll be here a day or two."

"*Whoa.*"

"Don't get me started."

"No worries. Just take care of yourself."

"I'm being told I have no choice about that. Talk to you later." Sam closed the phone. "How long do I have to be here?" she asked Anderson.

"Three to four days, depending on how you do and if there're complications."

"What kind of complications?"

"Infection, for one, but we'll try not to let that happen."

"Try really hard."

"Yes, ma'am."

"Babe, I texted Terry to tell him what's going on, and he suggests we release a brief statement before the media catches wind."

"I haven't even told my sisters or Celia or my mother."

"Do you want me to text them?"

"I guess," she said, becoming resigned to the fact that this was really happening.

"This is what I'm saying to them. 'Hi there and sorry for the group text, but Sam slipped on ice, fell in the parking lot at work yesterday and managed to fracture her hip. She's having surgery this afternoon at GW and will be here three to four days. She is not happy about this, as you can imagine. Please pray for both of us.'"

"Look at you, joining the comedians," she said as Anderson snickered. "I'll remember all the people who thought this was funny. There's nothing wrong with my rusty steak knife."

"Duly noted," Nick said. "I sent it."

"You should tell Eli and Scotty, too."

He pushed some buttons on the phone. "Done."

Sam's phone rang with a call from Tracy.

Sam answered with one of her dad's trademark sayings. "Kelly's Pool Hall, eight ball speaking."

"*Seriously, Sam?*"

"Yep."

"*Jeez...*"

"I know. No sex for weeks." She took great pleasure in watching Nick's smile fade. "Nick is just realizing that."

"*Figures that's what you're thinking about.*"

"I'm thinking about a lot of things, and none of them are good."

"*This is not gonna be pretty,*" Tracy said.

"No, it isn't, but I will be."

"Well, that's a given."

"Trace! Four to six weeks!"

"Ugh. That blows."

"Totally."

Anderson, who'd stepped out of the room, returned with a female doctor.

"I gotta go. Nick will keep you posted."

"Love you."

"You, too."

CHAPTER FIFTEEN

"Sam, this is Dr. Jane Thurston. Dr. Thurston, Sam Holland Cappuano, and her husband, Nick, who you may recognize."

"It's such an honor to meet you both." Dr. Thurston shook hands with them. "I'm sorry about the circumstances, though."

"Are you the one who's going to fix this for me?" Sam asked.

"I am."

"How soon can I get back to normal?"

"Four to six weeks."

Anderson gave her an "I told you so" look that earned him another glare from Sam.

"That's too long. I need to get back to work before then."

"You can go back to work in a wheelchair before your hip is fully healed."

There was no way she was going to HQ in a wheelchair. "There has to be some other way, something faster…"

"There isn't. It's a fairly serious injury, as I'm sure you can tell from the pain you must be in."

"I don't have time to be injured. I just caught a new murder. I've got four kids and this first-lady thing to deal with. I can't be laid up for *six weeks*."

"I warned Dr. Thurston that you would be her most exasperating patient ever," Dr. Anderson said. "And I told her you hate needles."

"Thanks for preparing her for me."

"I'll get you back on your feet as fast as I can, but you have to do what you're told, or you'll only extend the rehab even longer," Dr. Thurston said.

"She'll do what she's told," Nick said. "I'll see to it."

He'd pay for that later.

"When is this surgery happening?"

"In an hour. We don't like to let hip fractures linger for too long, as complications can arise. The nurses will get you prepped, and an anesthesiologist will be in to see you shortly. There'll also be some paperwork to complete giving consent for the surgery."

"This just gets more fun by the minute."

Dr. Thurston patted her arm. "Hang in there. I'll see you in the OR."

"I can't wait." When they were alone in the room, Sam said to Nick, "This totally fucking blows."

"It sure does. I'm sorry you're going through this."

"We're both going through it since it's going to put us out of business for weeks."

"Oh, no, it won't," he said with the devastatingly sexy grin that had made him the fantasy of women around the world since he'd been catapulted into the Oval Office. "We'll just have to be creative."

"Nick... I don't want to have surgery. I hate this."

He sat carefully on the edge of the bed and held out his arms to her.

She leaned forward to fall into his embrace and breathed in the scent of her love. "Bust me out of here."

"Not happening. It's in my best interest to get you pinned back together so everything works the way it's supposed to."

"Don't make me laugh when I'm pissed off."

"I'll try not to. Just hold on to me. I'll be right there with you through it all."

"You've got your security briefing."

"Only because that briefing can't be done just anywhere, I'll go to the White House while you're in surgery and be back by the time you're out. You won't even miss me."

"Yes, I will."

Anderson returned with a nurse he introduced as Mindy. "She'll be setting up your IV and getting you ready for surgery. And yes, I warned her about you."

"I'm not worried," Mindy said with a peppy smile that had Sam gritting her teeth, even as she appreciated that Mindy didn't freak out the way people normally did when encountering the first couple. "What happened there?" She pointed to Sam's upper arm.

"Oh, I got shot right before Christmas. The stitches come out in six days."

"You're having a week!"

"I'm giving you ten punches on your frequent-flier card for the busted hip," Anderson said.

"Go away," Sam said. "You're enjoying this too much."

"Nah, not really," he said, chuckling. "We're all better off when you're out catching killers."

"Exactly! That's why I don't have time for this."

"Trevor has a statement ready to go out to the media," Nick said. "What do you think?" He handed her his phone.

First Lady Samantha Cappuano slipped on ice yesterday afternoon, fell and fractured her right hip. She's undergoing surgery this afternoon at the George Washington University Hospital and is expected to make a full recovery within four to six weeks. The first couple asks for privacy as the first lady recovers.

"Is that okay?"

"No, but I guess you can release it. People will find out soon enough that I'm a klutz with a busted ass."

Mindy giggled.

"Don't repeat that," Sam said.

"My lips are sealed, ma'am."

"And don't call me ma'am. My name is Sam."

"Sam, I need to start an IV. Have you had one before?"

"Unfortunately, yes, and I hate them."

"We'll do it in your hand, and I'll numb it up for you. You shouldn't feel a thing."

True to her word, Sam didn't feel a thing, and thank goodness for that, because needles freaked her out on the best of days, and this was certainly not the best of days.

"Have you had surgery before, Sam?" Mindy asked.

"Nothing like this. Just a few unpleasant fertility procedures that didn't work."

"They'll ask you a hundred times which hip they're operating on, so be ready for that. It's how we keep mistakes from happening."

"What kind of mistakes?"

"Like operating on the wrong hip."

"That happens?"

Mindy patted her shoulder. "It won't happen today."

Sam's phone rang.

Nick checked the caller ID. "Scotty."

Sam held out her hand for the phone. "Hey, pal."

"Well, this is a fine mess, huh?"

Laughing, she said, "You said it."

"Damn, Mom. Surgery and everything?"

"I don't do anything halfway."

"I guess not. Don't worry, though. We'll take care of you when you get home."

"Aw, thanks. Not how I wanted to spend the vacation."

"You suck at vacation. We all know that. Don't worry about anything. Eli and I are taking care of the twins, and we're going out to build the snow fort after lunch."

"Thanks for helping with them."

"I love having siblings. It's so much fun. We'll come see you later."

"I'll be here. Thanks for calling. Love you."

"Love you, too, and don't give the doctors any lip."

"What? Me give people lip?"

They hung up laughing.

She took calls from Celia, both her sisters, her mother and Shelby before Mindy told her it was time to go. Sam reached for Nick, suddenly full of anxiety.

"It's okay, babe. Just relax and let them take care of you. I'll be here when you wake up." He leaned over the bed to kiss her. "Take good care of my clumsy cop. She means everything to me."

"It's out of my hands this time."

"Love you."

"Love you, too."

Mindy asked for a number the doctor could call to update him when the surgery was finished.

Nick gave her Sam's cell phone number and took the phone with him.

She and an orderly wheeled Sam out of the room toward the operating suite. As they navigated corridors, people stopped what they were doing to watch the first couple go by.

"Gotta love the goldfish bowl," Nick muttered, giving her hand a squeeze.

The predictable comment made her smile and settled her nerves. With him by her side, she could get through anything. Even surgery for a busted fucking hip, of all things.

. . .

AFTER SENDING SAM INTO SURGERY, Nick wanted a stiff drink. Seeing his usually unflappable wife seriously undone had rattled him. A fractured hip, of all things. The doctors had told him the surgery would take three hours, followed by another hour in recovery before he could see her.

"Let's go home," he said to Brant, even though he'd prefer to wait at the hospital. He had to do the security briefing, and setting up a secure space at GW would be too involved.

"Yes, sir. The main entrance and the door we used to get in are overrun with media since the statement was released, so we're looking for a better way out."

While Vernon and Jimmy remained posted outside the operating room, Brant and the other agents escorted him through a random exit that hadn't been discovered by the press.

On the ride back to the White House, he glanced at Twitter and found an outpouring of concern for Sam and their family. She would hate being the center of attention but would appreciate the well-wishes. He took a call from Terry.

"How's she doing?"

"Pretty well, all things considered."

"It's such a bummer."

"She'd say literally."

"Yes, she would," Terry said, laughing. "I wanted to tell you I heard from the FBI that they have LeRoy Nevins in custody on the bomb."

"That name rings a bell."

"It should. He's the one who's been ranting to anyone who will listen that Americans shouldn't have to live under an unelected president."

"Ah, right. It's all coming back to me now. So, he went so far as to build a bomb and leave it at the gates?"

"The FBI isn't saying much other than they have a suspect in custody, and they believe it was related to him. Whether he was the one who left the bomb remains to be determined."

"Well, that's something, I guess. I'm on the way back now."

"I heard. You need to make a statement about the storm and the resources the federal government is making available, etc. Will is writing something for you now. They're saying it could take a week to get the region back up and running."

"Wow. In Massachusetts, it would've taken a day. We never got a second snow day."

"Welcome to the Mid-Atlantic, where snow is a full-on calamity."

"I always find that amusing. I'll be there in ten."

As soon as he ended the call with Terry, his personal BlackBerry rang with a call from Freddie.

"How is she?"

"Not happy, as you can imagine."

"In other words, you took one for the team with her today."

"Yes, I did, but she's going to be fine, and I have no doubt she'll bounce back quickly."

"But she's gonna be hell on wheels—literally—until then."

Nick chuckled. "Quite possibly."

"Will you text me when we can visit?"

"Absolutely. Thanks for checking on her."

"I already miss her, but if you tell her I said that, I'll deny it with every fiber of my being."

Smiling, Nick said, "I already miss her, too. I'll check in later."

"We'll be waiting to hear."

He ended the call as the SUV pulled through the gates at the White House. Inside, he went directly to the Situation Room to take care of business so he could check on the kids and then get back to the hospital by the time Sam woke up.

Teresa Howard, the national security advisor he'd inherited from President Nelson, was waiting for him, as were General Michael Wilson, the chairman of the Joint Chiefs of Staff, and the other advisers he met with each morning to review global security risks.

Each of them asked after the first lady and expressed their concern for her.

"Thank you all." Nick took his seat at the head of the table, with Terry seated to his right.

"She's in surgery now, and as you can imagine, I'm eager to get back to the hospital. Let's get this done."

GONZO UPDATED the murder board with the information gathered thus far in the Olsen investigation. He'd started a column for similar cases, including the one Detective Lucas had brought them, as well as the earlier one that had been tied to their case by DNA.

"What's the latest?" Cruz asked when he came into the room, where Jeannie was also working on a laptop.

"Dani and Gigi reviewed every call, text and email on Audrey's phone from the last year and didn't find anything other than the ongoing beef with a teacher she worked with that the boyfriend mentioned," Gonzo said. "The guy liked to tell her she was young and naïve and didn't 'get it.' He, of course, was much older and wiser and knew better in all situations. There were some texts from Audrey to Wes complaining about how the guy had something to say to her at every staff meeting and how she thought of him as a bully."

"We need to talk to him," Freddie said.

"I talked to him," Gonzo said. "He was with family all day yesterday and never left the house. Multiple family members can vouch for him."

"Crap," Freddie said, taking a seat. "So that leaves us with no one in her life who would've had motive for murder."

"It leaves us with most likely a random attack by a guy who's done this before," Gonzo replied. "Lindsey ran the DNA found on Audrey through national, state and local CODIS and checked it against the rape kit from Lucas's case to find they're a match. But nothing new popped from CODIS."

"You should look at FDS," another voice said.

Gonzo and Cruz turned to find Chief Marshal Jesse Best taking up most of the space in the doorway.

"FDS?" Gonzo asked. "What's that?"

"Familial DNA Searching," Best said. "Simply put, it's when you run the DNA you have through the system to look for close relatives. That can lead you to someone who's already in prison or has submitted DNA in a previous investigation. From there, you work backward through the person's male relatives until you find the one you're looking for."

"Ah, right," Gonzo said. "I've heard about that."

"I've been reading about it," Freddie said. "It's been used in several cases that never would've been solved otherwise, but DC and Maryland outlawed the practice."

"How come?" Jeannie asked.

"Fear of it targeting a disproportionate number of minorities, and the FBI has been slow to embrace it. The NDIS can't be used for familial searching," Freddie said, referring to the National DNA Index System.

"How does FDS work?" Jeannie asked. "I haven't done the research yet."

"Say for example a perp's brother is in the system," Freddie said. "In that case, a familial match on them can lead us to the guy who did our crime, but it's not without controversy. For instance, say the family doesn't know that the person whose DNA is in the system had committed a crime. This process would 'out' the first person, because we'd have to disclose what led us to the second person."

"I can see how that could get messy," Jeannie said.

"Very, or if we target an entire group of siblings, for instance, we put them all through an investigation in the effort to find the guilty one," Freddie said. "Or maybe we uncover a previously unknown paternity situation."

"People have raised privacy concerns as well as Fourth and Fourteenth Amendment concerns regarding illegal search and seizure and equal protection," Best said.

"How so?" Jeannie asked.

"Requesting samples from family members who haven't committed a crime, for instance, puts their DNA into the system, and again, the disproportionate representation of minorities in CODIS and the many issues associated with that."

"I see," she said. "Well, if we have a serial rapist on the loose who's escalated to murder, we might be able to make a case for an exception to the local law prohibiting the use of FDS."

"It's definitely worth considering," Best said. "Cases like this one are usually the exception to the rule when it comes to new technology. In my experience, when there's a violent predator likely to strike again and all other investigative options have been exhausted, jurisdictions are willing to consider it, even with laws on the books."

"That's true," Freddie said. "If we can present a strong rationale for the use of the technology in this one isolated case, we might be able to get them to make an exception."

"Or if you happen to get a hit on a similar case in Virginia," Best said. "FDS is legal there."

"That's an interesting angle," Gonzo said. "Let's widen our search to see if there're other unsolved sexual assaults within a three-hundred-mile radius and go from there. Thanks for this, Jesse."

"Sure thing. The only downside is it can take months to do a full search of all the databases. You have to get in line."

"Months, huh?" Gonzo said. "And in the meantime, we've got a rapist-murderer getting away with it."

"You keep working the case while you wait," Best said.

"I guess so," Gonzo said.

"Is the LT around?" Best asked.

"You must not have heard that she's having surgery for a fractured hip," Freddie said.

"Oh shit, really?"

"Yeah, she fell on ice in the parking lot yesterday and thought it was just bruised. Today, she found out otherwise."

"Well, damn, that's unfortunate. I wanted to talk to her about the Deasly case. When will she be back?"

"We're not really sure," Cruz said. "In the meantime, Sergeant Gonzales is in command."

"A word, Sergeant?"

"Of course," Gonzo said. "Be right back."

"Detective McBride, can you join us?"

Jeannie got up to go with them.

CHAPTER SIXTEEN

Once they were in Sam's office with the door closed, Jesse glanced at Jeannie. "This is turning into a very big deal."

"How so?" she asked.

"We've linked Daniella Brown and her boyfriend, Xavier Iker, to a human trafficking ring that's been on our radar for a year. We believe that the babies and children found with Carisma were going to be trafficked and that others before them already were."

Jeannie took a seat, seeming shocked. "How many are we talking?"

"Possibly hundreds," Best said.

"Oh my God," Jeannie whispered.

"You cracked open one hell of a hornet's nest, Detective," Best said. "Congratulations on a very significant accomplishment."

"What happens now?" Jeannie asked.

"We're following the trail, hoping to recover as many of the children as we can, but that'll take some time."

"How did Carisma fit into it?" Gonzo asked.

"Brown thought of Carisma as her own child. The others were commodities."

"I feel like I'm going to be sick," Jeannie said. "All that time that went by from when she was first abducted…"

"This is on Stahl," Gonzo said.

"It's on all of us," Jeannie replied sharply. "We all failed those kids."

"We're putting together a task force of federal, state and local officers," Jesse said, "to find as many of them as we can and reunite them with their families. Iker's computer has been a treasure trove of information."

"If we can help at all, let us know," Gonzo said.

"You've already helped," Best said. "I spoke to Chief Farnsworth about a commendation for Detective McBride."

"Thank you," Jeannie said, although she didn't look happy.

"I'll keep you posted," Best said. "Give my best to the LT."

"Will do," Gonzo replied.

After Best left the office, Gonzo said to Jeannie, "You should be really proud of the work you did here."

"Then why do I feel like I'm going to vomit?"

"Because this stuff is horrifying and disgusting."

"And because if Stahl had given a flying fuck about Carisma eleven years ago, we could've prevented all those poor babies from being thrust into hell."

"Yeah," Gonzo said, sighing. "That, too."

"I don't know what to do with my outrage over this, Gonzo. As a Black woman, soon to be a mother… How could he just *ignore* her?"

"I don't know. I'll never understand how someone could *fake* an investigation into a missing kid. Would you consider talking to Trulo about how you're feeling?"

Jeannie shrugged. "Sam says I have to, so I will."

"Despite all this, we still have a job to do, and if you're going to have trouble doing it, that's what he's there for."

"Yeah, I guess. I'll take care of it."

"Keep me in the loop, okay?"

"I will."

After she left the room, Gonzo stared out into the pit for a long time, thinking about the horrors they faced on the job. Some were worse than others, and he was concerned for his colleague and friend, who'd already dealt with significant trauma on the job. While he was temporarily in charge, he would keep a close eye on her and make sure she talked to Trulo.

SAM DIDN'T KNOW where she was or what was going on when she opened her eyes to bright lights overhead. A low, dull hum of pain radiated from her right side, and when she tried to move, a woman was there to tell her to stay still. Who was she? Where was this place? What was happening?

"Mrs. Cappuano, how are you feeling?"

"Who are you?"

"I'm your nurse, Mindy. Remember me from before?"

She didn't. "No."

"You had surgery on your fractured hip, and it went very well. Dr. Thurston will be in to see you in a few minutes."

It was all coming back to her now. *Four to six weeks. Motherfucker.* "Where's Nick?"

"He's waiting to see you."

"Can you get him?"

She patted Sam's shoulder. "Of course."

Sam closed eyes that were too heavy to keep open. The next time she opened them, she was in a different room, and Nick was standing next to her bed, running his fingers through her hair.

"There you are," he said with a relieved smile. "Don't leave me like that again. I missed you."

"Where'd I go?"

"Three hours of surgery and another hour in recovery is a long time for me to be without my Samantha."

"That's not as long as a workday."

"When I can text you or call you if I need a fix."

Sam rolled her eyes.

"There she is, my sweet, sassy, sexy cop."

"I'm gonna be super sexy for the next four to six weeks."

"There's never a time when you're not sexy. I have news you're going to like."

"What's that?"

"A crackpot named LeRoy Nevins is in custody on the attempted bombing."

"What do we know about him?"

"That he doesn't approve of me being president and decided to leave a bomb at our gate to make sure I was aware of his disapproval."

"Are they sure it's him?"

"The FBI is sure enough that they released the update to the media this morning, and it's all over the news that they got the guy. He's saying he didn't do it, wouldn't waste his time, etc."

"They wouldn't have released news of the arrest if they weren't sure."

"That's what I thought, too, based on my extensive firsthand experience with police work."

Sam smiled. "You're learning by osmosis."

"I love the way you rub off on me."

"It's gonna be a while before I can rub off on you."

"Not that long."

"Long enough. Nick?"

"What, honey?"

"The crackpots scare me. That they hate you just because you did your job and took over for Nelson when he died."

"I know it's easy for me to tell you not to worry about it."

"Like it's easy for me to tell you not to worry about me?"

"Just like that but try not to worry. The Secret Service is incredible, and they're not going to let the crackpots get anywhere near me."

"You promise?"

"I promise."

"I want my phone to check in with Gonzo."

"Not yet. You need to rest. You just had surgery."

"I've been resting half the day—you just said so. Now give me my phone."

"Is this what the next month is going to be like with you?" he asked as he fished her phone out of his pants pocket.

"I suspect it'll get much worse than this before it's over."

"Oh joy. I can't wait."

"And just think, you're working at home, so you can tend to me between meetings."

As he handed her the phone, he leaned over the bed to kiss her. "I love nothing more than tending to my gorgeous wife regardless of her foul moods."

Only he could make her giggle after having fucking surgery on her fucking *broken hip*. "Can you raise the bed?"

"They told me not to touch it yet."

"I hate this place and everyone in it."

"Even me?"

"Not yet, but I'm sure I'll hate you, too, before long."

"Good to know," he said with a chuckle.

Flat on her back in a hospital bed, Sam put through a call to Gonzo.

"Hey," he said. "How'd it go?"

"Fine. Where are we with Olsen?"

"Honestly, Sam. Take a day off."

"Answer the question, Sergeant!"

"Lindsey has tied the DNA collected from Olsen to the case Lucas brought us and one other, and we're checking it against several other unsolved sexual assaults in the region. Olsen's mother is hoping to get here tomorrow and wants to see her daughter."

"Ugh," Sam said.

"I'll take care of her. Don't worry. We also had a visit from Jesse Best, who heard us talking about DNA for a suspect who's not in the system and suggested we look into FDS."

"They outlawed that in the District and Maryland."

"Right, but as Jesse said, if we find a related case in Virginia, it's legal there."

"Ah, good thinking. We'd have to exhaust all other options before we could even consider making a case for FDS with the mayor."

"Right, and the downside is FDS can take months."

"Did we get anywhere with the cameras in the park?"

"They were covered with snow at the time of Olsen's murder, so we got dick there. We're going back tomorrow around the same time as the murder to canvass, hoping someone saw something. No one was out today because of the snow."

"Today has totally sucked donkey balls in every possible way."

"Yep. Finally, and I've buried the headline here, but Best told us that Jeannie's bust has led to a child trafficking ring that's possibly involved hundreds of kids over the years."

"Oh God."

"Jeannie is upset about it, that people ignored Carisma for so long and what we could've stopped if only Stahl had given a fuck about her."

"She's not wrong."

"No, she isn't. She said you told her to meet with Trulo. I'll stay on that."

"Please do. And I'll talk to her as soon as I can."

"That'd help. Best is recommending Jeannie for a commendation."

"She certainly deserves that and much more for this bust. Back to the case... What about the guy at Olsen's school who was hassling her?"

"He has an alibi for the entire day."

"I didn't like him for it anyway. Anything else?"

"Not that I can think of. The snow slowed us down today, but we'll be back at it in the morning."

"I want to be kept in every loop. I'll be working from home as soon as I can."

"Got it. Let us know when we can visit."

"Probably tomorrow."

"Will do. Hope you feel better soon."

"I feel fine," Sam said.

"Because you're still numbed up," Nick said.

"They gave me the good drugs."

"Be careful what you take," Gonzo said, speaking from experience.

"I hear you. Send an update to the squad, will you?"

"Yep. Talk to you tomorrow."

"Yes, you will."

She slapped her phone closed. "Did you update the kids and my family?"

"All set. The hospital is being overrun by flowers for you."

"Seriously? People are sending me flowers?"

"Hundreds of arrangements arrived after we posted the news. I told them to bring us the cards so we can acknowledge the gifts as well as a few of the arrangements to brighten up your room and then distribute the rest to other patients."

"Wow. That's really nice."

"My first lady is beloved."

"No, our president is beloved, and his wife benefits by association."

"Don't sell yourself short, sweetheart. People admire you for you. Nothing to do with me."

"Whatever you say, Mr. President. Do I have to write thank-you notes?"

Smiling, he curled his hand around hers. "We have people who can help us with that."

"Thank God."

A female doctor entered the room. Sam recognized her from before but couldn't recall her name.

"Thurston," Nick whispered.

"How do you do that?"

"Samantha superpower."

Sam tightened her grip on his hand. "How'd it go, Doc?"

"Very well. It was a routine surgery."

"For you, maybe."

The doctor laughed. "You're young and strong, and I expect you'll bounce back very quickly from this, unlike our older patients who sometimes never regain complete mobility. The most important thing is to follow the directions I'll give you and those of the PT, who'll be in to see you tomorrow. That's when the fun really begins."

"Can't wait. Can I sit up a little?"

"Sure." She raised the bed slightly, enough to keep Sam from being flat on her back.

"What are the things squeezing my legs?"

"Compression stockings to keep you from developing blood clots."

Blood clots! Did the fun ever end in this place? "Well, that's good, I guess. Am I allowed to eat? I'm starving."

"We ordered dinner for you, and it should arrive as soon as we get you up to your room."

"That's good. Thanks. When can I go home? We have an elevator at our place, so that's good, right?"

"That's very good." She smiled at how Sam referred to the White House. "Let's see how you are in a day or two. It's going to depend on how quickly PT can get you mobile on crutches or a walker."

"A walker... Jeez, this just gets even better."

"Most of my patients hate the crutches and love the walker."

"And how old are they? Thirty-six or seventy-six?"

"Mostly the latter," the doctor said, smiling.

"I rest my case."

"We'll send you home with a raised toilet seat, too," Thurston said, grinning.

"My husband will leave me if you turn me into an old lady."

"He's not going anywhere, and you know it," Nick said.

"You two are as lovely as you seem in the media."

"*I'm* lovely." Nick grinned at Sam. "*She's* a bear."

"That's true," Sam said. "I'm a bear on a good day, and this is most definitely *not* a good day."

"It can always be worse, as you certainly know, as well as I do," Thurston said.

"Don't make me feel guilty for wallowing in self-pity."

The doctor laughed. "I'll check on you in the morning. In the meantime, you're in the hands of my very capable residents, who'll be by to see you. I've instructed them not to be starstruck by the two of you."

"Thank you for that."

She handed her card to Nick. "Call me if you need me. My cell number is on there."

"Thank you for everything, Doc."

"My pleasure."

"Her pleasure..." After the doctor left the room, Sam crossed her arms. "What about my pleasure or lack thereof for *four to six weeks*?"

"I'd never let my baby go that long without pleasure."

"This *sucks*, Nick. Like, sucks-the-biggest-of-gigantic-donkey-balls *sucks*."

"I know, but we'll make the best of it, like we always do. Don't worry about anything. Four to six weeks is a blip in the grand scheme of things."

Sam knew that was true, but the weeks stretched before her like an eternity, keeping her from her favorite things, such as chasing murdering scumbags, playing with her kids and having as much sex as possible with her gorgeous husband.

It *sucked*. That was her story, and she was sticking to it.

CHAPTER SEVENTEEN

After a restful night blissfully provided by the good drugs, Sam found out the next morning when the physical therapists arrived that the suck had only just begun. They wanted her up, out of bed and moving when that seemed all but impossible. And the good drugs had worn off by then.

She'd sent Nick home last night to be with the kids, and he'd promised to be in as soon as he could to spend the day with her. Thankfully, he was mostly on vacation this week and had the time to hang with her. Scotty had texted earlier to say they'd be in to see her after lunch.

Sam hoped she lived that long as the therapists put her through the paces of gently moving her surgically repaired hip. They had her holding on to a chair and moving her leg in a variety of directions that hurt like a mother-effer.

By the time they settled her back in bed with promises to be back later for another round—oh joy—Sam was weak and sweaty and more pissed off than she'd been in longer than she could remember. That she couldn't even blame this on a murdering scumbag was the worst part.

Her spirits were raised considerably when her entire squad arrived, bearing a dry-erase board that immediately improved her mood.

"You guys know what I need," she said.

"Yes, we do," Gonzo replied. "We figured we'd rescue the nurses by letting you do some work."

"Wise move. I think they've already had enough of me."

"I can't imagine how that can be with your sunny disposition and love of all things medical," Freddie said as he placed a coffee and a bag of doughnuts on her tray.

Her mouth watered when she caught a whiff of sugary goodness. "Excellent sucking up." She took a bite of a jelly doughnut and sipped her coffee. "Now tell me everything I've missed. Leave nothing out."

They went through everything they had so far, which was basically nothing.

"We're doing the canvass in the park later today at Audrey's usual running time, but we're not sure what that'll yield, as most of the paths are still unpassable from the snow, so the regulars might not be out."

"Work the perimeter of the park, too," Sam said. "If they can't run on the paths, they might run nearby."

"Good idea." Gonzo made a note. "I'll ask Patrol for help. What else you got?"

"How hard have we looked at the boyfriend?" she asked.

"Not that hard," Freddie said. "He seems legit from all appearances."

"I've learned not to trust appearances. Let's take a go at him and make sure his story holds up. Nothing confrontational. Just checking the boxes. That kind of thing. Ask for permission to dump his phone."

Gonzo added it to his list.

"Look at his brother, too." Her gut was telling her they were both clear, but women were often murdered by their domestic partners, so it was worth considering. "What else is going on? How was Gigi's first night back?"

"She seemed fine this morning," Cam said. "Tired, but otherwise good."

"Make sure she doesn't overdo it," Sam said. "We don't want any setbacks."

"Will that apply to you, too?" Freddie asked.

"Shut your face. We're talking about Gigi, not me."

"Got it."

"Go back to work, and let's do this again tomorrow. Same time."

"We'll be here."

"Jeannie, can you stay for a minute?"

"Sure."

After the others had left, Jeannie pulled up a chair to Sam's bedside.

"I heard you're taking the news Best brought yesterday pretty hard."

Jeannie shrugged. "Just another day at the office."

"Don't do that. Don't downplay it. It's a big deal."

"I'm getting nothing but accolades for the bust, but I'm not proud of how long it took us to find Carisma, or how many others had to suffer because Stahl didn't care about her."

"I hate how this happened. All we can do now is our best to make things right."

"Our best is never going to be good enough for the Carismas of the world or their families. I'm having a serious existential crisis over this, Lieutenant. To do this job day in and day out, to see what I see and experience what I do, I need to believe we're the good guys, but to find out that sometimes we're not... I'm sick over it."

"I know," Sam said, sighing. "I am, too. I was so afraid my dad played a role in this."

"He didn't. His name was nowhere in the files. There was a Captain Rosa, who was the chief of d's at that time."

"Rosa," Sam said. "I've heard the name, but I don't remember much about him."

"I want to do some digging on him."

"Do it quietly. Report anything you find to me, and we'll figure out a plan together."

"If we find out that retired sergeants, lieutenants, captains, deputy chiefs and chiefs intentionally ignored cases like Carisma's, I'm going to want to ruin them."

Sam had never seen Jeannie as fierce or as determined. "If they did, I'll help you ruin them."

SAM WAS SENT home on New Year's Eve, frustrated that her team was no closer to a suspect in Audrey Olsen's case than they'd been days ago.

Scotty, Eli and the twins surrounded her with love and flowers and books and kept her company through an afternoon of movies and popcorn in the theater. She refused to take to her bed, even though she was exhausted and in pain.

The twins were extra snuggly with her, seeming relieved to have her home. She gave them her full attention, which she was so rarely able to do.

After dinner, they played a fierce game of Candy Land that Scotty won after accusing Sam of cheating—again. "You have to watch her," he told the twins. "She sends you to get her a drink and then stacks the cards so you get sent all the way back to the start."

Sam shook her head as the twins giggled. "Who do you believe? Me or him?"

"*Him*," Nick and Eli said as the twins giggled some more.

She loved to hear them laugh and to see them enjoying the family they'd cobbled together after their parents' tragic deaths. And now that they'd fended off the custody suit from their money-hungry relatives, Sam felt like they could relax and look forward to the future together.

Just before midnight, Nick came into their suite with a wheelchair and a blanket.

"What's going on, Mr. President?"

"I'm keeping a promise to my wife that I made two years ago on a rooftop across town."

"Are we going to K Street?"

"It turns out we have our own rooftop lookout with an even better view than we had at K Street. Are you game?"

She was tired, sore and aching, but she wouldn't miss an adventure with him. "Always."

"Your chariot awaits, my love."

After he got her settled in the chair, he bundled her up in a winter coat and put the blanket over her lap. "Comfortable?"

"Yep." She ached fiercely, but she wasn't due for another pain pill yet. However, she kept that hidden from him since he had gone to some trouble to stick to their tradition.

Nick wheeled her to the elevator and up to the third floor, where the Secret Service waited to accompany them onto a roof deck she hadn't known about before this. When they were settled, the agents stepped back into the shadows, always watching, but out of sight.

"When we set this tradition two years ago, I didn't expect to be doing it on the roof of the White House or in a wheelchair," Sam said.

Nick produced a folding chair and sat next to her. "The wheelchair is temporary. You'll be back to kicking ass and taking names in no time."

"It's weird to be unable to do so many things I normally do. It gives me a bit of perspective on what my dad dealt with after his injury."

"I'm sure it does." Reaching for her hand, he kissed the back of it. "I skipped the champagne since you're still taking pain meds."

"Thanks for arranging this."

"A tradition needed to be upheld, and before we hit midnight in one minute, I want you to know how much I appreciate you and the way you've supported me this year. A lot of wives would've run for the hills when their husband suddenly became president. But not my wife. She was a trouper."

"She complained *a lot* behind your back."

His ringing laughter made her smile. God, she loved to make him laugh. "For which I would soundly spank her, except she has a busted ass."

"Raincheck?"

"Yeah, baby." He leaned in to kiss her as the sky exploded with fireworks that Scotty and Eli had gone to watch on the South Lawn. "This is gonna be our year. I feel it."

"What does that even mean? How can we top this last year? You're the freaking president."

"We're going to top ourselves. I feel it in my bones."

"Well, my broken bones are saying enough already."

"Never enough. If I have you right here next to me, I can do anything, even be the freaking president. And you, my unstoppable love, are going to have another remarkable year. I just know it."

"An okay year would be fine with me."

"Nah, we're shooting for the stars, babe."

"This is already our third New Year's, and look how far we've come from when you were promising me one year in the Senate, and then we could get back to normal. Ah," she said on a deep sigh, "weren't those the good old days?"

His eyes sparkled with amusement. "I can think of only one way to shut you up that never fails." With his fingers on her chin, he tipped up her face to receive his kiss. Leaning his forehead on hers, he said, "Happy New Year, love, and cheers to us and our amazing family."

"Cheers to us."

JANUARY CAME at them like a tsunami of activity, obligations and grueling physical therapy at the hands of a sadist named Nancy, who came to the White House daily. Sam and Nick hosted their first state dinner as president and first lady for the German chancellor, which had been on the schedule long before President Nelson passed away. The pomp and ceremony of the evening reminded Sam of the night she and Nick got engaged in the Rose Garden, during an earlier state dinner for the Canadian prime minister. Fortunately, she'd graduated to a cane by then and didn't have to be on a walker in the photos.

Stahl refused to meet with any of them, so that'd been a dead end. Farnsworth and Malone did the interview with Darren that put a spotlight on Stahl's malfeasance as they assured the public they'd be looking into everything he'd ever done. That seemed to take some of the heat off the recent revelations that had come to light after the arrest of Daniella Brown.

Sam's friend Roni Connolly started as the new communications director in Sam's White House office, and Sam and Nick attended the first meeting of Nick's new task force on gun violence at which he pledged his full support to working with leaders on all levels to come up with sensible policies to address the problem. The Senate, back from holiday recess, took up the nomination of Gretchen Henderson to be Nick's vice president, and the White House dealt with the blowback about yet another unelected official, not to mention one who was even more inexperienced than the president, possibly leading the country as vice president.

On Martin Luther King Jr. Day, Sam stood by Nick's side in the Roosevelt Room as he delivered remarks on the enduring legacy of the civil rights leader.

"Martin Luther King Jr. wanted us to believe that we could do better, be better, and in some ways, we have. In others, we have a very long way to go to achieve the goals he set for us with his stirring words and unflinching commitment to equality for all. We are a better nation because of Dr. King and his sacrifice, and we owe him a debt we can never fully repay. Every time we reach out a hand in friendship and compassion to someone whose life experiences are different from ours, I'd like to think we make him proud."

Sam listened to him with so much pride for his stirring words and the passion with which he delivered them. The more she watched him embrace the presidency, the more she loved him—and she wouldn't have thought that was possible.

After his remarks, they attended a reception for civil rights leaders and members of the King family in the East Room.

Later that afternoon, Sam was relieved to head for the elevator to get back upstairs, where she could get off her aching hip. How much longer would she be constrained by her stupid injury? "This is getting so old," Sam said as she leaned against the wall of the elevator, relieved to take weight off the healing joint.

"You're so much better than you were," Nick replied. "Back to desk duty tomorrow. Are you excited?"

"Can't wait to get back to normal, although I've kept up fairly well with everything these last few weeks. We're at a complete standstill with the Olsen case, and I'm ready to start from scratch on that." Detectives had continued to canvass the Rock Creek Park area every day at four o'clock, looking for people who might've seen Audrey on the day of her murder. Only one person had recognized her from the photos officers had shown them, but the woman hadn't seen anything that could help them. "It's so frustrating to have nothing to go on."

"I'm sure you guys will figure it out."

"The further we get from the day it happened, the less likely that becomes. I want to be able to tell Audrey's mother what happened to her only child."

Eli came out of his room, wearing a backpack and pulling a rolling suitcase. He was on his way back to Princeton for the spring semester. "You guys aren't going to believe what happened."

"What?" Sam said, almost afraid to ask.

"Remember when I told you about my former girlfriend, Candace?"

"Of course," Nick said. "What about her?"

"She turned eighteen today, and the first thing she did was call me." The young man had tears in his eyes. "She apologized for the ordeal her parents put me through and said she's never stopped thinking about me or caring about me." Her parents had had him charged with statutory rape when he was seventeen and Candace was fifteen, after they learned the two of them had been having sex. He hadn't seen or talked to the young woman he loved in the three years since then.

Sam hugged him. "I'm so happy for you, Eli."

"I still can't believe it. I was so hoping I'd hear from her."

"This is such great news," Nick said, hugging him.

"I'm going to call her back from the car, but I wanted to say goodbye to you guys, Scotty and the twins before I go." He hugged them both again. "Thank you for a great Christmas and vacation, for the adventure of living in the White House, for the family you've given me and the twins, for all of it. I, um, well... I love you guys."

Sam was ridiculously moved by his heartfelt words. "We love you, too. So much. We can't wait to have you home again."

"Especially for spring break so you can go to Bora Bora, right?" he asked with a cheeky grin.

"You said that, not us," Sam said.

They shared a laugh before he went to find Scotty and the twins to say his goodbyes.

The entire family went downstairs, Sam and Nick via the elevator since stairs were still a challenge for her, to see off Eli. Before he got into the Secret Service SUV for the ride back to Princeton, he hugged them all again, giving extra attention to the twins, who clung to him.

"I'll be back in a couple of weeks," he told them. "I promise. And I'll FaceTime tonight at bedtime."

He held them for five more minutes before they were ready to let him go.

Sam wiped away a tear as she watched them. The poor babies had been through so much, and Eli was their bridge between the past and the present. It was always hard for them to let him go when he had to return to school. And she could see that it broke his heart to leave them.

"Love you guys all the way to the moon and back again," Eli said as he kissed them both and wiped away their tears. "I'll be back before you miss me."

Aubrey shook her head. "No, you won't. I already miss you."

"After this," Scotty said to the twins, "let's go throw snowballs for Skippy to fetch." Looking up at Sam and Nick, he added, "She can't figure out why she can't catch them. It's so funny." They'd gotten another six inches of snow the day before, and the kids had been thrilled.

"That sounds like fun." Nick picked up Aubrey while Scotty lifted Alden so they could wave to their brother as his three-car motorcade departed. "Let's go upstairs and get your snow pants on. I'll help with boots."

The three of them took off in a rush of energy and excitement that made Sam laugh. She took the arm that Nick offered for the walk to the elevator. "Thank goodness for Scotty. They've already shaken off Eli's departure."

"I was just thinking the same thing. Our boy has become an amazing big brother."

"Yes, he has."

Nick pushed the button to summon the elevator.

"I'm looking forward to being able to do stairs again."

"You're getting there."

"Such a stupid injury," she said for the nine hundredth time.

"Eh, shit happens. So, after the kids go out to play, you wanna take a nap?"

"Like a sleeping nap?"

"What other kind is there?"

Sam laughed at the heated look he gave her. "I could use a nap. I'm still recovering, you know."

Upstairs, they followed the sound of squealing children, who were chasing Skippy around while Scotty tried to corral them to put on snow pants.

"They're impossible," he declared.

Sam was glad to see they'd shaken off the sadness of Eli's departure rather quickly and was certain Scotty's attention had made a big difference. He was so good with them. "Guys, let's get your snow pants on so you can go play before the snow melts."

She sat on Alden's bed and helped him into the pants while Scotty helped Aubrey. Nick handled boots, and within a few minutes, they were ready to go.

"Give me five," Scotty said, "and then we're outta here. We're gonna hit the bowling alley after this. We've got a big afternoon planned, don't we, guys?"

"We do!" Aubrey said. "We're very busy. And Ms. Florence said we can bake cookies tomorrow. I can't wait!"

"I love cookies," Alden said, grinning.

Sam gave his belly a playful poke that made him laugh. It amazed her daily that she couldn't seem to remember what life had been like before the twins and Eli joined them a few months ago.

They sent the kids off to play in the snow, under the watchful eyes of their devoted big brother and the Secret Service.

Sam took the hand Nick offered her and followed him into their suite.

CHAPTER EIGHTEEN

Nick shut the door and then tossed a log on the fire one of the ushers had started earlier. "Alone at last."

"We're alone every night," she reminded him as she sat next to him on the sofa.

He drew her in close to him and planted a kiss on her neck that made her shiver. "It's never enough."

"You might want to see a doctor about that."

"I never want to be cured of my mad, crazy love for my gorgeous wife."

"We'd never want you cured of that. What would I ever do if you didn't love me in a mad, crazy way anymore?"

"That's something you never need to worry about. The longer we're together, the worse my affliction seems to get."

"In this case, worse is better."

"Worse is much better."

With a deftness that never failed to amaze her, he had them both naked and heading for their bed in a matter of minutes.

"Tell me if anything hurts."

"I have this ache..."

"The good kind or the bad kind?"

"The very best kind."

"I've missed this so much," he said as he pressed his muscular body against her. Despite their best intentions, Sam had been in no mood for anything sexual since her injury. The pain had put a damper on everything, even her favorite things.

"I have, too. Sorry to be such a drag these last few weeks."

"Baby, you were hurt. You weren't a drag. And P.S., to my great shock, you were also an excellent patient."

Laughing, she gave him an elbow to the gut. "I hated every minute of being a patient, and I'm going to hate every minute of being on desk duty for the next month. I've added ice in parking lots to the list of things I hate the most—flying, needles and ice."

"We hate ice."

"We hate ice more than flying."

"Wow. That's big."

Sam curled her hand around his erection. "Speaking of things that are big..."

He groaned. "It's not going to take much to..."

Sam stroked him and loved the way he lost his train of thought.

"Are you up for being creative?" he asked.

"Always."

"Can you turn onto your left side?"

"If you help me."

When he had her positioned the way he wanted her, he curled up behind her and ran his hands over every inch of her fevered skin until he had her on the verge of begging for relief. "Nick..."

"What, honey?"

"Don't 'what, honey' me. You know what I want!"

"Does it go something like this?" He began to push into her from behind.

"*Yes,*" she said on a long exhale, grasping the arm he had around her. "It goes *just* like that."

"Missed this so much," he whispered. "Don't break any more bones, you hear me?"

"Mmm, no more broken bones."

He cupped her breast and toyed with her nipple and then slid his hand down to caress between her legs.

As always, he played her like the Sam expert he was, coaxing her until she was biting her lip to keep from screaming when the pleasure rolled over her in deep, intense waves.

He pushed into her, groaning as he let himself go.

For a long time afterward, he held her close as their bodies cooled and their breathing returned to normal.

"You feel okay?" he asked.

"I feel divine."

"That was the goal."

"Your naps are the best."

"We aim to please at Naps-R-Us."

Sam laughed and snugged back against him, wanting to be as close to him as she could get after so many weeks without the thing they both enjoyed so much. "Thanks for putting up with me and my crankiness while recuperating."

"I love you and your crankiness."

"You're a rare and special man," she said, turning his usual line about her around on him.

"I'd have to be to tame you."

"You're perfect for me in every possible way."

"Likewise. Nice how that worked out, huh?"

"It's the nicest thing in my whole life."

ELI GAVE himself half an hour in the car to calm down, get his emotions under control and think about what he wanted to say before he called Candace.

She answered on the first ring. "Hi," she said, sounding shy and uncertain.

"Hi. I can't believe I'm talking to you."

"I've been counting down to today for three long years while having no idea if you even wanted to hear from me after what my parents did to you."

"All I've wanted was to hear from you. I've been so worried about you."

"I was worried about *you*, which is why I never snuck a call. I was sure they were monitoring my phone, and I was afraid of getting you in trouble again."

"It means a lot that you were thinking of me."

"I thought about you all the time. It's been really hard. I barely speak to either of them."

"Wow. That must've been rough."

"It's been awful. A very, very long three years."

"Are you still living with your mother?"

"For right now. I've been working like a fiend to save up for an apartment."

"Come here," Eli said before he took even a second to think about it. "I've got my own place at Princeton. You can stay with me."

"Eli…" She released a nervous-sounding laugh. "We can't just pick right up again. Can we?"

"Why can't we? We both know we didn't do anything wrong. We fell in love, and if the way my heart is racing just from hearing your voice is any indication, nothing has changed. At least not for me."

"I thought for sure you'd have someone else by now."

"There hasn't been anyone else."

"Don't tell me what you think I want to hear."

"I'm telling you the truth. There hasn't been anyone for me since you."

"Elijah..." Her voice caught on a sob. "I'm so, so sorry for what they did to you. I'll never forgive them for it."

"You will. Eventually."

"No, I won't. I won't ever forgive them for treating you like a criminal."

"Did you hear about what happened to my dad and Cleo?"

"I did, and I wanted so badly to call you, but I was so afraid they'd cause more trouble for you if I did. I was so heartbroken over it."

"It was horrible."

"And the twins are living with the first family."

"They're the most amazing people. Sam met them while she was working the case and took them home with her when they needed somewhere to be, and they've been like family to us ever since. I just left the White House to head back to school."

"It's so crazy that you're staying at the White House!"

"I know," he said with a laugh. "I still can't believe it myself. And I've got a Secret Service detail, which is a bit of a drag, but they're cool and try to give me my space. I'd, um, understand if all this was too much for you. My life has changed a lot since you saw me last."

"It's not too much, but please don't feel obligated—"

"Obligated is the last thing I feel when I think of you. I just want to be with you. That's all I've wanted from the beginning. I've missed you so much. You're the best friend I've ever had."

"Me, too. All of that. Me, too."

"Come to New Jersey. Be with me."

"What about school? I don't want to distract you."

"Please come and distract me. You can take some classes, too, and that way, we'll both have to study."

"You're sure?"

"I've never been surer of anything. I can't wait to see you. How soon can you get here?"

"Would tomorrow be too soon?"

"I suppose I can wait that long. Do you need me to get you a ticket?"

"I can do it."

"Send me your flight info, and I'll pick you up. Fly into Newark or JFK."

"Are we really going to do this?"

"I'm in if you are."

"I'm in. You really haven't dated anyone else?"

"Nope. What about you?"

"I haven't either."

"Is it tomorrow yet?"

Sam returned to work in the morning, bringing her trusty cane and asking Vernon and Jimmy to drive her, as she wasn't yet cleared to drive herself.

"Nice to see you getting back to normal, Lieutenant," Vernon said as he navigated the SUV through rush-hour traffic.

"Thanks. I'm ready to get back to it." She was insistent that they not use flashing lights or anything else to get her through the traffic faster. The last thing she needed was her colleagues seeing her getting special treatment. She could only wonder what many of them thought of the first lady continuing to work for the department. If there were any sort of major objections, she was unaware of them and happy to stay that way.

Her first stop was at the morgue to check in with Lindsey.

She jumped up to greet Sam with a hug. "Hail to the queen! She's back!"

"Hush with that foolishness. What goes on around here?"

"The usual nonsense. I heard Ramsey is back today, too."

"He is? Ugh, I hadn't heard that."

"Yep. Apparently, it happened overnight. The union filed suit to reverse his termination, and the judge granted a stay, allowing him to come back to work until the case is heard."

"That's just great. This is why we have people on this force who'd ignore a kidnapped kid for eleven years, because we have no way to get rid of the bad ones."

"I still think we'll get rid of him," Lindsey said. "It's just going to take longer than we'd like."

"Him spending even one more day on this job is too much."

"I agree, and a lot of other people do, too. From what I've heard, there's an uproar over allowing him back, so we're not the only ones who feel this way."

"I guess that's something, anyway."

"What's the latest from the marshals on the trafficking ring?"

"They're still working it, tracking down kids who've been missing for years."

"Of all the things we deal with, I think that might be the one thing that's more revolting than murder."

"Agreed. Well, I'd better get cracking. Got a long to-do list for today."

"Don't do too much too soon."

"Yes, Mom. Thanks for the welcome back."

"Glad to have you. It's not the same around here without you."

"That's nice to hear. I'm sure plenty of people were happy to have a break from me."

"Not that I heard."

As one of Sam's closest friends at work, Lindsey wouldn't hear if people were sick of Sam. "I'll check in later."

"Have a great day!"

"Thanks, you too."

Sam made her way—slowly—to the pit and stopped short at the sight of balloons floating above the cubicles. "Uh, what's all that?"

Her entire squad was there to greet her with applause and a huge WELCOME BACK banner to accompany the balloons. They'd also brought in coffee and doughnuts to mark the occasion. "Wow, thanks, guys. You missed me." She pretended to dab at tears. "You really missed me."

"For some strange reason, we did." Freddie handed her a coffee. "It's not the same around here without you riding roughshod over everything."

"I'm back on the horse today, albeit with a cane and limited duty."

"We'll take what we can get, LT," Gonzo said. "I'm very happy to turn over management of this unruly crew back to you."

"Thanks for all you did to keep things running smoothly."

"We're extremely frustrated to have made no real progress in the Olsen case," Gonzo said.

"Let's hit the conference room and start from scratch before we send Dani and Gigi home."

When everyone was settled with coffee and doughnuts, Sam took her place at the head of the table. "Thank you all for holding down the fort, for the visits, the flowers, the good wishes. I really appreciate you guys. Give me the rundown on where we are."

Gonzo and Freddie gave an overview of everything they'd done, from canvassing to reinterviewing everyone in Audrey's life.

"The boyfriend and his brother are clear," Gonzo said. "They're both heartbroken over her murder. In addition, they voluntarily offered DNA so they could be eliminated as suspects."

"Guilty people don't do that," Sam said, feeling frustrated.

"No, they don't."

"So we've got this guy on three sexual assaults and a murder," Sam said, "and not a single lead."

"Yes," Gonzo said, his expression grim. "I keep going back to what Best suggested about FDS."

Sam shook her head. "That's not an option."

"What if we made a case for a special exception to get a violent predator off the streets?" Cameron asked.

"We can try, but it'll be a long shot."

"I say it's worth the long shot," Gonzo said, "if it gives us something we didn't have before."

"I'll take it to the captain and chief and see what they have to say," Sam said. "In the meantime, let's go back over everything again— phones, financials, witness statements, all of it. Let's make sure we haven't missed anything."

"Yes, ma'am," Jeannie said for all of them.

Sam left the conference room and went into her office, which Gonzo had unlocked earlier. As she sat behind her desk, she released a deep breath full of relief to be back to her home away from home.

A knock on the door had her looking up at Dr. Anthony Trulo. "The rumors are true. The lioness is back in her den."

Laughing, Sam waved him in. "She is. Still on the cane and on limited duty, but back nonetheless."

"We'll take you any way we can get you." He sat in her visitor chair. "You're feeling better?"

"Much. I don't recommend the fractured hip."

"I've heard it's a bitch."

"It was, and so was I after it happened. With no one to blame but myself."

"I hate when that happens."

"Thank you for keeping an eye on Gonzo and Jeannie in my absence. They both report you've been very helpful to them."

"Glad to hear that. Waiting for the trial to conclude has been tough for all of us, especially Gonzo. And the news about the trafficking just gets worse all the time, as you know."

"It's unbelievable."

"That it is," Trulo said.

"Jeannie seems to be doing better than she was."

"It's a process. Accepting the faults of others that led to disaster isn't easy."

"No, it isn't."

"Speaking of that process, I came down to remind you the next meeting of the grief group is tomorrow night, if you're able to attend. No pressure, though. Everyone knows you're still recovering."

"I'll try to make an appearance. I'm going to invite the boyfriend of our latest victim to attend. We're getting nowhere fast in that case, so it might help Wes and his brother to have the outlet."

"Everyone is welcome, as you know." He stood to leave. "Nice to have you back. It's very dull around here without you."

"Thanks, Doc."

Trulo had no sooner left than Freddie appeared in the doorway. "We've got a body in the south end of Rock Creek Park, near Adams Morgan."

CHAPTER NINETEEN

"You're not allowed to come with us," Freddie said as Sam followed him and Gonzo to the main doors.

"I'm just going to watch." She'd sent a text to Vernon to let him know she'd be riding with Sergeant Gonzales. "You'll do all the work, which is really how it ought to be anyway."

"I'm not responsible for any setbacks," Gonzo said as he unlocked his new black Dodge Charger.

"Duly noted."

"This car is so fresh," Freddie said.

"Christina calls it my midlife-crisis car," Gonzo replied.

"I'm ready for a midlife-crisis car." Freddie bent to get into the back seat, leaving the low-slung front seat for Sam. "I can't find anything cool that I can afford."

She eyed it with trepidation "I, uh, I might need a hand here."

"I got you covered." Gonzo came around to the passenger side and helped Sam ease down to the seat.

She was about halfway there when her judgment kicked in. "Stop."

Gonzo froze.

"Pull me back out—slowly."

When she was standing upright again, she waved to Vernon. "I'll go with them."

"See you there. Cruz, get in the front seat. I'm not your chauffeur."

Frustrated and embarrassed, Sam walked over to the SUV.

Vernon held the back door for her and gave her an arm up.

"In case I haven't mentioned it before, this totally *blows*."

"I believe you've said that a time or two."

"A time or two hundred."

"Happy to drive you until you can drive yourself. No sense railing against that which we cannot change."

"Don't steal my fun. Railing is one of my favorite hobbies."

"Rail away," Vernon said, grinning as he closed the door.

They followed Gonzo through traffic to K Street, passing the lounge where she and Nick had celebrated their promotions to lieutenant and senator two New Year's Eves ago. What a long, strange trip they'd taken together since then, Sam thought. If she'd known then where it all was leading, would she have still gone all in with him?

Hell to the yes. No question. He was worth every crazy twist and turn in the road that had led them to living in the White House. After ten minutes back with him six long years after she'd first met him, she'd known she'd never be happy with anyone else. He was it for her. The only thing she'd change about these last few years was that her dad would still be alive.

She'd give anything to see him wheeling through the halls of the White House like he owned the place.

When tears filled her eyes, she shook off thoughts of her late father so she could get back into the mindset needed for the victim they were on their way to. The weeks away from the job had made her brain go soft, even as she'd stayed engaged from the sidelines. Though she still had limitations, being back on the front lines beat being unable to work.

Vernon brought the SUV to a halt behind Gonzo's car and jumped out to give her a hand.

"Thanks a lot," Sam said.

"My pleasure. Don't overdo it, kid."

"Wouldn't dream of it."

"Sure, you wouldn't."

Sam appreciated his sarcasm. She made her way slowly and carefully to the tape line being minded by an officer she didn't recognize.

The young woman lifted the yellow tape for her. "Lieutenant."

Sam glanced at her name tag. "Thank you, Officer Wisdom. That's a great name."

"Thank you, ma'am. It's an honor to meet you."

"Likewise." Sam made her way over uneven terrain she shouldn't have been walking on to where Freddie and Gonzo stood over the body. When they parted to let her in, she noted the half-naked young woman and let out a swear under her breath. "Not again."

"Afraid so," Gonzo said, sounding as frustrated as she felt.

"The case for FDS just got stronger," Freddie said.

"True." Sam leaned in for a closer look. "What do we know about her?"

"Her name is Ling Woo, age twenty-seven, with a Georgetown student ID and a DC driver's license. Lives about six blocks from here in a third-floor apartment on Ward Place."

They took photos and waited for Lindsey to arrive.

"Again?" Lindsey asked as she viewed the body.

"Apparently," Sam said.

They'd released multiple warnings about a sexual predator targeting Rock Creek Park, but that hadn't stopped Ling or other women from continuing to live their lives despite the threat. Sam didn't blame them. Why should they live in fear? It infuriated her that anyone in their city had to live that way, and she was more determined than ever to stop this guy.

A short time later, they made their way back to the cars, stopping to question everyone they encountered, asking if they'd seen or heard anything.

"Someone has to have seen *something* at one of these scenes," Gonzo said.

"Since I can't do stairs, I'll go back to brief the media and make an appeal for info," Sam said. "You guys track down her people."

"I'd rather brief the media," Freddie said.

"So would I," Sam said.

Vernon helped Sam back into the SUV. "Where we headed?"

"To HQ please."

"You got it." When he was in the car, he glanced at her in the mirror. "Is this one related to the other?"

"We won't know for certain until we get DNA, but it looks to be."

"Damn it."

"You said it." Sam called Malone. "We've got another sexual assault-murder."

"Shit. Where?"

"South end of the park this time, by Adams Morgan. We need to put out yet another alert to the community, and I want to talk to you and the chief about using FDS to try to track this guy down."

"That's gonna be a tough sell, Sam. The mayor is adamantly opposed to it."

"And for good reason. I agree there's a disproportionate number of minorities in the system, but if there's something we can do to catch this guy before he rapes and kills another woman, why wouldn't we at least try?"

"You're preaching to the choir. She's the one you have to convince, along with the U.S. Attorney."

"I'll work on that."

"Word on the street is that the FBI report is coming tomorrow. Avery asked if he could have a few minutes with us at the end of the day today. Can you be there?"

"Yeah, I'll be back soon," she said, even as worries about what would be in that report had her anxiety spiking.

NICK HAD CALLED the meeting of his closest advisers—Terry, Derek, Christina, Trevor and George, his speechwriter—to reveal the first cut on the State of the Union speech he wanted to give. He'd kept his cards close to the vest on the speech, intending to write most of it himself so he could give it the tenor and tone he wanted. He handed out the copies he'd asked one of the administrative assistants to make for him.

"This is what I'd like to do," he said, sitting back while the others reviewed the draft.

At one point, Terry looked over at him, brow raised in surprise.

"I love this thing about the airplane," Christina said.

"I do, too," Derek said. "That's genius."

"Thanks," Nick said, appreciative of their feedback. While his family had slept, he'd labored for hours every night for the last few weeks to hammer out the speech that would define his first year in office.

"I think this is…" Trevor shuffled the pages. "It's remarkable, Mr. President. I wouldn't change a word of it."

"I have to agree," George said. "There's nothing I could do to this to make it better than it already is."

"Terry?"

"I love it," he said. "Of course I do. It's just that I worry it might be a little too honest, if you know what I mean."

"That's the beauty of it," Derek said. "The things he shares here could only have come from him, from his heart, and it's important that the American people hear those things so they can know who he really is. That's how we beat back this drumbeat of people saying he's too young, too inexperienced, not elected by anyone, illegitimate. If he gives them this insider view of who he really is, it'll help to overcome some of that."

"It's risky," Terry said.

"I'm aware," Nick replied, "but don't forget, I'm not worried about my political future. I'm sitting in the catbird seat already. If all I ever have is these three years, then so be it. That's more than I ever dared to dream possible."

"I'd like to run it by Dad," Terry said, referring to retired Senator Graham O'Connor.

"I've already sent it to him," Nick said. "He loves it and approves of my plan."

"Then I guess you have a consensus," Christina said. "It's beautifully done."

"Thank you. I appreciate the feedback."

Derek, Trevor, Christina and George left a few minutes later, leaving Nick alone with Terry.

"What're we hearing from the Hill on Gretchen's meetings with the senators?"

"It's going well so far. We're getting the expected pushback on her inexperience, having never held elected office and sitting a heartbeat from the presidency, but no one can quibble with her education, her political pedigree or her command of the issues."

"Inexperience is looking to be the theme of our administration."

"You have an opportunity to show the world that inexperience doesn't mean incompetence."

"Let's hope we can pull that off." Nick would never admit to anyone, even his closest aide, that the weight of the matters that crossed his desk every day had him running on anxiety-fueled adrenaline as he considered a wide range of issues with impacts that couldn't be easily measured or articulated. The responsibility of it all sat on his shoulders like a boulder every moment of every day and night.

Sam arrived at HQ at the same time as FBI Special Agent-in-Charge Avery Hill.

"You're getting around better," he said to her.

"Better every day. I'll be glad to lose the cane."

"I'm sure."

"Have you come to ruin our lives?"

"Not at all."

"Well, that's a relief, I guess."

Avery walked at her pace as they made their way to the chief's suite, where a large group of lieutenants and captains had gathered in the conference room.

Lieutenant Archelotta raised his chin at her. "Good to see you, Holland."

"Good to be seen. Note to self—don't break your hip."

"I've heard it's a bitch."

"You've heard right." She sat in the chair Captain Malone held for her. "Thanks, Cap. Nice to see you all."

"Welcome back," Higgins from Explosives said.

"Thanks."

"Glad to hear the FBI caught the bomber," Higgins added.

"Me, too."

"Agent Hill," Chief Farnsworth said, "this is your meeting."

"Thanks, Chief. I want to thank you all for your cooperation over the last few months as my team conducted its investigation. It's never easy to be under scrutiny, especially outside scrutiny from a rival agency. Our report will reflect that spirit of cooperation and genuine effort on the part of leadership to identify and address problems while supporting the diverse workforce that makes up this department. We spoke with numerous people at all levels and roles, from the librarian and psychiatrist to Patrol to SVU to IT to Homeland Security to Internal Affairs. What we found is a group of hardworking, dedicated professionals who strive to provide the best safety and security possible for the District, its residents and the many visitors who come each year to visit the nation's capital.

"That said, we found deficiencies as well. Some of them you're aware of, including a deep backlog of untested rape kits, unsolved kidnappings, assaults, burglaries and murders dating back at least a decade or more in some cases. We're painfully aware that not every crime is solved in a way that brings satisfaction to the victims and their families. We've identified several former officers with the greatest percentages of unsolved cases, and in light of the recent successful conclusions to the Worthington and Deasly cases, we recommend the department employ significant resources to resolving as many of these cold cases as possible.

"Within the outstanding cases, we found a disproportionate number involved minority victims, and I expect that when the report is released, that could be the headline the media fixates on. I wanted the opportunity to tell you, face-to-face, that racial disparity is an area that needs work throughout the department. As you know, this is an issue of concern in departments and law enforcement agencies across the country. We recommend additional training in the areas of diversity, implicit bias, cultural assumptions and fair and impartial policing.

"We found no other significant deficiencies in the areas of leadership or command and recommended that the new deputy chief be hired from within the ranks of the current department. If you have any questions, I'm happy to take them."

"Thank you, Agent Hill, for taking on this project and for your fairness and open-mindedness," Farnsworth said. "As with any agency made up of thousands of people from a wide variety of backgrounds, we have our strengths and weaknesses. We're more than willing to address the weaknesses to improve our track record in the areas of concern identified by your team. I speak for everyone in this room when I assure you that your recommendations will be received in the spirit in which they're intended and will be taken seriously by all levels of command."

The meeting ended a short time later with the chief vowing to implement enhanced training for all personnel and to take a hard look at unsolved cold cases.

"Could've been much worse, I suppose," Archie said as he and Sam walked toward the pit.

"I was thinking the same thing. It's a relief that they backed the brass, which seems to protect the chief."

"Yeah, for sure. We've had enough upheaval around here without them giving him the boot."

"I wouldn't want to do the job without his support."

"Me either. Heard you caught another homicide-SA."

"We did, and if the DNA matches the earlier cases, we're going to make a plea for an exception to the FDS policy."

"Let me know how I can help. That technology is fascinating."

"Will do."

"By the way, I never laughed so hard in my life as I did at that *SNL* sketch."

"That topic is firmly off-limits in this building."

"Haha," Archie said. "You wish." He walked away humming the "My Humps" tune.

Freddie and Gonzo entered the pit from the other side as Sam came in with Archie. Both men still wore winter coats, their expressions grim.

"As always, notifying friends and relatives that a loved one has been murdered ruins a perfectly good day." Freddie unzipped his coat. "We talked to Ling's roommates, who are shocked and devastated. She's the first of her family to go to college, and her parents are in China. We're going to need to arrange for a translator before we call them. According to the roommates, the parents don't speak any English."

Sam thought of people half a world away, going about their business, not knowing their daughter had been raped and murdered in Washington. Her heart broke for them and for the hopes and dreams that had died along with Ling.

"By all accounts, Ling was a quiet person who kept to herself. Didn't date, had a small circle of friends in the Neurosciences Department and rarely socialized. Her roommates say she spent most of her time studying or in her lab. She just went back to running recently as a New Year's resolution to exercise more."

"And they said she was brilliant," Gonzo added sadly. "They're coming in shortly to identify her."

"I want to find this guy," Sam said, "and stop him before he can do this again. He keeps getting away with it, which has made him brazen. We warned women to stay away from the park, and he knows we're watching, but he does it again. He knows we can't tie the DNA to him, so he's careless. He wants us to know it's him every time—and he wants us to know he's gotten away with it—again."

"He'll keep doing it until we stop him," Gonzo said.

"Hold that thought." Sam turned to head back the way she'd come with Archie, stopping at the captain's office. "Come with me."

"Yes, ma'am," Malone said. "Whatever you say, ma'am."

They arrived at the chief's suite.

"He's still with Agent Hill," Helen said. "Should I interrupt them?"

"Yes, please," Sam said.

"She's in charge around here," Malone added.

Helen's wide-eyed gaze darted between them, as if she was unsure what was going on. "Chief, Captain Malone and Lieutenant Holland are here and need to see you right away." She put down the phone. "He said to go on in."

"Thanks, Helen," Sam said as she followed the captain into the chief's office.

"What's up?" Farnsworth asked Malone.

"Ask her. She's the one who ordered me to attend this meeting."

Avery huffed out a laugh. "That sounds about right."

"We have two dead women and four sexual assaults. We haven't got the DNA back from the most recent victim, but we believe it's going to match the other three. Our guy isn't in the system, which of course he knows. He's getting ballsy. He's getting away with it, so he'll keep doing it until we stop him. We have no witnesses, no usable film and not a single lead as to who this guy is. I'd like to try FDS to see if we can get a familial link to lead us to a suspect."

CHAPTER TWENTY

Farnsworth shook his head. "It's not allowed here, as you know."

"I want to request a special exception. This is the type of case that's solved by this technology."

"I understand, but the city council, mayor and U.S. Attorney have been united in their opposition to it."

"I'd like to formally appeal to them for an exception in this case. How do I go about doing that?"

Farnsworth considered the question. "Put it in writing and include as many details of each related assault as you can. If you show the mayor and U.S. Attorney what this guy is doing to these women, it may help to sway them that we need to try something outside the box to find him."

"I'll get right on that."

"No promises," he added. "It'll be a tough sell. The mayor has been adamantly opposed to using FDS in criminal investigations. She spearheaded the bill that outlawed it when she was first on the city council."

"I understand the objections and agree with them in most cases. This isn't most cases. We've got a sexual predator who's escalated to murder. If we don't find a way to stop him, he'll kill again."

"You're preaching to the choir, Lieutenant. Get busy making a case to take to city hall."

Sam nodded, thankful for once to be on desk duty so she could personally oversee this project. "I hear you. We'll make sure there's no way she can say no. Will you come with me to meet with her?"

"Do I hafta?" the chief asked.

Sam laughed at the look of agony that accompanied the question. "Yes, you hafta."

"Fine."

"At least the FBI report isn't going to skewer you on the BBQ."

"There is that. While you're here, I want to talk about the other homicide cold cases."

"I planned to ask Detective Green to do a formal review and triage for us. We'll work our way through them between other priorities."

"U.S. Attorney Tom Forrester is asking for a formal review of all the convictions associated with Stahl's cases as well."

Sam blew out a deep breath. "That could get very ugly."

"It's already ugly," Malone said. "It could get uglier."

"Ask Detective Green to keep us informed on what he finds."

Sam hobbled to the door. "You got it."

"Lieutenant."

Sam turned back to the chief. "Yes, sir?"

"It's so good to have you back. We missed you around here."

"Aw, thanks. It's good to be back."

As she made her way slowly back to the pit, she came face-to-face with the last person in the world she wanted to see—Detective Ramsey.

"Well, if it isn't Little Miss Thing. You must be *thrilled* to see me back after all you did to get me fired."

Sam kept walking as if he hadn't said a word, but she picked up the pace to get away from him as fast as possible.

"Love the cane," he called after her, "but a broomstick would've been more appropriate."

Sam wanted to ask how his divorce was going, but since she couldn't kick his ass if it came to that, she kept her mouth shut and let him spew his garbage.

"Better get used to having me back," Ramsey said, "because I'm here to stay."

"What's he saying?" Freddie asked when she came into the pit.

"I wasn't listening."

Freddie laughed. "I can't believe we have to put up with him again."

Sam shrugged. "Whatever. I'll ignore him until he goes away for good after he's found guilty of vandalizing my office. He can't help himself." She turned to Detective Green. "Can I have a word, please?"

Cameron jumped up. "Sure."

Sam went into the office. "Close the door."

He shut the door and took a seat. "What's up?"

"I'd like to put you in charge of reviewing Stahl's homicide cases."

"The cold ones?"

"All of them."

"Whoa."

"The U.S. Attorney wants to look at every conviction that came from Stahl's investigations. Not to mention, we've got defense attorneys filing for reviews of old cases."

"That could be a big deal."

"It's already a big deal."

"Yeah, I suppose it is. I'll dive right in. Can I have help?"

"Jeannie and Matt can help you. I'll partner up Cruz and Gonzo until I'm back to full steam."

"I assume we're doing this in addition to active cases?"

"You assume correctly."

"Got it."

"I'll let the others know the plan. Appreciate you taking the lead on this."

"Thanks for asking me."

"Keep me in the loop on anything you find."

"Yep, will do."

"On another front, how are things with Gigi?"

His entire demeanor softened as he smiled. "Things are great. Never been better, in fact."

"Happy to hear it. She's doing all right?"

"I think so, but you should ask her. She's very anxious to get back to full duty."

"I'll talk to her. Sometimes we say we're fine when we're not because we want back in the game so badly. I've been guilty of that myself—and probably will be again with this damned hip thing."

"She's much better than she was, but there's still a fragileness to her that wasn't there before. And she'd hate me for saying that."

"I'd never repeat it, but I hear what you're saying. Jeannie was like that for a few months after she was assaulted. As cops, we live under the assumption that we can take care of ourselves in all situations. It's a shock to the system to realize that's not always true."

"I hadn't thought of it quite like that, but you're right."

"I usually am."

"God, I walked right into that, didn't I?"

Sam flashed him a big grin. "That was a softball. Thanks for the insight. I'll talk to her, too, and I won't mention that I spoke to you."

"That'd be appreciated. I'm walking a fine line in this new relationship between wanting to support her and wanting to protect her."

"She's lucky to have you."

"I'm the lucky one, Lieutenant. Thanks for giving me a nudge in her direction when I needed it."

"I do what I can for my people."

Smiling, he stood. "Glad to be one of your people. I'll keep you posted on the Stahl situation."

As he was walking out, Gonzo came in. "What was that about?"

"I put him in charge of reviewing Stahl's cold cases and convictions."

"I would've done that."

"I know, but I need you to be my legs in the field for a few more weeks. And that sounded weirder than I intended it to."

Gonzo laughed. "I understood what you meant. What're we doing about this rapist-murderer?"

"We're writing a detailed justification for FDS that we'll take to the mayor. Can you do the part about the two prior assaults? I'll do Olsen and Woo."

"I'll do it right now."

"Thanks."

Sam spent the next several hours summarizing the report on Audrey Olsen's rape and murder, focusing on the more brutal elements of the attack. *While the perpetrator covered her mouth with his hand, he raped and sodomized her before strangling her.*

If that one sentence wasn't enough to convince the mayor to let them use FDS, Sam wasn't sure anything would be.

She stood and went to the door. "Before we take this to the mayor, I want to talk to the two women who survived," Sam said to Gonzo.

"They've already been thoroughly interviewed," Gonzo said.

"Not by me."

THE NEXT DAY, Sam asked Kaitlyn Oliver to come to her, since Kaitlyn lived in a third-floor walk-up in Foggy Bottom, and Sam couldn't do stairs yet.

"I appreciate you coming in," she said when Kaitlyn was seated at the conference room table with a bottle of water in front of her. They had turned the murder board around so Kaitlyn wouldn't have to see the details of the Olsen and Woo cases.

Sam had asked Jeannie to join her, hoping Kaitlyn might be more comfortable speaking to two women. Not to mention Jeannie had survived a similar attack. "This is Detective Jeannie McBride."

"I wish we were meeting under different circumstances," Jeannie said.

Kaitlyn nodded. "Me, too."

Sam noted that Kaitlyn's hands trembled as she wrapped them around the bottle. "We're sorry to have to put you through this again, but we just want to be sure that we have all the information."

"I don't mind. If it helps to catch him, I'll do whatever you need."

"Can you take us through it from the beginning?" Sam asked gently.

"Yeah, sure. I was, um, out for a walk in the snow. I'm one of the few people who grew up here who loves the snow. I can't get enough of it. Although... It'll never look the same to me again after this." She swiped at a tear as if it made her angry. "I was distracted, had my face turned up to the snow, breathing in the cold air and just enjoying it so much. He got me from behind and had me deep into the trees in a matter of seconds. I hit the ground hard, facedown." She rubbed at a spot on her cheek where a faint bruise remained from the attack two weeks ago. "Everything I'd learned about self-defense was worthless. He had me completely immobilized in a matter of seconds."

Sam reached over to open the bottle of water. "Take a sip."

Kaitlyn drank from the bottle and used the tissue Jeannie handed her to wipe her eyes. "Sorry."

"Please don't be," Jeannie said. "I still cry every time I think about it happening to me."

Kaitlyn seemed startled to hear that.

"And trust me, I know how to defend myself, too."

The young woman drew in a deep breath and released it slowly. "That's the part I wrestle with. I knew what to do, but when it was happening, I was just frozen with fear."

"Anyone would be," Sam said.

"It's just... It's hard to talk about it."

"We understand, and we're so sorry to put you through it—again," Jeannie said. "But since he's since committed two homicides, the case is now ours. We just want to be sure we have every detail we need."

"I can't stop thinking about the girls he killed," Kaitlyn said softly as she wiped away tears. "That could've been me."

"Take all the time you need," Sam said, forcing herself to be patient with the traumatized young woman.

"He covered my mouth with one hand and pulled my pants off with the other. He tore my underwear and jammed the fabric in my mouth. I started to hyperventilate because I couldn't breathe." She took another deep breath. "He raped me while keeping his hand over my face the whole time. I remember being so cold and not being able to breathe. And that it hurt—a lot. I thought it would never end."

"Do you have any idea how long it lasted?" Sam asked. That was one thing she hadn't seen notated in the reports.

"I've gone over it in my mind a thousand times, and I just don't know how long it was. It felt like an hour at the time, but it was probably more like ten or fifteen minutes. Long enough for him to rape me twice."

Which led Sam to believe the man they were looking for was young and recovered quickly—or that he'd taken medication.

"Did you see him at any point?"

"No, he was behind me the entire time. I was facedown on the ground."

"Did he say anything?"

"Not a word."

"Tell us how you got away from him."

"I struggled the whole time, kicking and fighting him. At one point, I connected with something, and he grunted and loosened his hold on me. Just for a second, but that was all I needed. I jumped up, pulled the fabric out of my mouth and stumbled away, screaming for help. I was in a state of panic, sure he'd come after me, but he didn't. Two joggers came to my rescue and called the police. One of them was female, and I recall her helping me get my pants back on while the guy she was with looked away."

Sam wanted to know where the perp had gone while all that was happening. How had he managed to sneak off with people around? Someone had to have seen something. She made a note to bring in the couple who'd assisted Kaitlyn for another interview.

"Is there anything else you remember? Even something as random as a scent or what color his coat was or anything at all that stood out."

"I can't think of anything."

"Did he have gloves on?"

"He did."

"Was there any scent you recall from when his glove was over your face?"

She shook her head. "No."

Sam pushed her business card across the table. "If anything else comes to mind, please call me."

Kaitlyn took the card. "I'm sorry I can't give you more to work with."

"We have more than we had before. Thank you for coming in and reliving it once again."

"It was really cool to meet you," Kaitlyn said with a sad smile. "My friends and I are big fans."

"Thank you."

Jeannie walked her out, and when she returned to the pit, Sam called her into the office.

"Shut the door."

"What's up?"

"I know that had to be hard for you to sit through."

Jeannie shrugged. "I'm okay."

"You're sure?"

"Brings it all back, but it's nothing I can't handle. What's next?"

"I'd like to speak to the couple who assisted Kaitlyn."

"I'll call and ask them to come in."

"Call the other victim, too. Moira. If I'm going to make a compelling case for FDS, I should speak to everyone involved."

She started for the door. "I'll make the calls."

"Jeannie."

She turned back. "Yes?"

"If this gets to be too much, please say so. I can have Erica help me."

"I've got it, but thanks."

As Sam watched her go, she vowed to keep a close eye on her friend and colleague. This case was striking too close to home for her.

CHAPTER TWENTY-ONE

S am was about to leave for the day when Gonzo appeared in the
office doorway. "Jury's in. I'm not sure what to do."

"What do you want to do?"

"I think I'd like to be there when the verdict is read."

"Then let's go."

"You don't have to come."

"Yes, I do, but can we have Vernon and Jimmy take us? I can't
manage that sled of yours."

"Sure. My hands are shaking. It's probably better if I don't drive."

"Gonzo."

He turned back to her.

"Even if the worst possible thing happens, which it won't, we know
who killed Arnold."

Nodding, he said, "Yeah."

"Keep the faith."

"Trying to."

Vernon pulled the SUV up to the federal courthouse fifteen
minutes later.

Gonzo got out and then gave Sam a hand.

"Thanks."

They walked up the ramp and into a media scrum in the lobby.
Reporters started calling Sam's name the second they stepped inside.

Vernon and Jimmy ran interference, delivering them to the
courtroom they needed with minimal fuss.

"Sometimes having Secret Service protection doesn't suck," Sam said to Gonzo.

"True that."

Arnold's parents, sisters and girlfriend greeted Sam and Gonzo with tearful hugs.

"Thank you for being here," his mother said. "Your support means everything to us."

"We wouldn't be anywhere else right now," Sam said, hugging the other woman.

The courtroom was soon called to order, the jury filed in, the verdict given to the bailiff and to the judge. The defendant was ordered to rise, and the judge ran through the motions of reading the verdict and then asking the jury forewoman how they'd found the matter.

"Guilty, Your Honor."

The same verdict was recorded on three additional charges as the Arnolds wept silently.

Thank God, Sam thought as she squeezed Gonzo's hand.

The jurors were thanked for their service and dismissed, sentencing was set for March 23rd, and the guilty man was led away in leg chains. When the judge pounded the gavel to signify the end of the proceedings, Sam turned to hug her friend.

"You did it. You got him."

Gonzo nodded as tears slid down his face. "Yeah. We got him."

The Arnolds hugged them both and thanked them for the tireless pursuit of justice on behalf of their son and brother.

"We'll see you for the anniversary?" Sam asked.

"We'll be there," Mr. Arnold said. "We're excited to visit the White House."

"We're looking forward to it." They'd decided to have it there so that Nick could attend without a big hassle, and when they'd offered the idea to the Arnold family, they'd been thrilled. One of the best aspects of their new situation was sharing the White House with the people in their lives.

Sam and Gonzo followed them out and stood by their side when they gave a statement thanking the U.S. Attorneys who'd prosecuted the case and their son's colleagues in the Metro PD, especially his beloved partner, Sergeant Tommy Gonzales, Lieutenant Sam Holland, former Detective Will Tyrone and the other Homicide detectives, who'd seen them through their darkest hours.

"We have to believe our son is looking down on all of us," John

Arnold said, "and is proud of the battle we fought for justice. This conviction doesn't bring back our son..." His voice caught, and he took a second to collect himself. "But there's comfort in knowing that no one else's son or daughter will be killed by this vile career criminal."

They stood by while U.S. Attorney Tom Forrester praised the team of prosecutors who'd worked tirelessly to convict Sid Androzzi. "The murder of Detective Arnold was one of the most brazen and senseless killings I've seen in my career, and it gives me and my team tremendous satisfaction to see the man responsible for ending the life of this promising young man convicted on charges that'll ensure he never again sees the light of day outside of prison."

Sam couldn't seem to stem the swell of emotion that overtook her, listening to the Arnolds and Tom. She was taken right back to the terrible first hours after learning Arnold had been killed and the nightmare that had unfolded for Gonzo in the ensuing months. Justice for the victim could be a hollow win for their loved ones, because it didn't bring back the person they'd lost. *Hollow* was a good word to describe how she felt now that Arnold's killer had been convicted.

While the gathered media shouted questions at her, many of which had nothing to do with Arnold or the conviction, Vernon, Jimmy and Gonzo surrounded Sam and escorted her back to the waiting SUV.

"They're still asking about Nick bringing me back on *Marine One*," Sam said to Gonzo when they were settled in the back seat. "They're not letting that go since he hasn't given them anything else to gripe about in the meantime."

"They'll be all over the FBI report tomorrow."

"That ought to change the narrative for a few days." Sam laughed even as more tears threatened. "I'm an emotional basket case since the verdict was announced."

From the front seat, Jimmy handed her a tissue.

"Thank you."

"We're so happy to see that scumbag convicted," Vernon said.

"We are, too." Sam glanced over at Gonzo, who was looking out the window. "How're you feeling?"

"Relieved, empty, sad, happy. The full gamut."

"We've had a year to process this, and sometimes I still can't believe it happened. I can only imagine how you must feel."

"It's surreal. I keep thinking he's going to come bounding into the pit with some stupid joke he heard on the radio on the way in that he just has to share with me."

Sam laughed. "That sounds about right."

"He always had a joke that I never had time for. I wish I'd made the time."

"I could see how he drove you mad," Sam said, "but I could also see him becoming a much better detective and man for the time he spent with you."

Gonzo looked over at her. "You really think so?"

"Oh, hell yes. He grew in leaps and bounds under your guidance."

"Half the time, I wanted to shoot him myself," Gonzo said, grimacing. "I hate to say that out loud."

"I get it. He was like a big puppy following you around, hanging on your every word, wanting your approval."

Gonzo wiped away a tear. "And I let him be slaughtered on my watch."

"You didn't let it happen, Tommy. Don't say that. You would've taken that bullet for him if you could have."

"Yeah, I would've. I just wish I'd treated him better when I had the chance."

"You treated him exactly the way you should have as his training officer. You think I don't beat the shit out of Cruz daily? But like Arnold did with you, Cruz knows I love him like a brother, and everything I say and do on the job—well, almost everything—is about making him a better detective."

"I did love him like a brother, but I never told him that."

"You didn't have to, Gonzo. He knew. Of course he knew."

"I really hope so."

"Let's hit the grief group meeting together. I think we both could use the support tonight."

"I just need to make sure Christina doesn't mind." He pulled out his phone for the first time since they'd left court. "Damn, more than two hundred messages about the verdict." He put through a call to his wife. "Hey. Yes, I'm okay. Relieved and all that. Sam suggested we attend the grief meeting tonight. Do you mind if I'm a little late?" After a pause, he said, "Thanks, baby. I'll be home soon. Yeah, me, too. It's a huge relief. Love you, too." To Sam, he said, "She's sobbing."

"A lot of people were heavily invested in the outcome of this trial."

Nodding, he said, "I appreciate the support. Not sure where I'd be without my friends and family—including my blue family."

Sam knew the loss of Arnold would stay with them both for the rest of their lives. There was no getting around that. They'd had to learn to live with the grief, the heartache, the regrets that would also stay with them forever. He'd been under their command. No matter the outcome of the trial, they both felt responsible.

The entire squad had stayed long after their shift ended to be there when Sam and Gonzo returned to HQ. Carlucci and Dominguez had come in early, and the group greeted them with hugs and words of support for Gonzo, whose eye-witness testimony had been so critical to achieving justice for Arnold.

Chief Farnsworth and Captain Malone came in, both shaking Gonzo's hand.

"I don't feel right accepting any kind of congratulations for this," Gonzo said. "We did what needed to be done, but it doesn't change anything. Not really."

"It makes it so that thug can't do this to anyone else," Freddie said. "That matters."

"Yes, that's true," Gonzo said.

"We're going to hit the meeting upstairs," Sam said. "Anyone else who wishes to join us is more than welcome."

The entire squad came to support Gonzo at the meeting, which was well attended by many of the regulars. Sam was glad to see Audrey Olsen's boyfriend, Wes, had accepted Sam's invitation to attend, along with his brother. Hearing Wes speak about the strain of not knowing who'd killed his girlfriend made Sam even more determined than ever to get the man who was terrorizing women in her city.

It was well after eight by the time Sam got home and took the elevator to the residence. She looked in on Aubrey and Alden, who were both sound asleep, and was sad she'd missed kissing them good night. But she'd been where she'd needed to be tonight, with her squad as they helped Gonzo through another difficult day in the journey he'd been on since losing his partner so senselessly.

She stopped at Scotty's room and knocked on the door.

"Enter!"

"Hey," she said. "Sorry to be so late getting home."

"We heard about the verdict. How's Gonzo doing?"

"As well as can be expected. Days like today, even with good news, bring it all back, you know?"

"I'm sure. I didn't know Detective Arnold that well, and I still feel sad today."

Sam went to sit gingerly on the edge of his bed and leaned into his hug. "I really needed that. Thank you. Did you have a good day?"

"As good of a day as you can have in the eighth grade."

Sam laughed, ruffled his dark hair and scratched Skippy behind the ears. "Get some sleep, you two."

"You, too. Love you, Mom."

"Love you, too."

Love you, Mom. Had three words ever meant more to her than those did?

In their suite, she found Nick in his office, bent over a pile of correspondence. She cleared her throat to let him know she was there.

He turned to her, smiling, and her heart skipped an actual beat at the sight of him in the sexy dark-framed reading glasses he'd recently acquired.

She fanned her face. "Those glasses really do it for me."

"Is that right?"

"That's right, Clark Kent."

He stood and came to hug her, leaving the glasses on. "Rough day, huh?"

"It was a strange day. Full gamut of emotions."

"Thank God he was convicted."

"Yes, definitely. But like Gonzo said, it doesn't bring Arnold back."

"No, but you got justice for him and his family, and that matters."

"We're trying to tell ourselves that. What went on around here today?"

"Nothing much."

Sam laughed. "Right. Is the fate of the free world secure for another day?"

"It is, although the North Koreans are continuing to vex me. But I don't need to think about them now that my lovely wife is finally home." He shut off the light on his desk and directed her into their sitting room. "Are you hungry?"

"Starving."

"Stand by."

While she sat on the sofa and put her right foot on a pillow, he called for her dinner. Life at the White House had its perks.

"How's the hip?"

"Aching."

He went into their bathroom to get her two Motrin and returned with the pills and a glass of water.

Sam took the pills. "Thanks."

"Did you do too much today?"

"Define 'too much.'"

He gave her a stern look. "I knew you'd overdo it."

"I was very glad to be back. This case that's now got four victims—that we're aware of—is making us all crazy. Tonight, at the grief group, Audrey Olsen's boyfriend, Wes, had us in tears talking about how difficult the not knowing is. We've got to find this guy."

"You will. I have every confidence."

"We're hoping to try something we've never done before."

"What's that?"

"Family DNA search."

"How does that work?"

"We run the rapist's DNA through the system, looking for familial matches. The guy we're looking for isn't in the system, but a family member might be. If we can isolate the family, we can work from there."

"That's fascinating."

"It's also illegal in DC and Maryland."

"Why?"

"Due to the disproportionate number of people of color in the system, it often targets minorities unfairly and involves innocent people in a murder investigation."

"But if it can get a vicious criminal off the streets, why wouldn't they at least try it?"

"That's the argument we're taking to the mayor and U.S. Attorney. It'll be a tough sell. The mayor is adamantly opposed. She spearheaded the legislation to outlaw it."

"I have to believe she'll want to do whatever it takes to find this guy before he kills again."

"I sure hope so, because we've got jack otherwise. None of the usual effort has yielded even a single lead. He attacks from behind, so even the two women who survived the attacks didn't see anything."

"Damn, that's got to be frustrating."

"It's beyond frustrating, and it's been more than a month since Audrey was killed. One of the victims who survived is too traumatized to be interviewed, so we have nothing from her. Jeannie brought in the couple who assisted another victim and got nothing new."

"You and your team are doing everything you can to get answers for Wes and the other victims, babe."

"Everything we can just isn't enough in this case."

CHAPTER TWENTY-TWO

Cameron had been preparing for this night for weeks, biding his time until Gigi seemed stronger and more like her old self before taking the next step with her. They'd dined at one of his favorite restaurants, which was only two blocks from his apartment complex, so they'd walked.

On the way home, he'd put his arm around her and kept a careful eye out for black ice. They'd had enough injuries to last awhile, and now was the time for new beginnings.

"That was so good," she said. "Thanks for dinner."

"You're welcome."

"I need to start doing some cooking so you'll know I can."

"I'm not worried about whether you can."

"You've been feeding me for weeks now. The least I can do is return the favor."

"Feeding you has been my pleasure. You don't owe me anything, Gigi."

"Yes, I do."

"Nope."

"Yup."

Cam loved everything about being with her, even "arguing," if you could call it that. He couldn't help but compare this relationship to the last one he'd been in and find that one lacking in every possible way. When he thought of Jaycee, he cringed and gave thanks for not doing something stupid, like marrying the wrong woman.

Since he was thinking of her—which he tried hard not to do since she'd slashed his tires and then insulted Gigi—he couldn't believe it when he saw her sitting on the stairs to his townhouse.

He froze.

Gigi looked up at him.

Cameron handed her his keys. "Go inside and stay there."

"Cam..."

"Please go, Gigi."

"I'll be listening, and if there's any trouble, I'm calling Dispatch," Gigi said so Jaycee would hear.

When she'd gone up the stairs and into his place, Cameron turned his gaze on his ex. "What do you want?"

"I need to talk to you."

"We have nothing to talk about."

"Yes, we do. I'm pregnant."

"It's not mine."

"Yes, it is."

"No, it isn't, Jaycee."

"How can you know that?"

"Because this is another ploy to get me back, and I'm not coming back. Even if you're pregnant and the baby is mine, which I highly doubt, I'm not coming back to you."

"If you want to see your kid, you'll do what I say," she said in the ugly tone that had so surprised him when he'd first heard her disparaging Gigi's ethnicity.

"Not happening. Honestly, Jaycee, you could be pregnant with triplets and I wouldn't care. Now that I've seen who you really are, I've got nothing more to say to you."

He started up the stairs, stepping around her.

"You can't *honestly* want *her* more than you want me."

"Not only do I want her more, I love her like I've never loved anyone. Now get out of here before I report that you're violating the no-contact order. We gave you a break the last time. We won't do it again."

"What break did you give me? I got charged and had to go to court!"

"Whose fault was that?" He turned back to face her. "I'm going to say this in the simplest possible terms—go away. Leave me alone. Or I'll make your life a living hell."

"Too late. You already have."

"Nah, you did that all on your own. You have one minute to leave, or I'm making a call to Dispatch."

"Cameron! Don't do this!"

He stepped into his condo, closed the door and locked it.

Gigi stood waiting for him with his pug, Jeffrey, at her feet.

Cameron looked out the window by the door to see what Jaycee would do. He was relieved when she walked down the stairs and headed for her car. "I was so wrapped up in you that I didn't notice her car in the lot," he said, chilled by the realization. "I'm sorry about that."

"I'm not."

Surprised, he turned to her. "No?"

She shook her head. "Thanks to her, I found out you love me like you've never loved anyone."

Immediately flustered, he started to say something, but the words died on his lips.

Gigi laughed. "I did hear that right, didn't I?"

"Yeah," he said gruffly. "You did, but I'm sorry you had to hear it like that."

"Again, not sorry."

She came to him, wrapped her arms around his neck and went up on tiptoes to plant a soft, sweet, sexy kiss on him. "Best thing I've ever heard."

"Really?"

Nodding, she kissed him again.

"Best thing I've ever felt."

"Same."

Pulling back, he looked down at her. "So, what you're saying is that you feel the same way?"

"I do."

Cameron hugged her tightly, breathing in the rich, fragrant scent that would forever remind him of his love. "I never knew it could be like this. I had no idea."

"I spent years with the wrong guy, so I had no clue either." She pulled back to look up at him. "Is it weird to be slightly glad that things with him blew up so I could find this?"

"We're not even slightly glad that you got hurt so badly, but the rest I'm down with." He tipped her chin up to receive a kiss that started off slow and sweet and quickly became about the desire that had been simmering between them for weeks. "Gigi..."

She pressed her curvy, sexy body against him. "Yes, Cameron?"

"I, uh, forgot what I was going to say."

He loved the sound of her laughter, the way her dark eyes lit up with mirth, how her smile left a deep groove on the right side of her face. He loved everything about her. "I should've been looking into your gorgeous eyes the first time I told you I love you. It shouldn't have happened that way."

"I'll never forget the first time I heard you say it—or the second. Do we need to talk about what she said?"

"Nope. She's not pregnant."

"How do you know?"

"She's got a 'life plan' that she sticks to faithfully, and that includes no kids for another five years and long-term birth control."

"Is it possible she tricked you somehow?"

"I haven't done anything with her in months. She'd be showing by now if she was pregnant by me. And that's enough about her." Cameron smoothed his hands down her back to cup her ass, lifting her into his arms, planning to take her straight to bed, until Jeffrey whined, reminding Cam that he hadn't been outside yet. "Damn it. That was gonna be so smooth, too." He set Gigi down as she laughed.

"It'll keep."

He clipped the leash on Jeffrey, and after taking a good look around to be sure Jaycee was gone, he walked him outside, hoping the dog wouldn't have to sniff every bush in the complex before he peed. Thankfully, Jeffrey was cooperative, taking care of business in a matter of seconds and heading for the stairs, eager to get back to his new favorite person.

They found Gigi curled up on the sofa, waiting for them.

Jeffrey bounded toward her, full of excitement, as if he hadn't seen her in a year.

Cameron understood how he felt. He sat next to her and laughed when Jeffrey planted a wet kiss on her face. "He loves you as much as I do." It was freeing to finally be able to give voice to feelings that'd been almost painful to contain.

"I love him, too."

"Jeffy, that's enough," Cameron said. "Go lie down. Go on. My turn."

The dog gave him a hurt look but did as he was told.

"Phew, I thought I was gonna have to fight him for you."

"There's enough of me to go around."

Smiling, he kissed her and lost himself in her enthusiastic response. He ended up on top of her, which gave him pause.

She stopped him when he tried to move to the side. "I'm fine, Cam. Don't treat me like I might break. I won't."

"Promise?"

"I promise." She drew him into another kiss, her hands sliding under his shirt making him shiver from her touch. "Take this off."

He sat back to remove his shirt and then reached for her sweater.

Gigi helped him remove it.

They'd done this much before, but anything else would be new. As he gazed at her lush breasts contained by a lacy bra, the angry red incision on her abdomen was a reminder to go easy, to take it slow, to treat her with the reverence she deserved. He released the front clasp on her bra and pushed the cups aside to reveal the full breasts that had fired his fantasies for weeks now. Her dark nipples stood at full attention, and as he bent his head to touch his tongue to one and then the other, he decided this was shaping up to be the best night of his life.

GIGI HAD NEVER EXPERIENCED the kind of desire she felt for Cameron. Over the last few weeks, it had built between them to the point that it was nearly painful to think about him without wanting him this way. Hearing him say he loved her like he'd never loved anyone—even if he was saying that to his ex—was the best thing she'd ever heard from anyone. Not that she was surprised to hear he loved her. He'd been demonstrating that to her every day since she'd been badly hurt by her ex-boyfriend.

As she'd recovered from her injuries, Cam had been nothing but patient, kind and devoted. They'd spent hours kissing and touching each other until she'd felt like she'd die if she had to wait any longer for what they both wanted.

"Cam."

"Hmm?"

"I want... I need..."

"What, honey? Tell me."

"I want you. Now." To make her point, she reached down to cup his erection, giving him a squeeze to make sure he understood what she was asking for.

"Are you sure?"

"If I were any surer, I'd spontaneously combust."

"We can't have that."

"Please, Cameron. I'm totally fine, and I want this. I want *you*."

He tugged on the button to her jeans.

Gigi pushed them off, leaving her in a tiny pair of panties that matched her bra. And yes, she'd planned for this outcome tonight, determined to move things forward before Jaycee had taken care of that for her.

"You're so fucking sexy, Gigi. You have no idea how crazy you make me."

"I think I know, since you make me just as crazy."

He helped her out of the panties and tossed them aside before leaning over to press his tongue to her core.

She was so primed that one stroke was all it took to trigger an orgasm that had her moaning and thrashing.

Jeffrey barked, which made them laugh.

"Should he be seeing this?" Gigi asked as she tried to catch her breath.

"Hold that thought." He put a blanket over her. "I'll put him upstairs."

Cameron got up to relocate the dog and returned, wearing only boxer briefs that hugged his large erection. He tossed a strip of condoms on the coffee table.

Gigi licked her lips and held out her arms to him.

He pulled the blanket back and came down on top of her, devouring her with deep, drugging kisses that had her squirming under him, desperate for more.

"Cam..."

"Yes, love?"

"I want you right now."

He drew back to remove his underwear and roll on a condom.

Gigi watched him, taking note of every detail of his muscular body, wanting to remember this for the rest of her life. But then he was pushing into her, and that required her full attention. Holy shit. He was huge and hot and hard and perfect. Nothing had ever felt this good.

She moaned, and he paused.

"Did I hurt you?"

"You'll only hurt me if you stop."

"Got it." He grinned as he pushed into her. "How do you feel?"

"Amazed."

"Yeah?"

She looked up at him and nodded. "That I might've missed this..." Her eyes filled. "I would've hated to miss this."

Cameron rested his forehead on hers. "Me, too." As he shifted his weight to press into her again, the living room window shattered, spraying shards of glass all over them. A brick landed a foot from them. "What the fuck?" He withdrew from Gigi and got up, glass falling from his back as he made his way to the broken window.

"Cam! Your feet!"

Gigi reached for her phone on the coffee table and called 911, while Jeffrey barked frantically upstairs. "This is Detective Dominguez. I'm with Detective Green, and someone just threw a brick through his window. Can you send Patrol, please?" she asked, giving the address.

"They're on the way, Detective. Do you need EMS?"

"No, thank you."

Cameron carefully made his way back to her, his outraged expression one she'd never seen before as he handed her sweater to her. "I'm sorry."

"Don't be." Gigi put on the sweater, because it was quickly getting cold in there, and reached for her jeans.

"Wait. Don't move." He pulled a huge shard of glass from her hair and put it on the coffee table. "I'm going to fucking nail her to the wall for this."

"I'll help you."

Sam woke to a text from Detective Green letting her know what'd happened overnight at his home. *I'm a hundred percent sure it's Jaycee. She was waiting for us when we got home last night, told me she was pregnant, and it was mine. I told her I didn't believe her and said to get lost. The brick landed a foot from where Gigi and I were, glass all over us. No more "favors" for her. Patrol is looking for her. No sign of her at her place or her parents' house.*

Agree on no more favors, Sam said. *I'll be in shortly and will do whatever I can to help.*

"What's going on?" Nick asked.

"Cameron Green's ex threw a brick through his window last night, just missing him and Gigi."

"And he knows his ex did it?"

"They'd had an encounter with her, even though both detectives were under a protective order that was supposed to keep her away from them. She's a psycho. She's already slashed his tires and spent a night in lockup. I had a talk with her and thought we'd reached an understanding. Apparently, that's not the case." She leaned over to kiss him. "Morning."

"Morning, and welcome to another day in paradise."

"Yep. It never ends in our version of paradise."

"Do you honestly never think about the day when none of this will be our problem?"

"I can't envision that, no matter how hard I try. What will we *do* with ourselves?"

His hand landed on her abdomen under her shirt. "I can think of a few things."

"We can only do so much of *that*. What do we do with the other twelve hours we're awake?"

"I'm sure we'll find something interesting."

"More interesting than what we're doing now? I doubt that."

"So, what you're saying is that these are the best years of our lives, and everything else will pale in comparison?" Nick asked.

"Well, I hope not, but that's probably true. Adrenaline junkies like us don't just come off it without some withdrawal issues."

"I'm not an adrenaline junkie. You are."

"Yes, I am, and I can't imagine giving that up, as frustrating as it can be at times like this. And with that, I must get going. Today's the day we're making our FDS case to the mayor, and I need to go over everything again beforehand."

"Good luck with that. I hope you can convince her to give it a try."

"Me, too. If we can't, I'm not sure we'll ever get this guy."

"You will, but who knows how many more women will be attacked and murdered before you do?"

"That's exactly the point I plan to hammer home."

"No one hammers things home quite like my cop." He smiled as he kissed her. "Want some company in the shower?"

"Always."

"How much longer until we can go back to doing it in the shower?" he asked a few minutes later as they stood together under the warm water.

Sam grimaced at the thought of assuming that position. "Not for a while yet."

Wrapping his arms around her, he held her close. "This will have to suffice in the meantime, and it's hardly a consolation prize."

"Note to self—a broken hip is the ultimate cockblocker."

His low chuckle made her smile. "Thanks for this perfect start to what promises to be another crazy day."

"Always a pleasure to start the day naked with you, even if my hip is cockblocking us."

"We'll make up for it in Bora Bora."

"God, I can't wait for that. And in the meantime, I owe you—as well as several family members and friends—another weekend at Camp David to make up for the lost vacation."

"Let's do that after the State of the Union."

Sam kissed him. "It's a date."

CHAPTER TWENTY-THREE

Vernon and Jimmy delivered her to the morgue entrance just over an hour later. She'd helped get Scotty and the twins up for school and had breakfast with them before leaving Celia in charge until they would leave with their respective details. Thank God for Celia, who was always there when Sam needed her and seemed to be loving her new life in the White House. She'd told Sam that everyone she knew was jealous that she got to live there and be part of their grand adventure.

Sam was glad she saw it that way. After they'd lost Skip, she'd worried about Celia, who'd not only been his wife but also his devoted caregiver for the last four years. It gave Sam great pleasure to give her beloved stepmother something exciting to partially fill the gaping void Skip's death had left in both their lives.

The move to the White House had done that for Sam, too, if she was being honest. It had shaken things up and removed them from their Ninth Street homes, where the ramps they'd never need again were a constant reminder of their loss.

Sam stepped through the door by the morgue and nearly ran smack into Ramsey. She recoiled, her hip twinging in response to the unexpected movement.

"Get out of the way," he growled as he brushed by her.

"I'm not in your way."

He slammed out without another word, thankfully.

"What's going on?" Sam asked Lindsey, who'd stepped out of the morgue.

"I heard he had a screaming fight with Erica Lucas, but I haven't gotten any of the details."

"I'll see what I can find out. What else is going on?"

"I finished the exam on Woo and sent the report over."

"Anything new?"

"Nothing other than confirmation that the DNA matches the earlier cases, and he's not at all concerned about leaving his calling card behind."

"That's because he's not in the system, and he knows it, so he's confident he's going to keep getting away with it."

"Son of a bitch," Lindsey said. "Where are you with trying FDS?"

"Meeting with the mayor later this afternoon to make the case."

"Good luck. I hope you can sway her. This guy is getting high off his own success. It's only a matter of time before he strikes again."

"I agree. Did you hear what happened at Green's last night?"

"Everyone is talking about it. I saw him and Dominguez together at the Christmas Eve party, but I hadn't heard they were officially a couple."

"It's a recent development that's not going over well with Green's ex-girlfriend. She'd decided they were getting married and had even gone so far as to book a venue, which was news to him."

"Wow, that's pretty effed up."

"She's a piece of work. She disparaged Gigi's ethnicity to me when I had words with her the last time we had her in lockup."

"Ew."

"Exactly. She showed her ass in a big way, and he heard the whole ugly thing. I just feel sorry for Cam and Gigi that they're dealing with this on top of everything else they've already been through with her ex."

Lindsey shook her head in dismay. "They're certainly being tested."

"Yep. Let me go see where we are in tracking down his ex."

"Have a good one."

"You, too, Doc."

Sam arrived in the pit to find everyone standing around Green's cubicle as he updated them on the goings-on the night before.

"The brick just missed hitting us," he said, running his fingers through his hair, which was standing on end. His usually pressed-and-polished appearance was disheveled, and he looked as if he'd been up all night.

"Any sign of Jaycee?" Sam asked him.

"Nothing yet. I've looked in all the usual places."

"You shouldn't be the one looking for her, which you know," Sam said.

"I just looked. I would've called for backup if I'd seen her."

"You've notified airports, train stations, bus depots, etc.?"

"Everything."

Sam should've known. He was nothing if not thorough.

His cell phone rang, and he pounced on it. "It's Jaycee's mother." He took the call, putting it on speaker. "Mrs. Patrick, thank you for returning my call."

"I can't believe Jaycee would do something like this, Cameron."

"She's already slashed my tires."

"What?"

"She didn't tell you she spent a night in jail after that?"

"No, she didn't. She's been extremely upset since you broke up with her, but this…"

"She's more than upset. She's dangerous. She almost hit me and my new girlfriend with the brick, not to mention the shattered glass all over us."

"How do you know it was her?"

"She was waiting for me outside my place when we got home last night. I told her again it was over between us and asked her to leave before I called the police. The brick came through my window half an hour later. It's being tested now for prints to see if they match what we have on file for her. I strongly suspect it'll be a match."

"I'm so sorry, Cameron." The woman sounded tearful now. "She hasn't been herself."

Sam wanted to object to that. She suspected *this* was the real Jaycee, not the sweet, unassuming side she'd shown Cameron before he'd ended things with her.

"She told me she was pregnant and tried to pass it off as mine. If she is pregnant, there's no way it's mine. We haven't been together that way in months."

"I… I don't know what to say."

"Can you help us find her before she makes this worse somehow?"

"Y-yes, of course. Whatever I can do."

"Mrs. Patrick, this is Lieutenant Holland. Detectives Cruz and McBride are on the way to your house. When they get there, please call Jaycee and ask her to come home. Tell her it's an emergency. Will you do that?"

"Yes, I will. I just… This isn't the girl I raised."

After hearing the hateful things Jaycee had said about Gigi, Sam had so much she'd like to say to that, but she bit her tongue. The goal was to find and arrest Jaycee, not antagonize her mother.

"The detectives will be there shortly. Please don't do anything until they arrive."

"I won't."

"Thanks, Mrs. Patrick," Cameron said. "I'll be in touch." He ended the call and looked up at Sam. "I hope this works."

"One way or another," Sam said, "we'll find her."

THE MAYOR MOVED their meeting to earlier in the day. Sam rode to city hall with Farnsworth and Malone in a police SUV.

"Nothing like being followed by the Secret Service," the chief said as he glanced in the side-view mirror.

"They're good to have around in a pinch," Sam said.

"Listen to you," Malone said from the driver's seat, "getting all Zen-like about having a detail."

"I've gotten used to them, and they're very good about staying out of my way. Not to mention, it's been convenient to have them drive me around since the hip thing happened."

"We're all glad you have extra eyes on you, Lieutenant," Farnsworth said. "Your sky-high profile gives me nightmares."

"I know it's not ideal, but I'm making it work."

"Not ideal," Farnsworth said on a huff of laughter. "That's putting it mildly." He glanced over his shoulder at her in the back. "The mayor will try to hard-sell you on the deputy chief thing again. You know that, right?"

"What? No, she won't. We put that to rest."

"*You* put it to rest. She hasn't. It's come up again several times since she first proposed it. She wants you."

"I told her I don't want it, and I haven't changed my mind about that."

"You should consider it, Sam," the chief said. "It'd get you off the streets, which is more dangerous than ever for you now that Nick is president."

A streak of panic cut through Sam, leaving her breathless. "Sir, with all due respect, I *do not want* to be deputy chief."

"For what it's worth," Malone said, glancing at her in the rearview mirror, "I agree with him."

Sam took a deep breath and tried to calm herself before she said things to her bosses that couldn't be taken back. "I understand you're concerned and that you both feel extra protective toward me because my dad is gone, and you were his best friends. But please... Don't encourage her on this. I'd rather retire than be the deputy chief, and I'm not in any way interested in retiring either."

"We do worry about you," Malone said. "More than any other officer on our team. Everyone knows who you are, and you'd make for a very appealing prize."

"Which is why I have the detail—and a partner. I appreciate the concern. I really do, but I'm fine. Nothing needs to change."

Sam's BlackBerry dinged with a text from Nick. *Nevins has been arraigned on federal terrorism charges and threatening the life of the president. The ATF found bomb-making materials in his house and tied him to the device that was left at the gates. One less thing to worry about.*

That's good news, she replied, wishing she could tell him her new worry—that the captain and chief would insist on moving her to an admin role that didn't interest her in any way. But he'd know it was because of him, and he'd hate that. So she kept it to herself, even as the panicky feeling stuck with her. They couldn't force her to take a job, could they?

That question spiked her anxiety. "What happened with Ramsey and Lucas?" she asked, eager to change the subject.

"She took over his cases after he was fired, and now he wants them back," Malone said. "Lucas has made progress on them and didn't want to give them up. He went off on her, and I sent him home."

"Is she okay?"

"She's fine. She sat back and let him do what he does and didn't say a word, according to witnesses."

"Good for her." Sam made a mental note to check in with her friend later. "If the mayor wants a great deputy chief, I still say it ought to be her. She's one of the best officers I've ever worked with."

"I'd hate to lose her in SVU, though," Farnsworth said. "She's excellent with the victims."

"That's true," Sam said, regretting she'd mentioned the deputy chief position again.

Fortunately, they arrived at the Wilson Building at 1350 Pennsylvania Avenue a few minutes later and parked in a VIP area.

Vernon and Jimmy pulled in behind them, and Vernon got out to accompany her inside.

They secured their weapons at the security checkpoint, were

screened by a magnetometer and their belongings put through an X-ray machine.

Heads turned and people expressed surprise at seeing the first lady as they walked to the mayor's suite. The attention only reinforced the chief and captain's argument, Sam thought. *That's just what I don't need.*

They were shown to the mayor's conference room and offered refreshments.

"We're fine, thanks," the chief said for all of them. After the admin left them, he said, "That's the first time I've ever been offered refreshments here. They're dazzled by you, Lieutenant. I need to bring you with me more often when I meet with the mayor."

"I'm too busy for that stuff." She read a text from Freddie. *At the Patrick house, the mother called her, told her it was an emergency. Waiting to see if she'll come.*

Be prepared for anything, Sam replied. *She's unpredictable.*

That's what Cam said, too. Good luck with the mayor.

Thanks. Waiting for her now.

Mayor Monique Brewster came into the room, thanking them for coming in earlier than planned. To Sam, she added, "Nice to see you again, Lieutenant."

"You, too, ma'am."

"It feels strange to have the first lady calling me ma'am," Brewster said on a laugh.

"You're still my boss, ma'am."

"I suppose that's true."

The chief chuckled. "As I like to say, ain't nobody the boss of her."

The mayor laughed.

"That is just not true," Sam said. "And the reason we're here is because we need your help on a case."

"My help? What can I do?"

"You've heard about the recent sexual assaults and murders in Rock Creek Park, I assume."

"I have," the mayor said with a sigh. "It's terrible."

Sam had come ready for this. She placed photos of the women who'd been raped and murdered on the table in front of the mayor, introducing each of them to her. "Audrey Olsen was a teacher who devoted her spare time to teaching English as a second language to immigrant children. She'd lived with her boyfriend, Wes, and had dated him for five years, since they were nineteen. He told me he was planning to propose to her on Valentine's Day, which was, incidentally, the day they met.

"This is Ling Woo, a biomedical engineering graduate student at Georgetown, the first of her family to attend college and, by all accounts, a brilliant scientist. She'd recently started running again as a New Year's resolution. Both women were assaulted and murdered in Rock Creek Park. These other two victims were 'lucky' to escape with their lives but are dealing with trauma that'll stay with them forever. Kaitlyn Oliver told us she doesn't feel safe anywhere, even in her own home. And Moira Kaull is so traumatized, we've yet to be able to interview her. These four victims have one thing in common—they were all attacked from behind by the same man in the vicinity of Rock Creek Park."

"What can I do to help get this guy?" Brewster asked.

"We've exhausted our usual investigative techniques, having spent countless hours canvassing the park and surrounding neighborhoods, reviewing thousands of hours of video, interviewing forty potential witnesses and thoroughly investigating each of our victims."

"Oh Lord. You have *nothing*?"

"Nothing except his DNA, which doesn't help us unless the man has been arrested in the past, which he hasn't been. We'd like you to authorize an exception to the District's prohibition on using familial DNA searches in police investigations and allow us to run his DNA for a familial match."

Brewster was shaking her head before Sam completed the sentence. "Absolutely not."

"We understand and respect the many objections to the use of FDS," Sam said. "However, we're at a standstill in this case, and we believe the killer is becoming more confident because he's getting away with what he's done. He knows he's not in the system. He knows we're not any closer to him today than we were after the first assault. He's emboldened by that reality, and he'll kill again unless we stop him. You can help us stop him, ma'am."

Brewster sat back in her seat, deflated. "I have so many concerns about this technology, which is why I wrote the resolution that outlawed it. A majority of the people with DNA on file are minorities, which stacks the deck unfairly."

"I realize that and agree with your objections," Sam said. "I'm not asking for a rollback of the resolution. I'm asking for a one-time exception."

"And if it works in this case, you'll be back again."

"You have my word that we will do that only if we've already exhausted every other possible option," Farnsworth said.

The mayor touched each of the photos of the four women who'd been attacked. "I don't know what to do."

"Please let us search for a familial match." Sam slid a piece of paper across the table to her. "Sign the waiver making an exception in this one case. Let's stop this monster before he can kill another innocent woman."

Brewster stared at the paper for a full minute before she pulled it toward her and signed it. "Please don't make me regret this."

"We won't," Sam said. "But if we make a match, we'll need to disclose that we were given an exception. That's apt to cause some blowback for you."

"I can handle that if you catch this guy."

"We'll do our best. Thank you, ma'am."

"Before you rush off, have you given any more thought to my offer of a promotion?"

Sam, who'd been on her way to a clean escape, sat back down. "No, ma'am. Honestly, I haven't thought of it again since the day we last spoke about it. My position hasn't changed since then. I don't want the job."

Farnsworth gave her a look.

"Even if I'm honored to have been considered, ma'am."

"I really wish you'd consider it, Lieutenant. It's an amazing opportunity to put a woman who's truly earned it in a position of leadership within the department."

"I agree," Sam said. "As long as that woman isn't me."

"You're the one I want."

"And I appreciate that, but if that's the only job I'm allowed to do, I'd leave the department."

Brewster tipped her head as if she hadn't heard that right. "For real?"

"As real as it gets," Sam said. "I believe people are born to do certain things. For some of us, it takes us a while to figure out what that thing is. I've always known what my thing is. From the time I was a little kid following my dad around, I wanted to do what he did. I wanted to find the killers and lock them up. It's not just what I do, ma'am. It's *who I am*. If I can't do that job for the District, I'll find somewhere that I can do it."

Sam held the other woman's gaze for a long moment, determined not to be the first to blink.

Brewster finally sighed and looked down at the table. "I figured it was worth one more shot before I moved on."

"There're many outstanding female officers in the department who could fill that role honorably," Sam said. "I'd be happy to help you with a short list of candidates, including my own colleague in Homicide, Detective McBride."

Brewster's eyes lit up at the mention of Jeannie, the star of the moment. "Do you think she'd be interested?"

"I'd be delighted to ask her."

"Please do that and get back to me, if you would. Even before the recent investigation that yielded such remarkable results, I was certainly familiar with Detective McBride's work, as well as her resilience. Not to mention, I'd love to see a Black woman in a command position."

"I'll let you know what she says." Sam glanced at Farnsworth and Malone, hoping they'd help to extricate her from the meeting so she could get back to work.

"Thank you so much for your time, Monique," Farnsworth said. "We deeply appreciate your support."

"Please get this guy."

Sam gathered up the photos and put them back in her file folder. "We'll do everything we can."

She put through a call to Gonzo the second she stepped outside the mayor's suite. "Green light on FDS. Get that moving with Lindsey and the lab."

"What about Forrester?" he asked of the U.S. Attorney.

"The chief spoke with him about it. He said if Brewster okayed it, his team would accept any evidence it produces." Before they'd gone to the mayor, they'd had to be certain the team prosecuting the case would be on board with the investigative tactic. "Give the go-ahead to the lab for a familial search. Tell them we have the signed exception from the mayor and will send it over as soon as I get back to the office."

"I'm on it. Let's hope it gets us something—and sooner rather than later."

"Fingers and toes are crossed. Any word from Cruz and McBride?"

"Not yet."

"If this woman is unhinged enough to throw a brick through a window, knowing there're two cops inside, what'll she do when she's cornered?"

"That's what I'm afraid of."

CHAPTER TWENTY-FOUR

F reddie and Jeannie sat at the kitchen table with Mrs. Patrick, who stared at her phone, seemingly without blinking.

"She always calls me right back. *Always.*"

"Are you able to track her?" Jeannie asked.

"I tried that. She's turned off her location. She never does that, because she knows how I worry about her. Do you think something has happened to her?"

"I think she's trying to avoid being arrested—again."

"Cameron is trying to make her look bad to make himself feel better about dumping her right before their wedding."

"Mrs. Patrick, there was no wedding. Cameron never asked her to marry him and had no intention of proposing."

"You people need to leave my home. Clearly, you're on the side of your colleague and are trying to make my daughter into something she isn't. I thought he was such a nice young man."

"He's a very nice young man," Jeannie said, "and your daughter threw a brick through his window last night, narrowly missing him and another officer who was with him."

"You can't prove it was her!"

"Actually, we can," Freddie said. "We're testing the brick right now to see if her prints are on it. They're on file from when she was arrested."

Jeannie's phone chimed with a text. "We've received notification that her prints are on the brick."

"This is a setup!"

"No, it isn't." Freddie struggled to stay patient when he wanted to arrest the woman for being obtuse. If only that were a chargeable offense. "We need to find her before this gets worse. Where would she be?"

The woman folded her arms over her ample bosom. "I have no idea."

"You're not helping her by stonewalling us," Jeannie said. "In fact, if you know where she is and don't help us find her, you can be charged as an accessory."

That seemed to permeate the aura of denial the woman had been putting forth. "She couldn't have done this," she said with much less conviction than she'd shown thus far.

"She did do it," Jeannie said. "Where is she?" When Mrs. Patrick didn't reply, Jeannie slapped her hand on the table, making her startle. "*Where is she?*"

"She... You should check... her grandmother's house."

"Write down the address." Freddie pushed a notebook and pen across the table to her. "And make sure it's correct. You've wasted enough of our time."

After she wrote down the address in Stafford, Virginia, Freddie stood, grabbed the notebook and pen and headed for the door.

"If you tell her we're coming," Jeannie said as she followed him, "we'll be back to arrest you." When they were outside, Jeannie said, "For fuck's sake."

"That's exactly what Sam would say."

"I learned from the best—and so did Jaycee, apparently. No wonder she is the way she is if that's her mother. The girl probably got away with everything short of murder growing up, and now thinks she's entitled to have whatever she wants—even a man who doesn't want her."

"That about sums it up."

While Freddie drove, Jeannie called Malone with an update on their progress. "Can you request a warrant in case she makes this difficult?"

"Yep. Contact Stafford County to back you up, and keep me posted."

"Will do." Jeannie ended that call and placed another to Stafford to request backup, adding, "It's important to keep the cars hidden until we arrive so we don't tip her off."

"Understood. We'll send two cars right away and request they hold back until you arrive."

"Thank you."

"What a freaking waste of time this is," Jeannie said. "We've got better things to be doing than chasing down a lunatic who can't take no for an answer."

"We're on hold with the serial rapist case until we get the FDS results," Freddie said. "And P.S., good job with the mother."

"She was pissing me off. If I ever lie to cops on behalf of my kid, give me a slap upside the head, will you?"

"I suspect that won't be an issue for you or your future child."

"I'd smack the crap out of my kid if they behaved the way Jaycee has."

"I hear you. Me, too."

When they arrived in the grandmother's neighborhood, Jeannie called Stafford County to let them know they were pulling up to the address.

"Our officers are ready to provide backup, Detective."

"Thanks again."

Freddie and Jeannie parked on the street and walked up a long driveway.

"That's her car." Freddie pointed to a white Nissan Altima. "I remember it from the time we watched Cam play football when he was seeing her."

They waited for the Stafford officers to join them.

"Can you take the back?" he asked Jeannie and two of the officers.

"Yep."

"Be ready for her to run."

"I hope she does," Jeannie said as she went around to the back of the house with two of the Stafford officers, while the other two stood off to the side as Freddie knocked on the door.

When an older woman answered, he showed her his badge. "I'm looking for Jaycee Patrick."

"She's not here."

"Yes, she is. That's her car. Can you please ask her to come to the door? It's either that, or we're coming in after her."

"You can't come in here without a warrant."

Freddie held up his phone as if to say he already had the warrant, though he was still waiting. She didn't need to know that. "What's it going to be? The easy way or the hard way?"

The woman stepped back from the door and turned. "Jaycee! Come here right now."

A flash of movement inside caught Freddie's attention. "She's heading for the back door," he called to the other officers.

He bolted from the front porch and ran around the house to help Jeannie take her down as she came out the back door. They had her facedown on the ground and cuffed before she knew what hit her.

"That was fun," Jeannie said as Jaycee screamed about police brutality.

"Most fun I've had all day."

"I'll have your badges for this," Jaycee said, her face purple with outrage.

"Knock yourself out," Jeannie said as they walked her back to the car to transport her to the city jail.

They thanked the Stafford officers for their assistance and were heading back to the District in a matter of minutes.

"Can you text Cam to let him know we got her?" Freddie asked. "Tell the others, too."

"Yep."

Jaycee shrieked all the way back to DC, while they ignored her.

CAMERON CALLED GIGI AT HOME. "They've got her."

"Well, that's a relief. Where was she?"

"Hiding out at her grandmother's in Stafford. Cruz and McBride arrested her and said she made quite the scene."

"Why am I not surprised?"

"I'm so sorry about all this and what she interrupted."

"You have nothing to be sorry about, Cam, and we can pick right up where we left off the next time we have a night off together."

"I'm not going to like working opposite shifts."

"I could move to days with a different unit," she said.

"You like this one."

"I'm sick of working nights, though."

"Let's not do anything hasty. We'll figure it out."

"How soon will Jaycee make bail?"

"Probably by the end of the day."

"And then what?"

"I hate to say it, but we need to be on our guard—all the time. She's proven how unstable she is. I don't want to scare you, but she blames you for our breakup even though you had nothing to do with it."

"Don't worry about me. If she's stupid enough to come for me, I'll be ready for her."

"That scares the hell out of me, Gigi. You can't let anything happen to you right when we've finally got everything we've ever wanted."

"Nothing will happen to me. I wouldn't miss this with you for anything."

Cameron blew out a deep breath as the sleepless night started to catch up to him. He ran his hand over the stubble on his jaw. "I'll call you later?"

"Please do and try not to be upset about Jaycee. This has nothing to do with us."

"Keep telling me that, okay?"

"Anytime you need to hear it. Love you."

"Yeah," he said, suddenly emotional at hearing those words again. "You, too."

As he ended the call, Sam came into the pit and made her way over to him. "I heard they got her."

"They did."

"And she's making a stink."

"Not surprised. What I want to know is how long will it be before she makes bail, and how am I going to do anything but worry about Gigi? Jaycee's convinced she's been wronged and is blaming everyone but herself." He looked up at Sam. "After what Gigi went through with her ex, this is the last thing she needs to deal with. How do I make it stop?"

"I wish I had an easy answer, but I'm afraid you have to ride it out until she gets the message that it's over with you."

"I don't know what I'll do if she goes after Gigi."

"Maybe you need to talk to Jaycee again when they get back. Look her in the eye and tell her again that it's over and nothing will change that, especially slashing your tires or throwing a brick through your window."

"I suppose it can't make anything worse to try that again." Although the thought of having to see her after what she'd done made him sick.

"I'm sorry you're going through this."

Cameron sat up a little straighter, determined to shake off the drama. "I'm sorry to bring this crap to work with me."

"Where else would you bring it?"

"I heard you got the green light on FDS. I can't wait to see what that does for us."

"I just hope it does *something*."

"Yeah, me, too."

WHEN FREDDIE and Jeannie returned with Jaycee in custody half an hour later, Sam heard her before she saw her.

Sam stepped out of the office. "Shut up."

The blonde woman recoiled as if no one had ever spoken to her like that before.

"I thought we'd reached an understanding the last time you were our guest in the city jail."

"I didn't do anything! These officers should be arrested for how they treated me—and my grandmother."

"Jaycee, you threw a brick through Detective Green's window last night, and we can prove that. Your fingerprints are all over it. So quit with the woe-is-me nonsense."

"You can't prove it was me."

Sam glanced at Freddie, who seemed as annoyed as Sam felt. "We can prove it was you, and you're being charged with malicious mischief and violating a protective order. If you keep it up, we'll add threatening the lives of two police officers to the charges, which is a much bigger deal. Do you know what a *felony* is, Jaycee?" Sam purposely spoke slowly, the way you would to a child or a dimwit. She wasn't sure which word best described Jaycee.

"Yes, I know what that is," she said through clenched teeth.

"You're *this close* to being charged with two of them." Sam held her fingers together. "Do you know what kind of time you'll do if you're convicted on felony assault charges? It could be as much as a decade, possibly longer because you certainly won't get time off for good behavior. So I'd suggest that you shut the fuck up before we add to the charges. You got me?"

"I didn't do *anything*."

"So you say. Cruz, put her in interview one."

He gave her a questioning look.

Sam used her chin to tell him to do it.

"Cameron, do what you can. Freddie will go in with you."

"Thank you, Lieutenant."

SAM DUCKED into the observation room, eager to see how Cameron would handle this ridiculous situation. She felt for him. He was one of the most professional officers she'd ever worked with and knew how upset he had to be that his ex-girlfriend was causing trouble for everyone.

Malone came in and closed the door. "What's the plan?"

"Cam is going to try to convince her to knock this shit off. If I don't like what she says, I'll ask the USA to up the charges to felony assault of police officers."

When Cameron stepped into the interrogation room, Jaycee visibly brightened, shifting out of the slump she'd fallen into, her gaze taking him in hungrily, so hungrily that Sam immediately feared that nothing he could say would persuade her to leave him alone.

"What's it going to take?" Cameron asked Jaycee, hands on his hips and annoyance in his tone. "What do I have to do to get you to leave me alone?"

"You don't mean that! You said you loved me, and I believed you!"

"I did love you. I don't anymore, and if you think slashing my tires, insulting my new girlfriend or throwing a brick through my window is going to 'bring me around,' you're insane."

Her eyes flashed with outrage. "I am not insane. You made promises to me."

"No, I didn't. I never promised you anything but a good time, and you know that. We never talked about marriage or anything beyond basic dating."

"Were you banging her at the same time you were doing me?"

"What? No, I wasn't banging anyone else, and you know that, too."

"One minute, you were with me, and the next, you were gone. It's because of her, right? That..."

"Don't say another word about her," Cameron said. "This has nothing to do with her and everything to do with us and what wasn't working for me."

"What wasn't working for you? What changed?"

"I don't know, Jaycee, but it was a realization, over time, that we'd run out of steam."

"Because you found someone you liked better than me."

"That didn't happen until after we were done. I was honest with you when I told you I wanted out. I'm not going to change my mind, and your harassment is only making me wonder what I ever saw in you in the first place."

"Don't say that," Jaycee said, tears spilling from her eyes. "You don't mean that!"

"Yes, I do. This has to stop. We gave you a huge break the last time, and you still came back for more. My boss is considering felony charges because you attacked my house knowing there were police officers inside. You'll do years in jail if she pursues those charges. Is that what you want?"

"What I want is *you*. What I want is what you promised me."

Cameron took a deep breath and held it for a second before releasing it. "Then I'm sorry, but I can't do anything to help you. Detective Cruz will call your lawyer if you let him know who you'd like to represent you."

"I don't need a lawyer."

"Yes, Jaycee, you do." Cameron walked out of the room, ignoring her cries for him to come back.

Sam left the observation room and went to meet him in the hallway. "You did everything you could—more than she deserved."

He looked at the floor, seeming defeated. "What're you going to do?"

"Since she's unable to see reason and unlikely to stop this, I recommend we ask the USA to file felony charges. But only if you agree."

"I hate this. I hate everything about it, especially having you involved."

"It isn't your fault."

"Why does it feel like it is?"

"It's not. You were straight with her. She didn't like it. That's on her, not you."

"I'd never consider felony charges if it wasn't for Gigi."

"For what it's worth, I think you're right to be concerned about her."

"If anything happened to her because of me…"

"It wouldn't be because of you, Cameron. Tell me you know that."

"I do, but…"

"Let me talk to the AUSA and see what they want to do about charges. In the meantime, I want you to go home and get some rest."

"No, that's okay."

"That wasn't a request, Detective. Go home. We'll take it from here."

He stood up straighter. "I'm sorry about all this."

"No apologies needed. Take care of yourself, get some rest, shake it off and come back in the morning."

"Thank you, Lieutenant."

Sam nodded and watched him go, noting the unusual hunch to his shoulders.

"That was well done, Lieutenant," Malone said when he joined her in the hallway.

"Were you eavesdropping, Captain?"

"As a matter of fact, I was."

Sam smiled. "The poor guy. He's always so professional. Having this invade his workplace is tearing him up."

"He'll be all right."

"After she makes bail, I'd like to temporarily put some officers on him and Detective Dominguez. Just to be safe."

"I'll run that up the flagpole and let you know. Were you aware of his relationship with Detective Dominguez?"

"Not only was I aware, but I was also the one who made *him* aware of it."

Malone's brows furrowed in confusion. "How's that?"

"I saw something happening there he wasn't fully aware of yet and gave him a subtle push."

"I wasn't aware that you were capable of subtlety."

Amused, Sam said, "I have many hidden talents."

"I'm not touching that. We have no concerns about an interoffice romance?"

"They work different shifts, neither reports to the other, and both are exceptionally professional. I'm fine with it."

"Excuse me, Lieutenant?"

CHAPTER TWENTY-FIVE

S am turned to find Jesse Best looming in the hallway. "Hey, Jesse. How's it going?"

"I wondered if I could have a word with you and Detective McBride? You're welcome to join us, Captain."

"Sure," Sam said. "Let me get her. We'll meet you in the conference room."

"You go ahead," Malone said. "I'll save you some steps and get her."

"Thanks."

"How're you doing?" Best asked.

"Much better than I was, but ready to be rid of the cane that makes me feel ninety."

"Don't rush it. My dad had the same injury and had no patience with the rehab and ended up having a second surgery."

Sam grimaced. "That would suck."

"It did, and truthfully, he was never the same after that. Do what you're told, Lieutenant."

"For once in my life?"

He grunted out a chuckle. "You said that. Not me."

Sam took a seat at the table across from Best. "Are you okay? You look exhausted."

"I haven't slept in three days, but that's not uncommon."

Before Sam could express shock at that, McBride and Malone came in and closed the door.

"Detective McBride, I wanted to give you an update on the

Carisma Deasly case, which has become the Daniella Brown and Xavier Iker case. We've tied them to more than two hundred missing children and young adults. We suspect there'll be more before we're done."

"Jesus," Sam said on a whisper.

"Carisma is due to be released from the hospital tomorrow and will be going home with her mother. They've asked to see you, Detective."

"I... I'll call LaToya and set it up," Jeannie said.

"We're holding a press conference tomorrow at our office and would like to have you there, since this is technically your case, your bust," Best said.

Jeannie glanced at Sam, who nodded. "You definitely need to be there."

"Thank you for including me," Jeannie said.

"We wouldn't be where we are right now without your fine work, Detective. I'll send you the details of the press conference as soon as I have them." Best got up to leave the room. "See you tomorrow."

"He's not long on small talk, is he?" Sam asked.

"Never has been," Malone said. "But the man is good at what he does."

"What's his story, anyway?" Sam asked. "I've worked with him for years but hardly know him."

"His younger sister was kidnapped when they were kids. She wasn't found, but he's never stopped looking for her. His entire professional life is fueled by his obsession with missing people, especially his sister."

"Wow," Sam said, deeply moved. "I don't know how people can bear to live when their loved ones are missing. I'd go mad."

"I would, too," Jeannie said.

"While we have you," Sam said to Jeannie, "we had an interesting chat with the mayor this morning. Your name came up."

"How so?" Jeannie asked, brows furrowed.

"First of all, she was impressed—as we all are—with your work on the Deasly case, but she also mentioned a job opening that she thought might interest you."

Jeannie gave her a wary look. "What opening is that?"

"Deputy chief."

Sam enjoyed watching Jeannie's expression go completely flat with shock.

"*What?*"

"You heard me. She very much wants a woman in the post, and your name came up."

"What about you?"

"Can you picture me as the deputy chief?" Sam asked with a snort. "I'd be like a cat on a hot tin roof in that job, but I think you'd be great at it."

"Did she ask you first?"

"She mentioned it, but we all know I'd suck at it."

"Is this for real?" Jeannie asked, arms crossed.

"As real as it gets," Malone said.

"And the captains and the other higher-ups would be okay with a detective being promoted over them? Can that even happen?"

"It's not the norm," Malone said, "but the mayor's the boss. She wants a woman, and we're sadly lacking in women at the captain rank."

"There're other female lieutenants."

"None who have recently brought down a massive human trafficking ring," Sam said, "or survived a brutal attack that led to other high-profile arrests. She wants you."

"Because I'm Black—and female."

"That doesn't hurt anything," Malone said, "but without your accomplishments, your name wouldn't be in the mix."

"This is for real," Jeannie said, sounding incredulous. "Like, she really wants me?"

"She really does." Sam handed her the business card from the mayor. "She'd like you to call her."

Jeannie stared at the card for a long moment before she took it from Sam. "I, uh... You guys... *Seriously?*"

Sam laughed. "Dead seriously, and you should consider it, Jeannie. You're going to be a mom. This would take you off the streets and give you—more or less—a day job with regular hours."

"Congratulations," Malone said. "I hadn't heard about the baby."

"Oh, sorry," Sam said, wincing. "I didn't mean to blab."

"It's fine," Jeannie said. "People will find out soon enough, and thank you, Captain. We're excited." She took a deep breath and blew it out as she glanced his way. "Tell me the truth... Would people accept me as the deputy chief? People who are currently sergeants, lieutenants and captains?"

"At first, it might be rocky," Malone said. "I won't lie to you about that, but I think you could handle it. If you show up, do the job and don't let the promotion go to your head, which you won't, eventually people won't remember that you were promoted over more-senior officers. The bottom line is that the mayor is impressed by you and wants you for this position."

"Thank you for your candor, Captain. I need to speak to Michael about this before I call the mayor."

"Let us know what you decide," Sam said, "and congratulations. I couldn't be happier for you or prouder of you—and not just now, but always."

Jeannie blinked rapidly as if trying not to cry. "Goddamned pregnancy hormones."

Sam laughed. "Go call your husband and tell him the news."

"He's going to think I'm lying. Hell, *I* think I'm lying. I sure didn't see this coming. Thank you again, both of you, for your support."

"You got it," Sam said. After Jeannie left the room, she glanced at the captain. "I love when good things happen to good people."

"Which makes you an outstanding boss and friend, because most people would be envious of a colleague being promoted over them."

"I'm not at all envious of anyone who gets that job. Don't forget... I've had a bird's-eye view of what it's like moving from the streets to the admin suite. My dad hated that job for the first two years. He was bored senseless."

"I remember that," Malone said with a chuckle. "I had to talk him into coming to work most days."

"He was miserable, talked about retiring constantly. He even asked the chief to demote him back to detective, but Uncle Joe talked him out of that."

"Joe wanted his best friend riding shotgun. He admitted to being selfish about that, and over time, Skip grew into the job."

"I never would have. You know that, right?"

"Yes, Sam, we all know that. You're right where you belong here."

"I'll be very happy to spend the rest of my career in this office. I can't imagine anything I'd rather do than this, and on that note, can you check to see where we are with the FDS?"

"That's going to take months, well at least the national search will. The local one might be back sooner."

Sam moaned. "Why does it have to take so long?"

"We're asking multiple agencies to run our sample through their databases. We've told them it's 911, but I'm sure everyone who asks for this says that. We just have to be patient."

"And while we're being patient, we have to hope this guy doesn't kill again."

. . .

JEANNIE GRABBED her phone off her desk and told Matt she'd be right back. In a state of disbelief, she walked out to her car, got in and turned the engine on for heat. Then she took a couple of calming breaths before she called her husband.

"Hey, baby, this is a nice surprise."

They normally didn't talk during the day when they were both busy at work.

"Jeannie? Hello?"

"Sorry, I need to talk to you."

"Is everything okay? Are you all right?"

"I'm fine, but something happened just now…"

"You're freaking me out, sweetheart. What's wrong?"

"It's something good, at least I think it's good. I don't know."

"Quit talking in riddles and tell me what's going on."

"The mayor has asked me to consider being the deputy chief."

"Holy *shit*, Jeannie! That's amazing! I told you the Daniella Brown bust would turn out to be a good thing for you."

"It's not just that. She wants a woman. That I'm a Black woman makes me that much more appealing."

"Baby, you'd rock that job, or any job for that matter. They know how great you are, or they'd never be talking to you about this."

"You're not even slightly biased, though, right?" she asked, amused by his enthusiasm.

"I know how hard you work and how dedicated you are to the job. Others see that, too."

"I'm not sure I should do this."

"Why not? What's the downside?"

"I'd be skipping three ranks and suddenly outranking people who've been here a lot longer than I have. They'd probably cry foul. It's apt to be more headaches than anything, but the upside is it would get me off the streets and into a regular nine-to-five kind of job."

"That's a huge upside, especially with the baby coming."

"I know."

"Do you want the job?"

"I don't even know. It's not something I've considered for even a second, because it never occurred to me that I'd be offered it."

"Well, now you have, so you need to think about it. What does it entail?"

"It's a lot of admin stuff, budgeting, interaction with city hall, the council, that kind of stuff. I wouldn't be doing as much actual police work."

"Would you miss it? The police work?"

"I would, but I'd still consult on cases as needed, so I wouldn't be completely cut off from it, and after the Deasly case... I've just been so heartsick over that. As deputy chief, I could ask to oversee the review of Stahl's old cases to keep my hand in things."

"It sounds to me like you might be interested."

"Do you really think I could do it? That I could handle the blowback from the officers who'll cry foul about me being promoted over them?"

"I think you, my love, can handle anything that comes your way. You've already proven that countless times."

"I can't believe we're even talking about this. When I came to work this morning, I sure as hell didn't see this happening."

"I think you'd look super sexy in the white shirt, baby. Would you make me ask for permission to come to bed every night?"

Jeannie laughed. "You bet I would—and I'd make you salute me."

"I'd be happy to. This is such marvelous news. I couldn't be happier for you—or myself, because worrying about my pregnant wife chasing murderers is the stuff of nightmares."

"Am I going to call the mayor, then, and tell her I'm interested?"

"Only if it's what you really want, but my vote is an enthusiastic hell yes. They need you in a command role in that department. You could help fix the problems the FBI report identified and clean up Stahl's mess in addition to so many other contributions. You'd have real power to make changes."

"That part definitely appeals to me." She let out a nervous laugh. "I guess I'm going to do this."

"Congratulations, love. I'm so, so proud of you."

"Don't congratulate me until it happens."

"I'm congratulating you on being asked, and it *will* happen. If you make that call to the mayor, you'd better be ready for that."

"Jeez, am I really going to make that call?"

"Yes, you are. Now go do it and let me know how it goes. I'll be dying until I hear back from you."

"Don't do that. I need to keep you around."

"Then hurry up and call me back. I love you so much, and I couldn't be prouder."

"Thanks for the support. I love you, too. Here goes nothing."

"Call me back."

"I will."

Jeannie ended that call and gazed at the business card with the direct line to the mayor written on it in ink. She dug deep, searching for the Zen she'd worked so hard to find after being kidnapped and assaulted. Alas, there was no Zen or chill to be found in this surreal moment. Before she could talk herself out of it, she dialed the number and listened to it ring.

"Monique Brewster."

For a second, Jeannie was so surprised that the mayor herself answered that she forgot what she needed to say.

"Hello?"

"This is Detective Jeannie McBride."

"Detective McBride! I'm delighted you called."

"Thank you for thinking of me. I'm in shock, to be honest."

The mayor's laughter helped Jeannie to relax a bit. "I don't know why you'd be shocked after orchestrating some of the most important arrests in recent memory. Everyone is talking about you, Detective, and in the best possible way."

"Thank you, ma'am."

"I've been following your career since the earlier incident that we don't need to rehash now. But let me just say I admired the way you handled yourself after that, and your superiors have nothing but praise for you and your work. It's an honor to offer you the deputy chief position if you're interested."

This was it. "I'm interested—and nervous. It's not every day that a detective is promoted three ranks. I expect to have some pushback from my colleagues."

"Which I'm sure you'll handle with the aplomb and professionalism you've exhibited thus far. I made it clear from the beginning, after Conklin was relieved of his position, that I wanted a woman in the job. Your boss turned me down cold, twice, but she enthusiastically recommended you, as did Captain Malone and Chief Farnsworth."

That brought tears to Jeannie's eyes. She had so much love for Sam Holland as a boss and a friend and tremendous respect for the captain and chief. "That's nice to hear."

"So, have I found my new deputy chief of police?"

"I should mention I'm expecting my first child this summer."

"We can work around that, but thank you for letting me know—and congratulations."

"Thank you. We're excited, and now this is happening."

"Does that mean you accept my offer?"

"I believe it does."

"Excellent! We'll hold a press conference at city hall in a day or two to announce the news. In the meantime, tell the people you need to tell so they hear it from you. The deputy chief works closely with me and my office, and in the wake of the FBI report, it's safe to say we have hard work to do. I'm looking forward to doing that work with you, Deputy Chief McBride."

Hearing that title attached to her name for the first time would go down as one of the most amazing—and surreal—moments of Jeannie's life. "Thank you for your faith in me, ma'am. I'm looking forward to working with you."

"Likewise, and please, call me Monique. I'll be back in touch about swearing you in, and in the meantime... Jeannie, you might want to see about acquiring new uniforms."

"I'll do that. Thank you again."

"My pleasure."

Jeannie ended the call and sat for the longest time in her car, trying to process that this was really happening before she remembered Michael was waiting to hear from her. She pressed his name at the top of her Favorites list.

He answered on the first ring. "So?"

"How does Deputy Chief McBride sound?"

"I think it sounds wonderful. Aw, baby, I'm so proud, I'm bursting."

"There'll be a swearing-in ceremony at city hall in the next day or two. Can you be there with me?"

"I wouldn't miss that for anything."

CHAPTER TWENTY-SIX

S am called Freddie into her office. "I want to start over—again—with this investigation, and I want you to help me do it."

He eyed her skeptically. "Help you how?"

"Let's hit the streets with Vernon and Jimmy driving us. Let's do what we do while we wait for FDS, which can take months. We don't have months with this guy raping and murdering women right under our noses. He's brazen. He does this in a public park where anyone might hear them scream for help. That tells me we're looking for someone who's fearless, who thinks he's unstoppable and untouchable. Let's go find him."

"I hate to be the one to remind you that you're on desk duty and not allowed to work in the field."

"I don't need to be reminded of anything, Detective. We're going to walk out of here like we always do, and you won't say or do anything to draw attention to what we're doing. You got me?"

"Playing devil's advocate, but what if someone comes at us, and my partner is unable to defend herself or me? What then?"

"We're going to talk to the families and friends of the victims. Who's going to come at us?"

"Someone is always coming at us."

"Go get your stuff and be cool. I mean it. Don't tip anyone off, or I'll partner up with someone else for this mission."

Rolling his eyes, he turned to see to her orders.

They were leaving the pit when Jeannie came in, looking wide-eyed and amazed.

"I talked to her," Jeannie said to Sam. "And I accepted."

"Yes!"

"What's happening?" Freddie asked, his gaze darting between them.

"You may as well tell everyone at the same time." Sam turned to return to the pit. "Listen up, everyone! Jeannie has something to tell you."

Gonzo, Cruz and O'Brien gave her their full attention. Green, Dominguez and Carlucci would find out soon enough.

"Mayor Brewster has asked me to take the deputy chief's job, and I've accepted her offer. And no, I can't believe this any more than you can."

"Holy *shit*, Jeannie," Gonzo said. "That's fantastic. Congratulations."

"I'm so happy for you, Jeannie," Freddie said. "And so proud."

They hugged her and celebrated her until Jeannie was wiping away tears. "Thanks so much, you guys. I'll need your support when everyone else finds out and complains about me being promoted over sergeants, lieutenants and captains."

"Let them complain," Gonzo said. "We all know firsthand that you've earned this."

"I love you all so much. Please tell me you'll still be my best friends."

"Always," Freddie said, speaking for all of them.

He and Sam left through the morgue door a few minutes later and got into the SUV. Sam recited Wes Hambly's address, which Jimmy punched into the GPS.

"Thanks, guys."

"No problem, ma'am," Vernon said.

"This is pretty sweet," Freddie said of the Secret Service SUV.

"Don't get used to it. I'll be back to driving you in no time."

"I plan to enjoy this while it lasts. I bet Vernon will be more sympathetic to my regular need to eat than you are."

"His regular need to eat happens hourly, Vernon, so don't be too sympathetic."

Vernon cackled with laughter.

"Don't ruin it for me," Freddie said. "So, what's the plan with Hambly?"

"To ask all the same questions again. And then we'll take our show on the road and talk to Woo's friends. I never got to interview them the first time around, so I'll start fresh."

"If we're going to be dealing with grieving friends and family all day, I'll need food. Lots of it."

"You see what I deal with, Vernon?"

"I see it, and I empathize. Young Jimmy is equally ravenous."

"And does he eat nothing but crap and not gain a pound, like my partner?"

"Yep. Life isn't fair."

"I say that every day."

"We can hear you," Freddie said for himself and Jimmy, who was laughing in the front seat.

"Good, then hear this—your disgusting diet will catch up to you someday, and I'm living for that day."

"Don't be a jealous cow, Sam. I've told you before it's not a good look on you."

Vernon and Jimmy both cracked up.

Sam smiled at her partner, thrilled to be back to doing what they did together after weeks of being sidelined. This was what she'd needed to set things right in her world—a case to sink her teeth into and some bickering with her partner. "How about our girl Jeannie, huh?"

"I'm so thrilled for her. But I can't help but wonder why the mayor didn't ask you."

"She did. Twice. I turned her down both times. Can you imagine me in that job? I'd lose my mind. Three weeks of convalescence leave nearly wrecked me. I was going crazy wanting to get back in the game. Being stuck behind a desk is my idea of hell."

"It'd be mine, too. Do you think Jeannie will be okay with it?"

"Maybe not a couple of months ago, but things have changed. Don't let on that I told you, but she's expecting her first baby, and this comes at a good time. It'll get her off the streets and into a job with more regular hours."

"That's great news. No one deserves all these good things more than she does."

"That's a fact. After Sanborn attacked her, I worried she'd never bounce back. Not only did she bounce back, but she came back stronger than ever. The Brown bust is a big fucking deal, and anyone who objects to her being promoted over more-senior officers will have to admit that a bust like that is a once-in-a-lifetime thing and results in opportunities like this."

"She'll be great at it."

"Yes, she will. I wish my dad was here to see one of my detectives being put in his old office."

"He's here, and he knows. Hell, I wouldn't put it past him to be orchestrating the whole thing."

"Yeah, true," Sam said, feeling emotional suddenly. The grief hit her at the strangest of times, such as when she was celebrating the promotion of a dear friend and colleague. She had to shake that off when her phone rang with a call from Roni Connolly.

"Hey there."

"How're you doing?" Roni asked.

"Very well, and you?"

"I'm good. Settling into the new job and figuring out my way around the White House."

"Glad to hear it. I'm going to be a little scarce in the East Wing for the next little while. Things are nuts at work, as usual."

"No worries. I wanted to let you know that, per your request, I'm meeting with Scotty after school to talk about Skippy's Instagram platform and how we can help him manage it."

"I can't believe how popular that dog is," Sam said. "Nick says she's the most popular member of the family."

"People love her, and they love Scotty's story as well, but we need to help him wrangle the massive outpouring that comes with it."

"Thanks for taking that on, Roni. Running a dog's Instagram account isn't in your job description."

"It falls under 'other duties as assigned.'"

Sam laughed. "I suppose it does. How're you doing otherwise?" Roni had been widowed suddenly in October when her husband, Patrick, was hit by a stray bullet on 12th Street.

"I'm doing all right. I've joined a local group called the Wild Widows, made up of young widows supporting each other. They reached out to me through a friend of my sister's, and so far, they've been great. It helps to connect with people who get it."

"I can see how that would help. What's with the name, though? The Wild Widows."

"It's taken from the Mary Oliver quote, 'What is it you plan to do with your one wild and precious life?'"

"Ah, I love that."

"I know, right? While I have you, I wanted to share some other news with you."

"What's up?"

"Well, it seems that when Patrick died, he left me a very special gift in the form of a baby due in June."

"Oh, Roni... That's wonderful. It is wonderful, right?"

"It is, although it took me a minute to get to wonderful. The idea of raising a child on my own is daunting, but I'm excited and nervous and all the things."

"We'll all be there for you. Everyone in your life will be there."

"You have enough going on without worrying about me."

"I will worry about you, and you can't stop me."

"If you insist," Roni said, laughing. "I'll keep you posted on Scotty and Skippy."

"I do insist and thank you for taking that on. You're the best."

"Glad to do it. I think it'll be fun. Talk soon."

"Skippy's Instagram account is the highlight of my day," Freddie said after Sam slapped her phone closed.

"I've only heard about it and how it's getting out of hand, but I've never seen it. Show me."

"For crying out loud, Sam." He called up the account on his phone and handed it to her. "Do you need me to show you how to navigate?"

"I think I can manage." She scrolled through the photos and videos of the adorable dog who'd stolen all their hearts. "Does that say that Skippy has two-point-two *million* followers?"

"It does, and that's why you had to get your staff involved."

"I've heard him say it's gotten big, but Jesus Christ above."

"Sam!"

"What? That was a *prayer*, Freddie. Duh."

"Sure, it was."

"But really... Two-point-two million followers for a dog?"

"She's not just any dog. She's the first dog."

"People are crazy."

"Yes, they are. They're crazy about you, your husband, your kids, your dog. Did you see how there's been more than thirty-two million views of the *SNL* skit on YouTube?"

"Dear God. That was mortifying."

"But so, so funny. I've never laughed so hard in my entire life."

"It was not funny."

"Yes, it was. Ask Vernon and Jimmy. Was it funny?"

"We're not allowed to comment on that," Vernon said diplomatically, "but if we were, I'd have to say it was indeed amusing."

"You're supposed to be on my side, Vernon."

"Always, ma'am, but that skit was funny."

"Ha!" Freddie said. "I told you."

"I hate everyone."

"Even Nick?"

"Especially him. None of this would be happening if he hadn't become the damned president." As she said that, she realized she'd come to trust Vernon and Jimmy enough to speak freely in front of them. "Except I can't hate him when I love him so much."

"That's a problem," Freddie said.

"Sure is."

They pulled up to Wes's place a few minutes later, and Sam's stomach immediately clenched at what they had to do there. "We'll be back shortly," she told Vernon.

"Take your time. Jimmy, stay with the car."

"Yes, sir."

Vernon helped Sam out of the car.

"I said I didn't need a detail, but I'm thankful for you every day. I hope you know that."

"It's an honor to work with you, ma'am."

"Sam. My name is *Sam*."

Smiling, Vernon said, "Yes, ma'am."

"Ugh." Sam walked with Freddie and Vernon up the stairs to the home Audrey had shared with Wes. "I hate how slow I am."

"You're moving better than you were."

"It's still too slow."

"Slow and steady wins the race."

"Whatever you say."

It took eight minutes to climb the flight of stairs that led to Wes's apartment.

Sam raised a finger, telling Freddie to give her a minute to catch her breath before he knocked. She ended up needing two minutes, all the while swearing silently over how much it sucked to be injured. "Go ahead."

Freddie knocked.

The person who came to the door barely resembled the guy they'd met weeks ago. His hair was long and scraggly, he had almost a full beard, and his eyes were dead looking. When he saw it was them, he brightened ever so slightly. "Did you get the guy who killed Audrey?"

"Not yet," Sam said, aching as his eyes went dull with disappointment. "We wondered if we could talk to you again."

"Um, sure. My place is a mess. I, ah, haven't been doing much."

"That's okay."

They followed him into a pigsty. That was the only word for the condition of the apartment. It bore no resemblance whatsoever to the home he'd shared with Audrey. Sam hurt for him, for her, for what had been so senselessly lost.

He cleared a place for them to sit on a love seat across from the sofa where he was clearly spending most of his time.

"When we find ourselves in situations like this, without leads to follow, we start over," Sam said. "We take it from the top as if we haven't done anything, and we go through it all again. I'm sorry to put you through it, but we need to reinterview you to make sure we didn't miss something the first time around."

"You don't have *any* leads?"

"No, we don't. We have his DNA, but it's not in the system. We've received special permission from the mayor to run a familial DNA search on the samples we have, hoping to find a relative who's been arrested in the past and has DNA on record. But that's a long shot that can take months, and we don't have months if we want to find this guy before he kills again. So, we start over."

"Whatever you need to do," he said.

They went over every detail again, drilling down into every random tidbit, but they didn't learn anything new.

"All I do is think about her, about her routine and her friends and the people she interacted with every day, and I can't come up with a single thing that would've led to something like this. Everyone liked her. She was sweet and kind and... I just don't know how to go on without her."

The comment gave Sam an idea. "I have a friend who was recently widowed. She's joined a group of young widows, and she just told me it's been very helpful to her. I can connect you with her if you think it might help."

"I'm not a widow, though."

"Aren't you? You were going to spend your life with Audrey, and now you're not. I'd say you qualify. Would you mind if I gave my friend Roni your number?"

He shrugged as if he couldn't care less. "Sure."

"Thank you for seeing us. I'm sorry we had to put you through it again."

"Whatever it takes to get this guy, not that it'll bring her back, but it'll give us some comfort to know he's not out there living his life while she's dead. And I don't want anyone else to go through the hell we are."

Freddie gave Sam an arm to help her up.

Wes walked them to the door.

"Keep coming to the grief group meetings. It helps to connect with other loved ones who've been touched by violent crime. It's helped me."

He looked confused for a second. "Oh right. Your dad."

"Yes. We'll keep you informed of any developments. Hang in there, Wes."

"I'm trying."

After the door closed behind them, Sam said, "Well, that did nothing but reopen his wound."

"It was a good thought to connect him to Roni. That alone might make it worth the trip."

"I suppose. We've had some frustrating cases, but this one is the worst ever."

"Yeah, it's right up there."

They went next to the apartment Ling Woo had shared with three other Georgetown graduate students. Only her roommate Lily was home when they arrived on the third floor after another slow, painful climb for Sam.

"Is there news?" Lily asked.

"No." Sam explained about starting over when the leads ran dry. "Would you mind if we interviewed you again, just to be sure we have everything?"

"Of course. Whatever I can do. We're all still in shock. Ling was the sweetest girl. She'd do anything for anyone. We called her the house mother. She was always cooking for us and cleaning up after us and taking care of us." Her voice broke as she sat on a red sofa. "We had no idea how much she did until she wasn't here anymore."

"We're so sorry for your loss."

Lily used a tissue to wipe away tears. "Thank you. It's so senseless, you know?"

"We certainly do."

"What can I do to help?"

"We know you and your other roommates went over everything with the first detectives you spoke with. Do you mind if we do that again?"

"No, not at all."

They spent the next hour reviewing the notes from the first

interview, discussing Ling's routine, the people she saw every day, her weekend job at a nearby coffee shop. Detectives had spoken with close friends, classmates, lab partners and coworkers, who had all said the same thing. Ling had been a brilliant student with a bright future ahead of her as well as a nice person who got along with everyone in her orbit.

"There's one thing that nags at me," Lily said almost as an afterthought.

Sam sat up straighter. "What's that?"

"About a week and a half before she was killed, we were at a bar one night. It was rare for her to come out with us, but we were celebrating our roommate Cassie's birthday, so she came. We were at a bar a mile or so from campus, and we met up with a bunch of guys that Cassie knows from high school. She grew up here in DC. One of them, this guy Shane, was hitting on Ling. She wasn't interested, but he didn't let that stop him from bugging her all night."

"In what way was he 'bugging her'? What was he doing?"

"Asking her to dance with him, not taking no for an answer, buying her drinks she didn't want. That kind of thing. Cassie told the other guys to do something about him, but they were all drinking and partying and didn't care that their friend was being a dick. Ling and I ended up leaving so she could get away from him."

"How did he react when he realized you were leaving?"

"He followed us out of the bar, yelling that she'd be sorry for missing out on a chance to be with him."

"You heard him say that? She'd be sorry?" Sam asked, her backbone buzzing with the tingles that came from finally catching a break.

"I did."

"Why haven't you mentioned this before?"

"I'd forgotten about it until just now. I'm so sorry. Everything has been so awful since Ling was killed. My thoughts are all over the place."

"How can we find this guy?"

"Cassie would know."

"Where is she?"

"Working at Tucker's Steak House down by the Feds stadium. She's not allowed to look at her phone during her shift, or I'd text her. I can get you the address."

"I know where it is," Freddie said. "What's her last name?"

"Richardson."

"This was helpful," Sam said. "Thank you so much."

"I wish there was more I could do."

"You've given us more than we had coming in here. If it turns out that Shane was involved in her murder, we'll need you to testify."

"Whatever I can do to nail the bastard who took her from us."

CHAPTER TWENTY-SEVEN

They left Lily with promises to keep her apprised of the investigation. Back in the SUV, Freddie gave Vernon the address of the restaurant.

Sam put her head back and closed her eyes for a second as pain radiated from her hip. She was doing too much and would pay for it later, but they finally had *something* to work with, so she couldn't stop now.

"I could go talk to Cassie if you want to go home," Freddie said.

"Not going home." From her coat pocket, she found the pain pills she'd stashed there earlier and downed them with water from one of the bottles Vernon and Jimmy kept in the back of the SUV. The agents were handy to have around. She hadn't needed pain pills in a while, so taking one felt like a setback. But she'd learned to stay ahead of the pain.

When they arrived at the restaurant, they had to deal with the stunned reactions of staff and patrons alike when they realized the first lady was there.

Sam and Freddie showed their badges to the hostess. "Lieutenant Holland, Detective Cruz, MPD. We're looking for Cassie Richardson."

"Is she in trouble?" the hostess asked.

"No, she isn't. Can you get her for us, please?"

"Sure."

The hostess took off on heels so high, she could hardly walk.

"I don't understand the allure of heels that high," Sam said. "They must be five or six inches. That makes no sense."

"Heels make no sense to me in general, but I sure do love what they do for my wife's spectacular legs."

"Ew."

"What? My wife's legs are in fact spectacular."

"Knock it off."

"You started it."

"Is everyone staring at me, or does it just seem that way?"

"They're all staring."

"Awesome. Where's that hostess?"

Sam went around the hostess stand and made her way to the back of the restaurant, where the hostess was conferring with a dark-haired young woman. "Are you Cassie?" Sam asked the woman.

"I am."

"Get lost," Sam told the hostess, who gave her a testy look.

"Do it," Freddie said. "You don't want to make her mad."

During the long weeks on the sidelines, Sam had forgotten how fun this job could be with him as her wingman.

Sam introduced herself and Freddie to Cassie. "Is there somewhere we can talk?"

"Is this about Ling?"

"Yes."

"Will you keep an eye on my tables?" Cassie asked another waitress.

"Sure," she said, eyeing Sam.

Cassie led them to a break room and closed the door.

"We spoke with Lily at your apartment, and she mentioned an outing for your birthday at which a guy named Shane was hassling Ling. Do you know where we might find him?"

"I don't really know him."

"Lily said he came with guys you know."

She nodded. "Yes, that's right."

"Can you please ask them where we might find him, only don't tell them who wants to know?"

"Of course." She went to a locker and retrieved her cell phone.

An older woman came into the room. "What's going on here? Is she in trouble?"

"No, she isn't. As I'm sure you know, her roommate was murdered. She's helping us with something, so leave us alone."

"Make it quick," the woman said.

"Pleasant," Sam said after the woman left the room with a loud slam of the door.

"She's a real joy to work for," Cassie said sarcastically. She thumbed through her phone and sent a text. Her phone chimed a few seconds later.

"His name is Shane Ramsey. He lives with his parents in Columbia Heights."

The name Ramsey sent a shaft of electricity down Sam's backbone. Not to mention, Columbia Heights wasn't far from Rock Creek Park.

"This is helpful," Sam said when she recovered from the initial shock of hearing that name. What were the odds of Shane being related to the sergeant? *Please God, let there be no connection to him.* "Ask where else we can find him besides home."

She sent the text and then waited. "He works for an auto repair shop."

Sam wrote down the address, which was also close to the park.

"And hangs out at a bar near work called Woodrefsens."

"Thank you very much. If they ask why you want to know this stuff, please don't tell them."

"No problem. Do you think he had something to do with Ling's murder?"

"We don't know yet, but it's the first solid lead we've had."

Tears immediately filled Cassie's eyes. "If her death had a connection to me, I'll never forgive myself."

"It had nothing to do with you. If this guy is tied to it in some way, that's on him, not you."

"Still... He met her through me."

"No matter what, it's not your fault, Cassie."

"We all loved her so much," Cassie said softly. "I can't believe I have to go on with my life, go to class and work and study for exams, like nothing's happened when the worst thing ever has happened."

Sam handed her a card Dr. Trulo had made to give to victims of violent crime who might benefit from their grief group. "Our next meeting is in two weeks. Please come if you think it will help."

"I will. Thank you."

Sam left her with a promise to keep in touch with her and her roommates about the investigation. The woman who'd interrupted them waited at the hostess stand. As they approached, she held up her hand to stop them.

"I don't care who you are, you can't come into my place of business and interrupt one of my waitresses like that."

"Detective Cruz, am I allowed to come in here to interview a material witness in a murder investigation?"

"Yes, you are, Lieutenant."

"And will I arrest anyone who gets in my way?"

"You often do, ma'am."

The woman glared at her. "You think you're so cool."

"I don't think it. I know it. Now get out of my way before I have no choice but to arrest you. And if you hassle that young woman, whose roommate was brutally murdered, I'll come back and arrest you myself."

Sam pushed past her and headed for the door, feeling pretty good about herself for the first time since she'd fallen on ice and broken her hip.

"That was awesome," Freddie said when they'd stepped into the cold.

"In case I forget to tell you, I appreciate how you always have the lines memorized."

"I do what I can for the people."

She shot a look over her shoulder. "*Your* lines. Not mine."

When they were in the car, she turned to him. "Tell me Ramsey doesn't have a son named Shane."

He did some poking around on his phone and then glanced at her. "Wish I could."

"Son of a *bitch*."

"Son of an asshole, you mean."

"Why, young Freddie, you said a swear!"

"In this case, it's warranted. What's the plan?"

Sam pulled out her phone and put through a call to Malone. "This is above my pay grade," she said as he picked up the call.

"What is?" Malone asked.

"The fact that my investigation has led me to Ramsey's son Shane."

"Stop it. Are you for real right now?"

"Real as it gets."

"Fill me in."

Sam told him what they'd learned from Ling Woo's roommates.

"And we're sure the guy's name is Shane Ramsey?"

"We're sure. They mentioned he lives with his parents in Columbia Heights. Is that where Ramsey lives?"

"Hang on."

Sam heard him doing some clicking around on his computer. "Yes," he said with a sigh.

"How do we play this?"

"I don't want you anywhere near Ramsey's house or his kid. Come back in, and we'll figure out next steps. And P.S., what're you even doing in the field?"

"Detective Cruz needed some assistance."

Freddie glared at her.

She shrugged and smiled. "We'll be back shortly." After she flipped the phone closed, she stared out the window, thinking about how they should play this unlikely turn in the investigation.

"Thanks for tossing me under the bus."

"That's my favorite place to toss you."

"Believe me, I know. As annoying as you are, it's nice to be getting back to normal around here."

"Agreed. Being sidelined doesn't look good on me. Neither does physical therapy, which is now right up there with flying, needles and ice as my least favorite things."

"But they got you back on your feet."

"In the most painful way possible."

Vernon dropped them at the morgue entrance.

"Thanks for the assist today," Sam said to him and Jimmy.

"Glad to help."

"They're not so bad," Sam said to Freddie as they walked into HQ.

"Not so bad at all, and Vernon already loves you like a daughter."

"You think so?"

"Absolutely."

"That's sweet. I miss my dad so much."

"I miss him, too. I can't imagine what it's like for you and your family."

"You were family to him, too, Freddie. You know that."

"I'd love to ask him what the heck we do about this latest development."

"Yeah, he'd definitely have an opinion."

When they reached the pit, Sam said, "Everyone to the conference room. Freddie, call the captain—and the chief."

"Oh, hello," Gonzo said. "What's up?"

"You won't believe it."

"Do we have a lead?"

"Do we ever."

They waited fifteen minutes for the chief to arrive. "Sorry, I was on a call with the mayor, who's busting her buttons over the big news. Detective McBride, we're so proud of you."

"We *so* proud," Sam added. "My dad would be thrilled to see you in his old office."

"Thank you all. Your support means everything to me—and I'm going to need it when the word gets out that a detective is being promoted three ranks."

"We've got your back," O'Brien said. "Couldn't be happier for you."

"Back to business." Malone used his chin to gesture to the chief. "Tell him what you told me."

"Our investigation has led to Ramsey's son Shane."

Gonzo gasped. "Shut. *Up.*"

"We're not saying he's our guy. We're saying he hassled one of our victims in a bar about ten days before she was raped and murdered. The night they met he told her she'd be sorry she wasn't receptive to his advances."

"That makes him our first person of interest," Jeannie said.

"It does. And since Ramsey has a massive hard-on for me—"

"Disgusting," Freddie muttered.

"—Gonzo, I want you and Jeannie to find Shane Ramsey and bring him in. Captain Malone, I need you to go directly to a judge with what we have to get a warrant for his DNA. He threatened her, and she turned up dead a short time after. That should be enough to get a warrant, but I don't want any nosy courthouse people or the sheriff's deputies that work there talking about this before we have it locked and loaded."

"I'll take care of it," Malone said. "Find him somewhere other than the house where he lives with his parents and make sure he has no time to notify anyone he's being brought in. Let's keep this quiet until we know for sure if he's involved."

Sam gave Gonzo and Jeannie the address of the auto repair shop where he worked as well as the name of the bar where he was known to hang out.

"We're on it," Gonzo said.

After he and Jeannie left, O'Brien went back to the pit, leaving Sam and Freddie alone with the captain and chief.

"Check to see if he has any kind of record," Malone said to Freddie.

He got up to use the computer in the conference room. "Sealed juvie."

Farnsworth blew out a deep breath. "If he's our guy, this is gonna get complicated."

"You know how we have to have our DNA on file so we can avoid crime scene confusion?" Sam said.

"What about it?" Malone asked.

"We've already requested FDS on the local database," Sam said.

"That'd include everyone associated with the department, so if there's a hit, we'll know it soon enough."

"That's true. I'm not sure whether to hope for or against a hit that ties him to Ramsey," Malone said as the others grimaced.

Patience had never been Sam's strong suit, but she feared she'd lose it entirely waiting for the DNA searches to yield results. Why did everything have to take so long when there was someone out there raping and murdering innocent women?

"It goes without saying that even talking to Ramsey's son will make this thermonuclear," Farnsworth said. "Let's proceed with utmost caution."

"Understood." Sam's heart gave a lurch at the thought of Ramsey's reaction to his son being brought in for questioning in one of her cases. *Thermonuclear* probably wasn't a big enough word to describe this situation.

To Freddie, she said, "Get on the computer. I want everything you can find about this guy. I want to know where he went to high school and when, his social media stuff, everything you can find, and make it fast."

"On it."

Since she had time for a break, she went into her office, closed the door and sat behind her desk, wincing at the pain radiating from her hip. She pulled the BlackBerry out of her pocket and sent a text to Nick. *Call me if you have a minute to talk. Nothing urgent.*

The phone rang a minute later, making her smile simply because she got to talk to him. "Hey."

"Hey, yourself. What's going on?"

"You aren't going to believe it."

"Lay it on me."

She told him about the possible connection to Ramsey's son.

"No way."

"Right?"

"Holy shit, Sam. What's the plan?"

"Gonzo and Jeannie have gone after the son and are bringing him in for questioning."

"Won't that send his father into orbit?"

"We're trying to keep it quiet until we know if he's our guy."

"How will you figure that out?"

"We need a warrant to get a DNA sample from him, which is in the works. He's not apt to give us that voluntarily, and the warrant isn't assured, so we're thinking outside the box. We may check our DNA sample against his father's to see if there's a familial match."

"Christ, Sam. What if it is him? His father will claim you guys framed him."

"Which is why we're doing this as by the book as by the book gets."

"Just be careful. That guy has it in for you even when you're not looking at his son for being a serial rapist and murderer."

"I know. In other news, I'm off the hook with the mayor on the deputy chief's job because she offered it to Jeannie."

"No way! That's amazing. Is she going to do it?"

"She is. We're very excited for her."

"I can imagine. Tell her I said congrats."

"I will. What goes on over there?"

"Other than my VP nominee getting skewered on the Hill?"

"Is she?"

"It's bad. She's handling it as well as she can, but they're ripping her apart, digging into every aspect of her life, her marital woes, all of it."

"God, I hate that. What the hell do her marital woes have to do with what kind of vice president she'll be?"

"It has nothing to do with it, but they're digging into that stuff because their only other reason for opposing her is that she's even more inexperienced than I am."

"Inexperience isn't disqualifying, is it?"

"No, but they're doing their best to discredit her in every way they can think of."

"Probably doesn't help that she's a woman either."

"Nope."

"Even though I've had my doubts about her, I find myself rooting for her, because if there's anything I hate more than misogyny..."

"You hate airplanes and needles more."

"And black ice and physical therapy. They've been added to the list."

His laughter made her go warm all over. "I guess you'll be late for dinner, huh?"

"Looks that way but tell the kids I'll tuck them in when I get home."

"Will you tuck me in, too?"

"Absolutely. I can't wait."

"Love you, babe. Watch your back with that jackass Ramsey."

"I will. Don't worry. And I love you, too. See you soon."

CHAPTER TWENTY-EIGHT

Nick ended the call with Sam and sat back in his chair behind the Resolute desk, thinking about the ongoing threat to Sam presented by that son of a bitch Ramsey. Just when they thought they'd gotten rid of him once and for all...

A knock on the door preceded Terry walking into the Oval Office.

"What's the good word, Terry?" Nick asked, eager to think of anything other than Sam being in danger at work.

"I wish there was a good word, Mr. President. We received a call from Henderson's team that she's considering withdrawing from consideration."

"Oh no. No, no, no. She can't do that. Can you get her on the phone for me?" Gretchen's nomination had been Nick's first big decision as president, and he was determined to get her confirmed.

"Let me see what I can do." Terry left the office and went to the reception area to speak to one of the assistants, returning ten minutes later. "She's on the line now."

"Thanks." Nick picked up the extension on the desk. "Gretchen, thanks for taking the call."

"Of course, Mr. President."

He could hear it in her voice, the weary resignation that came with taking a beating from the Senate. "I understand you're wavering."

"I knew it'd be rough, but this is just too much. After all the progress my ex-husband and I have made toward repairing our relationship enough to be good co-parents... He doesn't deserve this."

"No, he doesn't, and you should issue a statement saying just that."

He glanced at Terry, who nodded and pulled out a pen to take notes. "Put the truth out there from your point of view. Say something like 'while I understand the Senate has a job to do in making sure I'm qualified to be your next vice president, I believe my family should be off-limits in this process. Yes, my ex-husband and I went through a very difficult divorce, but that's long in the past, and we've repaired our relationship to the point where we're able to be excellent co-parents to our beloved children.' Or something like that. What do you think?"

"Yes, I suppose I could do that, Mr. President."

"Terry wrote it down. I'll have him shoot it over to your team, and we'll issue our own statement in support of you. Please don't give up, Gretchen. You and I both know you're more than qualified to fill this role, and it's the job of the politicians to sling the mud. That goes with the territory for both of us."

"Yes, but I wasn't prepared for them to savage him. His recovery is fragile. I worry this'll result in a setback."

"If you come out strong in support of him, I have to believe that'll help. He's probably more concerned about your opinion of him than anyone else's. At least that's how I'd feel if I were him."

"That's true. We'll do the statement. Hopefully, that'll take some pressure off."

"Please don't quit, Gretchen. We're all so excited to make you the country's first female vice president."

"Thank you for your support, Mr. President. I won't do anything without discussing it with you first."

"Fair enough. I'll speak with you soon and will hopefully see you sooner for the swearing in."

"From your lips to God's ears, sir."

Nick put down the phone.

"Good job in talking her off the ledge," Terry said.

"Sometimes I hate this town."

"Only sometimes?"

Nick grunted out a laugh. "Most of the time."

GONZO AND JEANNIE approached the garage where Shane Ramsey was employed and showed their badges to the first person they encountered, a short man with brown skin and the name Jesus on his shirt. "Sergeant Gonzales, Detective McBride, MPD. We're looking for Shane Ramsey."

"He's working in the third bay," the man said in heavily accented English, gesturing to the left side of the garage. "What's he done?"

Gonzo ignored the question. "Gracias."

As they approached the third bay, he picked out Ramsey from the other two men he was with because he resembled his father, with the same wispy brown hair and beady eyes. Gonzo would try not to hold that against him. They flashed their badges again.

"Shane Ramsey?"

"Yeah, that's me. Did something happen to my dad?"

"No, he's fine. Can we speak to you for a moment outside?"

Shane glanced at his coworkers. "Um, sure." After wiping greasy hands on a red rag, he followed them outside. "What's this about?" His breath made vapor clouds in the cold.

"We have some questions we'd like to ask you downtown. If you come with us willingly, we won't cuff you out of professional courtesy to your father." The idea of extending any courtesy to Ramsey made Gonzo want to vomit, but he did it anyway to accomplish the goal of this mission.

"What kind of questions?" he asked, his gaze darting between Gonzo and Jeannie.

"The kind we want to ask downtown." Gonzo stared into the younger man's eyes, determined not to blink or look away.

Shane blinked. "Does my dad know about this?"

"No."

"He won't be happy when he hears you guys brought me in."

"Okay." After another beat of silence, Gonzo said, "I'm about one second from cuffing you and making a scene."

"Let me tell them I'm going."

"Detective McBride will take care of that."

While Jeannie went inside, Gonzo escorted Shane to the car and held out his hand. "I'll hang on to your phone until we get to HQ."

"Don't you have to have a warrant to take my phone?"

"Hand it over, or I'll cuff you."

"I'm not giving you my phone."

Gonzo had him cuffed, relieved of his phone and in the back seat of the car before Shane knew what hit him.

"My dad will make you so sorry you did this."

Gonzo slammed the door in his face.

"All set," Jeannie said when she rejoined him.

"You know what they say about the apple and the tree? This one didn't fall far. I ended up having to cuff him because he wouldn't give me his phone. We don't need him tipping off his father that we're bringing him in."

"You think we can keep a lid on that?"

"We sure as hell can try." After they were in the car and on their way back to HQ, Gonzo called Sam to let her know.

"How'd it go?"

"As you'd expect."

"Did he drop his father's name?"

"Several times."

"O'Brien has gone to find out where Ramsey is so we can avoid him on the way in. I'll call you in a few with the intel. If we decide to arrest him, we'll get one of the central booking clerks to process him in our interview room."

"Got it."

IT'D TAKEN Candace two days to pack her life in California into three suitcases for the trip to New Jersey.

Eli had thought he'd go crazy watching the seconds, minutes and hours tick by until he could see her again. He'd been a disaster in class, completely spaced out and unable to think of anything other than Candace coming to stay with him indefinitely.

She'd called him in tears the night before after yet another vicious argument with her parents. This time, however, she was eighteen, and they couldn't stop her from leaving or tell her who she was allowed to care about.

The fight had been so bad that Eli had put her up in a hotel near LAX for her last night in California so her parents couldn't do something drastic, like lock her away to keep her from him. Until he received the text saying she'd boarded the plane, he'd been unable to eat, sleep, study or take a deep breath.

He'd skipped a class to meet her plane at Newark, getting there two hours before she was due to land. For the first time since his profile had been elevated by Nick's ascension to the presidency, Eli was recognized by strangers at the airport.

"Oh my God," one lady said. "You're Elijah... The president's... Betty, *look*! It's *Elijah*!"

He smiled at the two women, uncertain of what to say to them. What was he to the president, anyway? Nick and Sam referred to him as their bonus son, which he loved. Apparently, that had made him famous.

The Secret Service agents with him kept the women from getting too close.

"That was a first," he said to Nate. Eli had liked the younger agent since he first met him and had requested that Nate lead his detail when it became necessary for him to have one.

"Won't be the last time," Nate replied as they took seats in a waiting area. "You never mentioned why you're skipping class to come to the airport."

"It's the first class I've ever skipped," Eli said. "When I went to Princeton, I promised my dad I'd never miss a class unless I was truly sick—and he said being hungover didn't count as truly sick."

Nate laughed. "Good for him."

"He told me I'd been given the priceless gift of a top-level education, and he expected me to take it as seriously as I'd ever taken anything."

"It's impressive that a man with his resources had such beliefs," Nate said.

"He never forgot where he came from, or how he'd had to rebuild after the company that made him wealthy imploded. It was imperative to him that I have an education to fall back on if all else fails, and I'll do the same with the twins. That's what he'd want."

"He'd be proud of you for the way you've stepped up for them," Nate said.

"Thank you. They mean the world to me. And the reason we're here is that my girlfriend, who I haven't seen in years, turned eighteen two days ago, which means she can decide for herself who she wants to be with."

"Whoa. When was the last time you saw her?"

"Three years ago."

"Damn, Eli. Man…"

"Yeah, it was ugly." Uglier than he'd ever admit to the agent who'd begun to feel like a friend. "I can't wait to see her."

"You guys kept it together all this time?"

Eli shook his head. "She wasn't allowed to talk to me—and vice versa. I talked to her for the first time in years two days ago."

"I'm amazed."

"We've picked up right where we left off, or at least it felt that way on the phone the last few days. I'm worried about what it'll be like when she's here."

"I'm sure it'll be great."

"Thanks for listening to me go on about it. These last few hours have been torturous."

"I could tell you were dealing with something." Nate offered him sunflower seeds. He was always eating something healthy.

"No, thanks. Yeah, the last couple of days have been intense. I couldn't believe it when she called me Monday. I wasn't sure if I'd hear from her when she turned eighteen. Turns out she was counting the days like I was."

"I feel like I'm watching a rom-com or something."

"Stop," Eli said, laughing.

"No, really, only this one has my full interest."

"I hope we don't disappoint you."

"You won't. While we're talking about rom-coms, do you mind if I ask you something wildly inappropriate?"

Eli glanced at the always super-professional agent. "Um, sure?"

Smiling, Nate said, "It's inappropriate in the sense that I shouldn't be talking to you about it."

"I sort of think of you as a friend since we're together every day."

"Likewise, which is why I feel comfortable asking you what you think of the first lady's niece Brooke."

"Oh, um, I don't really know her all that well, but she seems nice. Why?"

"Well, it's like this. A while ago, she was babysitting at the Ninth Street house. We got to talking, and we've kind of been talking ever since."

"Very interesting. And then I moved you to New Jersey, so you probably don't see her very often."

"I saw her while we were in DC over the holidays, and P.S., you did me a huge favor careerwise asking for me to head up your detail, so thanks for that."

"Are you going to see her again?"

"I sort of feel like I need to have a conversation with the first lady before I do, but the thought of that makes me cringe."

"She's so cool, though. You know that."

"I do, but this is a strange situation I find myself in."

"I can see that. Would you like me to talk to her about it?"

"Oh God, no. I'd never ask you to do that."

"You didn't ask. I offered."

"Ugh, it's so unprofessional for me to be having this conversation with you, or to be interested in dating the first lady's niece. I should've left it alone after I met her."

"If something is meant to be, it'll be. I remember my dad saying that after he met Cleo. They went through a lot to be together, and they were so happy. Like Sam and Nick... They're happy like that, too. Knowing them like I do after these last few months, I'm pretty sure they'd be okay with you wanting to date Brooke."

"You think so, huh?"

"I do, and I'm more than willing to mention it to her, if you'd like me to."

"I feel like I'm fifteen again, angsting over a girl."

"So, we never stop doing that?"

"Apparently not. But if you wanted to mention it to her, in the coolest way possible, I wouldn't object."

"I got you covered. It'll be fine. I'm sure of it."

When he heard the announcement that Candace's flight had landed, Eli shot out of his chair, startling Nate.

"Easy, big fella. What'd I tell you about sudden movements?"

"That they stress you out."

"Yeah, so don't do that."

"Sorry. I just can't wait to see her."

"I know, but it takes forever for people to get off airplanes these days because they take everything they own with them. It'll be another twenty to thirty minutes."

Sighing, Eli sat back down to wait. Fourteen minutes later, she texted to say she was on the way to baggage claim, where he was meeting her. "She's coming. I'm going to stand up now, if that's all right with you."

Smiling, Nate said, "Go right ahead. You've waited long enough for this."

Eli was surprised he didn't hyperventilate in the minutes it took for Candace to appear at the top of the escalator. *Oh my God*, he thought. *She's even more beautiful than I remember.* In three years, she'd gone from a gorgeous girl to a stunning woman. Long dark hair fell in shiny waves around her shoulders, her big brown eyes lit up with delight at the sight of him, and her smile... It still made his knees go weak, the way it had from the first time she directed it at him.

As she walked toward him, he went still as a huge lump landed in his throat, and tears flooded his eyes.

And then she was in his arms, bringing the scent he'd dreamed about during the long years apart.

In that massive, bustling airport, there was only her, only them. They stood there for the longest time, holding each other as people moved around them, grumbling about them blocking the corridor. He couldn't care less if they were annoying others.

Eli finally pulled back to look down at her and was touched by the tears on her face that he brushed away. "You're so tall!"

Laughing, she said, "I had a growth spurt."

"You're beautiful."

"So are you, even more so than you were before."

"I can't believe you're here. Tell me I'm not dreaming this."

"If this is a dream, I'm going to be really pissed off when I wake up."

Eli laughed and framed her face with his hands. He stared at her for a long, breathless moment before he kissed her. In deference to where they were, it was a soft, sweet kiss, but it was their first kiss in more than three years and perhaps the best kiss of his entire life. "I still love you," he whispered when he pulled back from her.

"I still love you, too."

He hugged her again, even tighter than the first time, wanting to weep with the sweet relief of having her back in his arms and his life. "Let's go home."

CHAPTER TWENTY-NINE

In preparation for Gonzo and Jeannie interviewing Shane Ramsey, Sam printed out photos of Ling Woo alive and dead. She lingered on the autopsy photo, filled with rage over what had been done to such a vibrant young woman. Maybe she would've been the one to cure cancer, Alzheimer's or Parkinson's. So much promise snuffed out. Was it because Shane Ramsey couldn't accept that she'd rejected him?

Sam wanted it to be that simple, but other things nagged at her. What was his connection to Kaitlyn, Audrey and Moira?

She put through a call to Kaitlyn. "This is Lieutenant Holland."

"Oh. Hi. Is there news in my case?"

"Possibly. Do you know a guy named Shane Ramsey by any chance?"

After a pause, Kaitlyn said, "I don't think so."

"Would you mind if I sent you a photo of him?"

"Sure."

"Give me your email."

Sam sent the photo she'd pulled from Shane's Instagram account with Archie's help. And yes, she knew stuff like that was easy, and she ought to be able to do it herself, but whatever.

Kaitlyn gasped. "He works at the place where I get my oil changed. He flirted with me, but I didn't encourage him and don't know his last name."

Sam's backbone buzzed. "If we can make this case, I may need you to testify to him flirting with you and your lack of encouragement."

"If it means he gets put away forever, sign me up."

"I'll be in touch." Sam ended that call and dialed Wes's number. "Did Audrey know a guy named Shane?"

"Not that I know of."

"Where did she take her car when it needed service?"

"She had a place in Columbia Heights that she liked."

More backbone buzzing. After confirming the address of the shop was the same place Ramsey worked, Sam said, "Did she ever mention anything about the shop that made her uncomfortable?"

"Not that I can... Wait. After the last time she went, she said she wasn't going back there because a worker looked at her funny and gave her the creeps."

"You're sure that's what she said?"

"I'm positive."

"But she never mentioned his name?"

"I don't think she knew it."

The backbone buzzing had reached roar status. "This is very helpful, Wes. Thank you."

"Do you have him?"

"We might be getting closer."

Sam thanked him, promised to be in touch and then used the intraoffice system to call Captain Malone. "I've got more. Both Audrey and Kaitlyn had encounters with Shane Ramsey."

"What kinds of encounters?"

"I showed Kaitlyn his photo to determine if she knew him. She recognized him from the garage where he works. She said he flirted with her, but she didn't encourage him. Audrey's boyfriend, Wes, said she used to go to that same garage until a worker looked at her funny and gave her the creeps. She said she wasn't going there again after the last time. He couldn't say for sure that the guy was Shane, but who else could it be?"

"Any of the other guys who worked there, Sam. The judge shot us down for the DNA warrant. He said we don't have enough, and this won't change his mind."

"Two of the women have reported encounters with Shane that we can back up with witness testimony. How is that not enough?"

"A defense attorney would have a field day with this flimsy case, and you know it. We need it nailed down, and we're not there yet. We're closer than we were. I'll give you that."

"We have a matter of minutes before Ramsey finds out his son is under suspicion for this. After he's involved, we won't be able to get near Shane. He'll be free to rape and kill again."

"If we have to spring him, we'll keep eyes on him around the clock. But we're getting ahead of ourselves. Ask him if he'll voluntarily give us a DNA sample so we can clear him. If he refuses, maybe that'll work in our favor."

"Him willingly giving us his DNA is about as likely as me winning a million dollars in the lottery."

"I thought you didn't play the lottery."

"I don't! That's my point! We have to find a way to hold him while we investigate further."

"Keep working the case and doing what you do. That led you to this guy in the first place. In the meantime, I'm working it from my end and will keep talking to the judge."

"Okay." Sam returned the receiver to her desk unit, wondering what Malone was up to. Before she had a second to think about what it might be, she heard shouting outside her office and got up to see what was going on.

Jeannie and Gonzo had a man by the arms who was screaming for someone to get Sergeant Ramsey.

So much for keeping it on the down-low.

When he saw Sam standing in the doorway to her office, he said, "You're the bitch who's always trying to ruin my dad!" He strained to break free of the tight hold Gonzo and Jeannie had on him. "Is this how you get even with him? By arresting his son?"

Sam let him go by without comment. If she were to reply, she might say that she had zero interest in his father and a ton of interest in rapist-murderers.

They put him in interview one.

"Matt, go in and keep an eye on him, please," Sam said.

O'Brien stood. "Yes, ma'am."

Sam updated Gonzo, Jeannie and Freddie on what she'd learned from Kaitlyn and Wes.

"He's our guy," Gonzo said, his eyes lighting up.

"The judge shot down our warrant, and Malone said even with this new info, it's not enough to go back to the judge. We need more."

"Then we'll get more," Gonzo said fiercely.

"Call Patrol and ask for a couple of officers outside interview one. I don't want anyone interrupting us. We also need to get one of the AUSAs here to listen in. I've got a call into their office. Let's take our time and do this right."

She no sooner got those words out than Sergeant Ramsey came bursting into the pit, eyes blazing.

"What've you done with my son, you fucking whore?"

Before Sam could come up with a witty, cutting response, Captain Malone moved into place between them. "Move along, Sergeant. Union or no union, I'll kick your ass out of here so fast, you won't know what hit you."

"*Where is my son?*" he hissed, making an obvious effort to not rip Malone's head off.

"Sergeant, you have five seconds to get the fuck out of here, or I'll have you arrested," Malone said.

Sam stood in the doorway to her office, arms crossed, unblinking as Ramsey glared at her with unfettered hatred.

"Three, two, one," Malone said. "Detective Cruz, please take Sergeant Ramsey into custody."

"I'm going," Ramsey spat at Sam. "But if anything happens to him, I'll own this place."

After he stormed off, Sam said, "I was really looking forward to watching Detective Cruz arrest him."

"Let's move this along," Malone said. "If Shane's not our guy, I want him out of here ASAP."

"He's our guy," Sam said. "I'm sure of it."

"Now all you have to do is prove it."

RONI CONNOLLY'S favorite meeting of the day happened at four o'clock, when Scotty Cappuano and his dog, Skippy, came to the office to, as he put it, "take a meeting."

Scotty was a handsome fourteen-year-old, and Skippy a sweet, full-of-energy yellow Lab mix puppy.

"Ladies, I apologize in advance for anything she does while she's here," Scotty said after he entered the first lady's East Wing office suite. "She's incorrigible." Stopping, he glanced at Roni and asked, "Did I use that word right? It was one of our vocabulary words last year, but that was a lifetime ago."

"If you mean you can't do a thing with her, then you used it right."

"Excellent," he said, grinning. He had dark hair and eyes and bore a faint resemblance to his father, even though he was adopted. The first time Roni met him, she'd noticed how he'd affected his father's expressions and mannerisms, which she'd found so endearing. "My mom tells me you guys can help me deal with her exploding social media accounts. Dad says I'm going to start an international incident if I make the wrong kind of comment there, so

I need all the help I can get. Not to mention the mail. She gets more than my dad does!"

"We heard that," Lilia said. "Let's see what we can do to help you manage that."

Roni and Lilia spent a delightful hour with Scotty and Skippy, who was indeed incorrigible, but so cute, too. They were both covered in blonde dog hair by the time they had a plan in place to manage Skippy's fame that would involve Scotty keeping them in photos and videos while they handled the messaging. Scotty said he had to head upstairs to the residence to get a jump on his dreaded algebra homework.

Before he left, he solemnly shook hands with them. "Thank you so much for being willing to help us."

"It's a pleasure," Roni said sincerely. Running an Instagram account for the first dog sounded like the most fun anyone could ever have at a job. "I'll be in touch with some thoughts about how we can show the two of you together, and with the twins, as we go forward. People love the narrative of a boy and his first dog."

"Especially a boy who was adopted himself," Scotty said.

"Absolutely."

"Excellent. You know where to find us if you need me and the superstar."

"Good luck with the algebra," Roni said.

He scowled as he headed for the door to the suite. "I'm counting on my dad to outlaw it."

"What an awesome kid," Roni said to Lilia after he left.

"He really is, and Skippy is beyond cute. I love how he named her for Sam's late dad."

"It's all so sweet. Running that account will be a blast."

"I agree," Lilia said, smiling, "but we'd better see about a lint brush for the office."

With Sam, Malone, Farnsworth and AUSA Hope Miller positioned in observation, Gonzo and Jeannie entered the interrogation room, where Shane Ramsey paced like a caged animal.

"What the hell do you want with me?" Shane asked the second the door closed behind Jeannie.

"Have a seat," Jeannie said.

"I don't want to!"

"I wasn't asking."

Shane jerked out a chair, sat down hard and folded his arms, all while glaring at Jeannie. "Now tell me what the fuck I'm doing here."

Gonzo put down the photo of Ling Woo from when she was still alive. "Remember her?"

Shane looked at the photo. "No. Should I?"

Sam couldn't help but notice how he seemed diminished somehow by the sight of that photo. "Why isn't he asking for a lawyer?" Sam asked.

"I was just wondering the same thing," Malone said.

"Is he too stupid to know he should?" Sam asked.

Gonzo pointed to the photo. "You met her at Rialtos when you were there with your friends, and she was with hers for Cassie Richardson's birthday party. Ringing any bells?"

He shook his head. "I don't remember her."

"Let me fill in some blanks for you," Gonzo said. "According to her friends, you were hitting on her somewhat relentlessly. Buying her drinks she didn't want. Asking her to dance. Refusing to take no for an answer. It was so intense, she chose to leave rather than put up with you."

Shane kept his gaze fixed on the photo.

"When you realized she was leaving, you told her she'd be sorry she didn't give you a chance. Do you remember that?"

"Nope. I meet a lot of people."

"Do you hassle a lot of women like you hassled her?" Jeannie asked.

"Some women don't understand the concept of having fun. They're so uptight, they can't get out of their own way."

"And you see it as your duty to get them to relax?"

He shrugged. "Since when is buying a woman drinks a crime?"

"Does it bother you when you buy a woman a drink and she's not appreciative?"

"Lack of common courtesy is a problem in our society."

"That sounds like something his father would say," Sam said.

"Just thinking the same thing," Malone replied.

"When women fail to show you the courtesy you think you deserve, how does that make you feel?" Gonzo asked.

"Disrespected."

"And when you feel disrespected, what do you do?"

"What can you do? People suck. That's never going to change."

"Would you agree to provide a sample of your DNA so we can

eliminate you as a suspect in Ling Woo's murder?" Gonzo asked as he placed an autopsy photo of Ling on the table.

Shane recoiled from the visual. "What the fuck? Her *murder*? I didn't murder anyone!"

"Then you won't mind submitting a DNA sample, then, right?"

He stared at the photo for a long time without blinking. "I'd like to call a lawyer."

"Damn it," Sam whispered.

"Who would you like us to call?" Gonzo asked.

"Roland Dunning. He's a family friend."

"That's Conklin's lawyer," Sam said with disgust. "Figures he's a family friend of the Ramseys."

"We'll call him," Gonzo said.

He and Jeannie got up and left the room.

"And now we wait," Sam said as frustration pulsed through her.

CHAPTER THIRTY

Cameron Green had used the unexpected day off to think rather than sleep. Though he was as exhausted as he could recall being in years, the adrenaline buzzing through his system had made sleep impossible. During the long day of introspection, he'd come to a difficult and painful conclusion.

He needed to take a step back from the new relationship with Gigi.

Although the thought of that made him ache like he never had, this latest incident with Jaycee had proven she wasn't done with him. He wanted to believe she'd be so frightened from being arrested a second time and charged with felonies that she'd leave him alone, but he'd thought the first night in jail would've been enough to get that point across. That she'd thrown a brick through his window, knowing two cops were inside, proved she was seriously unhinged.

He had no way to compel her to get the help she desperately needed and couldn't risk Gigi being hurt by her.

His whole body ached at the thought of not being with Gigi. He'd never been in love like he was with her. When he recalled the other women he'd thought he "loved," whatever that had been, it hadn't been love. This... With Gigi... This was love. He had to keep her safe from whatever Jaycee did next.

That brick had come too freaking close. He felt sick when he recalled the sound of the window smashing, the brick that'd landed only feet from them, as well as the glass that had covered them. What if the brick had hit her? The possibility of her being hurt because of him was unimaginable, especially after what her ex had done to her.

She was just getting back to normal after that incident. He couldn't let anything else happen to her.

He absently scratched Jeffrey behind the ears as he reveled in the sweet memories of making love to her. Nothing had been like it was with her, even if it had been interrupted in the worst possible way. It'd been almost spiritual, a homecoming of sorts, a certainty that he was exactly where he belonged with the person he was born to love.

His eyes filled with tears as the reality of having to give up Gigi to keep her safe settled on him like the heaviest weight he'd ever carried.

The ringing doorbell startled him.

Jeffrey leaped off the sofa, barking.

Cameron got up, went to the door, looked through the peephole and saw Gigi on his porch. That was all it took to raise his spirits considerably, until he remembered his plan to take a step back. His heart shattered, but it had to be done.

After unlocking the dead bolt and opening the door, Cameron stepped aside to let her in. He looked around the parking lot before closing and locking the door again. He'd put a sheet of plywood over the broken window until he could get it replaced.

"I heard you got sent home," Gigi said.

"Yeah."

"Are you okay?"

"Just great. You?"

"I was worried when you didn't respond to any of my texts or calls."

He'd heard the phone but had been too lost in his depressing thoughts to deal with it, which was unlike him. Homicide detectives were never off duty. "Sorry."

"What's going on, Cameron?"

The idea of the step back had seemed much better in concept, when she wasn't standing right in front of him, looking fresh and beautiful and exhausted, probably from worrying about him. "Nothing. I just think, you know... Things are weird, and it might be better if we..." He shrugged. It had made perfect sense until he had to explain it to her.

She came to him, laid her hands on his chest. "Don't do this. Don't push me away in some misguided attempt to keep me safe."

He should've known she'd see right through his flimsy attempt. "That's not what I'm doing."

"Isn't it? The thing with Ezra happened because it never occurred to me that he might hurt me. I misjudged him, and he caught me in a moment of shock. I haven't misjudged Jaycee. I know who she is and what I'm dealing with."

Cameron felt his resolve wavering.

She reached up to caress his face. "Don't forget I'm a cop, too. I can take care of myself, despite recent evidence to the contrary."

"I know you can."

"Then please have faith in me and us, and don't do this honorable shit where you think you're protecting me by leaving me. All that's going to accomplish is you breaking my heart when you promised me you wouldn't."

He dropped his head onto her shoulder. "If you were hurt… Again…"

"I won't be. I know what she looks like and what she wants. I know to look out for her and to be careful. The only way I get hurt here is if you tell me I can't have you anymore. So don't do that."

"I don't want you anywhere near this."

"Too late. The only place I want to be is with you. If we let her drive us apart, then she wins, and that bitch *cannot* win. Do you hear me?"

Cameron wouldn't have thought it possible to laugh but leave it to Gigi. He raised his head and gazed into gorgeous brown eyes gone fierce with determination. "I hear you."

"I heard Sam is hitting her with two felony assault-of-police-officer charges," Gigi said. "Although it'll probably be pleaded down to lesser charges, the thought of ten years in prison ought to put a scare into her."

"Let's hope so."

"I love you, Cameron. All I want is more of what we've started. I want everything with you."

He put his arms around her and held her close. "That's all I want, too."

"Then let's have it. Let's live large and love big and have all the things we both deserve, and to hell with anyone who'd get in our way."

"I ought to be worried about how quickly you were able to talk me out of a plan I was pretty sold on."

"That plan was stupid, and you knew it, which is why I could talk you out of it so easily."

Smiling, he brought his hands up to frame her face. "I love you, too. I think maybe I have from the first time I ever saw you." He hadn't let himself entertain the possibility then because they'd both been in other relationships. But now there was nothing standing in their way except a crazy ex who wouldn't leave them alone.

"Nice how that works out, huh?"

"Nicest thing ever," he said as he kissed her.

"Let's do it properly this time." She took his hand and led him up the stairs. "Which way?"

"Left. End of the hallway."

"I love how you make your bed when most guys don't know they're supposed to."

"Of course I make my bed. I'm not a savage."

Gigi laughed. "No, you're pressed and polished and perfect. Will you iron for me when we live together? I hate to iron."

The words *live together* nearly stopped his heart. "When are we going to live together?"

"As soon as I can pack up my stuff and sublet my place. Yours is nicer, and I assume you own it?"

"I do."

"I rent mine, but I'll pay half the mortgage. Don't worry."

"So, I've gone from wanting to take a step back to living with you in the span of ten minutes?"

She pulled his T-shirt up and over his head and then ran her hands over his chest and abdomen. "Keep up, Cam. Things are moving fast."

Laughing, he stood back to watch her strip down to lacy, sexy underwear that made his mouth go dry. The healing scar on her abdomen enraged him when he recalled how she'd gotten it. "You're so fucking hot, Gigi. I look at you, and I can't believe you love me."

"Believe it." Gigi helped him out of his track pants and boxer briefs and sat on the bed, drawing him in so he was standing right in front of her. She nuzzled his erection, running her tongue from top to bottom. "Don't push me away, Cameron."

He buried his fingers in her silky dark hair. "That's the last thing I want, especially when you're doing that."

"How do you feel about this?" She took the tip into her mouth and sucked hard.

His head fell back on his shoulders. "I feel very good about that."

She took him as far as she could, until the tip bumped against her throat.

"Gigi," he said on a gasp. "Let's do this together."

Slowly, she pulled back until he popped free of her mouth. They fell onto the bed, and he was inside her within a second.

He stopped when he realized what he'd done. "Shit. Sorry. No preliminaries."

She gripped his ass to hold him deep inside her. "Doing that to you was all I needed."

He gazed down at her looking up at him with so much love. "How'd I get so lucky to find you?"

"We both got lucky, and we're going to stay that way."

As he moved in her, he held her gaze and felt as if he was truly making love for the first time in his life. The other time didn't count because they'd gotten interrupted. This was a whole new experience, and he was determined to make sure neither of them would ever forget it.

He made it last as long as he could before reaching between them to help her cross the finish line. The feel of her flesh tightening around his was all he needed to fall into an orgasm for the ages. He came so hard, he nearly forgot to breathe.

And then he had a startling realization. "We forgot the condom."

"That's okay. I'm protected."

The information allowed him to relax ever so slightly. "You got me so fired up, I didn't give it a thought, and that's certainly a first."

"You're not in charge of protecting me, remember?"

"Yes, I am."

"No, you're not. I am, and if we'd needed a condom, I would've said so. Now knock off the alpha shit and snuggle me."

Since there was nothing he'd rather do, he said, "Yes, dear."

She patted his back. "That's better."

THE LAWYER SHANE RAMSEY requested couldn't get there until the morning, so he'd be their guest in the city jail overnight. While Freddie took him downstairs to get settled, Sam headed home, confident they had their killer. For tonight, anyway, he was off the streets.

She took the hand Vernon offered to help her into the SUV. "Thank you."

"Pleasure, ma'am."

"Sam."

"Yes, ma'am."

"Honestly. It's just us. Call me Sam."

"It's not just us, ma'am. Young Jimmy is watching and learning."

"Vernon would skin me alive if I called you anything other than ma'am, ma'am," Jimmy said.

"Now you're double-ma'aming me."

The agents laughed.

"How was your day, ma'am?" Vernon asked, glancing at her in the mirror.

"I think we got our guy. And get this—he's the son of a sergeant who hates my guts for reasons known only to him."

"Wow," Vernon said. "That's complicated."

"As hell, but if he raped and murdered those women, I'm going to nail him to the wall."

"You've got DNA, right?"

"Yeah, but we need a sample from him that we didn't get before he lawyered up, and it certainly won't happen voluntarily now that the lawyer is involved."

"What I don't get," Jimmy said, "is if he's innocent, why wouldn't he give the DNA to prove that?"

"There's always a fear of being framed, I suppose," Sam said, "but that's a good question. If someone was tying me to rapes and murders I didn't commit, I'd hand over my DNA to prove I had nothing to do with it. But people don't trust us to always do the right thing, and with good reason, I suppose. That's another way that the few bad apples ruin things for the rest of us."

"Heard your friend Detective McBride is in line for a big promotion," Vernon said, glancing at her in the mirror.

"Yeah, she is. I'm thrilled about it. She's one of the best cops I've ever worked with. The department needs someone like her in a top-level role. She'll make us all look good."

"Did they ask you?" Jimmy asked.

"Twice, and I said 'thanks, but no, thanks' both times. I'd go mad in that job. My dad hated it at first. He grew into it, but the transition from street cop to desk jockey was rough for him. I'd never adjust to that."

"I can't see that for you," Vernon said. "Hope that's okay to say, ma'am."

"It's okay to say because it's the truth. I'm doing the job I was born to do, and I know that sounds self-important or whatever, but it's true."

"We can see that, ma'am," Vernon said. "You're very good at it."

"Thanks." Ugh, she was going to have to replace Jeannie so soon after filling the spots left by Arnold's death and Tyrone's resignation. The thought of undertaking that process again thoroughly depressed her. Nothing ever stayed the same, as much as she might wish it would. Change made her twitchy. There'd been a lot of it lately, more so than at any other time in her life. From Arnold and her father dying, to the twins and Eli joining their family, to Nick's new job and the subsequent move to the White House... It was a lot on top of a lot.

Tomorrow night, they would host a one-year remembrance for Detective Arnold on the anniversary of his tragic death. With that in mind, she put through a call to Gideon.

"Hi, Sam," he said. "I was just about to text you."

She was thankful that the chief usher at the White House was the one person in her new orbit who'd agreed to call her by her first name when it was just the two of them. "Hi there. I wanted to check in about tomorrow night."

"I just went over the final plans with the kitchen, and we're good to go for all of Detective Arnold's favorites—pizza, hot dogs, chicken wings and chocolate cake."

"That sounds perfect."

"I also added salad for those concerned about their arteries."

"Good call," she said, laughing. "I appreciate you overseeing the plans for this."

"My pleasure. We'll have everything ready at seven, and I've cleared the guest list with the Secret Service. They'll have the list at the gate."

"Thank you for taking care of everything."

"No problem. I'll see you then, if not before."

"Have a good night."

"You, too."

Ten minutes later, Vernon pulled the SUV into the White House complex and was stopped at the gate to show his badge and reveal his passenger before they were waved through.

"Why don't they do that every time?" Sam asked.

"They don't like to be predictable."

"Huh. Interesting."

Before Vernon could get there to help her, Sam was out of the SUV and standing on her own two feet, the cane tucked under her arm even as her hip ached like a bitch.

"Look at you go, ma'am." Vernon smiled like a proud papa. "You won't be needing us to drive you around for much longer."

"No offense but thank goodness for that."

"None taken," he said, laughing. "Have a nice evening."

"You guys do the same. Thank you for all you do to keep me safe."

"It's an honor, ma'am."

"My name is Sam!" she said over her shoulder as she walked away with the cane still under her arm. Inside, she was greeted by Dustin, one of the younger ushers. As she eyed the staircase to the residence, she decided she wasn't feeling that ballsy and headed for the elevator.

"Can I get that for you, ma'am?" Dustin asked.

"I've got it. Thank you."

"As you wish, ma'am."

Sam arrived to silence on the second floor, which meant everyone was probably upstairs in the conservatory, their favorite gathering spot. She sat on the bed and sent a text to Nick. *I'm home. Just getting changed and finding some food.*

Dinner is in the oven for you. I'll come down to get you.

How long would it be, she wondered, before an innocuous sentence from him, such as *I'll come down to get you*, wouldn't make her heart skip a beat? Hopefully forever. Since he was on his way, she stayed seated to wait for him.

He came through the door two minutes later, wearing sweats and his favorite ratty Harvard T-shirt, looking very much like her husband and not the leader of the free world. When he smiled at her, she could forget he belonged to the entire country. Right now, he was only hers.

She held out her arms to him, and he came to her, wrapping her up in his special brand of love.

"Tough day?" he asked.

"Aren't they all?"

"Are you okay?"

"I am now." Before she'd had him to come home to, the idea of clinging to any man would've been unthinkable. Now the clinging was as necessary as breathing. "What's for dinner?"

"Tenderloin and potatoes."

"My mouth just watered."

"Let me get it. You can eat upstairs while the kids have their ice cream."

"Sounds perfect."

She stood, took a second to make sure her legs were under her and then went to lock up her weapon. "Lead the way."

They stopped in the small kitchen to get her plate from the oven and then used the elevator to get to the third floor, where another small kitchen housed the ice cream.

"Have you heard anything from Eli?" she asked.

"Only that Candace was due to arrive in New Jersey today."

"I guess we won't be hearing from him for a while."

Nick smiled. "Probably not."

"Have we established an opinion about her moving in with him?"

"I don't think we're allowed to," Nick said. "He's twenty, and we're not paying for the apartment or the tuition. Even if we were, I'd have a hard time working up an objection after what they've been through. I do think there needs to be a fatherly conversation about keeping his eye on the ball with school and all that."

"Agreed."

"I'll take care of that in the next few days."

"Imagine how excited they must be," Sam said.

"I can't wait to meet her."

CHAPTER THIRTY-ONE

Elijah had cleaned his apartment until it sparkled, while recalling the series of events that had led to him having his own place. After they'd put him under their protection, the Secret Service had insisted he move to a more secure location, which had meant leaving the roommates he'd had since freshman year. He'd been furious about that, but had gone along with it because he hadn't wanted to cause trouble for Nick or Sam.

Now he was thankful to have his own place, because Candace could live there with him without three other guys underfoot.

"This is so nice!" she said when he gave her the five-minute tour.

"It's not much, but it's home. For now, anyway."

"I love it, Eli. It's so cozy."

"Can I get you something to eat or drink? I got an Instacart delivery to stock up on the black licorice you love and your favorite iced tea, although it's hard to find the unsweetened kind here for some reason." He felt like he was talking too much.

She moved so she was standing right in front of him. "I can't believe you remembered that stuff."

"I remember everything. I've relived every second we spent together at least a million times since I last saw you."

"I have, too. I tried to focus on the good parts and not the rest."

"Same. I rarely think about the bad stuff because it upsets me so much."

"I feel like I need to say this again, at least one more time before we move on from it, but I'm *so, so* sorry for what they did, Eli. I hate them for it, and they know it. Our relationship will never recover from it."

"You have nothing to be sorry about, and at some point, you ought to forgive them."

"I'll never forgive them for having you charged with statutory rape when our relationship was consensual and built on true love."

Hearing her talk about true love made his heart flutter. "Before I lost my dad and Cleo the way I did, I would've agreed with you. Fuck them and what they did to us. But now… Now, I think you ought to find a way to put things back together with them."

"I just don't know if I can. I'm still *so* angry with them. The last three years have been pure hell. I haven't said more than 'yes,' 'no' or 'maybe' to them since the day you were charged. When they found out I was coming here, to you, they went ballistic. I'm not sure it can be fixed, but I do hear what you're saying, and I'm also so sorry I wasn't here for you when you lost your dad and Cleo."

"It was brutal. I'll never forget that call from the FBI."

"I cried for days when I heard about it from Dalton. He called to tell me."

Dalton had been Elijah's best friend during the summers he spent in California with his mother.

"It was rough. Then I found out they'd left me as the guardian for Alden and Aubrey, and we fell into this situation with the Cappuanos."

She took him by the hand and led him to the sofa. "How did that happen?"

Over the last few days, they'd talked about so many logistical issues with her coming to New Jersey that they hadn't gotten a chance to talk about much else. "As you probably know, Sam is a homicide detective with the DC Metro Police Department, and when she encountered the kids in the hospital after the fire, she offered to take them home. She and Nick were already licensed foster parents from when they first took in their son, Scotty."

"It's funny to hear you call the president and first lady Sam and Nick."

"That's who they are to me."

"Is it so cool to visit the White House?"

"Yeah, it is. It's weird to think of that as home, but since that's where my brother and sister live, it's home."

"I read about Cleo's parents and sisters trying to get custody of the twins."

"That was almost as big of a nightmare as losing my dad and Cleo in the first place. I was so scared I was going to lose the twins, too. Thank God my dad had the best lawyers money could buy, and their will was airtight. They wanted me—and only me—to be responsible for the twins. There wasn't an ounce of wiggle room in the way it was written. It's like they knew it'd be challenged by Cleo's money-grubbing family and made sure it couldn't be broken. And Nick's lawyer friend, Andy, was incredible defending the will and the custody agreement."

"Your parents must've had a lot of faith in you."

"They knew I love the twins as much as they did. I can't wait for you to meet them. They're so cute. And Scotty has become like a little brother to me and a big brother to them. It's only been a few months, but the six of us are already a family. It's amazing when I think about how it all went down."

"The photo they released of your family on Christmas Eve was so sweet. I couldn't stop staring at you. I can't believe how much you've changed since I last saw you."

"I haven't changed that much."

"Yes, you have. You've gone from a handsome boy to a gorgeous man."

"Candace... I wish you knew how much I missed you and wanted you and loved you and thought of you for all this time."

"I do know, because I did the same. I followed your social media."

"I followed yours! It was like a lifeline."

"Right?"

"I kept waiting to see you with a new guy. I wasn't sure how I would deal with that."

"There couldn't have been anyone else while you were still out there somewhere."

She launched herself into his outstretched arms.

He caught her and hugged her as tightly as he could without hurting her. With her back in his life, he felt like he could truly breathe again for the first time since he last saw her.

"Eli?"

"What, honey?"

"Will you please take me to bed? All I want is to be with you the way we used to be—and with no worries about getting caught this time."

"There's nothing I'd rather do." He stood and helped her up. "I'm not going to wake up and find out that I've dreamed about you again, am I?"

"You dreamed about me?"

"All the time. It was torture. I'd wake up, hard as a rock, thinking you were here, and it was crushing to realize it was only another dream."

She reached up to put her hands on his face and drew him into a kiss that nearly made him whimper from the need that overtook him. "Does that feel real to you?"

"As real as anything has ever been." He lifted her into his arms and walked into the bedroom, putting her down next to the bed. As they kissed and laughed and pulled at clothes, Eli realized he was truly happy for the first time since the last time he'd seen her. Yes, he was still dealing with heartbreak and grief over the senseless murders of his father and stepmother, but with Candace back in his life, even that became easier to manage.

She made everything better, like she had from the first day he met her. She was just as he remembered her, only curvier. Her breasts were fuller, her body that of a grown woman now, and as he'd been before, he was dazzled by her.

They landed on his bed in a jumble of arms and legs that quickly sorted themselves into perfect alignment for what they were both dying for.

"Shit, I need a condom."

She stopped him from getting up. "I'm on long-term birth control. I did it two weeks ago. We're covered."

"How could you do that when you weren't eighteen yet?"

"I lied."

Smiling, he kissed her with three years' worth of longing and desire. "This might be quick."

"Who cares? We can do it anytime we want now."

They skipped most of the preliminaries to get to the main event, and with his body joined to hers, Eli felt as if he'd died and gone straight back to the paradise he'd found with her long before either of them was ready for it. "Oh God, Candace... This is just how I remember it, only better."

"*Yes.*"

He closed his eyes and surrendered to the bliss, hoping that this time, it would last forever.

. . .

IN THE MORNING, Sam woke early to find Nick curled up to her, his arm around her waist. He'd been called back to work again the night before to contend with yet another issue with the North Koreans and their missiles.

She covered his hand with hers, floating in the predawn moments before another frantic day began. This one would end with a remembrance of their beloved Detective Arnold, killed one year ago already. How was that possible? While the year had gone quickly, it felt like forever since she'd last seen the endearing young detective who'd been so eager to please.

"What're you thinking about?" Nick asked in the gravelly early morning voice that only she ever got to hear. She loved that voice.

"Arnold. A year today."

"God, that's right. Hard to believe it's already a year."

"I was just thinking how I feel like I haven't seen him in much longer than that."

"It's been a rough year all around."

"Sure has, but we got through it."

"Because we have this," he said, holding her closer as his erection pressed against her back.

She squeezed his arm. "I don't know what I'd ever do without this."

"Same."

"My hip is feeling much better if you want to attempt some old-school morning fun."

"*Oh*, old school, you say?"

"Three cheers for good old missionary."

"Hip, hip, hooray."

"You had to bring the hip into it."

Chuckling, he moved so he was on top of her, gazing down at her with the heated hazel eyes that were like windows to his soul. All she ever saw in them was love and tenderness and utter devotion. "If that phone rings right now…"

"Shhh, don't even say it."

"Tell me if anything hurts."

"You'll be the first to know."

He kissed her neck and had her fired up in a matter of seconds. Add that to his list of superpowers, the ability to light her fire with a minimum of effort.

Sam raised her left leg and slid it to the side, hoping to give him enough room to get things done.

He slid into her with the effortlessness that was so much a part of who they were together.

"I've missed being able to look at you when we do this," he said.

Sam gazed up at him, ferociously handsome in the early morning light. "Mmm, same." His hair was standing on end, his face covered in scruff, and if she'd ever seen a more gorgeous man, she couldn't recall. She liked him this way even more than she loved him pressed and polished and ready for world domination. This guy belonged only to her, and she loved him more than life itself.

"Samantha," he whispered in her ear. "My love. My life. My everything."

She held him close as they rocked together, chasing an explosive finish that left them breathless and gasping.

"Holy moly," he said after a long silence.

"We're so good at that, even with a bum hip."

"That's going to be the highlight of my shitty day."

"Mine, too."

"How's the hip?"

"What hip?"

Nick smiled down at her, brushed his lips over hers and said, "Get up, lazybones. World domination awaits."

Sam closed her eyes. "Five more minutes."

The next thing she knew, he was kissing her awake, bringing the scents of his cologne and minty-fresh toothpaste with him.

Without opening her eyes, she looped her arms around his neck and rubbed her face against his freshly shaven cheek. "Let's call in sick."

Laughing, he said, "I wish we could, but we have kids to get up and shit to do. Vacation will be here before we know it, and we'll spend the entire week in bed."

"Promise?"

"That's a promise I can't wait to keep."

"I'm counting the days."

"Me, too. Now get up before we make everyone late."

"You're very bossy this morning, Mr. President."

"Someone's gotta keep this train on the tracks, and it ain't gonna be you."

Since she couldn't argue with the truth, she dragged herself out of bed to hit the shower.

. . .

AFTER BREAKFAST with the kids and seeing them off to school with their details, Sam kissed Nick goodbye and rode to HQ with Vernon and Jimmy. She probably had two more weeks to go before she'd feel confident driving herself, which gave her something to look forward to.

They pulled up to the morgue entrance as Sam's phone rang with a call from Jeannie.

"What's up, Deputy Chief?"

"Not quite yet," Jeannie said with a nervous laugh, "but that's why I'm calling. The swearing-in is at four today at city hall. Can you make it?"

"I wouldn't miss that for anything."

"I just bought the white shirt," Jeannie said with another laugh. "I still can't believe this is happening."

"Believe it. You've earned it. What does your family think?"

"They're losing it! My mom hasn't stopped crying since I told her."

"I love it," Sam said, chuckling. "I've just gotten to HQ. I'll see you at four and, Jeannie?"

"Yes?"

"I'm so fucking proud."

"That means everything to me, as you know," Jeannie said, sounding tearful. "None of this would be happening for me if it wasn't for you."

"Sure, it would."

"No, it wouldn't, Sam. You put me back together on the job after the attack. I never would've come back without you and the support of our squad."

"We love you."

"Same. So much."

"I'll see you at four. We'll all be there to cheer you on today and always."

"Thank you for everything."

"You got it." Sam slapped her phone closed, feeling like a proud mama bear. "Deputy Chief McBride. What a thing."

"It's wonderful," Vernon said. "The way you support your officers is lovely."

"They're my people."

"They're lucky to have you."

"And vice versa. I'll see you after a bit."

"Looking forward to seeing her sworn in."

"I am, too."

"Have a good day at the office, ma'am."

"Thanks." She wondered how they didn't go mad with boredom while she was at work. Inside, she ducked into the morgue to check in with Lindsey. "How's it going?" Sam asked her.

"No complaints. You're getting around better."

Sam did a little jig that she instantly regretted. "Got to do it missionary this morning."

"Hallelujah," Lindsey said, laughing. "That's progress."

"Sure is. You don't know what you've got till it's gone, you know?"

"I get it, but I'm sure you've found ways to work around it."

"My husband is nothing if not creative."

Lindsey fanned her face. "Is it getting warm in here?"

"Does it ever get warm in this icebox? On another note, what're you hearing about McBride's promotion?"

"A lot of grumbling. *A lot* a lot."

"Ugh, I wondered how bad it would be."

"Your old friend Offenbach was heard saying just what we need is you having another ally in the chief's suite."

"He's still pissed because I caught him having an affair when his wife was expecting their fifth—or was it sixth?—kid."

Lindsey smiled. "No doubt."

"You think it'll die down?"

"Eventually, but Jeannie's going to have to stay tough and soldier through. The media is saying the only reason she got the job was because the FBI report identified racial disparities."

"That's bullshit! Brewster wanted a woman—and even mentioned wanting a Black woman—for the job long before the FBI report hit."

"You're preaching to the choir, my friend."

"If Jeannie could survive what Sanborn did to her, this shit will seem like a cakewalk in comparison."

"That's true. Our girl is made of true grit. She'll get through it."

"Let's keep an eye on her in the meantime."

"Will do. In other misogyny news, things have been ugly for Henderson, huh?"

"That's what I hear. I didn't get a good vibe from her, but I hate what they're putting her—and her family—through."

"Terry said the statement she issued, as well as Nick's in support of her, helped somewhat."

"Does he think she'll be confirmed?"

"Yeah, they've got the votes, so she just has to endure the rest of the hearing."

"Would they be doing this to a dude?" Sam asked. "Tearing apart his ex-wife in 'service to the country'?"

"Probably not like this, but it's high time we had a female in one of the top jobs. I give Nick props for making that happen."

"I just hope he doesn't live to regret it."

"How so?"

"I don't know. Just that strange vibe I got from her. Nick says I have to give her a chance because my ten seconds in her presence isn't enough to form an opinion."

"That may be true, but that gut of yours is rather legendary."

"Which is why I worry." Sam shrugged. "But I have bigger concerns today, such as nailing a rapist-murderer, and with that, I must get to it. Have a good day."

"You, too. Give 'em hell."

"That's the plan."

Sam arrived to unusual quiet in the pit. "What's up?"

Gonzo turned to her, his expression grim. "We had to bounce Ramsey."

"What? Why?"

"It came right from Forrester. We didn't have enough to hold him, and he didn't want to jeopardize future prosecution. Yada, yada."

"That's fucking bullshit!"

"You know that, and I know that…"

Sam was fuming.

"What's the plan, boss?" Cruz asked when he joined them.

"Since he won't give us a sample willingly, and the judge wants more before they'll give us a warrant, we'll stalk him until we get a sample of his DNA. Anything he discards is open game, no warrant required."

"Don't you think his father has schooled him on how to avoid that?" Gonzo asked.

"Probably, but even people who know better screw up. The second he does, we'll be right there to nab him."

CHAPTER THIRTY-TWO

With overtime authorized by the chief, Sam organized her squad and a team of ten Patrol officers into twenty-four-hour shifts to keep eyes on Shane Ramsey. Because she was still on limited duty, she was unable to be one of the officers following him, but that didn't stop her from joining Gonzo and Freddie while they took the daytime shift watching the garage where he worked. Freddie had driven his dad's SUV that day, which made it possible for Sam to go with them. Gonzo's Charger was still off-limits to her healing hip.

"This is gonna be deadly boring," Freddie said as he peered through binoculars.

"Boring but necessary," Sam said.

"Reminds me of what I was doing a year ago today," Gonzo said from the passenger seat.

The comment hit Sam like a punch to the gut. "Gonzo... I'm sorry. It never occurred to me. If you want to go back to the house—"

"Stop. I'm fine. I'm just saying it's a reminder of what we were doing."

"I can't believe it's a year already," Freddie said. "I woke up thinking about that day."

"I wake up thinking about it every day," Gonzo said. "And before you jump all over that, it's not as bad as it was. Mostly, I try to remember the good stuff and not how it ended."

Sam had no idea what to say to that.

Apparently, Freddie didn't either.

"I'm okay, you guys," Gonzo said. "I swear."

"Would you tell us if you weren't?" Freddie asked.

"I would. I promise. If I've learned anything this year, it's to ask for help when I need it. That was a bitter lesson, but one that'll stay with me."

"I'm glad to hear you say that," Sam said. "We're all so driven to prove to the world we can handle anything that we forget to be human sometimes."

"True, and we all know how trying to muscle through it went for me," Gonzo said. "I'm lucky to still have a job and a family after the dust settled."

"You still have both because we all love you," Sam said. "And would do anything for you."

"That's what got me through."

"We're going to have to be tough for Jeannie over the next few months," Freddie said. "Word on the street isn't great."

"So I heard," Sam said, "but whatever. They can fuck off and deal with it. There's a new deputy chief in town, and she's going to be incredible."

AT THREE THIRTY, they handed off the watch of Shane Ramsey to Sam's friend Officer Charles and her partner, Officer Dickinson, with specific instructions on what to do if they saw him discard anything.

"You have gloves and evidence bags?" Sam asked.

"Yes, ma'am," Officer Charles said. She'd made a friend for life in Sam after the incredible job she did planning Skip Holland's police funeral.

"When you hand off to the next shift, make sure to ask them the same thing."

"We will," Officer Charles said. "Give our congratulations to Deputy Chief McBride. She's such an inspiration to me and other young Black female officers."

"I'll tell her. It'll mean a lot to her." Sam glanced toward the garage where Shane had been working all day. "He knows we're watching him. Be safe out here, and don't forget what we suspect he's done."

"We'll be careful."

While Gonzo and Freddie headed for the SUV, Sam paused as a thought occurred to her. "Have you taken the detective's exam, Officer Charles?"

"I have and passed with flying colors. I'm just waiting for an opening."

"I've got one in Homicide as of today. We should talk."

The young woman's expressive eyes went wide. "Seriously?"

"Absolutely. Come see me next week."

"I'll do that. Thank you so much."

"You got it." Confident she'd left the investigation in capable hands, Sam rode with Freddie and Gonzo to city hall.

"You gotta love the circle of life," Freddie said, "with Jeannie being sworn in as deputy chief on Arnold's one-year anniversary."

"He'd be so proud of her," Gonzo said.

"He'd be proud of you, too, and how you fought for and got justice for him," Freddie said.

Sam's emotions were all over the place as she listened to them and picked through the memories from the last brutal year. While much had been lost, so much had been gained, too, including a new appreciation for one another and the blue brother- and sisterhood they shared. They were more than just her coworkers. They were as much her family as her blood family, and she loved them.

A commander probably shouldn't have so much love for the people who worked for her. Maybe that was a failing, but it was one she could certainly live with.

At city hall, they went through security, secured their weapons and made their way to the main hall, where the ceremony would take place. Seeing Jeannie wearing the deputy chief's uniform for the first time as she chatted with the rest of their squad brought tears to Sam's eyes and had her taking a step back to get it together before she embarrassed herself.

It came as no surprise to realize Freddie had followed her.

"Are you okay?" he asked.

"Yeah, it's just, you know... That particular uniform..."

"Your dad's uniform."

"Yeah." She took a deep breath and let it out. "He'd love seeing it on Jeannie."

"Yes, he certainly would. He's here with us. I'm sure of it."

Sam squeezed his arm. "Thanks."

He nodded. "Can't help but notice the turnout from HQ is kind of sparse."

"It's going to take time for people to come around to her in this role, but they will." At least Sam hoped so.

"You ready for this?" Freddie asked.

"As ready as I'm ever going to be."

They returned to the main hall and watched with pride as the mayor swore in their beloved friend as the District's new deputy chief of police. Jeannie's beaming husband pinned the bars on her shoulders and then hugged her tightly, whispering something to her that made her laugh through tears.

A rousing round of applause greeted the new deputy chief, who stood before the podium, seeming shocked and amazed by the turn of events that had brought her to this moment.

"One year ago today," she said when the applause finally died down, "we lost a wonderful friend and colleague. Would you please join me in a moment of silence for Detective AJ Arnold?"

Sam bowed her head and said a silent prayer for Arnold, her dad, his first partner, Steven Coyne, and all the officers who'd been lost on the job.

"We know our friend Arnold is telling corny jokes in heaven and making everyone he encounters happier just by being in his presence," Jeannie said. "Over the last year, we've learned that life goes on even in times of tremendous grief and sorrow. We also lost our beloved Skip Holland, who once held the title that now belongs to me. I'll strive every day to make him proud in my service to the department as your new deputy chief. Mayor Brewster, I thank you for the confidence and faith you've placed in me, and I vow to do everything in my power to be worthy of this tremendous honor. Chief Farnsworth, Captain Malone, Lieutenant Holland, Sergeant Gonzales, Detectives Cruz, Green, O'Brien, Carlucci and Dominguez, as well as my former partner, Detective Tyrone, I thank each of you for your unwavering support and encouragement. My years in the Homicide squad have been some of the best and most challenging of my life, and I give special thanks to our fearless leader, Lieutenant Holland, for her leadership and dedication to the men and women who work for her. There's no way I'd be standing up here without her friendship and guidance."

Again, Sam found herself holding back tears as Jeannie looked directly at her. She nodded and blew her friend a kiss.

"To my mother, sisters, brothers, nieces, nephews and my late dad, who's always with us, I thank you for a lifetime of love and support. And to my darling husband, Michael, who makes everything possible, I love you forever. Thank you all for this honor of a lifetime. I promise to do you proud."

Sam cheered and whistled and generally made a scene in support of her sweet friend. That something so wonderful could be happening on the same day they remembered the worst thing that'd ever happened on the job was almost too much to process.

Jeannie posed for photos with the mayor, the Homicide squad, Chief Farnsworth, Captain Malone, her family and other friends who'd come to support her ascension to deputy chief.

"See you all at my place after a bit?" Sam asked.

"I love the way you say that," Freddie said with a laugh. "Your place."

"Welp, that's what it is."

"We'll be there," Malone said for all of them.

JEANNIE'S SWEARING-IN had taken some of the gloom out of the occasion, which had turned into a remembrance and a celebration.

"It's so good to see you," Sam said, hugging Will Tyrone.

"You as well, Lieutenant."

"You're not a cop anymore. You can call me Sam."

Smiling, he said, "Old habits die hard."

"How's the security business?"

"Not as exciting as Homicide, but then again, what is?"

"Homicide has been a real thrill lately," Sam said sarcastically. "The fun never ends."

"I've heard about how you're looking at Ramsey's son for the rapes and murders in the park."

"We know it's him. We just have to prove it."

"My money's on you guys."

Sam had spoken with Officer Charles on the way home and had learned Shane was now at the bar he frequented in Columbia Heights. The officers had followed him inside and were watching him, hoping he'd abandon a beer bottle or glass that could be confiscated as evidence.

Of course, he knew what they were looking for and had made eye contact with Officer Charles as he'd wiped his beer bottle clean and handed it to the bartender.

He was as much of a bastard as his father was, only more so. To her knowledge, his father, as despicable as he was, had never raped or murdered anyone.

After everyone had eaten the Arnold-themed junk food, Sam stood with the microphone Gideon had made sure was on the large square table they'd set in the elegant State Dining Room. "Ahem," she said to get their attention. "I want to thank you all for being here tonight for what's turned into a two-part event. Part one is our solemn remembrance of our friend and colleague, Detective AJ Arnold, who left us far too soon one year ago today. As we have every day for the last year, we remember AJ's humor, the no-strings-attached friendship he offered each of us and his almost childlike enthusiasm for the job. We love him. We miss him. We will remember him always. I must also mention AJ's devoted partner, Sergeant Tommy Gonzales, who was instrumental in ensuring that the man who took AJ from us will never have the chance to kill again." Sam led an enthusiastic round of applause for Gonzo, who shook his head as if to deflect praise he didn't feel he deserved.

"Tommy, what happened to Arnold and to you is something we all fear every time we strap on the badge and hit the streets. You were tireless in your efforts to get justice for your beloved partner, and we're incredibly proud of you."

His wife, Christina, put her arm around him, and he leaned into her as he wiped away tears with the back of his hand.

"AJ's dad, John, would like to say something, so I'll turn it over to him."

Sam handed the microphone to John Arnold, who was seated next to her.

He stood and cleared his throat. "Thank you, President Cappuano and Lieutenant Holland, for this beautiful evening in honor of our son. He'd be amazed to see us celebrating him at the White House, of all places. Thank you, Gonzo, Jeannie, Will, Freddie, Dani, Gigi, Cameron, Captain Malone, Chief Farnsworth and the entire MPD for the way you've honored AJ over this last difficult year. Nothing can prepare a father, mother, sisters or devoted girlfriend for this kind of sudden, shocking loss. But the love and support we've received from AJ's brothers and sisters in blue has gotten us through it. He loved you all so much, and on behalf of our family, we thank you for the many ways you continue to honor his memory."

By the time he handed the microphone back to her, Sam had a huge lump in her throat and tears in her eyes. She would never get over the senseless loss of such a promising young officer.

Nick squeezed her hand as she stood to finish her remarks. "When we planned this event, we had no idea we'd also have something big to celebrate tonight, and that is the promotion of our wonderful friend and colleague, Deputy Chief Jeannie McBride."

Sam led a round of applause for Jeannie, who smiled as widely as Sam had seen her smile since her wedding day.

"Jeannie, we're so incredibly proud to call you our friend, our colleague and our deputy chief. And I just want to add… Skip Holland would be busting his buttons if he were here to see you wearing his former rank."

"Thank you, Sam, and everyone for your support. I appreciate it so much—and I'm going to need it going forward."

"You have it," Sam assured her.

After that, the butlers brought in chocolate cake and served after-dinner drinks. They ate, they reminisced, they laughed, and they remembered Detective Arnold even as they celebrated Deputy Chief McBride.

"How're you feeling, babe?" Nick asked Sam.

"Incredibly emotional. Freddie said it best earlier. It's the circle of life, and I don't think it's any coincidence that Jeannie was sworn in today, of all days."

"I don't think it was either. Skip's up there rubbing his hands together with glee after having orchestrated it all."

Sam rested her head on Nick's shoulder. "I wouldn't put it past him."

"Neither would I."

THE NEXT DAY, Sam was staked out again with Freddie and Gonzo, watching, waiting and hoping Shane Ramsey would fuck up.

"What if he never gives us anything?" Freddie asked.

"He will," Sam said with more confidence than she'd felt when she first settled on this surveillance plan.

Her phone rang with a call from Elijah, which she found odd. He rarely called her, especially during a workday. "Hey, what's up? Everything okay?"

"Everything is great."

"I take that to mean things are going well with Candace?"

"Couldn't be better."

"I'm happy for you, Eli. Truly."

"Thanks. It's been so great to be back together with her and to find that nothing has changed for either of us."

"Did Nick lecture you about keeping your eye on the ball at school?"

Laughing, Eli said, "He did, and I am. I'm calling you as a favor to a friend."

"How so?"

"You know that Nate is the lead agent on my detail, right?"

"I do." He'd been one of her favorites when he worked at the Ninth Street house. "What about him?"

"We were talking the other day, and he mentioned he's struck up a friendship of sorts with Brooke."

"*My* Brooke?"

"Yep."

"Do tell."

"I guess she babysat for you guys, and they got to talking. He said they've never stopped talking since then."

Sam was truly shocked to hear this news. She hadn't heard a single rumbling about that from Brooke or her mother, Tracy.

"Nate said he likes her a lot, but he feels like it's gotten to the point where he needs to have a conversation with you before it goes any further."

"How old is he?"

"Around twenty-seven, I think."

"That makes him seven years older than her."

"Would you object?"

Sam thought about that for a second. In the past, she might've had something to say about it, but after Brooke had overcome a violent attack at a party where multiple kids had been killed, her niece was not an average twenty-year-old. "That's not up to me. As much as I still think of her as a little kid, Brooke is a grown woman. I don't have any say over who she dates."

"I believe Nate's primary concern is one of propriety due to how he met her."

"I understand, but you can assure him there'll be no pushback from me or Nick. We think the world of him, and we'd only ask that he be kind to our niece."

"That'll mean a lot to him, Sam. Thank you. And he'd also want me to tell you he was absolutely *cringing* at the thought of me discussing this with you because it was so unprofessional."

Sam laughed. "I can imagine, but it was courteous of him to be concerned about what I'd think of it." She couldn't wait to call Tracy with this bombshell. "When do we get to meet Candace?"

"We'll be home soon."

"We'll look forward to that."

They said their goodbyes, and Sam immediately put through a call to Tracy.

"Hey, what's up?"

"That's what I'm calling to ask. Anything new or exciting over there?"

"Not that I know of."

"Interesting."

"What, Sam? You sound like the cat that swallowed the canary."

"I've stumbled onto a major scoop, and I'm not sure if I should tell you or wait until the person involved tells you."

"What the hell are you talking about?"

"I think Brooke might have a boyfriend."

"What? No, she doesn't."

"You should maybe check with her about that."

"What. Do. You. *Know?*"

"Do you promise not to flip out and let her be the one to tell you?"

"I promise."

"I mean it, Trace. I have a feeling about this... It could be a big deal for her."

"I hear you. I'll be cool. I swear."

"Remember Nate, the agent who worked at Ninth Street and now heads Eli's detail?"

"Yes, I know who you mean. Wait, you think it's *him?*"

"I know for a fact it's him."

"How old is he?"

Sam had to laugh that her first question was the same as Sam's. "Twenty-seven, Eli thinks."

"That would make him seven years older than her."

"Yes, I was able to do that math on my own."

"And Eli told you this?"

"He was doing recon for Nate, finding out whether there'd be objections on our part due to how they met."

"What did you tell him?"

"That Brooke is a grown woman who can make her own decisions about who she dates."

"I hate that that's true, but it is," Tracy said with a sigh.

"At least we know she'd be as safe as can be with him."

"That's something."

"That's everything, Trace. I got to know him well when he worked at the house, and he seems like a wonderful young man."

"And handsome as hell, if I remember correctly."

"That he is."

"I wonder why she hasn't said anything to me," Tracy said. "She's on her phone a lot when she's home from school, but I figured that's just what people her age do."

"Soon enough, he'll tell her the news is out. I'm sure you'll hear from her about it."

"Do you think it's serious?"

"Seeing as how Nate asked Eli to mention it to me, I'd say it must be. Eli said Nate was cringing over it because it was so unprofessional. Trace? Are you there?"

"I'm here. I'm just feeling super emotional about this. After what happened, I wondered if she'd ever be able to get past it to have a healthy relationship with a man, and to know that might be happening..."

"I'm right there with you, sister."

CHAPTER THIRTY-THREE

Brooke had left her last class of the day at the University of Virginia and was on her way back to her dorm when her phone rang with the special tone she'd set for Nate. As she dug it out of her tote bag, she wondered why he'd be calling in the middle of the day. They usually talked by FaceTime at night, sometimes for hours. At some point over the last few months, his calls had become the most important thing in her life.

"Hey," she said, breathless by the time she located the phone at the bottom of her bag.

"How's it going?"

"Good. You?"

"Very good."

"Uh, why are you calling me now?"

"Because I have news."

"What kind of news?"

"The kind where I might've gotten word to your aunt that we've become friends and found out she has no objection to it."

"Wait. You told my *aunt*?"

"Indirectly. Elijah actually told her."

"You did this without talking to me about it first?"

"I, uh... It's been really weighing on me, Brooke. I worked so hard to have this job, and I've been afraid of screwing it up."

"We've spent hours on the phone, and you never mentioned anything was weighing on you."

"I didn't want it to weigh on you, too."

"That's not how this works, Nate. I know you love to remind me that you're older and wiser and know best, but I'm not cool with you outing this to her without talking to me first. Do you understand that this news is now burning its way through my family?"

"Shit, Brooke. I'm sorry. I should've said something. The conversation with Eli just kind of happened, and I didn't really think it through."

"I'm getting a call from my mother. Wonder what that could be about?"

"I'm really sorry. Will you forgive me?"

"I'm not sure yet."

"Brooke... Don't forget the good news—your aunt doesn't mind if we see each other. And I'm not going to get fired for any of this."

"You haven't done anything that would get you fired."

"But I want to. I *really* want to."

Her blood went hot in her veins at the way he said that. "I'm not sure I can."

"I told you... Anything that happens between us will happen only when or if you want it to."

"What if it never happens?"

"I think it will. In time."

"What if you get tired of waiting for me to get over my shit?"

"I'll never get tired of waiting for you."

"You say that now."

"I'll say that always."

"Don't do that."

"Do what?"

"Act like this is a forever kind of thing."

"It sure feels like that to me. I've never spoken to any human being as much as I have to you, and I still have so much more I want to talk about with you."

Brooke sighed. "Nate..."

"Yes, Brooke?"

"You shouldn't say stuff like that."

"Why not?"

"Because!"

His laughter was one of her favorite things. She looked forward to his calls with the kind of heightened excitement that could surely be her downfall where he was concerned.

"I have next weekend off. Can I come see you?"

"My family is going to Camp David next weekend."

"Do you have to go?"

"No, but I was planning to."

"Could I convince you to hang with me instead?"

Most of their "relationship," if you could call it that, transpired on the phone through frequent FaceTime chats that kept him from getting too close even as she became closer to him than anyone alive. And yes, she could see how strange that was, but she liked it the way it was. "What do you want to do?"

"I could get a room near school, and we could... Go on hikes, go out to eat, go to the movies. I'd even be willing to go to the antique stores since I know you love that stuff. Whatever you want to do."

"You should..."

"What?"

The ache in her chest was so intense as to be concerning. "Be with someone who can give you what you need."

"I am with someone who gives me what I need, Brooke. And what I need is to spend more time *with* you rather than just talking to you." He softened his tone. "I understand what you're worried about, and this would be a no-pressure weekend. Just time to hang out and have some fun like we did in DC." They'd gone to the Smithsonian's Air and Space Museum and had pizza afterward. He hadn't even tried to hold her hand, which had been somewhat disappointing.

How many no-pressure weekends without sex would he engage in before he moved on to someone who hadn't been traumatized by violence?

"You know you'd be safe with me."

"How do I know that?"

"I'm a Secret Service agent," he said on a laugh. "Our motto is 'Worthy of Trust and Confidence.'"

"I'm more concerned about my emotional safety than the physical."

"You've got nothing to worry about there either."

She wanted so badly to believe him, but the feelings she had for him scared her.

"So, what do you say? Should we hang out next weekend? I can be in Charlottesville by Friday afternoon and would need to be back in Princeton by Monday at midnight."

That would be three nights and three days, since she didn't have class on Mondays... "I'd have to do some schoolwork."

"No worries. Whatever you have to do is fine with me, and I don't want you to stress out about this all week. It's just two friends hanging out and having fun. Don't make it bigger than that in your head."

That last part was what got her... He knew what she needed to hear. He understood. "I'd love to see you."

"Great," he said, sounding relieved. "I'll figure out the details. Do you promise you won't worry about anything?"

"I'll try not to."

"Trust me when I tell you that you have nothing at all to worry about where I'm concerned."

"I know."

"I mean it, Brooke. I don't want you to worry."

"Okay, I won't."

"Good. I'll call you later?"

"Talk to you then."

"No worrying!"

The phone beeped when he ended the call.

She remembered she'd missed a call from her mother while she was talking to him. Because Tracy would worry if Brooke didn't call her back, she put through the call.

"Hi, honey. How's it going?"

"Good, just between classes."

"How's everything else?"

"I know that you know about Nate, so stop trying to act so casual."

"Why didn't you tell me about him?"

"Because there was nothing to tell."

"Brooke... Come on. There must be something to tell if he felt the need to bring it to Sam."

"He shouldn't have done that. We're not at that point." Weren't they, though? Ugh, she hated the roller coaster of emotions that accompanied everything to do with him. "And I thought you wouldn't approve."

"Why not?"

"He's older than me, for one thing."

"Dad is older than me."

"By three years, and you were twenty-five when you met him. Nate is seven years older than me."

"You know what's good about that?"

"What?" Brooke asked, shocked that her mother found anything good in the age difference that had been a big reason she'd kept him hidden from her family.

"He's a full-grown man and not a boy pretending to be a man."

"That's what I'm afraid of."

Tracy laughed. "I'm referring to his maturity level."

"Which is a concern."

"Sweetie..."

"I know what you're going to say, and it's nothing I haven't told myself. Eventually, I'm going to have to be with a guy that way, and it may as well be with someone who truly cares about me."

"Does he truly care?"

"I think he does. He's very... kind."

"That's the most important thing. If I recall correctly, he's also very handsome."

"Yes, he is." Her roommates called him McDreamy after seeing him on FaceTime calls. "Are you *crying*?"

"No, of course not."

"Yes, you are. What's wrong?"

"Nothing. I'm just so happy for you that you've found a nice, kind, handsome man who makes you smile."

"Don't start planning the wedding, Mom. So far, it's just a lot of texting and FaceTime, and one time we went to Air and Space and got pizza. It's not a big deal." Even as she said those words to her mother, Brooke admitted they were a lie. It was already a very big deal, and she knew it.

"But it could be?"

"Maybe. I don't know. We're not there yet."

"We can talk more next weekend."

"About that... I don't think I'm going to make it."

"Why? What's going on?"

"Well, it seems Nate is coming down to 'hang out' for the weekend."

"Ah, I see. Is he staying with you?"

Brooke loved the way her mom asked that so casually. "No, he's getting a hotel."

"And you're freaking out about it."

"Trying not to. He made me promise I wouldn't."

"I like this young man."

"I like him, too."

"That's okay, you know, to like him."

"I'm trying to just be normal about it."

"Should you check in with Savannah?" Tracy asked, referring to the therapist who'd been so instrumental in putting Brooke back together after the attack.

"Maybe. I'm trying not to blow it up into a bigger deal than it is. I never expected casual texting to turn into something so..."

"Important?"

"Yeah."

"I love this for you, sweetheart."

"Thanks. I think..."

"Try to relax and just enjoy it. Falling in love is the sweetest thing in life, and I so want you to experience that."

Brooke suspected she'd fallen in love quite some time ago. Now she just had to figure out what she was going to do about it.

CHAPTER THIRTY-FOUR

On Monday morning, Sam met Tracy outside the U.S. District Court on Constitution Avenue for the preliminary hearing in their father's murder case. The charges had been upgraded to murder after he'd died of his wounds, four years after being shot on the job in a case that'd remained unsolved until after his death.

Celia and Angela had decided to let Sam and Tracy represent the family.

Sam hugged her sister. "How're you doing?"

"I'll be better when this is done."

"It's just a formality. The U.S. Attorney presents the evidence, establishes probable cause that the defendants should be tried, and then it should be bound over for trial."

"There's no chance it won't go to trial, is there?"

"Only if they plead out."

"What does that mean?"

"Accept a deal in which they'd plead guilty to the charges in exchange for a lesser sentence than they'd get if convicted at trial. We'd have to agree to that, and I haven't heard anything about a deal being on the table. The defense might approach the prosecution about a deal after they hear the mountain of evidence."

With Vernon and Jimmy escorting them, they headed for the stairs as someone called out to Sam.

She turned to see Alice Coyne Fitzgerald waving to her.

Sam waited for Alice to catch up and then hugged her. "I wasn't sure you'd be here."

"I won't miss a second of seeing the men who killed my Steven—and Skip—brought to justice." Skip's first partner and close friend had been shot on the job decades ago, and his killer had remained at large until Sam and her team tied his shooting to Skip's.

"Alice, this is my sister Tracy."

"I remember you as a little girl," Alice said, smiling at Tracy.

Tracy shook the woman's hand. "I remember you, too. It's nice to see you, although the circumstances suck."

"They do, but I've waited a long time for justice for Steven. I'm ready for this."

Sam wasn't sure she was ready to see the three men who'd been charged with killing her father, even if it had taken four years as a quadriplegic before he'd succumbed.

"It's surreal," she whispered to Tracy as reporters gathered outside the courthouse called to her, looking for a comment.

"What is?"

"That we're actually going to court to confront the men who shot Dad. For a long time, I thought that might never happen."

"It's thanks to you that it finally did."

"Me and a lot of others."

"But mostly you."

"Did you get to talk to Brooke?"

"I did, and I think this might be something significant with Nate."

"Wow, that's amazing. We all loved him when he worked at the house."

"That matters to me—and I'm sure to her. She said to tell you thanks for the invite to Camp David, but she's going to stay in Charlottesville next weekend."

"Any particular reason?"

"He's coming to visit."

"Ohhhh. Well, I don't blame her for blowing us off, then."

"I'm trying to keep my cool about this, but really... I'm so relieved that she's taking a chance on him after everything..."

"I know," Sam said. "Me, too. And he's a really *good* guy."

"That's all I've ever wanted for her—someone who could see how great she is and be patient with her."

Sam linked her arm through her sister's. "I can't wait to see where this goes."

"I know. Me, too. But we have to play it cool, or she'll cut us out of it."

"I can be cool. Can you?"

"I'm working on it."

In the courtroom, they sat in the front row with Alice. Sam braced herself to listen to the damning evidence she and her team had gathered to tie former DC councilman Roy Gallagher, his associate Mick Santoro and Dermott Ryan, the owner of O'Leary's, Skip's favorite bar, to the shootings of two police officers. Ryan's involvement stung the most. Skip had considered Dermott a friend and had made O'Leary's the preferred hangout for most of the MPD.

Right before the bailiff had asked them to rise as the judge entered, Freddie slid into the seat next to Sam.

Sam squeezed his arm to thank him for being there. Nick had wanted to come, too, but she'd talked him out of it, saying there'd be plenty of other hearings he could attend, and this one was just a formality.

Farnsworth and Malone came in a second later and took seats across the aisle. Sam wasn't surprised to see her father's two closest friends in attendance and sent them a grateful smile.

As Sam listened to U.S. Attorney Tom Forrester present the evidence that detailed how far the defendants had gone to protect their profitable gambling ring, it all came roaring back in a tsunami of emotion. The cold October Sunday morning, Celia's frantic call that her dad was unresponsive, Sam having to stop the EMTs from taking life-saving measures that were contrary to her dad's wishes, the unusual tension that followed with Celia, the need to tell people... Nick had been on his way home from Paris...

"Sam," Tracy whispered.

"What?"

"Why're you shaking?"

"Am I?"

"Yeah."

"Just thinking about that day last October."

"Don't do that."

Easier said than done.

It was no surprise that the case was bound over for a trial in September.

She watched the three men, wearing orange jumpsuits and leg chains, be led back to jail where they belonged.

"That wasn't as satisfying as I'd hoped it would be," Alice said. "Even if we got the outcome we wanted."

"It'll never be fully satisfying, because Dad and Steven will still be gone," Sam said.

"True."

They walked out together, ignoring the shouts from reporters, and hugged at the bottom of the steps.

"We'll see you soon," Sam said to Alice.

"Come by anytime. I'm always happy to see you."

"I'll do that."

"And bring your handsome partner," Alice said with a smile for Freddie.

"We try not to tell him he's handsome," Sam said. "He's already too full of himself."

As Freddie sputtered with outrage, the rest of them laughed.

"Be safe out there, you guys," Alice said before she left them. "I pray for you every day."

"Thank you, Alice," Sam said, hugging her again. "Take care."

"She's so sweet," Tracy said. "I remember how much Dad cared for her. Too much, as it turned out."

"He felt responsible for her after Steven was killed right in front of him. That put a lot of pressure on his marriage with Mom." That was another thing Sam had learned during the investigation, that the breakup of her parents' marriage had been as much on her dad as it had been on the mother Sam had unfairly blamed.

Life was so fucking complicated.

"We've got to get to work," Sam said. "I'll see you next weekend, if not before?"

"We'll be there. Mike is so excited to go to Camp David."

"Hopefully, the weather will cooperate this time."

"He's already checking the forecast and reporting to me daily that it's all clear."

Sam laughed. "That's funny. Have a good day, and keep me posted on what you hear from Brooke."

"I will, and thanks for sharing the intel."

"There was no way I could sit on that one."

After they waved off Tracy, Freddie said, "Mind if I catch a ride with you?"

"Not at all." She glanced at her partner. "Thanks again for being there this morning. Means a lot to me."

"I wouldn't have missed it."

Sam got into the back seat of the SUV, realizing she'd done that without pain or difficulty of any kind, which was an improvement.

"What was that about intel?"

"I found out Brooke is seeing Nate, the Secret Service agent."

"Wow, really? How'd you hear about that?"

Sam filled him in on the details.

"I like him for her," Freddie said. "He seems like a good guy."

"I agree. Tracy and I are trying to stay cool about it so we don't spook her into keeping the details from us."

Freddie laughed. "And how's that going?"

"We got this."

Vernon and Jimmy delivered them to Columbia Heights, where Gonzo was parked outside the garage where Shane worked.

Freddie got into the back of the Charger while Sam took the front seat, noting only a small twinge from her hip as she lowered herself into the low-slung seat.

"Another day in paradise," Gonzo said, looking through the binoculars.

"What's the good word?" Sam asked.

"Our boy has taken up smoking," Gonzo said.

"Has he now?"

"Yep. Here he comes, right on schedule at the top of every hour."

They watched, rapt, as Shane came out of the garage and lit up, his eyes darting around nervously, no doubt trying to find the cops who'd been watching him relentlessly for days now.

Sam used the binoculars for a closer look. "All we need is one cigarette butt to make this entire case."

"He's been careful not to leave any behind."

"How long can we keep up the twenty-four-hour surveillance?" Freddie asked.

"As long as it takes."

A WEEK OF SURVEILLANCE LATER, as Sam prepared for yet another deadly boring day of watching Shane Ramsey, Nick stood behind her in the bathroom, hands on her shoulders, gazing at her in the mirror. "You haven't forgotten about tonight, right?"

Sam stared at him in the mirror, desperately trying to remember what was on the schedule.

"Sam! The State of the Union is tonight, and I need you there. We have guests coming, including Cath Powell, the mom you met in Des Moines."

"Oh right. I knew that. I thought you meant something else."

"Don't lie to my face. You had no idea what I was talking about."

"I'm sorry. This case has me obsessed. I'm starting to worry that

Shane Ramsey will never fuck up." They'd dug deeply into his life, looking for anything that could tip the judge toward approving a warrant for his DNA, but had struck out on all fronts. IT detectives had watched hours of video trying to tie him to Rock Creek Park at the time of the attacks, but that too had failed to pan out. Frustration was running at an all-time high as they were certain he was their guy, but they still couldn't prove it.

"He will, and you'll get him."

"In the meantime, his father is threatening to sue the department for harassment. He says we haven't tried to find anyone else once we homed in on his son. That's because we know he did it. We're sure it was him."

"You'll get him. I know it. In other news, the Senate is poised to vote today to confirm Gretchen, and we have the votes, so that's a done deal, and we should make our goal of swearing her in before the State of the Union."

"Congratulations. I hope you two will be very happy together."

"That was frosty, babe." He smiled as he bent to kiss her neck. "Did Marcus send something over for you to wear tonight?"

"He did."

"What color is it?"

"Red, I believe."

"I love you in red, but then again, I love you in everything—and nothing. Especially nothing. Take the dress with you in case you run late."

"What? Me, run late?"

He rolled his eyes at her in the mirror. "This is one of the few first lady command performances. There's a reception at seven thirty at the Capitol to welcome the guests."

"I'll be there." She turned so she could put her arms around his neck. "Are you nervous?"

"Not really, and I should be. It's weird that I'm not."

"It's because you have faith in the speech you wrote, which I can't wait to hear."

When he'd offered to share it with her, she'd said she wanted to hear it in real time.

"I can't wait until it's over and we can have a weekend with our people at Camp David."

"Me, too. You'll be glad to know I've decided to fully embrace the camp this time and not worry one lick about work, even if we haven't nailed Shane Ramsey yet."

"I'll believe that when I see it."

"I know how much you need to get out of here, and I want you to relax and enjoy it. For that to happen, I have to relax and enjoy it, too, so that's what I'm going to do."

"That gives me even more to look forward to. Now, go to work and catch this guy."

"That's the goal." She went up on tiptoes to kiss him. "Love you."

"Love you, too. Don't stand me up tonight."

"Wouldn't think of it."

"Be careful with my precious cop. She's my whole world."

"Will do."

He hugged her tightly, kissed her again and left for the short walk to the West Wing.

She took the garment bag Marcus had sent, packed the required undergarments and shoes, as well as basic makeup in case she couldn't connect with the White House team for official fluffing, and went down to meet Vernon and Jimmy. She was thankful they were driving her today, because they'd know where she needed to be later.

Scotty would travel to the Capitol with Nick, and Celia already had his clothes ready for the big night. The twins had wanted to go, but it would be too late of a night for them, so they were staying home with Celia and would watch the speech on TV. Once again, Sam gave thanks for her stepmother, who made everything so much easier just by being there.

Speaking of people who helped make her life easier, Sam put through a call to Shelby.

"Hi there," Shelby said. "I was just thinking of you. Ready for the big night?"

"I will be once I get a big day at work taken care of."

"Still nothing on the Ramsey guy?" Shelby asked.

"Not yet."

"That's got to be so frustrating."

"It went past that a week ago. Now it's flat-out maddening. But anyway, I wanted to make sure you're set to come tonight."

"I wouldn't miss it. Thanks for asking me."

"Of course I asked you. I need all my people with me for this."

"I've heard people talking around here. They're saying the speech is remarkable."

"I'm looking forward to hearing it. And you guys are still good for Camp David this weekend?"

"Avery is so excited. Don't let on that I told you. He was crushed when the blizzard messed things up the last time."

"We'll get him there. One way or the other. If I get running late, can you meet me at the Capitol with Davida and Ginger?" The White House hair-and-makeup team would be critical for this event.

"Of course. Whatever you need."

"Thanks, I'll keep you posted."

"Sounds good. See you tonight."

Sam closed her phone. "You know where to take me later, right, Vernon?"

"We've got you covered, ma'am."

"That's good. I can't be late."

"We'll get you there. Don't worry."

"Okay, thanks."

Her phone rang with a call from Gonzo. "Hey, what's up?"

"We just got lucky."

She sat up straighter. "How so?"

"He forgot himself and tossed a butt aside. Freddie ran for it and nearly crashed into him when he came rushing back out after it, but he wasn't fast enough. Freddie bagged it, and we're on our way in with it now."

"Who's on him?"

After a slight pause, Gonzo said, "Oh fuck, we were so excited to get the butt to the lab that we didn't turn over surveillance to anyone."

"Let's get Patrol on him right away. He knows as much as we do what we're going to find on that butt. It's not going to take much to lose him."

"Shit," Gonzo said, groaning. "I should've thought of that. We were just so excited to get *something*."

"I would've been, too."

"I'll call Patrol."

"I'll see you at the house."

Sam slapped her phone closed and then opened it again to call Lindsey. "Gonzales and Cruz are on the way in with a cigarette butt that Ramsey tossed away. I need it analyzed for DNA ASAP."

"I'll get on it. Give me a couple of hours."

Those hours would seem endless while they waited for confirmation of what they already knew. "Will do. Thanks."

All Sam could think as they wove through traffic on the way to HQ was what if they were wrong? What if Shane Ramsey wasn't their guy? Then what?

CHAPTER THIRTY-FIVE

The ten minutes between the time Gonzo and Freddie left the garage and Patrol arrived were just enough for Shane Ramsey to bolt.

"Goddamn it," Gonzo said. "I can't believe we just took off. We didn't think."

"You were thinking about getting the evidence we needed back here as fast as you could after endless days spent waiting for a break," Sam said. "I would've done the same thing."

"You would've thought to call for backup before you left."

"Maybe not. Either way, we'll find him. Archie's trying to locate his phone now."

"You won't find him," Sergeant Ramsey said when he came into the pit, looking smug. "You'll never find him."

"Do you know what the police officer father does when his son is wanted for sexual assault and murder?" Malone asked him.

"I can't wait to hear this," Ramsey said.

"He tells his son to turn himself in and face the music, or he won't be a police officer for much longer."

"You keep trying to get rid of me, and you haven't succeeded yet."

"If you know where he is and you don't tell us, we'll charge you."

"Ah, but first you'd have to prove that I know where he is." He shrugged. "I have no clue."

Malone leaned in close so his face was half an inch from Ramsey's. "I don't believe you."

"That's not my problem."

"You know what's funny about this?" Sam asked.

Ramsey glared at her.

"We don't have to wait for the DNA to prove what we already know. Innocent men don't run. They let us test their DNA so we can prove they didn't do it. Shane's done us a favor by moving things along."

"People know better than to trust this corrupt department with their DNA. You all have a good day, now." Ramsey walked out of the pit, whistling as he went as if he hadn't a care in the world.

"Let's put eyes on him, his wife and his other kids," Sam said. "Since they know exactly where he is, maybe one of them will lead us to him."

The squad split up the assignment, with individual detectives assigned to Ramsey and his family members.

"No one goes after Shane alone," Sam said. "Call for backup before you do anything."

"Yes, ma'am," Cameron Green said as he followed Matt O'Brien out of the pit with Freddie and Gonzo right behind them.

They'd put Gonzo on the sergeant, since they shared the same rank.

"I want to be out there looking for him," Sam said to Malone when they were the last ones left in the pit.

"Let's go look, then," Malone said, surprising her. "It sure as hell beats sitting around here waiting."

With the captain at the wheel of his SUV, they looked everywhere they'd seen Shane Ramsey go over the last ten days—grocery store, coffee shop, bank, bar, restaurants, friends' houses and his parents' home, circling by the garage no fewer than ten times over the course of the frustrating tour.

Lindsey called at two.

Sam put the call on speaker so the captain could hear it.

"The DNA is a match," Lindsey said, "but we knew it would be."

"Yep," Sam said, feeling vindicated.

"We also got the familial report to the local database that linked him to Ramsey."

"Too little too late. If that technology is going to be useful in cases like this one, it needs to happen a hell of a lot faster than it does."

"I'm sure it will as they perfect it."

"Thanks for the info, Doc."

"Any sign of him?"

"No one has seen him, heard from him or has any clue where he might hide out if cops happened to be looking for him," Malone said.

"Good luck, guys," Lindsey said. "I hope you find him fast."

"Thanks."

They did the full circuit again. Sam scanned every face on every sidewalk, looking for a needle in a haystack. They went back and interviewed the same friends and coworkers of Ramsey's again, asking if they'd decided to do the right thing. They hadn't. "They're stonewalling us," Sam said as the afternoon began to fade into evening and the others reported no luck with Ramsey's family. "He's told the people in his life that we've been harassing him. They're not going to help us."

"Yeah, I'm sure he's had plenty to say about us."

Sam glanced at the digital clock on Malone's dash. Five forty-nine. She had an hour until she had to leave for the Capitol. She tipped her head back and racked her brain, trying to think of where he might be, reviewing every detail over and over and over again, until the facts of the case ran through her mind like a horror movie. Then it hit her. She sat up straight, as if she'd been zapped. "The park."

"What?"

"Maybe he returned to the scene of his crimes to hide out."

Malone reached for his radio to order as many officers as he could get to fan out for a grid search of the park, looking for Shane Ramsey.

It took thirty precious minutes to organize the search and send the officers on their way into the park with flashlights, K9s and infrared goggles that would help them see in the encroaching darkness.

Sam sat with Malone in his car, feeling guilty for the heat that kept them warm while their colleagues worked in the cold. Rank, her dad used to say, had its privileges. She took comfort in knowing that if it weren't for her still-healing injury, she would've been out there with them, rank or not.

Forty more minutes went by, making Sam officially late for the reception at the Capitol, before one of the officers reported in. "I've got him. He has a woman with him. He's stripped her naked and has a gun to her head. You can probably hear her screaming." The officer gave the coordinates, and the Special Response Team went in to provide backup.

Sam walked with Malone into the park, following the path the SRT had taken. She wished she could walk faster, but fear of a setback kept her cautious. "What time is it?"

"Almost seven."

She had half an hour, max, before she needed to be in the car with Vernon and Jimmy heading for the Capitol, and even that would make her late for the reception. She hoped Nick would understand that she couldn't leave when they were this close to getting their guy.

As they got closer to the location, they could hear the woman's piercing screams.

"Shane, we have you surrounded," the Special Response commander said. "There's no way out of here. You need to let her go."

"If you want her to live, let me out of here. She's got five minutes before I kill her."

Sam could see them now through the vegetation.

Shane had the naked woman in a chokehold, the gun pressed to her head.

"Please." The woman whimpered as she shivered uncontrollably. "Help me."

"Let her go, Shane," the commander said. "We want to get you out of this alive, but if you hurt her, we'll have no choice but to hurt you."

"Where's my father? I want to talk to him."

"We'll get him here, but that's going to take time. She's cold, Shane. Let her go, and we'll bring your dad in to talk to you."

"Get him on the phone," Shane said. "Now."

"I've got it," Malone said, putting through the call to Ramsey, his phone on speaker.

"What?"

"Your son wants to talk to you."

For a second, Ramsey said nothing.

"Sergeant! Your son is holding a woman hostage in Rock Creek Park and is asking to speak to you. *Do your job.*"

"Shane."

"Dad... They're trying to pin this on me. You have to do something."

"The DNA doesn't lie, Shane," Malone said. "Nobody is pinning anything on you."

"Why?" Sergeant Ramsey asked with less bravado than Sam had ever heard from him. "Why would you do this, Shane?"

"To get back at you, the mighty SVU detective who can't keep it in his pants. Like father, like son."

"*What?*"

"You heard me. I know what you did to Mom, cheating on her while preaching to me about the right way to treat a woman. I learned it all from you, Pops."

"No," Ramsey said, sounding horrified. "I never taught you to rape and murder."

"You couldn't find the guy who did it," Shane said, laughing now. "All that swagger and talk of power. I was raping women right under your nose, Daddy-o, and you had no way to stop me. Who's the powerful one now?"

"Let the girl go, Shane," Ramsey said. "Let her go and turn yourself in."

"You said you'd always have my back. Was that another lie?"

"Let her go, Shane."

"I've got a clear shot," Officer Offenbach, the sharpshooter, said through the earpieces they were all wearing.

Sam glanced at Malone. As the senior officer on the scene, it was his call.

Malone ended the call with Sergeant Ramsey since his pleas for Shane to let the woman go were only making the situation more fraught.

"Take him," Malone said.

A shot rang out, shattering the silence.

The bullet struck Shane in the forehead.

The frantic screams of the woman as she went down with him echoed through the wooded area. Officers rushed in, one wrapping his coat around the hysterical woman.

Sam went to the woman, helped her up and walked her toward the path. "You're all right."

Shane Ramsey's brain matter was all over her, reminding Sam of when that had happened to her after Clarence Reece was shot inches from her.

The woman was shaking so hard, she could barely move.

"Let us help you," Malone said to the woman. "Would it be all right if I carry you to the ambulance?"

The woman gave a quick nod.

Malone carried her down the path and delivered her to the waiting EMS. When he turned back, Sam noted his ashen complexion.

"Are you okay?" she asked.

Hands on his hips, he hung his head and shook it to say no. "I just ordered the killing of one of my officers' sons. I'm definitely not all right."

"He was going to kill her. You did the right thing."

"His father will make my life a living hell."

"He heard the confession, same as we all did."

"You think that's going to matter to him?"

"Ma'am."

Sam turned to Vernon, who pointed to his watch.

"I have to go," Sam said to Malone. "I have to be there for Nick tonight."

"Go ahead. I'm okay."

"I'll check on you after." Sam squeezed his arm. "You did the right thing, Captain. You saved her life. That was the only call you could make, and it'll hold up under scrutiny."

He nodded, but she could see that he was still troubled—and with good reason. He'd just ordered the son of one of his officers killed. Not to mention, she knew better than anyone what a formidable enemy Ramsey could be.

CHAPTER THIRTY-SIX

"Mrs. Nelson is here, Mr. President," Terry said.

"Any sign of Sam?" Nick asked as the clock ticked toward eight thirty. The reception for their invited guests was an hour in with no sign of his first lady.

"Not yet, but Lindsey texted to say they got their guy."

"That's good news." Before he went to say hello to Mrs. Nelson, he took a second to check his BlackBerry, hoping for a message from Sam.

Nothing.

Damn it.

"What's wrong, Dad?" Scotty asked when he joined him. "You're making a face."

"Just wondering if Mom will make it in time."

"She said she'd be here."

"She was supposed to be here an hour ago."

"I saw on Twitter that the police shot and killed the guy who was raping and murdering women in the park. That's probably why she's late."

"I hope she wasn't the one who shot him," Nick said, thinking of the trauma of taking the young man's life and how much Ramsey already hated her.

"I read it was a sharpshooter."

"Thank goodness for that."

"Besides, she's still on desk duty."

Nick glanced at his son. "How much you want to bet she was there when it went down?"

"I don't take bets I can't win."

"That's my boy."

"Congrats on your new vice president."

"Thanks, buddy. We got her sworn in before the State of the Union, which was the goal. What's Twitter saying about her?"

"People are excited about having a female VP, although the word 'inexperienced' is used a lot when your names are mentioned."

"I guess we'll have to prove ourselves to them the old-fashioned way, by getting the job done." Nick put an arm around Scotty's shoulders. "Come with me to say hello to Mrs. Nelson."

The crowd parted to let them through to Gloria Nelson and her daughter Camille.

Gloria hugged him. "It's so nice to see you again, Mr. President."

"You as well, and please, call me Nick."

"Thank you, Nick, for the kind invitation to be here tonight."

"We're delighted to have you. Scotty, you remember Mrs. Nelson and her daughter Mrs. Rothschild."

Scotty shook hands with them. "It's good to see you again. I hope you and your family are doing all right."

"Thank you, Scotty," Gloria said. "It's nice to see you, too. And we're doing as well as can be expected. Good days and bad days."

"I know how hard it is. I just lost my grandpa." He quickly added, "Not that it's the same thing as losing your husband."

"Grief is grief, my boy, and it stinks no matter who's been lost."

Scotty smiled up at her. "Yes, it sure does."

"It's very kind of you to think of us."

"It's kind of hard not to think of you guys every day, living where we are now."

Gloria tossed her head back and laughed hard. "Oh my goodness. How cute are you?"

"I don't mean any disrespect."

"None taken. The facts are what they are, and you're a very sweet young man." To Nick, she said, "This boy's going places."

"We agree," Nick said, giving his son a warm smile.

"If I pass eighth-grade algebra, that is."

"I hated algebra and all things math," Camille said. "What is the *point* of it all?"

"Thank you," Scotty said, offering her a fist bump in solidarity that she eagerly returned.

"Have you found the secret passageways in the residence yet?" Camille asked him.

Scotty's eyes lit up. "There're secret passageways?"

"Buy me a drink, and I'll tell you all about them."

"Later, Dad."

"What an impressive young man," Gloria said after they had headed for the bar. "That's the hardest I've laughed since David passed."

"We love him. He's everything to us and makes us laugh every day."

"I can see why you adore him. How's Sam doing? I couldn't believe when I heard about her broken hip."

"It's been an ordeal, but she's *this close* to back to normal and should be here any minute. They had a huge bust this afternoon, a guy they've been after for weeks."

"What an impressive family you have, Mr. President."

"Thank you. You'll hear me talk tonight about how I finally have it all now that I have them."

"I'm looking forward to it."

As Nick scanned the crowded room full of familiar faces, he saw no sign of the one face he most wanted to see, with just thirty minutes until he was expected in the House chamber. Would she make it in time?

SAM WAS IN A COLD SWEAT, stuffed into a tiny basement bathroom in the Capitol that Vernon had known about, trying to whip herself into first lady shape in time to face the public. Shelby had met her, bringing the hair-and-makeup team from the White House.

"Time check," Sam said.

"Eight thirty-five," Shelby said.

"Ugh, Nick is going to be so pissed I'm this late."

"He'll understand," Shelby said. "You got your guy."

Would he, though? He'd clearly said this was one of the few first lady command performances, and she couldn't show up looking like she'd been dragged through horse manure. After she'd changed into the red dress Marcus had sent, she slid her feet into her one pair of Louboutins and took a few steps, testing whether her hip would allow for the heels.

"I think I can do this," she said to Shelby as she emerged from the stall with her work clothes in a bundle under her arm.

"Do what?"

"Wear the heels. First time since the break."

"Are you sure that's a good idea?"

"Hell no, but I'm going with it."

Shelby took Sam's work clothes and put them in her huge tote bag.

Davida and Ginger, the White House hairstylist and makeup queen, appeared with a chair and the equipment they needed to make her presentable. Usually, she saw them one at a time, but with no time to spare, they attacked from the front and back, working with intense focus to get the job done quickly.

It was ludicrous, she knew, to be preparing for such an important event in a basement bathroom in the Capitol. Traditional first ladies probably spent an entire day getting ready for the State of the Union. She experienced yet another twinge of anxiety, knowing she'd never be a traditional first lady.

The only thing that mattered to her was being there for Nick.

"Shelby."

"Yes?"

"Can you please fish the BlackBerry out of my coat pocket and hand it to me?"

Shelby found the phone and gave it to Sam, who couldn't move properly to make the call.

"Um, could you please dial star six nine?"

The three women giggled.

"That's my husband's idea of funny. Please don't tell anyone that."

"We never would, ma'am," Ginger said. "And I think that's so cute."

"That's us," Sam said. "So cute."

Shelby made the call and handed the phone back to Sam.

She wondered if Nick would be able hear his phone ring with so many people around him.

"Hey," he said, sounding relieved to hear from her.

"So sorry I missed the reception, but I'm in the basement of the Capitol getting ready, and I'll be there for the speech."

"You're in the *basement*?"

"Vernon knew of a bathroom down here where I could get ready without attracting an audience."

"Only you, Samantha."

"I know. I was just thinking about how traditional first ladies probably spend an entire day preparing for this event."

"I bet there's never been one who caught a murderer on the same day as the State of the Union."

"That is probably a first."

"Congrats, babe. I'm glad you got him."

"Thanks. I think."

"I heard it got complicated."

"That's one word for it. I'll tell you about it later. In the meantime, tonight is about you and your big speech. I can't wait to hear it. Are you okay?"

"I am now. My first lady is in the basement. All is well."

"Sorry to make you wonder if I would make it in time."

"I was never worried. I knew you wouldn't disappoint me."

"Davida and Ginger are doing what they can to scrub the feral out of me."

His low chuckle made her smile. "I'll see you out there."

"Yes, you will. I love you so much, and I'm so proud of you, Mr. President. I can't wait for the rest of the world to see what I see when I look at you."

"Thanks, babe. See you soon and love you, too."

Sam ended the call and handed the phone to Shelby.

"I say it all the time, but y'all are too cute," Shelby said.

"We're not cute," Sam said, her lip turned up.

"You are," Davida said. "The cutest."

"Whatever you guys say."

When she was as presentable as possible, she thanked Davida and Ginger for the road call and followed Vernon to the elevator. Ten steps in, she deeply regretted the heels.

"What's wrong?" Shelby asked when they were in the elevator.

"The heels might've been a mistake."

"Do ya think?"

Sam made a face at her friend. "You think any heels that aren't pink are a mistake."

"True, but it's too soon for you to be wearing heels." She reached into the massive pink purse she never left home without and pulled out a pair of black flats. "Trade you?"

"God bless you, woman."

"I do what I can for the people," Shelby said, smirking.

Sam laughed as she swapped out the shoes, handing the priceless heels to Shelby, who stashed them in her bag. "That line is trademarked, but I'll allow it in this case."

"Gee, thanks."

Friends and family like Shelby would never know what it meant to her—and Nick—that they could be themselves with them amid the maelstrom that surrounded them since Nick became president—and even before that, if Sam was being honest. "Thanks for all you do, Shelby. I appreciate you so, so much."

"I love you—and your family. Everything I do for you is a pleasure."

Before she got off the elevator to step onto the world stage, she hugged her friend and then took her by the hand to keep her close for the next phase of the evening.

"FLOTUS arriving," Vernon said into his radio.

Thankfully, he knew just where she needed to be.

Sam wasn't surprised to see Lilia waiting for her outside a closed door.

"This is the balcony where you'll sit in the front row," Vernon said.

"You'll be with Scotty, Mrs. Nelson and several of your other invited guests," Lilia added. "I'll go with you and introduce you to everyone."

"Stay close," Sam said to Shelby and Lilia.

"We've got you covered," Lilia said.

"Do I look okay?" she asked Lilia.

"You look beautiful, as always."

"It took a village."

With her village supporting her, Sam felt as ready as she'd ever be to face the world as first lady of the United States.

CHAPTER THIRTY-SEVEN

Nick felt much calmer since the call from Sam. No other president could say his first lady had dressed for the State of the Union in a basement bathroom at the Capitol after catching a killer. All in a day's work for his Samantha, who somehow made the juggling of three jobs look effortless when it was anything but.

"Sam's in the gallery, seated with Scotty and Mrs. Nelson," Terry reported five minutes before they were due to be announced.

Nick breathed out a sigh of relief. With her there, he felt ready for the biggest moment of his career.

When all the other VIPs had entered the room, Brant and the rest of Nick's detail escorted him to the door of the House chamber.

"Good evening, Mr. President," the sergeant at arms said.

Nick shook the man's hand and smiled for the photo the White House photographer took. "Good evening, and thank you for having me."

"A pleasure, sir. Stand by." The man went inside the chamber to announce Nick to the joint session of Congress. "Madam Speaker, the president of the United States."

The announcement received enthusiastic applause, which surprised Nick. He'd expected a tepid reception, at best.

Here goes, he thought as he headed down the aisle, shaking hands with senators and representatives, people he knew well and others he didn't recognize. He made his way to the front of the vast room. There, he greeted his cabinet secretaries as well as the nine Supreme Court justices before taking the stairs to the dais to shake hands with Vice President Henderson and Speaker Carlin.

While he waited for the applause to die down, he glanced up to the gallery and saw Sam, looking gorgeous in her red dress and beaming as she clapped for him.

He smiled up at her.

She gave him two thumbs-ups.

How many times had he watched this speech on TV, never once imagining he might one day deliver it?

"Madam Speaker, Madam Vice President, our first lady. Members of Congress and the cabinet. Justices of the Supreme Court. My fellow Americans. I stand before you humbled and honored to have the opportunity to address you tonight as your forty-seventh president, to introduce myself to you once again and to chart the course for the first year of my administration. It's important to me that you know I wrote this speech myself. Every word of it comes straight from my heart.

"Behind me, for the first time in State of the Union history, are two women, our first female vice president, Gretchen Henderson, and our new Speaker of the House, Antonia Carlin."

He applauded the two most powerful women in America and knew a moment of pure satisfaction at having elevated the first woman to the vice presidency.

"Before we look ahead to the future, let us take a moment to remember my predecessor, President David Nelson, who spent his entire adult life in public service, as a senator from South Dakota and then as a president twice elected to serve this great nation. Gloria Nelson is here with us tonight, and I ask you to give her and her daughter Camille a warm welcome home."

Nick led the round of applause for Gloria, who stood next to Sam to receive it.

"Gloria, Sam and I thank you for your service as first lady as well as your grace and generosity to us during this difficult time for you and your family. We're proud to consider you a friend."

Gloria hugged Sam, blew him a kiss and waved to the audience that applauded her again.

"I'd be remiss if I didn't also acknowledge my own first lady, the incredible Samantha Holland Cappuano, who's made history as the first lady to be employed outside the White House, as the lieutenant in command of the Homicide division at the DC Metropolitan Police Department. Samantha, I couldn't be prouder of the important work you do as a police officer, as a gracious first lady and as a dedicated mother to our beautiful kids, Scotty, Aubrey and Alden, as well as our bonus son, Elijah. I love you so much, Sam, Scotty, Alden, Aubrey and Eli. I thank you guys for coming on this adventure with me and for giving me the family I'd never had until I had you."

Sam stood to receive generous applause. She waved to the crowd and used both hands to blow a kiss to him. When she urged Scotty to his feet to join her, the applause became even louder.

Scotty waved to the group, cute in his embarrassment and far too grown up all of a sudden.

"My fellow Americans, over the last two months, I've heard you as you simultaneously welcomed me as your president, disdained the way in which it happened and questioned my credentials as well as my intentions as an unelected president. Let me be clear. My only intention is to spend the next three years working for all Americans to keep you safe, to keep you prosperous and to keep you focused on our common goals of health, happiness and the pursuit of the freedoms upon which our great country was founded.

"I have no other agenda, goal or purpose beyond working every day that I'm blessed to hold this office to achieve those simple goals in each and every way that I can. We all know the problems facing our country are far from simple. We're more divided than at any other time in our history, except perhaps during the Civil War. These days, civil wars are fought online, on social media, in chat rooms and on dark webs. These civil wars may be less bloody, but they're every bit as destructive as cannons and artillery once were on battlefields.

"I've heard from those among you who question my legitimacy. I acknowledge that if I were an average citizen looking at how I ended up holding this office, I, too, might have questions and concerns. I am the youngest man to ever hold this office, and as such, some of you believe I lack the experience and gravitas to handle the job. I acknowledge and recognize those concerns, and all I can do to reassure you is promise that I will give you my very best every single day I'm in office. I'm surrounded by cabinet members, military leaders, advisers and staffers who know more than I ever will about their various areas of expertise. Their advice will not only be welcomed in my office, but it'll be accepted and acted upon. The first time I walked into the Oval Office as your president, I vowed to leave my ego at the door. This isn't about me. It's about all of you and how I can use the power entrusted to me as your president to continue the important work my predecessor began in the areas of education, housing, childcare, health care, prescription drug prices, transportation, climate change and national security, to name just a few areas of critical concern.

"Following the tragic school shooting in Des Moines, I'm determined to push for common sense solutions to our country's vexing problem with gun violence. I'll say it again—I am not looking to take guns from responsible owners, but we can and must do better at keeping guns out of the hands of people who shouldn't have them through enhanced background checks, red-flag laws, waiting periods and an increase in the age to purchase guns. If a young person can't buy a beer until they're twenty-one, they probably shouldn't be able to buy a weapon of war until then either."

An enthusiastic round of applause greeted that statement.

"I understand there are strong feelings on all sides of this issue, but I hope we can agree that our children, teachers and support staff need to feel safe in their schools, and the rest of us need to feel safe as we go about our daily business."

Another sustained round of applause greeted that statement.

"Tonight, we're joined by Cath Powell, who lost her children, Mason and Julia, in the Des Moines shooting."

Cath was greeted by the most enthusiastic applause yet. Tears slid down her cheeks as she accepted the outpouring and mouthed *thank you* to the audience.

"Mason was four years old and in preschool. He wanted to be a professional baseball player when he grew up and was the Pokémon card champion in his wide circle of friends. Julia, a six-year-old first grader, had her sights set on being a prima ballerina and baked the best chocolate chip cookies her family had ever tasted. What happened to Mason and Julia and the other children and adults gathered to see Santa was a heartbreaking example of what can occur when a mentally unstable person gets their hands on a gun. I think of tragedies as things we have no control over—hurricanes, tornadoes, fires, floods. A shooting in an elementary school is something we can and should have control over.

"With that in mind, I've asked Dr. Anthony Trulo, the staff psychiatrist at the Metropolitan Police Department and a close friend of the first lady's, to lead my gun violence task force, which will also take a hard look at mental health concerns. Dr. Trulo is here with us tonight."

Nick led a round of applause for the doctor, who stood to acknowledge it.

"The task force aims to bring together a bipartisan coalition to work on common sense solutions to make our country a safer place for everyone, especially for children like Mason and Julia. I ask for your patience and forbearance as we embark upon this important endeavor."

Nick spent the next twenty minutes touching on each cabinet area, introducing invited guests and telling their stories in the context of an ambitious domestic agenda. That was followed by ten minutes covering the greatest areas of foreign policy concern, including the latest missile testing in North Korea. "In this increasingly interconnected world, the most concerning threats we face are sometimes invisible in the form of cyberattacks, which have become a critical area of national security focus. Protecting our vital digital systems, our power grids, our water, fuel and transportation networks has become every bit as important as preventing more traditional attacks against the motherland.

"Behind every one of these initiatives is the dedicated, hardworking federal civil service made up of more than three million Americans who do everything from food inspection to air traffic control to processing of Social Security payments and tax returns to guarding against terrorism in all its many forms. Each day, our civil servants show up to do this important work on behalf of their fellow citizens, and we owe them a debt of gratitude."

He led applause that encompassed the entire room this time.

"Maybe after all this, you're still asking yourself—who is this guy? What does he know about my life, my struggles, my needs? I want to address those questions by telling you more than you've ever heard before about my life in the hope that you might see some of your story reflected in mine. My father, Leo Cappuano, is here tonight."

Leo stood to accept a warm round of applause even as he blushed from the attention. Nick had cleared what he planned to say with his father in advance and had received his support.

"Leo was two years older than my son Scotty is now when I was born. Needless to say, at sixteen, he was in no way ready to be a parent, which is how I ended up being raised in a one-bedroom apartment in Lowell, Massachusetts, by Leo's mother, who'd already raised her family and wasn't looking for a do-over. She kept me clothed and fed, but never missed an opportunity to tell me I was keeping her from enjoying the retirement she'd worked so hard for. I rarely saw either of my parents while I was growing up, although my dad has more than made up for that in the ensuing years. The one thing he did for me when I was a kid that I'll be forever thankful for was work a second job that allowed me to play hockey. That was my greatest joy in a childhood bereft of many others. My first bedroom was a dorm room my freshman year of college. My first Halloween costume was also that year, when I attended a college party. My first birthday party was the year I turned nineteen and was celebrated by the O'Connor family at their farm in Virginia. Senator and Mrs. O'Connor are with us tonight."

Nick led a round of applause for his adopted parents. "Everything I know about what it means to be part of a family came from Graham and Laine O'Connor, their sons, the late Senator John O'Connor and my devoted chief of staff, Terry O'Connor, as well as their sister, Lizbeth O'Connor Hamilton. I love you all very much, and I thank you for everything you've been to me."

After another round of applause for the O'Connors, Nick continued. "If you're struggling to get by, if you feel that the American dream has left you behind, if the mountain before you seems too steep to climb, I want you to know I understand. I've been right where you are. I know how exhausting it can be to face that same mountain day after day, thinking climbing it will never get any easier. I'm determined to do everything in my power to make that mountain more accessible to everyone who faces the daily climb. I want to hear from you about your struggles, your worries, the things that keep you awake at night. I promise I will read your messages. I may not be able to solve every problem you have, but I can't do anything if I don't know about them."

After another round of applause, he slowed the tempo for this next part, in which he'd make his case for legitimacy.

"Now, if you'll indulge me for a minute, I want you to think about the process of boarding a commercial airplane. You wait until your group is called. You step onto an airplane that will rush down the runway and lift you into the air, traveling five hundred miles an hour at thirty thousand feet, for however long it takes to get where you're going. You greet the flight attendants, make your way to your seat and buckle in for the ride. Usually before the flight departs, you hear from the people in the cockpit, whose job it is to deliver you safely to your destination. In most cases, you don't see their faces until you're disembarking, when you finally see the pilots standing at the head of the aisle to thank you for flying with their airline. You've just put your life in the hands of two people you'll probably never see again without having seen their faces beforehand or knowing a thing about their credentials. Many of us have probably flown with a commercial pilot on his or her first day at the controls, yet it never occurs to us to question whether they should be there. I'm asking you, my fellow Americans, to put the same faith in me that you regularly place into the hands of those nameless, faceless pilots.

"I'm asking you to believe that by working together, by focusing on the things that unite us rather than divide us, that we can make the American dream more attainable to all. I ask you to reach out to your fellow citizens with empathy rather than fear, with understanding rather than hatred, with celebration for the many things that make each of us unique and special. We're all Americans, descended from other countries and from former immigrants. We're all Americans regardless of our skin color, our sexual orientation, our religious beliefs, our political affiliations, and we're all in this together. If we rise, we do so together. If we fall, we go down together.

"No president can do this job alone. I certainly can't. I need everyone listening to me tonight to be part of this moment in time in which we get to decide what kind of country and what kind of people we're going to be. The week before President Nelson died, I announced that I would not run for this office in the next election. I haven't changed my mind about that."

A gasp went through the room.

"That said, if my party were to nominate me, and if you, my fellow Americans, were to elect me to a full term, I would willingly accept that honor and continue as your president for four more years. I will not campaign. I will not raise money. I will not travel around the country, asking you to give me a full term. That, my friends, will be entirely up to you. If all I ever get are the next three years to serve my country and its citizens, I'll consider that to be the honor of my lifetime. Thank you for your attention tonight, and for your support and encouragement as my family and I embark on this incredible adventure. I look forward to serving you with humility and grace and an optimistic view of the future.

"May God continue to bless our troops stationed around the world, as well as all of you, my fellow citizens, and the United States of America."

Nick was surprised as most of the room stood to cheer.

When he glanced up at Sam, he caught her wiping tears from her face as she smiled and accepted congratulations on his behalf from Gloria and the others seated with her.

If she was proud of him, he'd already succeeded beyond his wildest dreams.

EPILOGUE

W hen you couldn't wait for something to happen, time slowed
to a crawl. At least that's how it seemed to Brooke as she
counted down the days to her weekend with Nate. With each day that
passed, she became less nervous and more excited to spend time alone
with him. He'd sworn to her that if all they did was hold hands, he'd
be happy because he got to be with her.

How lucky was she to have found a man who understood that
trauma wasn't something you just "got over" on some preexisting
timeline? Her trauma was as much a part of who she was now as the
blood that ran through her veins. There would be no "getting over it."
Not now, not ten years from now, not ever.

It'd taken a lot of therapy to understand that new reality after the
attack, but because she'd done the work (well, her parents had made
her do it), she felt like maybe she might be ready to move into a
genuine relationship. But that was only possible because the other
person in that relationship would be Nate, whom she'd come to trust
implicitly.

He was patient, kind, understanding, indulgent and sweet—always
sweet. He'd worn down her defenses over months of texts, calls,
FaceTime conversations and a few strictly platonic in-person
meetings, as if he'd known that pushing her for too much too soon
would only push her away.

He got her, and that was such a priceless gift.

As she stood outside her dorm, waiting for him to arrive, she felt
only excitement for the time with him and none of the nervousness

she'd experienced when he'd first pitched the idea to her. He'd texted to say he was close and to watch for a black car, so when she saw a shiny black Mustang come into view, she figured that had to be him.

The car pulled into the half-circle drive in front of the dorm and came to a stop in front of her.

Nate jumped out to come around, shouldered her bag and opened the passenger door for her. "Hi," he said, smiling.

That sexy smile as well as the affection in his eyes took care of any remaining nerves. "Hi."

He had wavy dark hair, blue eyes and dimples. McDreamy, indeed, and even more so in person. "Are you going to get in?" he asked, seeming amused by the way she looked at him.

"I am, but first I want to do this." She stepped toward him, put her arms around him and rested her head on his chest. "Hi."

Nate returned her embrace, holding her tightly. "How're you doing?" Understanding how nervous she was about their plans, he'd continued to reassure her as their weekend together had drawn near.

"Much better now that you're here."

"I thought today would never get here," he said, echoing her thoughts on the matter. "Every minute felt like a week."

"Same."

"Do you have a ton of homework?"

"I did it all."

He pulled back to look down at her. "All of it?"

"Every bit of it. I didn't want to be distracted this weekend."

"Brooke," he whispered. "How is it that you get prettier every time I see you?"

"Do I?" Was it healthy for a heart to pound that hard?

"Yeah, you do." He tucked a strand of her dark hair behind her ear. "Let's get out of here."

She got in the passenger seat.

He stowed her bag in the trunk before getting in the driver's side and pulling away from the dorm. After reaching for her hand and joining it with his, he didn't say anything on the short ride to his hotel.

"Stay here for a sec. Be right back."

When he got back in the car, he drove around to the back side of the hotel, retrieved both their bags from the trunk and held the door for her when she preceded him inside. Their room was halfway down the hallway and was actually a suite with a kitchen and living area.

"The sofa pulls out to a second bed. I can sleep there."

Brooke ventured into the bedroom, which had a king-sized bed. She sat on the edge of the bed. "You can sleep in here. With me."

Nate came into the bedroom and stood before her, hands on his hips as he took her in. "I don't want to rush you into anything."

"You're not." She patted the bed, inviting him to join her. "You've been nothing but patient and kind and sweet with me."

He sat next to her, put his arm around her and kissed the top of her head. "You've become very important to me."

"Same." She rested her head on his shoulder, at ease now that he was there. "I'm not going to lie to you. I'm scared of having sex. I'm not even sure I can do it, because every time I think about it, my brain is overrun with images I've imagined to account for the attack I don't remember. And I know how bizarre that sounds, but I can't help it."

"We don't have to, Brooke. I meant it when I said that's not what this is about."

"I know you did, but I was thinking... Maybe what I need is to replace those images with different ones, special ones, so that when I think about sex, that's what I think of, not the horrible stuff."

"You're sure about this?"

She shook her head. "I'm not sure of anything, except that I want to try."

Nate leaned in slowly to kiss her for the first time, going all out to ensure their first kiss would be unforgettable. The spark that had simmered between them since the night they met ignited into a flame so quickly, she barely had time to react before they were reclined on the bed, arms and legs intertwined as one kiss became two and then a dozen.

"I knew it would be like this with you," he whispered.

"How is it?"

"Incredible."

They kissed for so long that Brooke lost track of time as she let herself experience pleasure and desire for the first time. The attackers had taken so much from her, but she refused to think about that awful night while in the arms of the man she loved.

His hand dipped under her sweater, making her shiver from the feel of his skin against hers. "Are you okay?"

"Yeah. Are you?"

"I'm much better than okay because I'm here with you."

She tugged on his oatmeal-colored thermal shirt. "Take this off."

He sat up to pull the shirt over his head, revealing defined muscles that made her want to touch him all over. "What?" he asked when he caught her staring at him.

"You're so hot."

"Shut up," he said, laughing.

"You shut up." She got up on her knees. "Can I touch you?"

He scooted closer to her. "I really wish you would."

Brooke ran her hands over his chest to his arms and then back again, before venturing down to caress rippling abdominal muscles.

He was so still, she worried he wasn't breathing.

When she glanced up at him, she found him gazing at her with blue eyes gone hot with desire. "Feels good," he said, sounding choked.

Brooke sat back on her heels and took off her sweater. She'd gone shopping with this moment in mind and loved the way he inhaled sharply at the sight of her sheer black bra. As she reached back, she wasn't sure where the courage was coming from, but she wasn't going to ask any questions. Not now, anyway. She unhooked the bra and revealed herself to him for the first time.

"You're beautiful, sweetheart." He brought her in close to him, her breasts pressing against his chest. "Beautiful, sweet, strong, brave, sexy."

He arranged them so she was on her back with him above her, continuing to whisper sweet words of comfort as he kissed her neck and chest and then the tip of her breast.

Brooke had never felt anything like the electrical charge that raced through her when he sucked on her nipple.

He stayed there for what felt like hours, kissing, licking, sucking until she was half out of her mind.

She was so far gone, she almost didn't notice when he unbuttoned her jeans or when he removed them and the panties that matched her bra.

He continued to kiss her all over, rendering her helpless to do anything other than lie there and wallow in the wonder of it all. Then his lips were on her inner thigh, moving toward the center of her desire.

Her legs fell open, almost as if someone else were controlling the movement, and when his tongue swept over her core, she came undone. The orgasm dragged her under, sucking the air from her lungs and every thought from her brain that wasn't centered in the place where he touched her with his tongue and deep thrusts of his fingers.

"Talk to me, sweetheart," he whispered. "Tell me how it feels."

"Amazing," she said, surprised she could speak at all.

He dipped his head and went back for more, making her come a second time before he withdrew from her. "Stay right there."

She couldn't have moved if the hotel were on fire.

Nate returned a second later, having shed his jeans and underwear and donned a condom.

Seeing him fully erect, Brooke swallowed the lump that suddenly appeared in her throat as she wondered how that would fit inside her.

"Are you sure about this, love?"

"Yes," she said, certain she would never regret taking this step with this man. She held out her arms to him, and he came down on top of her, starting all over with deep, devouring kisses that quickly had her craving more. "Nate... *Please.*"

The tight press of his cock between her legs had her gasping, surprised by the pinch of pain that accompanied the pleasure.

"Nice and easy, sweetheart." Nate brushed the hair back from her face as he gazed down at her with so much love. "We've got all the time in the world. There's no rush."

They were just the words she needed to hear as she struggled to take him in, to relax enough to allow this to happen, to not let the demons take over.

He'd been patient with her from the start and was again now, moving slowly and carefully until he'd entered her fully.

By then, she was having one orgasm after another, her body one gigantic nerve ending as he touched and caressed her until she was utterly mindless. It was safe to say that when she thought of sex in the future, it wouldn't be with horror.

"Brooke." His lips brushed over hers as he throbbed inside her.

She forced her eyes open and blinked him into focus. "Hmm?"

"I just want you to know..."

"What?"

"I love you. I really and truly love you."

"I love you, too."

He gathered her in close to him and began to move, teaching her one stroke at a time what it meant to make love.

AT CAMP DAVID, the weekend had begun with a huge surprise. Eli had come with Candace and an announcement.

"We got married by a justice of the peace two days ago," he said, seeming happier than he'd ever been.

"You did *what*?" Nick asked.

"We want to be together forever, and this way, nothing can stand in our way."

Nick glanced at Sam, silently asking how they should react to this unexpected news.

"Congratulations." Sam hugged them. "We hope you'll be very happy together."

"Thank you," Elijah said. "We're so excited and happy and all the things."

Thanks to the fortune his father had left behind, Eli could easily afford to get married at twenty, but Sam could only hope they hadn't been hasty.

Later that night, when she and Nick were in bed, he asked her what she really thought of Eli getting married.

"They've been through hell," Sam said. "If they've found peace with each other, then so be it. If it doesn't work out, they'll survive, although I have a feeling they're going to be fine. They're obviously madly in love."

"I'm worried he'll want the twins to live with them now that he and Candace are married."

The thought of that nearly stopped Sam's heart. "He's said he has no plans to uproot them, and we have to believe he meant that."

"That was before Candace came back on the scene. Now he has a partner who can help him raise them."

"Elijah has acted in the twins' best interest from the start," Sam said. "And he knows it wouldn't be in their best interest to remove them from our home and family. They're happy, healthy and thriving, despite the worst possible loss. He knows where they belong. Rather than worrying about things that aren't going to happen, let's celebrate gaining a bonus daughter."

"A bonus daughter. I like that."

"She's estranged from her parents, so we'll be her parents."

"This family of ours just gets more interesting all the time."

"Yes, it does."

"I've been meaning to tell you that since the speech, we've been overrun with interview requests. Everyone is talking about what I said at the end about not campaigning." The response to his speech had been unlike anything he ever could've expected, with praise for his sincerity and astonishment over his vow not to actively seek a full term, but to serve if elected.

"Because no one has ever said or done anything like that."

"Maybe it's high time they did. We waste so much money on campaigns that drag on forever. When I think of how many people that money could feed and house, it makes me sick. It's such a hideous waste."

"I'm so proud of my maverick husband," she said, grinning as she used the nickname the media had given him after the speech.

"As much as that nickname makes me cringe, it beats 'the unelected president.'"

"You shut that shit down with your airplane metaphor, which was so freaking perfect."

"Enough about me. How's Malone doing?"

"He's okay, I think."

He and Offenbach had both been placed on administrative leave while the Shane Ramsey shooting was investigated. "It was a clean shoot, and I'm sure they'll both be cleared of any wrongdoing. Sergeant Ramsey, on the other hand, is making as much trouble as he possibly can for all of us. Business as usual where he's concerned, even if he heard his son confess to the crimes before he was shot."

"Ugh, I hate that for you guys."

"Whatever. His son was a serial rapist-murderer who took a woman hostage. By taking his life, we saved hers. Those facts are irrefutable."

"You have the truth on your side, although this case reminds me a bit of John and Thomas." John O'Connor's son had killed him and the women his father had slept with in some misguided attempt to gain justice for his mother.

"I've thought that, too, and yes, the truth is on our side," Sam said. "Malone is using the suspension to try to find the captain who aided and abetted Stahl's efforts to hide the fact that he didn't do shit on the job. Captain Rosa seems to have gone missing, so we'll be digging into that next week."

"Do they think he was the one who helped Stahl?"

"Everyone else who was a captain or above at that time has checked out. Process of elimination has led us to Rosa, but now we just have to find him." Sam ran her hand over his chest absently as they talked. "In other things I've been meaning to mention to you, have you noticed anything between Roni and Derek at work?"

"Like what?"

"Just a vibe I've picked up on."

"I haven't tuned in to that vibe, but I will now."

"I like the idea of the two of them together."

"As long as you like it, that's what matters."

Sam laughed at the truth of that statement.

Saturday was all about fun and games—sledding, horseback riding for the kids, hiking and playing in the game room until long after the twins' usual bedtime. Sam didn't feel confined or cut off or anything else this time, as she gave in to the camp's relaxed vibe, determined to enjoy every second she could get with her family and friends.

That afternoon, she and Scotty held their long-postponed wrestling match at the Camp David gym, with Elijah serving as the impartial judge. Sam had to admit that Scotty more than held his own, but in the end, he was no match for her.

"Uncle, aunt, grandpa," Scotty said when Sam had his face pressed to the mat and his arms in a tight hold behind his back.

"We have a winner," Eli said. "Way to go, Sam, and nice challenge, Scotty."

"Give me a year," Scotty said, dusting himself off. "That's going to go very differently for you, Mom."

"I look forward to a rematch."

"Moms are supposed to let their kids win," he grumbled.

"Oh please," Sam said. "That's not how you want to win, and you say I cheat at Candy Land. Do you honestly think I'm going to *let* you win anything?"

"Obviously not," Scotty said with a good-natured grin.

"She's building your character, son," Nick said. "One humiliating defeat at a time."

"I'll be nice and humble by the time she's done with me," Scotty said.

"That's the goal." Sam gave him a one-armed hug and a kiss on the head. "Even though you're a wimp, I still love you."

"Hey!" Scotty said. "Those are fighting words!"

"Enough fighting," Nick said. "It's time for lunch."

Sunday morning, Sam and Nick had an early breakfast with Mike, Tracy, Terry, Lindsey, Harry, Lilia, Shelby and Avery at their Cedar cabin.

The kids watched a movie as the adults lingered at the table, enjoying second cups of coffee and the coffeecake Sam and Aubrey had baked the day before.

"Thanks again for having us," Avery said. "Camp David is the bomb."

"You know better than to say that word with the Secret Service within earshot," Nick said to the man who'd once infuriated him, but who'd since become a friend.

"Whoops," Avery said with a sheepish grin.

"An FBI agent should know better," Sam said with a teasing grin for Avery.

"I'm so off duty, it's not even funny," Avery said, snuggling his and Shelby's son, Noah, as he took a late-morning snooze.

"Where are Angela and Spence this morning?" Nick asked after he'd finished checking the headlines on his iPad.

"I don't know." Sam reached for her phone to text her sister. "She said they'd be here for breakfast. Maybe they decided to sleep in instead."

She'd no sooner said that than Angela came rushing in the door, looking white-faced and panicked. "Spencer won't wake up."

∽

DON'T DESPAIR! I won't make you wait long to find out what happens next! *State of Shock*, First Family book four, will pick up right where this one left off and will be out in three short months on December 20th! Preorder it now at *https://marieforce.com/stateofshock* to read it Christmas week. Also, if you haven't yet read Roni's story in *Someone Like You*, grab your copy at *https://marieforce.com/someonelikeyou*. Sam and Nick both appear in that book!

Join the State of the Union Reader Group at *facebook.com/groups/stateoftheunion3/* to discuss this story with spoilers allowed and encouraged and make sure you're also a member of the Fatal/First Family Group at *facebook.com/groups/FatalSeries* to be the first to hear series news and updates. Also, join the Book Club chat, with spoilers allowed, for *State of the Union* on Sept. 29 at 7 p.m. ET at *facebook.com/marieforcebookclub*.

A huge thanks to my good friend, retired Captain Russell Hayes of the Newport, RI, Police Department, who was such a huge help to me during the writing of this book, answering a million questions, or so it seemed. Russ is always there for me when I need him and has been part of my journey with Sam and my fictional MPD for nineteen books and two novellas. I couldn't write this series without his incredible help and support.

As I researched Camp David and *Marine One*, I enjoyed reading these books: *Inside Camp David: The Private World and Presidential Retreat* by Rear Admiral Michael Giorgione, CEC, USN (Retired), and *Inside Marine One: Four U.S. Presidents, One Proud Marine and the World's Most Amazing Helicopter*, by Colonel Ray "Frenchy" L'Heureux with Lee Kelley.

Thanks as always to the team that makes it happen for me behind the scenes: Julie Cupp, Lisa Cafferty, Jean Mello, Nikki Haley and Ashley Lopez. Kristina Brinton is the wonderful cover designer for this series, and I appreciate her amazing work at bringing Sam and Nick's stories to life on the covers. Thank you to Dani Sanchez and the team at Wildfire for the publicity help.

I'm thrilled to have Eva Kaminsky continuing as the narrator for the audiobooks for this series, and if you haven't yet experienced Eva's awesome work, check out the Fatal and First Family Series in audio. We're working to bring back some of the earlier Fatal books in audio, rerecorded by Eva, since the rights have reverted to me. The earlier titles currently not on sale will be returning over the next year or so.

Thank you to my wonderful editing team of Joyce Lamb and Linda Ingmanson, as well as my beta readers Anne Woodall, Kara Conrad and Tracey Suppo. Gwen Neff, my editorial assistant, helps me with continuity and fact-checking of past books, and her assistance has been invaluable as she read this book four times checking for everything. Thank you, Gwen! A huge shout-out to the Fatal/First Family Series beta readers: Kelly, Irene, Jennifer, Karina, Jenny, Mona, Marti, Ellen, Maricar, Viki, Kelley, Juliane, Gina, Elizabeth and Sarah.

And finally, I can't say enough about the fans of this series and how amazing you are. Your love for Sam and Nick keeps me going as we head toward the twentieth book in their story with no end in sight. Thank you for your amazing support of this story over the last twelve years. I love you all so much!

xoxo

Marie

ALSO BY MARIE FORCE

Romantic Suspense Novels Available from Marie Force

The Fatal Series
One Night With You, *A Fatal Series Prequel Novella*
Book 1: Fatal Affair
Book 2: Fatal Justice
Book 3: Fatal Consequences
Book 3.5: Fatal Destiny, *the Wedding Novella*
Book 4: Fatal Flaw
Book 5: Fatal Deception
Book 6: Fatal Mistake
Book 7: Fatal Jeopardy
Book 8: Fatal Scandal
Book 9: Fatal Frenzy
Book 10: Fatal Identity
Book 11: Fatal Threat
Book 12: Fatal Chaos
Book 13: Fatal Invasion
Book 14: Fatal Reckoning
Book 15: Fatal Accusation
Book 16: Fatal Fraud

The First Family Series
Book 1: State of Affairs
Book 2: State of Grace
Book 3: State of the Union
Book 4: State of Shock

Contemporary Romances Available from Marie Force

The Wild Widows Series—a Fatal Series Spin-Off
Book 1: Someone Like You
Book 2: Someone to Hold

The Miami Nights Series
Book 1: How Much I Feel *(Carmen & Jason)*
Book 2: How Much I Care *(Maria & Austin)*
Book 3: How Much I Love *(Dee's story)*
Nochebuena, A Miami Nights Novella
Book 4: How Much I Want *(Nico & Sofia)*
Book 5: How Much I Need *(Milo and Gianna)*

The Gansett Island Series
Book 1: Maid for Love *(Mac & Maddie)*
Book 2: Fool for Love *(Joe & Janey)*
Book 3: Ready for Love *(Luke & Sydney)*
Book 4: Falling for Love *(Grant & Stephanie)*
Book 5: Hoping for Love *(Evan & Grace)*
Book 6: Season for Love *(Owen & Laura)*
Book 7: Longing for Love *(Blaine & Tiffany)*
Book 8: Waiting for Love *(Adam & Abby)*
Book 9: Time for Love *(David & Daisy)*
Book 10: Meant for Love *(Jenny & Alex)*
Book 10.5: Chance for Love, *A Gansett Island Novella (Jared & Lizzie)*
Book 11: Gansett After Dark *(Owen & Laura)*
Book 12: Kisses After Dark *(Shane & Katie)*
Book 13: Love After Dark *(Paul & Hope)*
Book 14: Celebration After Dark *(Big Mac & Linda)*
Book 15: Desire After Dark *(Slim & Erin)*
Book 16: Light After Dark *(Mallory & Quinn)*
Book 17: Victoria & Shannon (Episode 1)
Book 18: Kevin & Chelsea (Episode 2)
A Gansett Island Christmas Novella

Book 19: Mine After Dark *(Riley & Nikki)*

Book 20: Yours After Dark *(Finn & Chloe)*

Book 21: Trouble After Dark *(Deacon & Julia)*

Book 22: Rescue After Dark *(Mason & Jordan)*

Book 23: Blackout After Dark *(Full Cast)*

Book 24: Temptation After Dark *(Gigi & Cooper)*

Book 25: Resilience After Dark *(Jace & Cindy)*

Book 26: Hurricane After Dark *(Full cast)*

The Green Mountain Series

Book 1: All You Need Is Love *(Will & Cameron)*

Book 2: I Want to Hold Your Hand *(Nolan & Hannah)*

Book 3: I Saw Her Standing There *(Colton & Lucy)*

Book 4: And I Love Her *(Hunter & Megan)*

Novella: You'll Be Mine *(Will & Cam's Wedding)*

Book 5: It's Only Love *(Gavin & Ella)*

Book 6: Ain't She Sweet *(Tyler & Charlotte)*

The Butler, Vermont Series

(Continuation of Green Mountain)

Book 1: Every Little Thing *(Grayson & Emma)*

Book 2: Can't Buy Me Love *(Mary & Patrick)*

Book 3: Here Comes the Sun *(Wade & Mia)*

Book 4: Till There Was You *(Lucas & Dani)*

Book 5: All My Loving *(Landon & Amanda)*

Book 6: Let It Be *(Lincoln & Molly)*

Book 7: Come Together *(Noah & Brianna)*

Book 8: Here, There & Everywhere *(Izzy & Cabot)*

Book 9: The Long and Winding Road *(Max & Lexi)*

The Quantum Series

Book 1: Virtuous *(Flynn & Natalie)*

Book 2: Valorous *(Flynn & Natalie)*

Book 3: Victorious *(Flynn & Natalie)*

Book 4: Rapturous *(Addie & Hayden)*

Book 5: Ravenous *(Jasper & Ellie)*

Book 6: Delirious *(Kristian & Aileen)*

Book 7: Outrageous *(Emmett & Leah)*

Book 8: Famous *(Marlowe & Sebastian)*

The Treading Water Series

Book 1: Treading Water

Book 2: Marking Time

Book 3: Starting Over

Book 4: Coming Home

Book 5: Finding Forever

Single Titles

Five Years Gone

One Year Home

Sex Machine

Sex God

Georgia on My Mind

True North

The Fall

The Wreck

Love at First Flight

Everyone Loves a Hero

Line of Scrimmage

Historical Romance Available from Marie Force

The Gilded Series

Book 1: Duchess by Deception

Book 2: Deceived by Desire

ABOUT THE AUTHOR

Marie Force is the *New York Times* bestselling author of contemporary romance, romantic suspense and erotic romance. Her series include Fatal, First Family, Gansett Island, Butler Vermont, Quantum, Treading Water, Miami Nights and Wild Widows.

Her books have sold more than 10 million copies worldwide, have been translated into more than a dozen languages and have appeared on the *New York Times* bestseller list more than 30 times. She is also a *USA Today* and #1 *Wall Street Journal* bestseller, as well as a Spiegel bestseller in Germany.

Her goals in life are simple—to finish raising two happy, healthy, productive young adults, to keep writing books for as long as she possibly can and to never be on a flight that makes the news.

Join Marie's mailing list on her website at *marieforce.com* for news about new books and upcoming appearances in your area. Follow her on Facebook at *www.Facebook.com/MarieForceAuthor*, Instagram at *www.instagram.com/marieforceauthor/* and TikTok at *https://www.tiktok.-com/@marieforceauthor?*. Contact Marie at *marie@marieforce.com*.

CPSIA information can be obtained
at www.ICGtesting.com
Printed in the USA
LVHW042054020922
727314LV00003B/90